THE
CRYSTAL
BUCEPHALUS

DOCTOR WHO – THE MISSING ADVENTURES

Also available:

GOTH OPERA by Paul Cornell

EVOLUTION by John Peel

VENUSIAN LULLABY by Paul Leonard

THE
CRYSTAL
BUCEPHALUS

Craig Hinton

First published in Great Britain in 1994 by
Doctor Who Books
an imprint of Virgin Publishing Ltd
332 Ladbroke Grove
London W10 5AH

ISBN 0 426 20429 8

Cover illustration by Alister Pearson

Typeset by Galleon Typesetting, Ipswich
Printed and bound in Great Britain by
Cox & Wyman Ltd, Reading, Berks.

Craig's Bit

In answer to everyone who's said 'What's a Buk...
Bucky... Bucket phallus?' it's pronounced Bew-sef-a-
luss. Get it? Got it? Good. It means 'ox-headed', and,
well, read the book. That'll tell you. Actually, it's
probably pronounced Bew-kep-a-luss, but that's another
story.

For the last goodness-knows-how-many months, I've
reviewed Virgin's output for Marvel's *Doctor Who
Magazine*, and now it's my turn to put my head on the
block. And I'll say this: writing a book is bloody hard
work! Thankfully, I haven't got to review this one – I'm
letting the boss do it. Anyway, without the following
people, it would still have been bloody hard work, but
nowhere near as much fun.

So, in alphabetical order . . .

Peter Anghelides (being an understanding manager and
friend), Lindsey Ashworth (modelling Hellenica Monroe
and golden lentil soup), Ian Bennett (showing me how
everything fits together), Ian Clarke (who could have
asked for a better Maitre D'?), John Furniss (helping me
come up with the idea in the first place), Andrew Hair
(fabulous, sweetie), Rikki Holland (being sensible in the
face of spam), the mysterious Mr J (you know why!),
Andy Lane (ripping it all to shreds), Gary Leigh (my first
big break), Paul Leonard (understanding this book better
than I do), Rebecca Levene (tireless support above and
beyond the call of duty), Alister Pearson (the spectacular
cover), Justin Richards (Earl Grey, Willy the Winebox,
and a constant ear), and Gary Russell (being an understanding editor and friend – you're the one reviewing
this!). And, of course, the rec.arts.drwho crew.

And, above all, James Lynch, for putting up with all of
this. I couldn't have done it without you, Jim. You make
a damn fine villain.

Dedicated to my Dad, who would
have been chuffed, and my Mum, who is.
I love you both very much.

Sed fugit interea, fugit inreparabile tempus.
(But meanwhile it is flying,
irretrievable time is flying)
Virgil – *Georgics*

Apéritif

Eight-thirty, and the restaurant was already full. But then, Beswicks was always full. Patrons in their Savile Row suits or Chanel, Quant or Biba frocks sat at the tables or in the private booths, while discreet waiters ferried the *haute*-est of *haute cuisine* from the kitchen. The unobtrusive lamps mounted on the wood-panelled walls showed off the sheer opulence to its best advantage: the whole place glittered, from the silver cutlery to the cut glass tumblers and champagne flutes on every table, and anything that didn't glitter simply glowed.

Neil Corridge was dining alone, his girlfriend's modelling career having forced her to fly to Paris at the last minute. Still, Coco had paid for her to travel on Concorde, and Neil couldn't really refuse Linda that, especially since he had just come back from an all-expenses-paid conference on the Côte d'Azur. He smiled as he thought about the trip, toying with his prawn cocktail and glancing around the restaurant. He recognized most of the guests — MPs, television actors and the like — but the couple on the table about eight feet away were new. Neil decided to pass the time by listening in on their conversation. In his line of business, any little snippets might be useful.

'Your drinks, sir, madame.' The head waiter placed the glasses on the table. The slim, attractive blonde was drinking sherry, while her companion, short, thuggish and generally unpleasant-looking, was obviously a whisky drinker. Obviously. He wore the expensive dinner suit the way a wolf would wear a fleece.

Beswicks was exclusive. Exclusive and expensive, and

1

Neil Corridge was exactly the sort of patron that the establishment catered for: a rich, successful, respectable businessman in the City. The couple on the adjacent table were a typical example of the lower class element creeping into society: new money, new values. And neither worth spit.

'I mean, where could I drink scotch like this in the Union?' The man was holding the tumbler up to the subdued lighting, watching as the amber sparkled within. Corridge internally congratulated himself. The Union, eh? The man was one of these hypocritical pinkos: all solidarity and 'up the workers' during the day, then eating and drinking the subs in places like Beswicks at night. Corridge continued his surreptitious eavesdropping.

'The simple pleasures of life, Monsignor Arrestis?' The woman's voice was deep and seductive. That, coupled with her high cheekbones and huge blue eyes, was almost enough to make Corridge give himself away by staring at her. He averted his eyes but continued listening. Monsignor? Italian? The Mafia? The man didn't look Italian: about five foot six, with thin wavy hair plastered to his scalp, long sideburns and big ears. Only the sleepy eyes gave any sense of menace; eyes that seemed to see nothing yet probably saw everything.

'Don't mock it, Diva. The whole purpose of the Crystal Bucephalus is to give people a taste of simpler times.' *Diva?* What sort of a name was that? And the Crystal Bucephalus? A disturbing thrill grew in Corridge's stomach. She was a high-class hooker, and this Bucephalus place was obviously a brothel!

'The Lazarus Intent believes that pleasure comes from within, Max,' she continued. 'It isn't limited to the few people who have the money or the power to afford it.' The Lazarus Intent? Was the woman one of these hippie types as well?

'That's what I like about the Lazarus Intent. All good intentions, founded by a messiah who single-handedly exterminated the Daleks.'

She sighed. 'Not that again. Why is it that you just love

2

bringing all of that up? Lazarus gave his life to the Sontarans so that the galaxy could know peace.'

Corridge frowned. Galaxy? What on earth were they on about?

'This lot don't seem to be doing so bad considering that their messiah won't be born for another three thousand years.' Arrestis looked up as a waiter approached the table. 'Yes?' he snapped.

The waiter, a plain fellow with sandy hair and a beaky nose, proffered a wicker basket containing a bottle of red wine. 'The patrons in Benefactor's Cubiculo have sent this over as a token of their good faith, Monsignor Arrestis.'

Corridge gave up. Their conversation was getting more and more bizarre by the second! Pledging never to eavesdrop again, he attacked the defenceless prawns.

'More well-wishers.' Arrestis grinned at Diva. 'Still, it's the price I have to pay for being the head of the Elective. What is it?'

Corridge broke his vow. He was right: the man was a Mafia godfather! From the faintly cultured but clearly English accent, he was probably a member of the British arm of the Family.

The waiter smiled with a slight bow. 'The Crozes Hermitage, sir, a 1935.' He placed the bottle on the table. 'An excellent vintage, I might add.'

'So I should hope.' Arrestis pointed a thumb at the bottle. 'Pour me a glass, woman. Earn your keep.' Corridge smiled; his guess was right: the Mafia boss and his prostitute.

She narrowed her eyes. 'I hope it chokes you.' She poured two glasses.

Arrestis sipped the red wine, a satisfied smile on his face. 'That's what I like about you, Diva. Your understanding nature . . .' His eyes bulged as he grabbed his throat, rocking back and forwards in panic.

'Max!' she screamed.

Arrestis began to make unpleasant rasping sounds, and guests and waiters turned and stared as he started to convulse. As his spasms became more intense, he toppled from his chair, dragging the table-cloth, crockery, cutlery and glassware with him.

Corridge jumped up and ran over. 'Is he all right?'

Reaching into her handbag, she pulled out a six-inch black rod. 'I've got to get him back to the Bucephalus!'

What good would getting him back to a brothel do? Corridge hefted Arrestis from the floor and placed him back in his chair. 'Let me call an ambulance!'

She pressed the red button on the end of the rod, and Corridge froze in disbelief as twin hoops of amber light materialized in the air around her and Arrestis.

Neil Corridge was dining alone, his girlfriend's modelling career having forced her to fly to Paris at the last minute. Still, Coco had paid for her to travel on Concorde, and Neil couldn't really refuse Linda that, especially since he had just come back from an all-expenses-paid conference on the Côte d'Azur. He smiled as he thought about the trip, toying with his prawn cocktail and glancing around the restaurant. He recognized most of the guests – MPs, television actors and the like. He looked over to the nearest table, about eight feet away. Empty. What a shame. He was in the mood for a bit of eavesdropping.

Hors-d'Oeuvre

'Cubiculo 455 requires a steward, please attend.' The Maitre D' reholstered his talkstick and sighed. Why hadn't the party asked for one when they first arrived? He caught his reflection in the polished surface of one of the Cubiculi and instinctively straightened his bow tie and tugged on his waistcoat. He chose to ignore the flabby, chinless neck and the bulging stomach; they were a sign of good living, and wasn't that what the place was all about? He smoothed down the neatly trimmed beard that just about covered his jowls, touched a finger to an errant strand of thinning hair and stepped back, finally satisfied with his appearance.

Cubiculo 455 was just one of the thousand Cubiculi that stood proudly on the white marble floor of the Mezzanine. Each one was a ten-foot tall, ten-foot wide cylinder of polished wood, the surface a marvel of engraving and marquetry inlay. They were arranged in concentric circles with ever-decreasing radii as they drew closer to the very centre of the Mezzanine, the *pièce de résistance* of the restaurant.

Rearing up above the Mezzanine in majestic splendour, it stood guard over the Cubiculi: 50 feet of painstakingly carved deep green crystal, the statue of Alexander the Great's warhorse glittered and scintillated in the light from the massive diamond chandeliers that hung from the delicately painted ceiling, and yet a deeper, softer glow seemed to emanate from within. The monument, set in an avenue of dark gothic columns, was so imposing that it had even given the restaurant its name: the Crystal Bucephalus.

'Good evening, Maitre D',' came the hissing voice.

His reverie broken, he turned to see a Martian senator in a black suit walking past, accompanied by one of the Bucephalus's stewards, the cybernetic servitors that acted as escorts for the galactic cognoscenti that frequented the Bucephalus. As always, their exotic design momentarily enthralled him: silver and gold satyrs with leering goat-like faces, their horns encrusted with diamonds. He clearly remembered the shock he had felt upon first seeing one, but the patrons seemed to admire their striking appearance – indeed, more than admire on a few occasions – so who was he to complain? Well actually, being the Maitre D', he had had every right to complain, but it had been one of the few arguments he had lost. He nodded in greeting to the Ice Lord and continued his constitutional about the Mezzanine.

The distant white walls weren't without their own charms: abstract statues on marble plinths stood every five feet, each one surrounded by colourful explosions of flowers, arranged daily by the greatest exponents of Chelonian floral engineering. Silver rose windows filled the spaces between the statues. The Maitre D' was especially proud of the windows: at least the designers had taken his advice on that particular matter.

He crossed between two rings of Cubiculi and spotted a familiar figure. 'How nice to see you again, Your Grace.' It was Tornqvist, the senior Prelector of the Lazarus Intent and arguably one of the most powerful figures in the echelons of galactic power.

'And you, Maitre D'.' The ginger-bearded man in the scarlet suit gave a sage nod. 'Any excuse to escape Clavidence.' He broke into a toothy grin at the Maitre D's shocked expression and slapped him on the shoulder. 'Only joking.'

The Maitre D' had to force himself not to cringe at the unwelcome physical contact, and matched the Prelector's grin. 'Of course, Your Grace. Enjoy your meal.'

'Feel free to join me for the cheese-board, Cubiculo Eleven.' With that, he beckoned his steward and walked off towards his chosen destination. Whenever that was.

Senators from the Union Presidium, Prelectors of the Intent, even the glorified thugs of the Elective: they all visited the Crystal Bucephalus. Indeed, such vaunted personages were the only citizens of the galaxy with sufficient money, power and influence to pass through the perimeter defences that encircled New Alexandria, the lifeless world that was host to the huge domed complex containing the Bucephalus and the hotel that surrounded it, the Emerald Syphax.

'Excuse me!' A shrieking voice like that could only come from one life-form, and the Maitre D's suspicions were confirmed when he looked round. The Alpha Centaurians were about five feet away, their six arms gesticulating furiously while their spherical heads bobbed wildly. Their single eyes were blinking at a frantic rate.

'Can I help you, Monsig . . . Signora . . .' He paused, desperately trying to remember the correct form of address for hermaphroditic life-forms.

'I am Senator Ipillis, and this is Senator Apilaris,' screeched one of the green aliens, pointing a flapping arm at its companion.

Why were they always green? he wondered. Green and reptilian. Martians, Chelonians, Earth Reptiles, Draconians . . . no variety. 'How can I help you?'

'Our steward seems to have vanished, and we can't find our Cubiculo,' Ipillis squeaked. 'Can you direct us to the right one?'

He suddenly remembered – and cursed himself for forgetting – that their steward had been recalled to carry an item of political bribery from the Benefactor's Cubiculo to 507. He should have assigned another from the stand-by pool, but it was too late now. He whipped out his talkstick. 'Maitre D' to webwork. Which Cubiculo has been assigned to Senators Ipillis and Apilaris?'

The measured tones of the webwork, the dissociated computer system that ran the important but invisible aspects of the entire New Alexandria complex, issued from the thin black talkstick. 'Cubiculo 001.'

7

He cursed silently, realizing that 001 was on the far side of the Mezzanine. 'Please assign a steward immediately. The senators are outside Cubiculo 225.'

'Understood. A steward will arrive in exactly 3.2 minutes.'

Should he wait with the senators or continue his traditional evening walk? Deciding that the senators were unimportant enough to be left to their own devices for a few minutes – the Alpha Centauri assembly to the Union Presidium on Maradnias was generally considered to be something of a joke – he took his leave and continued, reminiscing about his recent interview for the Union newsnet. 'In the Crystal Bucephalus, the decisions that govern the future of the galaxy are being made in its past.' It had made a wonderful sound bite, but behind it lay the truth. No one had any faith in the recognized government any more. The true decisions, the power-broking and spin-doctoring between the Union, the Elective and the Lazarus Intent, were made between the patrons in their Cubiculi, as the stewards passed gifts and promises from time zone to time zone. This was the true parliament.

'I beg your pardon, Maitre D'.' A steward was walking towards him, its silver hooves clopping on the marble floor. It seemed to be in something of a hurry.

'Yes?' He was puzzled. Why hadn't it communicated via talkstick?

'The patrons in Cubiculo 507 have activated the recall.'

507 – Arrestis and his woman. 'So? Patrons *are* permitted to return to the Crystal Bucephalus, you know.' Knowing Arrestis, he probably didn't like the wine that had been delivered. Still, he was the head of the Elective.

'According to the steward *in situ*, there was an incident. You are requested to attend Cubiculo 507 immediately.'

The steward's piccolo-voiced words made him freeze. In all the years that he had been the Maitre D', he had never been summoned to an *incident*. With panicked strides, he set off for 507. To make matters worse, 507 was also on the other side of the Mezzanine.

Stewards had already led Arrestis's woman from the Cubiculo, while others were carrying Arrestis out. As the Maitre D' approached, the three stewards that were kneeling over the body stood up. He gave them an enquiring glance. His main concern was to get all of this off the Mezzanine as quickly as possible, before any of the patrons got wind of the *incident*.

'Our preliminary diagnosis suggests that he was poisoned,' said one of the stewards melodically. 'We have been unable to identify the precise toxin.'

'Poisoned?' He looked down at the body. Arrestis's face was blue, a frozen mask of contorted fear.

'He's dead, isn't he?' The woman was staring down at the corpse with a strangely impassive look, a look that chilled him far more than Arrestis's look of horror.

'Signora, I assure you that I will instigate a full enquiry.'

'I have no doubt about that.' She held out the bottle of Crozes Hermitage. 'I thought you might want to look at this.' Her voice was cold and unemotional, and he could only assume she was in shock.

He passed the bottle to one of the stewards. 'Analyse that.' He returned his attention to the woman. 'Under the circumstances, might I suggest that you return to your suite in the Emerald Syphax? Forthcoming events might prove a little . . . distressing?' The faint questioning tone pressed home the point.

With a final look at Arrestis's prone form, she walked away from the Cubiculo. As she reached the next ring, she turned round to face the Maitre D'. 'I'm sure that the Elective would very much like to talk to whoever is responsible.' Then she was gone, her threat hanging tangibly in the air. He chose to ignore it: she was nothing more than an employee, and carried about as much weight with the Elective as Arrestis now did.

'Maitre D'?' A steward cantered up to him. 'There are traces of poison around the neck of the bottle. It resembles pyletheric acid, but possesses certain unique qualities. The Clerics of Ansaqi use pyletheric acid as a flavour enhancer, while the Floripscents –'

He held up both his hands. 'Please, spare me the lecture. Have the occupants of the Benefactor's Cubiculo left the Bucephalus?'

The steward cocked its head to one side as if listening, as it tapped into the webwork. 'There has been no transit either to or from the Benefactor's Cubiculo.'

The Maitre D's face assumed a rather cruel expression. For five years, senior members of all the major galactic powers had used the Crystal Bucephalus as an unofficial parliament. But the three groups had always followed a set of tacit laws: Maradnias, Clavidence and Hexdane in their perfectly balanced power triangle. Most importantly, there was to be no violence in the Bucephalus, either in the present or in the past. If the barbarians which beset the galaxy brought their jungle law to the Bucephalus, its very existence would be in jeopardy. And the continued prosperity of the Bucephalus was of paramount importance to the Maitre D'.

'Best to stamp this out quickly, then,' he announced to no one in particular. Then, to one of the stewards, 'Have a contingent of security stewards meet me outside Benefactor's.' And then, under his breath, 'No one is going to interfere in my restaurant.'

When the Maitre D' arrived, four security stewards stood around the double doors of the Cubiculo. Benefactor's was unique: installed at the request of the Benefactor himself, the Cubiculo was considerably more ornate than the others, with its inlaid patterns of gold and latinum. The only functional difference was that it had access to certain destinations from the Carte de Locales not readily available to the other patrons. The Benefactor himself had only ever visited the Bucephalus once; hardly worth the erection of a Cubiculo. And then a disturbing thought hit the Maitre D': he couldn't remember Benefactor's being assigned that evening. But they were in there, and he and the security stewards would ferret them out.

Security stewards were no different to the standard

model, apart from the psi-whips and stunners that hung from their belts. The last time that he had required such firepower had been the brawl between some ruffians from the Elective and a group of drunken Martians. That hadn't been pleasant. Seeing the stewards touching their stunners, he nodded. They unholstered the stubby weapons, but still held them at their sides.

He strode up to the double doors. To their left, an almost unnoticeable depression was carved between two inlaid panels. He pulled a small black cube, attached by a delicate silver chain, from the folds of his half-cloak and gestured at two of the stewards. 'As soon as the override closes the gate, bring them out.'

Inserting the override, he turned it like a doorkey, and immediately became aware of a faint humming, but only because it suddenly ceased. The two stewards opened the doors and entered the Cubiculo. Endless moments later, they emerged, stunners aimed at the three patrons.

The two men were both dressed in exquisitely embroidered jackets and silk pantaloons, with billowing white cravats around their necks. The younger man, a redhead, wore an outfit of emerald and gold, whilst the slightly older one was attired in a jacket of deep blue with a silver snake motif, his blond hair tied back in a short ponytail. An incongruous stick of what looked like celery was affixed to his lapel.

The woman, in a billowing dress of red silks and satin and bewigged in a powdered white pompadour, turned to the blond man. 'Okay, Doctor: get us out of this one.'

Entrée

One

Located on the very edge of the Mezzanine, Cubiculo 992 was one of the few Cubiculi that was not currently projecting the rich, famous or influential back through eternity. It had been booked, but Citizen Claas of the Draconian Republic had been forced to cancel. The news networks would report that Claas had resigned from the Draconian Government to spend more time with his wife and hatchlings; the Maitre D' knew that Claas's affair with Echthis, the consort of the Earth Reptile premier, had reached the ear of the Draconian President.

With a high-pitched whine, a brilliant blue light escaped through the cracks between the doors and the wall of the Cubiculo. The doors were flung open from the inside, and, silhouetted by the azure radiance that spewed from the doorway, a six-foot figure seemed to take its bearings. Then the light faded, and the figure was revealed. The overall impression was one of bulk: legs like tree trunks, arms like girders, and a domed head without any features. The entire ensemble was made from some blue, mirrored material which reflected the dark browns of the Cubiculi and the white of the Mezzanine marble in kaleidoscopic patterns.

Closing the doors behind it, the figure walked stiffly away.

'Trust Tegan,' muttered Turlough as the stewards prompted them, gently but firmly at gun point, towards a white door with a stained glass panel that was set in the even whiter walls. He thought back to his companion's

15

actions and couldn't help smiling: as one of the bejewelled androids had reached for her, she had thrust her wig in its face and run off into the distance.

'Her habitual urge to run first and ask questions later has proved advantageous in the past.' The Doctor gestured towards the tall fat man in the dinner jacket and cloak. 'Let's see whether our host can enlighten us.' He paused as the man unlocked the door and made for them to enter. 'Thank you,' said the Doctor with a curt nod. 'Come along, Turlough.'

At a glance, Turlough took in the heavy wooden desk, the leather chair, the pictures on the walls. The whole office screamed out the occupant's sense of self-importance.

Their captor gestured grandly towards the leather sofa that was placed with mathematical accuracy against one wall. 'Please, don't hesitate to avail yourself of my hospitality.'

'Pompous git,' whispered Turlough, before sinking into the burgundy leather. He liked the word 'git'. Tosser Armstrong had taught it to him.

Before the Maitre D' could say another word, the Doctor took the lead. 'Perhaps it would save time if I performed the introductions. I'm the Doctor.' He held out his hand in greeting. Withdrawing it at the lack of response, he continued, 'A man of learning and varied travel. This is one of my companions, Turlough. The third member of my little retinue is sadly absent from this cosy gathering, but she's called Tegan, Tegan Jovanka.' He paused for a second. 'She means well.' His roll-call complete, he smiled at the tall figure. 'And you?'

'I am the Maitre D'Hotel of this, the most exclusive restaurant that the galaxy has ever seen: the Crystal Bucephalus.' The heavy jowls wobbled with pride.

'Bucephalus? Hence the statue?' asked Turlough.

'Stop horsing about, Turlough. Let our host continue.'

'Doctor, you are not making this situation any easier.' The Maitre D's unflappable composure was clearly taking quite a pounding.

16

'I do apologize, Mr D.'

'Maitre D', Doctor . . .'

'Oh, I'm so sorry. We must preserve the social frame-work, mustn't we? Very well, I take it that this is going to be some sad excuse for an interrogation.'

The Maitre D's tone was deadly serious. 'I would like some answers. Now.'

'And I would like some questions.' The Doctor stood up, glaring at him. 'My companions and I were enjoying one of the finest French meals it has been my pleasure to experience, when this apology for a time machine scoops us up and dumps us in this farrago of glitter and bad taste. But do we get an apology for being chronologically displaced without permission? No, we do not. Instead, some overblown waiter and his mechanical men drag us off and accuse us of murder.' He paused for breath, but it wasn't long enough for the Maitre D' to get a word in edgeways.

'I think that just about sums up our side of the story. Now you can get the electrodes out, or the red-hot pokers, or is *peine forte et dure* more your line?' He slumped back onto the sofa, giving Turlough a satisfied smile as he did so.

The Maitre D' stared at the Doctor, trying to assimilate his outburst. 'Very well, Doctor, if you will allow me to explain the situation?' He stroked his beard. 'Earlier this evening, one of our most honoured patrons, Monsignor Maximillian Arrestis, was murdered.'

Aiming his voice towards the ceiling, he boomed out his command. 'Display the Arrestis's party's most recent visit to the twentieth century.' He turned to the Doctor and Turlough. 'Gentlemen, this is what happened.' He gestured at the spherical holographic display that had materialized above his desk. 'Witness their arrival.' They watched the hologram as a short, sleepy-looking man and a tall blonde woman stepped into the interior of a wood-panelled restaurant.

'This destination was specially chosen by Monsignor Arrestis; apparently his distant relatives owned it.' There was a momentarily raised eyebrow. 'I never realized that animals had family trees . . . never mind. This restaurant is on Ancient Earth.'

'Ancient Earth?' Turlough looked puzzled.

'When and where exactly?' asked the Doctor with a disarming smile.

'Webwork: please give the Arrestis party's selection from the Carte de Locales.' Realizing that the hologram was still playing, he barked another command. 'Freeze playback.'

'Playback frozen. Beswicks. Earth, 1968. London. The corner of Tottenham Court Road and Hanway Street –'

'Yes, thank you. Satisfied, Doctor?'

'Extremely. Pray continue.' He leaned back in the sofa and fixed his attention on the hologram.

'Thank you. Resume playback.' Within the holo-sphere, Arrestis and his companion allowed themselves to be escorted to their table.

Turlough shook his head. 'I suppose home movies are preferable to execution,' he whispered.

The Doctor grinned. 'Relax, Turlough. At least we're getting a chance to find out what's going on without guns being pointed at our heads.'

They sat back to watch the recording.

'Bloody floor!' muttered Tegan, stumbling for the ump-teenth time. Her impractical shoes had been abandoned ages ago, but her stockinged feet kept losing their grip on the marble. Although she had been glimpsed at least once by the goat-headed androids, she had managed to lose them, remembering her childhood antics with her friends in the orchard behind her uncle's farm. After her rapid escape from the trouble that they seemed to have arrived right in the middle of – stuffing that ridiculous wig in the goaty-thing's face had helped – she had aimed herself in the general direction of the opposite wall, about eight hundred yards away. She was now by the innermost row of booths, staring up at the statue.

'When I get my hands on you, Doctor, I'm gonna want

a full explanation . . .' She trailed off as she heard a noise. Peering round the curve of the booth, she saw another android escorting a party of three humanoid reptiles. Even after nearly three years of travelling with the Doctor – three years of Cybermen, Terileptils . . . Mara! – she still found the variety of alien life forms a breathtaking experience to witness. These were reptiles, with ridged heads and what seemed to be a third eye lodged in the forehead, and they looked like nothing on Earth. Shaking herself free of her enchantment, she slowly edged round the wooden booth in the opposite direction from the android and the aliens.

Hearing the sound of footsteps from the opposite side of the statue, footsteps that seemed to be heading in her direction, she darted over to the black base, hoping to keep the statue between her and the footsteps. Craning her neck, she caught a glimpse of the people responsible, if they could be called people. Two of them were the all-too-familiar androids, while the other three were yet another lot of lizard people. But these ones weren't the same: they seemed to have shells and helmets, like a cross between a Norman soldier and a crocodile. She drew back and looked the other way – and saw a flash of green vanish behind one of the booths, about twenty feet away. Something in Tegan's subconscious flashed a message, impelling her to find out more. Realizing that the androids and their lizard friends would be upon her in seconds, she ran.

The Suit watched Tegan as she dashed across the Mezzanine. Excellent. Not only Diva but the Doctor's friend as well: belt *and* braces. He stepped back as the stewards and their Martian charges walked by, oblivious to his presence. Behind the mirrored helmet, he smiled, glad that the heavy battlesuit was serving its purpose, rendering him undetectable from the Bucephalus webwork and, more importantly, from the stewards and patrons. Very soon he would reveal himself. But only to the right people.

The Suit lumbered off in Tegan's direction.

* * *

Turlough snorted. He and the Doctor had sat through a less than riveting account of some crime boss's murder, and, when it was over, that pompous prig had launched into his interrogation act, all accusing questions and cynical retorts.

'So, Doctor, let me understand this aright. You and your companions were dining at the Café de Saint Joseph, Aix-en-Provence, Earth, in the year 1791. Yet you claim to know nothing of the poisoned wine, or, unbelievably, of the Crystal Bucephalus.' He exhaled a deep blue cloud of aromatic smoke, and tapped the ash from his cigarette into the round marble ashtray on his desk.

The Doctor began to answer, the smoke catching in his throat. 'I'm pleased to see that your grasp of the facts is as impeccable as your office, Maitre D'.' He waved the smoke away. 'That really is a quite disgusting habit, you know. You should try giving up. I haven't touched tobacco for four incarnations.'

'Doctor, the Bucephalus is unique in the galaxy. There is no other restaurant that possesses our facilities.'

'Isn't that what unique means?' interjected Turlough.

The Maitre D' sailed on regardless. 'As I was saying, there really is no other explanation. You must have used the Cubiculo Grid.' He grinned a self-satisfied smile, like a little boy working out that one plus one equalled two.

'For the last time . . .' the Doctor's voice trailed off, and a surprised look flared briefly behind his eyes. Turlough became even more puzzled as the Doctor reached inside his jacket. 'I think this will put your fears to rest.' With an elaborate flourish, he pulled out a yellowing scroll, fastened by a large green jewel, and handed it to the Maitre D'.

He unfurled the scroll, retrieving his monocle from a small pocket in his waistcoat.

'What is it?' hissed Turlough.

The Doctor gave him a sly look. 'Patience is a virtue.'

The Maitre D' looked up from the scroll with a mixture of disbelief and shock, and held it out. 'Webwork: analyse!' he ordered. Immediately, a shaft of purple light shot from the ceiling and engulfed the scroll.

'The scroll is genuine,' said the artificial voice.

'Genuine?' he whimpered. Suddenly, a look of horror etched itself on his features. 'My dear Doctor, please accept my deepest apologies. If I had had the slightest idea . . . Naturally, this obscene questioning will cease immediately,' he said, returning the scroll to the Doctor. As he reached for it, Turlough snatched it away.

It seemed to be made of some sort of polymer resembling vellum, while the jewel that fastened it contained a holographic image of a familiar rearing horse. Turlough read the contents out loud. ' "This being a bond to certify that Doctor John Smith, traveller, holds a controlling share, to wit, one hundred per cent, in the business venture incorporated as the Crystal Bucephalus . . ." ' It was Turlough's turn to be shocked. 'You mean you own this place?'

He wasn't prepared for the Doctor's look of shame. 'Yes, Turlough, I'm afraid I do.'

'But how?'

'My balance at the First Galactic Bank occasionally gets embarrassingly large – compound interest and all that.'

'Isn't that a bit careless?'

The Doctor scowled. 'I'm a Time Lord, not a bank manager.' Passing over Turlough's look of amusement, he continued. 'Every now and then, I have to offload large amounts of it into ludicrous business ventures, ones with no hope of success.' A thought flashed unbidden into his mind: *How much money did I pour into the British film industry?*

Turlough interrupted his train of thought. ' "Ludicrous business ventures"? Such as "the most exclusive restaurant the galaxy has ever seen"? Oh, come on.'

The Doctor was valiantly trying to defend himself. 'I examined the prospectus very carefully. When I invested in this place I had no idea that it would succeed. I mean – a time-travelling restaurant? Who would have thought it stood a chance?' He shrugged. 'It appears I may have been a little . . . mistaken.' A discreet cough interrupted him. The Maître D' was putting his talkstick away.

'Doctor, I have taken the liberty of arranging light refreshments for you and your companion.'

'Thank you, Maitre D'. You've just guaranteed your continued employment.'

The Maitre D's face was a study in restraint. It was clear to Turlough that they were going to have problems with him.

Tegan skidded round the booth, her stockinged feet unable to get a grip. Slipping, she grabbed the booth to steady herself, and looked around, but couldn't see her quarry anywhere. And then she caught it, another flash of green peeking out from behind a nearby booth. 'Hey! Wait a minute!' she yelled. 'Don't run away!'

A tall woman stepped out, with long blonde hair and a gorgeous green dress, a dress that clung in a way that revealed every curve. A silver pendant in the shape of an infinity sign hung around her neck. She looked absolutely terrified, and had obviously been crying. 'Who are you?' she whispered.

Tegan walked up and held out her hand. 'Name's Tegan, Tegan Jovanka. And you?'

She nervously completed the handshake. 'I'm Diva. I'm . . .' She looked around with a faint air of panic. 'I'm on the run.'

'Join the club,' said Tegan. 'I've got a load of goat-shaped robots on my tail.'

'The stewards? Why, what have you done?'

Tegan shrugged. 'That's just it. One minute I was tucking into this really great French meal in an authentic French restaurant; the next thing I know I'm here, being accused of murder by some fat bloke with an attitude.'

'The Maitre D'.' Diva's face twisted in anger. 'Murder? Murder?' Before Tegan could react, the woman started laying into her. 'You killed Max! You cow!'

A fist hit Tegan in the stomach, knocking her backwards. And then the marble floor took a hand, and Tegan slipped and hit the ground, her head connecting with a dull thud. With a weak groan, she went limp.

Diva stood over her, but the anger seemed to drain out of her as she realized that Tegan was unconscious. Biting her bottom lip, she frowned, before dragging Tegan away from her extremely visible position to the area behind the Cubiculo that was a little less public.

The Suit was only three feet away. Behind the mirrored dome of his helmet, he broke into a smile. Diva stared straight through him and continued moving Tegan.

'Shall I be mother?' The Maitre D' picked up the silver teapot without waiting for an answer. The 'light refreshments' had arrived, courtesy of one of the stewards: plates of sandwiches, biscuits, and weird little blobs that made the Doctor think of the amoeboid civilization on Kappa Sendilon.

'Perhaps this isn't going to be quite the disaster that we imagined, Turlough.' The Doctor gratefully received the bone china cup and saucer, and sipped delicately. 'Ah, Earl Grey. Hot.' He grinned. 'I recommend it to all my friends.'

'Will you please excuse me one moment, Doctor, Monsignor Turlough? I still have the onerous duties of management to attend to.' His vast frame vanished through the office door.

'Aren't you forgetting a few things?' said Turlough.

'Mmm?' The Doctor picked up a sandwich.

'Not only is our resident walking disaster area still loose, but there is still the tiny matter of a murder.' His voice dropped to a whisper, 'And you still haven't explained how we got here. I mean, when you go for a meal, you don't normally expect to be snatched away by a time machine before the coffee and mints arrive.'

The Doctor nibbled a corner. 'You should try one of these, smoked salmon. All right, Turlough, I must admit that I'm not sure what happened. Somehow, we were intercepted by the Bucephalus, but I'd have to examine the innards of this place before I could come up with the answer. And as for Tegan, I have no doubt that she is handling herself with her usual aplomb.'

'But Arrestis's death?'

'We've acquitted ourselves perfectly, haven't we?' His voice was thoughtful, mischievous even.

'Only for the moment. Once the Maitre D' gets over the fact that you own this place, don't you think he's going to be a little suspicious? From what he's just told us, a bottle of wine was dispatched from the Benefactor's Cubiculo – a Cubiculo programmed for eighteenth-century France, and containing us – and ends up poisoning the head of this era's biggest crime syndicate.' He paused to sip his tea. 'It's obvious the sort of person he is. Even if you are his boss, he'll do everything in his power to bring you down.'

'I see. So, even if I do own this ghastly place, we're still top of the list of suspects?'

'Precisely,' agreed Turlough. 'And not only that, but do you seriously think that our dead kingpin won't have some pretty nasty friends?'

Placing his cup on the low table beside the sofa, the Doctor steepled his fingers beneath his chin. 'I take it that you're suggesting we involve ourselves in this little scenario?'

'Do we have a choice?'

The Doctor beamed at him. 'No, not really. With the TARDIS temporarily – not to mention temporally – displaced, we'll have to remain guests of the Maitre D' for a little while longer.'

Turlough broke into a broad smile. 'You had this all worked out, didn't you?'

'Oh ye of little faith. I just thought I might be able to apply my meagre gifts to the problem.'

Shaking his head in exasperation, Turlough laughed. 'You're incorrigible, do you know that?'

'Thank you, Turlough. I do my best.' He gave a boyish grin and leapt to his feet. 'Maximillian Arrestis was murdered in the twentieth century by a bottle of wine apparently dispatched from eighteenth-century France. Correct?'

'If we take the Maitre D's word for it.'

24

'I think you should curb your cynicism where that particular gentleman is concerned, don't you?' said the Doctor, patting him on the shoulder. 'As you've already pointed out, my ownership of the Crystal Bucephalus is a delicate matter to say the least.'

'All right, have it your way. I'll try to hold myself back.'

'Excellent, Turlough. So, we have the facts, and they offer a number of equally disturbing possibilities.'

'Such as?'

'Such as, Turlough, the precise moment that the wine was poisoned.'

'But who dispatched the wine?'

'Exactly.' The Doctor beamed, as if Turlough had solved the problem. 'That's part two of the problem. Part one has three answers: the three places where the poison could have been administered to the wine.'

Turlough counted them off on his fingers. 'The time zone programmed into Benefactor's Cubiculo, en route from that Cubiculo to Arrestis's time zone, or in 1968. Does it really matter?'

'It did to Monsignor Arrestis.'

Turlough snorted. 'That's not what I meant, and you knew it. Poison is poison.'

'The Crystal Bucephalus is designed to project its patrons into the past, but to prohibit permanent interaction in history.'

Detecting one of the Doctor's irritating non sequiturs, Turlough picked up one of the amoeba-like canapés and was nibbling a pseudopod. 'That's the bit I don't understand. If they can't interact, how can they eat, or order their meals? Or go to the toilet, come to that?'

'Turlough, Turlough, Turlough . . .' he sighed. 'Pay attention to detail. I said "permanent interaction". I would like to be more specific, but it does require a firm grasp of destiny mechanics, and I doubt that the Brigadier taught that at Brendon School.'

He wasn't amused. 'Don't patronize me, Doctor. I'm not one of these Earthlings that you usually surround yourself with. Or are you forgetting just who populated my planet in the first place?'

The Doctor grunted. 'Very well, I'll try to explain. Objects native to the space-time continuum have a reality quotient of one. At that level, they can fully participate in the goings-on around them, and actually make a difference. Patrons from the Bucephalus have a reality quotient of about 0.5. Any less than that, and they'd be phantoms, ghosts, what have you. But being "half real" allows the patrons to eat, drink and be merry, defecate, talk, kill, maim, marry, impregnate, whatever, and then return to the Bucephalus, with the time stream none the wiser. Too small a pebble to divert the river of destiny.' He gave Turlough an enquiring glance. 'Comprehensive enough?'

'Just about, I suppose. But why should that make any difference to where the wine was poisoned?'

Shaking his head in exasperation, the Doctor explained. 'If the wine was poisoned in Beswicks, the poison would also be unreal, which it clearly wasn't. Unless the poisoner had arrived in the 1960s under their own steam . . .'

'Another time traveller?'

The Doctor nodded. 'Still, let's assume that there hasn't been any interference in the time stream, shall we?' he stated, almost as if it were a mathematical hypothesis.

'Why?'

'Well, for one thing it involves an awful lot of paperwork.' Catching Turlough's cynical frown, he sat down in the red leather sofa. 'Call it a hunch, but I feel certain that this era contains all the answers. Who are our suspects?'

'I haven't the faintest idea.'

'Look around you.'

The Doctor's eyes gave him the clue. On the walls were framed pictures of the Maitre D' with what he presumed were galactic bigwigs, pictures which covered almost every available space.

'The galactic cognoscenti, Turlough. The most powerful people in Mutter's Spiral.' He gave a cursory wave at the photographs. 'Surely one of them would have had sufficient motive to want Arrestis dead?'

Turlough sank into the matching armchair to the right of the Doctor. 'It would help if I knew the set-up. I mean, I have absolutely no idea when we are.'

The Doctor wiped his mouth with a serviette. 'About six or seven centuries into the tenth millennium. The largest political organization is the Union, comprising the tattered remnants of the civil war that split the Federation apart. The galaxy is in the middle of a new dark age, where scientific development is confined to a handful of geniuses. The rest of the Union makes do with the rusting achievements of their forebears. The Crystal Bucephalus is the last shining star in a firmament that is rapidly guttering. Another hundred years, and the Union will go the same way as the rest of the galaxy. A millennium of barbarism.'

'Very optimistic. So we're standing on the cliff-edge of chaos, are we?'

'Poetically put. But even when civilization is collapsing, the various factions are all after their slice of what's left. Arrestis was the head of the Elective, a criminal syndicate that runs all the brothels, drug dens and gaming establishments in the Union.'

'And this other lot, the Lazarus Intent. More criminals?'

The Doctor gave Turlough a wry smile. 'Ostensibly quite the opposite. The Intent is a religious order that has been in existence for nearly five thousand years. They believe that their messiah died on the Sontaran Throneworld in the sixty-third century to save the Federation from annihilation.'

'And did he?'

'Come now, Turlough. Ben taught me that there are two things you never talk about in the pub: religion and politics.' Then he frowned. 'Actually, I don't have the faintest idea. I've always meant to pop back and have a look.'

Turlough decided to change the subject. It wasn't as if a 5,000-year-old religion was going to be particularly important, was it? 'So we have a galaxy-full of suspects, not a single motive, and we don't really know how the murder was committed in the first place. A brilliant position to be in.'

'So we should get things rolling,' said the Doctor, standing up and stretching his arms out. 'I think I ought to start poking around in the innards of this monstrosity: I might get a clue as to how Arrestis was murdered.'

'And me?'

The Doctor smiled. It did nothing to reassure Turlough. 'The Maitre D's job brings him into contact with a large number of people. The galactic cognoscenti . . .'

'Oh no.' He advanced on the Doctor. 'If you think I'm going to follow that bag of pretension around, and put up with his condescending attitude —'

'Yes, Turlough, I do think. Now, be a good chap and do as I ask. I'd like to get to the bottom of this *Grand Guignol*, and your assistance would be greatly appreciated.'

Turlough's face took on a look of resignation. 'I suppose so. Just don't blame me if I hit him, will you?'

'Do you really think that I'd ask you to carry out such an unpleasant task if I didn't think it was important?' He leaned forward, snorting. 'Something is going on here, I can feel it. And if we can tie up these particular loose ends before somebody else dies, then I'll be much happier.'

Turlough gritted his teeth. It just wasn't worth protesting, not when the Doctor was in one of his 'avenging Time Lord' moods. 'All right, Doctor, I'll do it. Just lead the way, and I'll follow the Maitre D' around like a puppy dog. Satisfied?'

The room was large and white: white tiled walls, white tiled floor, and functional white furniture. The only colour was centred around the sole occupant, an exotic-looking woman with wild black hair and smouldering brown eyes. Her skin was slightly olive, with full lips that were currently not smiling. She was sitting at a light-harp, an instrument that resembled a standard harp, save that its strings were delicate strands of multi-coloured light and, instead of music, it generated the harmony of pure logic.

'Damn you! I told you to make it brief!' Ladygay Matisse's vehemence was directed in front of her, towards the twelve-foot high and eight-foot wide Archway, also white, that stood in the centre of the room.

'He's the boss, Ladygay.'

At the sound of the bass voice, Matisse rose from the harp and looked round, straightening her black and gold kaftan as she did so. Seven feet of tanned muscle in a white judo suit blocked the doorway. The suit was tied round the middle with a brown belt. Thick black hair poured out from the neckline.

'Don't you think I know that, Garrett?'

'Sorry. Just trying to help.' He landed heavily on one of the chairs which immediately creaked in protest.

Matisse smiled and patted him on the shoulder. Garrett Byson, the giant with cropped hair and an equally cropped intellect; sometimes she felt more like a zoo-keeper than a scientist. 'I know, Garrett. I just can't help feeling that his passion for melodrama will be his undoing.'

Byson scratched his goatee beard, searching for a reply. He eventually found one. 'He's the boss, Ladygay.'

Matisse sighed. Slumping into the chair opposite Byson, she pummelled her eyes with her fists. It was definitely going to be one of those days.

'Tegan,' Diva hissed. Although she had managed to drag her into the gap between two of the Cubiculi, they were still a lot more visible than she would have liked. And she had been unconscious for almost twenty minutes. 'Tegan, wake up!' She knelt over her and gave her a soft slap across the face. To Diva's relief, her eyelids began to flicker. And then Tegan started trying to sit up.

'Hey, not so fast.' Diva gently helped her into a sitting position. 'That was quite a knock; there might be concussion.'

Tegan touched the back of her head and winced. 'You pack quite a punch.'

'That was the floor.' She gave a sheepish smile. 'I'm

sorry about that. When you said about the murder . . . I was there. The person who was murdered was Maximillian Arrestis.'

Tegan shrugged. 'Is that meant to mean something?'

Where had this woman been? 'Max is . . . was the CEO of the Arrestis Corporation, the front for almost all of the criminal activities in this part of the galaxy.'

Tegan whistled. 'And he's been murdered?' She sighed. 'And we get accused of the murder; typical. So where do you fit into all of this?'

'I worked for Max. I was his woman.'

'His woman? His woman? What sort of an expression is that?' snapped Tegan.

'Not so loud.' Diva put a finger to her lips. 'That was Max's way. No commitments. When he needed a companion, he put them on the pay-roll. I was the latest.' She closed her eyes. 'Not that that makes this any easier. To see him die in front of me —'

'Very touching.' The voice seemed to come from nowhere, a deep voice that was obviously coming through some sort of speaker. And then it happened. A man-sized region of empty space suddenly churned with mirrored streaks, as if someone had taken the fabric of space and time and given it a good stir.

Tegan gasped. 'What the hell?'

The disturbance suddenly condensed into what appeared to be a suit of battle armour, its surface reflective blue metal. A disruptor pistol was held in the thick fingers of the Suit's right gauntlet.

Diva jumped to her feet. 'Who are you?'

'You're both trespassing in the Crystal Bucephalus. That holds rather severe penalties.'

The muzzle of the disruptor flared.

Two

'I presume you'll want to visit the Grid Control Suite?' The Doctor spun round. The Maitre D' had entered the office with surprising silence for a man of his bulk. The Doctor gave him a disarming smile. 'Why would I want to go there?'

The Maitre D's eyes sparked with contempt, but his voice was even when he replied. 'My stewards tell me that you have expressed an interest in the "grubby workings of this edifice of kitsch".' Turlough grinned at the Maitre D's delivery of the Doctor's quote, but two pairs of warning eyes forced him to adopt a more respectful expression.

'Well, yes. It might help to put all of this into perspective, don't you think?'

'I am but a humble servitor, Doctor; I am not permitted an opinion.' But the Maitre D' sounded like anything but a 'humble servitor', thought Turlough.

'You're too modest,' countered the Doctor, injecting just the right amount of sarcasm in his tone. 'I'm sure that you're a man of deep passions.' Before the Maitre D' could respond, the Doctor threw his arm out to Turlough. 'While I'm looking at this fine establishment's technical infrastructure, I'm sure that you will have no objection to Turlough watching you at work, as you oil the wheels of the Crystal Bucephalus?'

That's it, Doctor, light the blue touch-paper and stand well back. Turlough braced himself for the inevitable backlash. It took approximately half a second.

Divesting himself of his earlier false modesty, the Maitre D' expanded like a preening baboon. 'Doctor, I am the Maitre D'Hotel of the Crystal Bucephalus, not

31

your paid lackey.' His voice leapt an octave. 'I do not take reprobates on guided tours!'

In response, the Doctor's voice dropped in tone, with a clear streak of menace colouring every word. 'Might I remind you who pays your salary? To all intents and purposes, you *are* my paid lackey. Do I make myself clear, Maitre D'?'

For a second, there was a loaded silence. Then he replied. 'As clear as crystal, Doctor. I shall return for Monsignor Turlough in a few moments.'

If Turlough hadn't known better, he would have sworn that the Doctor waited until the Maitre D' had reached the door before speaking. 'Ah, just one more thing –'

Turning, the Maitre D' seemed to be gritting his teeth. He said nothing, but his raised eyebrow was eloquence itself.

'Could you be so kind as to direct me to this Grid Control Suite?'

The disruptor pulse hit the wood of the Cubiculo about a foot to the left of Diva's head.

'The next time, that'll be your pretty little head.' The Suit pointed at the Cubiculo: a five-inch wide circle of light brown had vanished, revealing the dull metal that lay beneath the ornate surface.

Tegan had gingerly clambered to her feet. 'Now listen here, buster. I don't know what your game is, but you can't just start taking pot-shots at us.'

'I can and I will.' He gestured with the disruptor. 'Now move!'

The women walked forward in the direction the Suit had indicated. 'Well?' whispered Diva.

'We play along until we can see a break.'

'Is that a plan?'

'Let's just say it's worked before.' Tegan stopped talking as she felt the disruptor touch her back, its muzzle cold through the red silk of her dress. 'Okay, okay,' she protested. 'No need to hassle us.'

* * *

The Grid Control Suite was on the opposite side of the Mezzanine to the Maitre D's office, necessitating a walk through the avenue of gothic pillars and straight past the dominating crystal horse. The Doctor craned his head to look at the glaring nostrils and the concave cheeks as they sparkled in the light from the distant chandeliers. He couldn't help noticing that the emerald horse was radiating an inner light of its own. He shrugged; another puzzle for another time.

'Obviously somebody is an enthusiast of Alexander the Great,' he muttered. 'Rather a pity: the man was such a dreadful bore.' He ran a light finger over the surface of the black marble plinth that supported the statue. 'Now, if they'd consulted the owner, I would have come up with something a little less tongue-tying.' He continued on his way through the avenue of Cubiculi.

'Actually,' he said thoughtfully, 'I quite like the sound of "The Crystal Wombat".'

Inside his office, the Maitre D' was fussing around his desk, shuffling papers and pens in some bizarre semblance of a chess match.

'Queen's paper clip to Knight's pencil sharpener?' enquired Turlough.

'I beg your pardon?'

'Look, forgive me for asking, but is there some purpose to your sudden obsession with stationery rearrangement? I mean, you come back to your office and start reorganizing your desk; I thought that you had duties to attend to?' Turlough picked up a spherical paperweight and peered into its depths. He suddenly realized that it was a holosphere, containing the image of a stunning red-headed woman.

'Excuse me,' snapped the Maitre D', plucking the paperweight from his grasp. 'If you must know, I was looking for my talkstick.'

'You mean the talkstick that's in its holster strapped to your side? The talkstick that is exactly where you knew it was all the time?'

His face was inscrutable. 'Thank you, Monsignor Turlough.' But he still made no move from his desk, his fingers splayed out on the surface like fat spiders.

Leaning over the desk, Turlough's face was only inches from the Maitre D'. 'If that's all, I suggest we go. Or should I call up the Doctor?'

Raising his large frame from the mahogany desk, he transfixed Turlough with a look of sheer disgust. 'No need for veiled threats, Monsignor Turlough.' He made a theatrical show of checking his watch. 'It just so happens that this is about the time that many of the patrons request my presence at table.'

Turlough's voice was a study in innocence. 'Why, are you the cabaret?'

The Maitre D' turned on his heel.

On the opposite side of the Mezzanine, the Doctor was standing in front of two silver doors, emblazoned as ever with the rearing horse motif. Two of the goat-like stewards stood sentinel on either side, their impassive gazes locked onto the Doctor. He strode towards them, stopping when he was equidistant between them. 'Is this a private party, or can anyone join in?'

The stewards grabbed a handle each, and opened the doors. With a cheery grin, the Doctor breezed through.

The Grid Control Suite was a large oblong room, wood-panelled like a Tudor house. Three banks of oak lecterns stood to the Doctor's right, where six grey-garbed technicians busied around and ignored his presence. In the far left-hand corner, a less ornate Cubiculo stood idly by.

But his attention was drawn to what stood in front of him, opposite the now wood-panelled doors: twin interlocking spirals of light, stretching from a bronze plinth on the floor right up to the ceiling, 40 feet up, where another bronze plate seemed to devour them. The spirals were encased in a crystal pillar that reflected the white radiance in coruscating bursts of light. Around the plinth and reaching up around the pillar, a cradle of brass and crystal formed a kind of scaffolding, interlaced with thick golden ropes that snaked in and out of the bars. The Doctor lifted an eyebrow in uneasy recognition. 'Bladamite tubing; well, well, well,' he muttered.

He moved over to the instruments that surrounded the pillar in a semicircle. The controls that covered the surface were in keeping with the Jules Verne ambience: monitors framed with bronze, keyboards with large brass buttons, bronze levers topped with huge crystal knobs. Then again, surface sophistication was no measure of internal complexity: the Doctor thought fondly of the control room he had designed along the same lines as the Grid Control Suite, where block transfer computations and dimensional engineering were translated into a symphony of stained glass, brass rails and stained oak. Well, he'd liked that sort of thing once.

The Doctor stroked the controls, trying to calm some inner voice, but something was wrong, something was shouting out in protest, trying to get the ear of the time technician that lay buried within the Doctor. The time of the Union was somewhat of a blur to him, an era off the beaten track, but he did remember a paper by a couple of temporal scientists, Monroe and Lassiter, that was it. Their research had only got as far as the sort of temporal projection that lay behind the Bucephalus, with no suggestion in their work that it was anything more than a technological dead-end, like Whitaker's time scoop, Findecker's double nexus particle, and Blinovitch's chronal displacer.

'Of course, I should have realized!' he shouted, eliciting curious stares from the technicians. But he knew what bothered him about the Grid Control Suite. Someone was holding back: bladamite tubing, a positive cretathole converter – and the transparent cube with a sphere inside was definitely a psio-linguistic translator. All fundamental aspects of TARDIS technology. With the equipment laid out here in the Grid Control Suite, true time travel – interactive temporal transfer – was only a few blocks of exitonic circuitry away. Yet it seemed that the architect of the Grid had deliberately handicapped his own work, holding back from the logical development that the Grid promised, just so as not to exceed the researches of Lassiter and Monroe.

Fired with curiosity, the Doctor walked over to the lecterns. He selected the nearest technician, a short man with a bushy beard and curly red hair. 'Excuse me . . . ?'

The technician looked up. 'Technician Ottway. Look, I'm sorry, but patrons aren't allowed in here.' He began to glance around, probably hoping to summon a steward.

'Ah, no, I understand that, but I'm not a patron.' He held out his hand. 'I'm the Doctor. I own this place.' Seeing the technician's frown, he dropped his hand and continued. 'How else could I have got past the stewards?'

'You've got a point there. So, what do you want to know?'

The Doctor gave him a boyish smile. 'Oh, not much. I just wondered who was in charge of all this.' He waved a hand around dismissively.

'Oh, is that all? He's not here at the moment. He's in the Legion tank. Out of the door, straight on, then turn left at the Diamond Dobbin –'

'The what?'

'The statue. The Legion tank is behind the far wall.'

The Doctor turned away, then turned back. 'Sorry to bother you again, but who might I be looking for?'

The technician raised an eyebrow. 'I thought you owned the Dobbin?'

'I try to keep out of the business side of things. Leave it to the experts, that kind of thing.'

'Probably a good idea in this place. You want Professor Lassiter.'

'Lassiter? Alexhendri Lassiter?'

'The same. Anyway, I must get on: the negative plum-finity coils need tuning.'

The Doctor tried to feign a lack of understanding of a subject he had mastered centuries ago. 'Yes of course, sorry to take up so much of your time.' Lassiter. What was going on here? Walking towards the doors, an uneasy thought crossed his mind. If he remembered his training correctly, he mused, then he was supposed to shut the place down. He stopped and turned back, admiring mankind's stab at the secrets of Gallifrey. *Mankind, such an indomitable species* . . . It hadn't been that long since he'd uttered those words, and here was that very same species, on the threshold of conquering time itself. He compared that with his most recent experiences with the Time Lords: a shallow and terrified race quite prepared to sacrifice him rather than soiling their lily-white hands. And then there was Ruath, the Master, Omega himself . . .

'Sorry, chaps,' he muttered to no one in particular. 'You can do your own dirty work this time.' With that he set off for the Legion tank, and, hopefully, Professor Lassiter.

Tegan stopped. 'What authority have you got to arrest us, then?'

The Suit shoved his disruptor forwards. 'This authority.'

She held back her nervousness. 'I don't think you're anything to do with this place. You're just some sad man with a superiority complex who gets a kick out of pointing a gun at two so-called defenceless women.'

'Aren't we the amateur psychologist?' The blank helmet gave nothing away. 'Now keep quiet and move.'

'Hey!' Tegan screamed over the Suit's shoulder. 'Over here!' As she had expected – or rather, as she had hoped – the Suit turned to see who Tegan was talking to.

'Oldest trick in the book. Run!' Tegan grabbed Diva's arm and pulled her between two Cubiculi. As they turned into the gap, Tegan glanced behind and saw the Suit dissolve into a reflective swirl before vanishing completely. 'He's invisible again; he could be anywhere.'

Diva stopped and pulled off her shoes. 'We won't be going anywhere if I have to keep tottering around on these.' Throwing them at the base of one of the Cubiculi, she peered out, beckoning to Tegan as she did so. 'Over there. If we keep zig-zagging, we should be able to give him the slip.' This time, she grabbed Tegan's arm and started running.

They padded across the floor towards the next ring, taking care not to slip on the smooth marble. 'I hope that battle armour is as slow as I think it is,' said Diva as they ran. 'We're not exactly going to set any records skidding from Cubiculo to Cubiculo.'

'Battle armour? Is that what it is?' One space suit looked a lot like any other in Tegan's opinion.

'Class Seven osmidium battlesuit.' Diva stopped as they reached the next ring in. 'Not exactly standard issue, though: personal shroudfields are an optional extra.' She sucked a finger and decided upon a direction. 'Next ring!'

After another hectic sliding trip across the Mezzanine, they stopped behind another Cubiculo.

'You seem to know a lot about it.' Tegan looked around for their pursuer before remembering that he could have been standing next to her for all she knew. 'Battle armour, I mean.'

Diva gave a shrug. 'My father was a general in the Union Fleet. I was brought up reading about ship schematics and the latest in spacewear.'

Tegan grinned. 'Makes a change from Enid Blyton.' Ignoring Diva's quizzical frown, she stared around. 'Okay, soldier's daughter: where now?'

'I think we ought to find a steward and report this, er, Suit person. I think they'd be quite interested in an armed and shrouded intruder flitting about amongst the galactic glitterati, don't you?'

Despite the fact that Tegan didn't have a clue who the 'galactic glitterati' were, she couldn't fault Diva's logic. Apart from one point. 'You're forgetting one thing.'

'Which is?'

'I'm wanted for the murder of your boyfriend. Which I didn't do,' she added, raising her hands in the air.

'If you didn't do it, you haven't got anything to worry about, have you?'

Tegan gave a lop-sided smile. 'If you put it that way, no, I suppose I haven't.'

The Suit, two feet behind Tegan, rubbed his gauntlets together.

'Most of the stewards seem to be otherwise engaged,' Diva pointed out. Tegan realized that they hadn't seen a single one of the goat-like androids for ages. 'Still, if we try one of the offices on the outer wall we should be able to get some help.'

'Okay, so I get arrested. I'll just have to hope that the Doctor has performed his usual magic trick and charmed the pants off everyone.' She shrugged. 'So, what are we waiting for?'

As the women made for the wall of the Mezzanine, the Suit checked the head up display projected on the interior of his helmet. Yes, there was more than enough power in the sarium krellide cells for this little miracle. With darting eye movements, he deftly navigated through the menus until he found the particular defence panel he was after. Diva might have recognized his battle armour, but he doubted she was familiar with some of its more esoteric abilities. Such as being able to cast its shroudfield around nearby objects.

The Legion tank. Shown through the double doors by the androids, the Doctor cast an inquisitive look around. In yet another complete shift of architectural styles, the Legion tank was furnished like a Greek temple: fluted stone columns stood at the four corners, while the walls were decorated with alcoves containing various carved deities. The Doctor recognized a few: Zeus, Athene, Ares and Alexander the Great himself. The centre of the room was a sunken pit, some twenty-five feet by fifteen and five feet deep. It wasn't empty.

From the gun-metal block in the middle of the pit, thick cables snaked out to the creatures that surrounded it; the Doctor counted 20 of them. Black and furry, with octopoid appendages that seemed to grow in thickness before fading to almost nothing, they had a certain other-worldly, other-dimensional quality about them.

'Legions!' exclaimed the Doctor, recognizing the

multi-dimensional race and irritated that he hadn't made the connection sooner. He was a little surprised that they were still part of galactic society in the 108th century; considering how thoroughly unpleasant they had been in the twenty-seven hundreds, he'd expected them to have been imprisoned for at least a hundred and fifty thousand years, the standard Time Lord sentence for a crime of such magnitude. Their mercenary desires had led them to use their unique gifts to undermine the great business consortia that had ruled the galaxy, and, when they were exposed, their revenge had been brutal. The Doctor had a vague memory of the CIA sticking their oar in – oh yes, Mortimus, wasn't it? – erecting temporal inhibitors on their planet to prevent them from escaping. He could only assume that they had served their sentence. That would teach him not to read his mail.

His reverie was interrupted by a tap on the shoulder. He turned to see a man of average height, slightly overweight, with a big bushy moustache and short brown hair. The Doctor noticed the short ponytail and immediately remembered his own. The man was wearing a pair of black trousers and a white polo-neck jumper with an unfastened black waistcoat over it.

'Doctor Smith, I presume?' The man's voice was brimming with barely restrained enthusiasm.

He couldn't help smiling. 'Just call me "Doctor". And you are?'

The tubby stranger grinned infectiously. 'Alex. But if you want to be formal, I'm Professor Alexhendri Lassiter.' He offered his hand.

The Doctor shook the hand warmly. 'Professor Lassiter – Alex – how nice to meet you.' He gestured around the room. 'I was just admiring your handiwork.'

His grin grew even broader. 'I understand from the Maitre D' that you have some knowledge of temporal physics yourself.'

The Doctor stroked his chin thoughtfully. 'Oh, a passing interest, nothing more. Although I have read the paper on the LeFabvre equations by your good self and –'

'Hellenica Monroe.' A faint but unmistakable trace of bitterness coloured his voice. 'From that initial research, she and I finally came up with a theoretical basis for the creation of an interstitial motive bridge as an analogue reality for the Time Vortex.' He stopped to catch his breath.

'So, rather than passing directly through the Time Vortex, with the inherent risks of exposure to the time winds, you generate a pocket dimension, linking the Bucephalus with the target time zone.' The words were out before the Doctor could stop himself.

'Exactly. Time bubbles.' Lassiter was beaming. The Doctor got the feeling that it wasn't often that Lassiter got to speak with someone on equal scientific terms.

'Just so. But the Legions . . .' The Doctor waved his hand at the pit. 'Couldn't you develop a technological equivalent?'

'I'm afraid not; some things are beyond even me,' he said immodestly. 'Anyway, the Legions have just been released from a prison sentence, and this is their way of making amends.'

'Prison sentence?' How much did Lassiter know?

'The Time Lords,' said Lassiter as if it was obvious. 'You must have heard of them? A race of beings who exist at the dawn of time who don't like people messing around with time travel. From what I've read, the Legions abused their powers, and the Time Lords waded in and shut down their operation.' Lassiter gave the Doctor a wry look. 'Actually, I'm quite surprised that they haven't tried to shut me down yet!' He grinned. 'You're not a Time Lord are you?'

The Doctor smiled, but his hearts almost skipped a beat. 'Of course not. What do you take me for?'

'Only a joke, Doctor, only a joke.' He looked around the Legion tank. 'Anyway, what do you think of it all?'

'Oh, a monumental achievement, Alex.'

'This is nothing, just a way of keeping the bored galactic nobility happy.'

This did nothing to ease the Doctor's worries. 'But

41

surely you must be proud of your discoveries?'

Lassiter paused for a second, as if deciding what to say. When he finally spoke, it sent a shiver up the Doctor's spine. Giving him a friendly punch in the arm, he said, 'I do know that I couldn't have done any of it without your financial backing.'

The Doctor smiled, but there was no humour in it. For countless aeons, the Time Lords of Gallifrey had fiercely protected their secrets, as the Legions had found out to their cost. And he had provided the means for mankind to unlock their safe. *I might as well just build Lassiter a TARDIS and be done with it. Those stuffed shirts will definitely not be pleased with me.*

'Where are we off to, then?' Turlough was trailing behind the Maitre D' as he nodded and smiled at the few stewards and patrons that were still on the Mezzanine rather than sampling the pleasures of the past.

'I'm sure I must have mentioned my popularity?'

Turlough smiled unconvincingly. 'You could say that.'

'Well, the patron in Cubiculo 011 has specifically requested that I join him for the cheese-board, meta-phorically speaking.'

'How wonderful for him.' It was becoming increas-ingly difficult to be civil to the man. 'Shouldn't you be ensuring the smooth running of the Bucephalus?'

'Dear boy, it would be quite jejune of me to turn down such an invitation.' Turlough could see him puff up with pride. 'One does not ignore the whims of a Prelector of the Lazarus Intent. The Prelectors are second only to the Benefactor in the hierarchy of the Intent.'

'Where, I mean, when has he gone? Yes, and where, come to that?'

The Maitre D' pulled out his talkstick with an air of irritation. 'Webwork: Prelector Tornqvist's location.'

'Prelector Tornqvist is on Chardon, 4338. He is a guest of Wilhelm, König of the Wine Lords,' the deep voice informed them.

He returned his talkstick to its holster and nodded.

'Satisfied, Monsignor Turlough?'

'Wine Lords? And he's supposed to be a priest?'

'We are but the servitors of our charges,' he stated. 'Their caprices are not ours to question.'

'Very noble.' Turlough had had his fill of hypocritical religions on Trion. 'Oh well, each to their own. Anyway, can you answer me a question?'

'If it shuts you up.'

Turlough ignored him. 'How are the time zones located?'

The Maitre D' waved condescendingly at a nearby steward. 'In certain cases, such as that of the late Monsignor Arrestis, patrons will suggest a location, and we will do our utmost to ascertain its spatio-temporal coordinates. But most of the destinations are chosen from our pre-set Carte de Locales.'

'How was that put together?'

'Nine years ago, when we initially designed the Crystal Bucephalus, a search was made of the Union information net. All of the knowledge of all of the civilizations that comprise the Union – humanity, Alpha Centaurians, Earth Reptiles, Martians and the like – lies within the net.' He paused to nod at a steward. 'The search detected all references to places connected to the consumption of food, however elliptical: news broadcasts, historical texts, archaeological reports –'

'Years ago,' interrupted Turlough, 'I remember reading about an archaeological dig on one of the outer planets of my star system; Montaplure, that was it. They discovered the remains of a civilization that was devoted to the art of eating.'

'Monsignor Turlough, I am familiar with the complete Carte de Locales of the Crystal Bucephalus. Ancient Montaplure is one of our less exotic locales.'

Turlough ignited in fury at the pompous prig's dismissal of his anecdote. 'Why don't you just . . .' He trailed off, deciding that discretion was the better part of having an easy life. 'Why don't we look in on the Prelector?'

'A splendid idea, dear boy.'

Turlough trotted behind as the Maitre D' sailed away like a galleon in full sail.

'What purpose do they serve?' The Doctor was looking over his half-frames at the multi-dimensional creatures as they throbbed in and out of reality. His first-hand knowledge of the race was limited: he had met a Legion briefly on Earth in the 25th century, just before the Second Dalek War. That particular fellow had apparently been a typical example of his species: rude, arrogant and overbearing and, for once, he could quite understand the Time Lords' actions.

'The Legions possess a rare gift: they're capable of navigating through the Time Vortex. The twenty members of the Legion tank are responsible for plotting the courses of all of the active time bubbles. All of this,' Lassiter gestured at the rest of the equipment and presumably implied the Grid Control Suite as well, 'generates the time bubbles, and provides the motive force to drive them through the Vortex to the target time zone. The Legions create the paths that the bubbles are sent along.'

'Very ingenious, Alex.' It didn't ring true. Given the technological advancement of the Grid Control Suite, albeit suspiciously handicapped, he found it hard to believe that Lassiter was incapable of designing a cybernetic equivalent of the Legion tank. Even the Doctor's brief look at Grid Control had shown him equipment that was far beyond the exitonic navigator needed to replace the Legions. Lassiter was hiding something – but what? He looked at the cluster of truncated ionic pillars about ten feet away. Their surfaces were covered in keyboards and trackballs, switches and levers, all carved from pinky-grey stone. Yet another of the quaint anachronisms that Lassiter obviously found so fetching.

'Would you like some tea? I have a special blend imported from Caspar; I think you might like it.'

The Doctor smiled. 'How wonderfully civilized.'

* * *

'Are we there yet?' Turlough felt like they had walked past every Cubiculo in the Bucephalus. They were now on the outer edges of the Mezzanine, strolling past the tasteless statues and flower arrangements that were placed every few feet.

'Patience is a virtue. The Prelector is expecting me in about ten minutes. I have other calls to make before I indulge myself of his hospitality.'

'But the Crystal Bucephalus is a time machine. It shouldn't make any difference out here, should it?'

The Maitre D' smiled with a revoltingly smug grin. 'There you exhibit your ignorance of the true nature of the Bucephalus, Monsignor Turlough.'

'Well, pardon me for existing.' He decided that hitting the bloated bag of condescension was too kind. He'd go back to the TARDIS, set the coordinates for the planet of the exquisite torture creatures, and dump the pompous old bastard there. For goodness sake, I'm even beginning to think like a human, he decided. 'If you would care to explain?' he said tiredly.

'The Blinovitch Limitation Effect, or so I'm told. An hour here in the Bucephalus is equivalent to an hour in the target time zone. It makes everything neat and tidy.' He stopped. 'You'll have to excuse me. Even I am at the mercy of the forces of nature.' He made a praying gesture, and then pointed his hands toward six doors in the wall.

As Turlough tried to interpret the icons on each door, the Maitre D' vanished into the one marked by the eternal symbol of the gent's toilet. Turlough whiled away the general manager's micturational moments by trying to identify the other icons. He recognized the human women's toilet and the Draconians' — no females, naturally. But who would use the one with an icon that looked like a man with handles for ears?

Turlough's concentration was broken by someone behind him. He turned to see a tall figure, its skin like organic silver. It wore a sort of harness-cum-bodywarmer, a grey thing with pearly disks at the chest and groin. Facially, it had two blank eyes, a muzzle for a mouth, and a tube that started at one ear, went round the back of the head, and met the opposite ear. Turlough jumped back.

'I'm so sorry,' said the creature, a faintly synthetic tone in its voice. 'Did I startle you?' It walked up to the door and walked through the one that Turlough couldn't identify. Before it entered, it looked back. 'You really should learn to unwind.'

The Doctor sipped his tea with a look of pleasure. 'Absolutely delicious, Alex. Where did you say it came from?'

Lassiter had drawn up two reproduction Grecian chairs and was sitting opposite the Doctor. 'Caspar, in the Gelephatic Rift. Twin suns, you know.' It was also dreadfully expensive, but he had decided long ago that he deserved a few creature comforts in his exile.

'I must get a supply for the TAR . . . for my ship, I think.' He placed the cup on an adjacent console. 'Have you any idea what could have happened to Arrestis?'

'He was poisoned. Surely it's a matter for the Elective now.'

The Doctor raised an eyebrow. 'Perhaps. But my primary concern is where, or rather when, the poison was introduced.'

'I checked the memory logs of the steward that was assigned to Benefactor's: it was given the wine, took it to 507 and delivered it to Arrestis. Whereupon he died.'

The Doctor leaned forward. 'Who gave the steward the wine?'

Lassiter shrugged. 'That's the problem. It received the wine, but that's it. The logs don't show anything apart from confirmation that it was given a bottle of wine. As far as the steward is concerned, one moment it didn't have the bottle; the next, it did.'

The Doctor leaned forward in his chair. 'Interesting. I presume that its memories are quite coherent from that point on?'

'Got it in one. The poison couldn't have been introduced at any other point apart from Benefactor's.' Which doesn't do a lot to get you off the hook, Doctor, he almost added.

'As I suspected. I take it that the Bucephalus has records of who is in which Cubiculo?'

'What sort of an operation do you think I'm running here?' he snapped. 'Of course it does. And, before you ask, I checked the register. Benefactor's was booked in your name. 1791, Ancient Earth, France, to be exact.'

'Le Café de Saint Joseph, Aix-en-Provence,' the Doctor huffed. 'So all the evidence points to me?'

Lassiter raised a finger. 'It might look that way, except that I ran one of my diagnostics against the webwork.'

'And?'

'It's been tampered with. I'll admit that the culprit is clever: most people wouldn't have spotted it, but they aren't in my class. The diagnostic indicated that someone invaded the system nucleus of the webwork and had a good old play around.' He leaned back and cracked his knuckles. 'You've been set up, Doctor.'

'I suspected as much. Perhaps I can have a look . . .' He trailed off. 'I can't be sure, but –' Jumping up, he pointed at the pit. 'That Legion, there's something wrong.'

'How can you tell?' Even as he spoke, Lassiter realized that the Legion was shrinking, retracting into hyperspace.

The Doctor's voice took on a more forceful tone as he strode over to the lip of the tank. 'Alex, that Legion is ill. Disconnect it from the tank.'

'I can't. The systems don't permit –'

'Then make them permit!' he shouted. 'It's suffering from an infarction; it'll die unless you get it medical attention.' The Doctor vaulted into the pit and started examining the cabling that connected the Legion to the metal block. 'Don't just stand there, man, help me!'

'If it dies while it's connected up we'll lose all the bubbles it maintains,' Lassiter yelled, as he desperately typed away on one of the consoles.

'Then reroute its workload to the others.' The Doctor was looking at the Legion's connection to the central block.

'I'm trying, but the systems aren't designed for this!' He held out his hands in impotence. The Legions were an integral part of the Grid: without them, everything would fall apart.

The Doctor leapt back up and dashed over to his side and began entering a complex sequence of commands with the keyboard and trackball, watching the results in the holosphere above the pillar. Patterns of lights flickered across the board, while the holosphere pulsed at the same rapid rate as the Doctor's fingers. After what seemed like an age, the Doctor lifted his hands from the stone console. 'Try to stabilize what I've done here; I'll disconnect the Legion!' Jumping into the tank, the Doctor pulled the cables out of the oscillating ball of fur. 90 per cent of the creature had retreated into hyperspace, and the little that remained was trembling in an alarming manner. He dropped to his knees and sank his arms into the Legion: they disappeared up to his elbows. 'A particular form of artificial resuscitation,' he commented, almost certainly noting Lassiter's puzzled expression.

'I've called the medics: they'll be here any minute,' said Lassiter before returning his attention to the control panel.

'Thank you,' said the Doctor, getting to his feet. The Legion seemed to be slowly expanding, gently flowing outwards from wherever it had gone. 'I think it's stabilized.'

Lassiter ran nervous fingers through his moustache. 'Unlike one of the bubbles. Can you take a look?' The Doctor's attempt had succeeded, almost. The other Legions had taken on the additional workload relinquished by their sick colleague, all except one bubble. And all the indications showed that it was critically unstable.

'Can you close it down?' asked the Doctor, peering at the readings.

'Too much interference at the other end.' Lassiter could feel the sweat forming as he looked up from the console. 'We're going to lose it!'

48

The Doctor jabbed a finger at one of the holospheres that hovered above the pillar. Within, it showed all the details of the bubble. 'We must try to boost the integrity levels. Try an anchor beam.'

'But an anchor beam could disrupt the bubble.'

The Doctor's reply was as hard as diamond. 'Do it!'

'That looks important.' The two huge silver doors were about twelve feet away, set into the wall that encircled the Mezzanine. A rearing horse was engraved on each, and, more importantly, two stewards stood guard. 'Shall we make ourselves known?' asked Diva.

'If you're prepared to pay the bail,' said Tegan with a resigned air.

'What?' She was beginning to think that Tegan had stepped out of one of the Cubiculi, with her archaic speech patterns. 'It's now or never.' With that, she crossed from the outermost ring of Cubiculi towards the doors.

'Okay,' sighed Tegan. 'Wait for me.'

Diva stepped up to one of the stewards. 'Excuse me?' The steward's silver face looked straight through her, its burnished eyes focused on somewhere far behind her. Diva couldn't help shuddering. 'Excuse me!' her voice was louder. 'I'm talking to you!' She tapped the steward on the shoulder. It looked around, but still didn't register their presence.

'What's it up to?'

Diva frowned. 'I don't know. It's as if we're invisible.' Her eyes widened in realization. 'For the love of Lazarus, the Suit!'

Tegan obviously understood. 'You mean we *are* invisible?' She turned to face the Mezzanine. 'Where are you! Show yourself!'

'Tegan!' shouted Diva. 'What are you playing at?'

'Face it. He knows where we are. He's been following us since he vanished. Haven't you?' The last part of her remark was aimed at the empty space between the women and the Cubiculi.

'Very astute.' The Suit churned into existence in front of them. 'Ventriloquists throw their voices; I throw my shroudfield.'

Diva stepped forward. 'Who are you? You're not with the Bucephalus.' Fear tightened around her stomach. 'You – you killed Max, didn't you?'

'I could swear that you sound concerned.'

'Why did you kill him?' screamed Diva.

Tegan held out her hand. 'Don't lose your temper. That's what he wants: two screaming women he can dominate.' She mustered a hard stare at the featureless helmet. 'It won't work.'

'As much as I've enjoyed this little cat-and-mouse game, I've got better things to do.' He pointed a thumb over his shoulder. 'Over there.'

'The Cubiculi?' Diva began to have a horrible suspicion. 'You can't be serious.'

'Very. Now move!'

'The appointed hour and the appointed Cubiculo,' said the Maitre D', flicking a nonchalant hand at the carved booth. He walked up to the double doors and grabbed the handles.

'I'm quite looking forward to meeting the Wine Lords,' said Turlough.

'Oh no, I'm afraid that would be quite improper and quite out of the question. The invitation was for myself, and myself alone. I'd appreciate it if you could wait here.'

Turlough gave him a look of contempt as he pulled open the doors.

'And try not to cause any trouble, there's a good boy.'

'What about the anchor beam?'

'I can't get a lock. I'm losing it!' Lassiter's eyes scanned the holosphere; the outlook wasn't good. And, unless he was very much mistaken, there was something else amiss, almost as if something else – 'For Lazarus's sake, Doctor, do something!'

'Bear with me.' The Doctor's fingers rattled out a frantic staccato on the stone keys of the console. 'There,' he announced. 'I've sent a pattern enhancement pulse down the line. Is there any change?'

'Cubiculo 011 is still unstable,' whispered Lassiter. 'Prelector Tornqvist. Doctor, he's one of the most powerful men in the galaxy. If he dies –'

'The status of the bubble?'

He was shaking as he replied. 'Collapse imminent.'

'That's it!' Turlough grabbed the Maitre D's arm before he could enter the inky void that lay beyond the doors. 'I'm sick to the back teeth with your supercilious, pompous attitude!' He pushed past him and stepped through into . . . The Crystal Bucephalus had vanished. The room was cramped but luxurious, with carpeted walls and floors. Not only that, but his jacket and pantaloons had been transformed into a green robe, edged in silver. 'The planet of the Wine Lords,' he muttered.

A man in the same manner of clothing looked up from his plate of food, a quizzical look in his eyes. The insect-like creature in attendance took one look at him and fled the room in terror.

The Suit flicked open a panel on his wrist and pulled a cable from within, inserting the small block on the end into an almost invisible keyhole in the Cubiculo. But the blank helmet never wavered: he was watching Tegan and Diva from behind the reflective osmidium. He pulled the doors open, revealing the blackness that led to the Grid. 'In!' he ordered.

'You can't do this!' Diva protested.

'I can do anything I want.' He casually flicked the disruptor in her direction. 'Get in!'

'Why did you kill Max?' Diva's voice was wavering. Funny; she had never known that Arrestis meant so much to her.

'His life insurance? For the last time, get in!'

Diva and Tegan entered Cubiculo 992 at gun point.

He watched as they vanished into the blackness, then followed.

Perhaps the Prelector would have asked Turlough what he was doing there instead of the Maitre D'. Maybe he would have asked him to join him for a pastry parcel of larks' tongues and a glass of the excellent '69. As it turned out, all he could do was scream, as blood red hoops of light materialized around him, their extra-dimensional forces tearing at his body. And then Turlough joined in.

'It's too late.' Lassiter shook his head in resignation. 'The bubble's collapsed.' Another death at the Bucephalus, and he had been powerless to stop it.

'And the Prelector?'

Lassiter slumped into his chair. 'Not a hope. As soon as the bubble went, Tornqvist would have been exposed to the time winds; they would have ripped him apart. He wouldn't have stood a chance.'

The Doctor shivered. 'Yes,' he agreed, 'I can imagine.'

The brief squawk of his talkstick cut the silence. He pulled it from inside his waistcoat. 'Lassiter?'

'Alex: Sebastian here.'

'What is it?' A call from the Maitre D' was unexpected, unprecedented, even. It didn't bode well.

'I'm at Cubiculo 011.'

He was confused: how could the Maitre D' have known? 'What's happened?'

'It's the Doctor's friend. He fell into the Prelector's Cubiculo without an actuator rod. Is there any way to retrieve him? I entered the Cubiculo about a minute after he did, but there's no sign of Turlough or the Prelector.' The Maitre D's voice was matter of fact, a disturbing baseline to Lassiter's mounting horror.

For a long moment, Lassiter was silent. Then he replied. 'No, Sebastian, there isn't any way to retrieve him. None at all.' He looked at the Doctor, who was slumped in his chair.

'Katarina, Sara, Adric and now Turlough. Innocent

lives that I drag into my endless games. Innocent lives that I sacrifice for the games that I play with time and space.' The Doctor sank into the chair like a puppet with its strings cut. Sinking his head in his hands, he let out a low groan. 'Won't I ever learn?'

Three

___

Diva blinked twice, and found herself overwhelmed by a barrage of sounds and images that her mind desperately tried to interpret. Brightly dressed people milled around her, most of them with coloured bags on their backs.

'We're on Earth!' yelled Tegan with rising recognition in her voice.

Diva frowned at her but said nothing, still fascinated by their surroundings. They were definitely in some sort of a restaurant, but that wasn't surprising for the Crystal Bucephalus: obviously the Suit had thrown them into a Cubiculo that was occupied. Not that there was much chance of their recognizing another patron: the image inducers made sure of that. An Earth Reptile could have been standing next to them and they wouldn't have noticed it. A quick glance at their attire proved the effectiveness of the inducers: both gowns had been transformed into sweatshirts and leggings, with only the colours preserved, red and green.

'Are you listening?' Tegan gave her a gentle thump on the arm. 'This is London.'

London: the name sent her thoughts back to Beswicks and Max. Once again, she could see him clutching at his throat, his eyes bulging. She shivered. 'How can you be sure?'

'Because I've been here before. This is McDonald's on Oxford Street; I can see Claude Gill Books over the road.'

'McDonald's on Oxford Street: what an odd name for a restaurant,' she muttered. And what an odd place:

54

everything looked artificial, with tables, chairs and walls all in materials and colours that clashed and jarred most unaesthetically. Diva questioned the taste of the patron who had requested this place from the Carte de Locales, before remembering that Tegan was familiar with it: she decided to hold her tongue in case she offended her new-found ally.

'Over here.' Tegan started dragging her over to an unoccupied table, its drab beige surface covered with paper cups and empty plastic boxes. 'Quickly, before anyone else grabs it.'

They sat down in the plastic seats. 'So what year is this?' asked Diva, already feeling uncomfortable in the smooth chair.

Tegan looked around. 'At a rough guess, the mid-eighties – the 1980s. I was here in 1981, just before I met . . . Anyway, this looks a bit later.' She grabbed Diva's hand. 'But why are we here?'

Diva shrugged. 'I have no idea. Except . . .' Her voice was quiet. 'I'm pretty certain that the Suit killed Max. And I was Max's . . . mistress. Perhaps it's some sort of vendetta.'

Tegan raised an eyebrow. 'Great. Not only are we stranded in the twentieth century, but we've got a homicidal maniac after us.' She trailed off as she realized what lay behind her words. 'After us!' Tegan looked around in panic.

Diva nodded. 'I'd just about come to the same conclusion. But he could be anywhere and disguised as anyone.' She sighed. 'I suppose we'd better look out for anyone acting strangely.'

Tegan laughed nervously. 'Diva, this is London. Everyone acts strangely.'

'Feeling better?' Lassiter gave the Doctor what he hoped was an encouraging smile as he handed over another cup of tea. 'You gave me quite a turn.' But he couldn't prevent the tea from slopping into the saucer as his hand refused to shop shaking.

The Doctor took the cup with a steady hand. 'I'm sorry. It's just that, well, Turlough was a good friend. He and I had a lot in common.'

Lassiter tried to put some optimism into his voice. 'I'll get one of the Legions to do a full search of the Grid. He may still be –'

'Alive?' The Doctor's voice was quiet. 'I appreciate your concern, Professor Lassiter, but it's not worth the effort. Exposure to the time winds is invariably fatal. You and I know that.'

The scientist bit his lip. The Doctor's grief was understandable, but Lassiter had his own concerns. Something had gone wrong with the Grid, his marvellous, faultless Grid, and the Doctor's reactions during the Legion's infarction had been evidence enough that he knew as much, if not more, about temporal physics than Lassiter himself. Time scientists weren't exactly thick on the ground in the Union, and he could hardly ask for help from, well, certain people. If he wanted to get to the bottom of the mystery, his best hope lay with the owner of the Crystal Bucephalus. It was time for a bit of amateur psychology.

'Fine, Doctor. You just sit there and wallow in your own grief, and I'll try to sort all of this out. Hopefully, I'll be able to get to the bottom of these deaths before any more people get murdered.' Turning his back, Lassiter knew that he felt even worse than the Doctor looked.

Turlough was confused. One moment he had been with the Wine Lords, and the next he was in a large white room being glared at by a woman in a black and gold kaftan. She looked less than pleased to see him.

'You know, I could get the feeling that I've been hijacked,' he quipped. 'Could you tell me what's going on?'

She transfixed him, a hard glint in her eyes. 'Listen to me, young man. I have better things to do than stand here and explain the way the universe works. Come over here and be quiet.'

Turlough remained where he was, some tiny spark of rebellion actually overriding his natural cowardice. 'Not until you tell me –' He broke off as the woman snapped her fingers. A gargantuan white android, its surface made of interlocking metallic plates, appeared from behind her, its vast bulk moving in his direction. He hadn't noticed it before because its colour had blended it into the wall. Turlough did the only sensible thing.

'All right, all right.' He shrugged and walked over to her.

'A wise choice.' She looked up at the ring of holo-spheres that hovered above the light–harp in front of her. 'Ah, just what I wanted to see. Our next guest will now be joining us.' She sat down and plucked a brief arpeggio on the harp.

The interior of the Archway flared, an exhibition that briefly turned the room a biting blue. And then a silhouette materialized, back–lit in sapphire, before stumbling through the gateway. Turlough recognized the man immediately: he was roughly his height, with a ginger beard and brown hair cut in a flat-top. Turlough estimated that he was in his late thirties, by human standards. It was the Prelector, Tornqvist, his robes transformed into a scarlet suit edged with black, an ornate pendant around his neck.

Tornqvist looked at the woman and raised an eyebrow. 'Matisse? Fancy seeing you here.' There was no friendship in the reunion.

She returned a completely false, completely transparent smile. 'It's been a long time, Your Grace. Welcome to the Exemplar.' She turned her attention to Turlough. 'I suppose I ought to ask who you are?'

'Vislor Turlough. Who are you?'

The smile continued. 'Professor Ladygay Matisse, Monsignor Turlough.' She waved proudly and expansively around the white tiled room. She pointed to the huge man who had just entered the room. 'This is my assistant, Garrett Byson. Say hello, Garrett.' Byson nodded and gave a grunt.

The Prelector leant towards Turlough. 'By the way, don't be fooled by her professorship; it's an affectation,' he whispered. He looked up. 'And what, pray, is the Exemplar?'

Matisse finished her ministrations at the harp, watching as the strings faded in colour. She looked up at them, her face a mask of self-satisfaction. 'The Exemplar is a time machine, Your Grace. Just like Professor Lassiter's precious Crystal Bucephalus.'

'That's a real professorship, the University of Megalopolis Six,' muttered Tornqvist.

'So why are we here?'

'My, my Turlough, aren't we the inquisitive one? Especially since you weren't exactly on the guest list for our little gathering.'

'And I was?' asked Tornqvist.

'Yes, Your Grace. Most definitely. And when your time bubble collapsed, my Exemplar was there, a safety net to protect you from the ravages of the time winds. We've been expecting you. Turlough, on the other hand, is a bit of a gatecrasher.'

'I am getting rather sick of you, Professor Matisse,' he snapped.

'And you'll be a damned sight sicker if you ever talk to me like that again!' With a single gesture, Byson gripped Turlough's wrist in his huge hand. He twisted, and Turlough let out a rather embarrassing scream before the pain mercifully ceased. Matisse smiled again: this one was pure venom. 'Do we understand one another, Monsignor Turlough?'

His reply was chastened. 'Understood perfectly. But I'd still like to know why I'm here.'

'That's better. Ask nicely and you get a nice reply. You entered the Prelector's bubble as it collapsed. Since the Exemplar was locked on to it, you suddenly became a piece of excess luggage.'

'So what now? I take it we're hostages?' asked Tornqvist.

Matisse laughed. 'Oh, Your Grace, I'm hurt. You

58

and Turlough are guests here. We may not be able to provide the standard of service that you were used to at the Emerald Syphax, but I'm sure you'll be comfortable.' And then her voice dropped. 'Eventually. Garrett: escort our guests to Monsignor DeSalle.' And then, *sotto voce*, 'I understand that he is aching to try out his new equipment.'

Turlough shuddered.

'Definitely an infarction,' stated the Doctor, looking up from the system logs and stabbing at an intricate pattern on one of the screens. 'The Legion was lucky to survive.' Lassiter's harsh words had been successful, igniting a spark of interest which had soon been fanned into a hard determination.

'As I remember, luck didn't have a lot to do with it. Where did you learn to do that?' He could still remember the Doctor's successful resuscitation.

The Doctor was modestly dismissive. 'Here and there, Alex, here and there. How have the other Legions taken it?'

'They're very quiet. Still, they're off until the next shift in about ten hours. More importantly,' he touched the Doctor's arm, 'how are you feeling?'

'I have been better.' He straightened his blue jacket and adjusted the stick of celery. 'But I'll be a lot happier if I can find Tegan. Have you any idea where she could have gone?'

'I'm afraid not: she's not been seen since she flung her wig in the steward's face.' He smiled.

'Can't you track her?' said the Doctor angrily. 'For goodness' sake, man, what sort of set-up are you running here?'

Lassiter realized that he was throwing his own words back at him. 'Look, Doctor, I realize that you're upset, but she did run off.' He stopped as the doors to the Legion tank opened, revealing the Maitre D', flanked by two stewards. Lassiter began to smile, then recognized the expression on his face.

Before either the Doctor or Lassiter could say anything, the Maitre D' was towering over the Doctor, a weird look in his eyes. 'In all the time I have been Maitre D' of this establishment, nothing has ever gone wrong. And then you turn up, Doctor.' His voice was rising. 'And suddenly one can't walk round the Bucephalus without falling over corpses. Arrestis, Turlough, Tornqvist; three deaths in as many hours! What have you got to say to that, then, eh?'

'But –'

'And Alexhendri's Grid: years of smooth, uninterrupted running, then you throw a spanner in the works. Legions collapsing, ne'er-do-wells skulking around the Mezzanine –'

'But –'

'Thanks to you, the reputation of the Crystal Bucephalus, a reputation that I have built up to the point where it spans the Union, lies in tatters. Who will want to eat here, eh? Who? As soon as word gets out, this place will be blacklisted and I will be a social pariah!' His voice had reached a screech. 'And you've done this, Doctor, you!' He raised his arm, his fist clenched.

'Not permissible.' The silky voice of the steward was in counterpoint to the firm grip in which it held the Maitre D's arm.

'What?' he screamed. 'I'm the Maitre D'!'

'The Doctor is the owner of the Crystal Bucephalus. Our prime directive gives him authority over you.'

The Maitre D' seemed to shrink into himself like a deflating balloon. 'Over me?' he whispered. 'Over me?'

The Doctor stepped forward. 'I'm sure that we would all prefer this situation – and you will agree that we do have a situation – discussed without these constant threats being bandied about.' His eyes bored into the general manager, his voice quiet. 'Especially empty threats aimed at the owner of the Crystal Bucephalus. Do we understand one another?'

The Maitre D' fell silent, his chest rising and falling with rapid breaths.

'Perhaps this will persuade you. I can see why you're unwilling to ask for assistance from outside the Bucephalus.' He gave him an understanding look. 'I will offer you as much assistance as I can, but, for reasons of my own, I tend to shun publicity. When all of this is over, I would prefer my part to be kept quiet.' He raised an eyebrow. 'Can I count upon your cooperation?'

The Maitre D's face was unreadable when he replied. 'Under the circumstances, Doctor, I believe that would be an admirable solution. Your wish is my command.'

Lassiter frowned. Somehow, he couldn't see him giving up his authority quite so easily.

'Are we going to be much longer?' asked Tornqvist. 'This is all very tiresome.'

'Almost there,' grunted Byson.

'He said that five minutes ago,' whispered Turlough. 'For all we know, we could be walking round in circles. It's not as if there are many landmarks.' He gestured at the walls. Since leaving Matisse's control centre, all they had seen had been the same, plain, whitewashed brick walls, with occasional black doors to break the monotony, but no windows. There was no way of telling whether they were on a spaceship or on a planet. Then again, Turlough couldn't recall many spaceships made of brick.

'We're here.' Byson stopped them with an outstretched arm. They were in front of yet another black metal door. 'Monsignor DeSalle's laboratory.' He pronounced each syllable with care and then thumped the door.

Turlough looked at the black, riveted door and shuddered: it reminded him rather too much of the dungeons underneath Sir Ranulf's castle. Suddenly the door opened.

A short, thin man peered at them from the darkness beyond. 'Ah, Your Grace. And Monsignor Turlough, isn't it?' He had protruding eyes hidden behind thick glasses, and a pinched and ascetic face: a face that Tornqvist imagined was capable of great cruelty. He was immediately reminded of Lazarus's experiences with the Vians and shuddered.

'Welcome to my humble establishment,' said DeSalle with a disturbingly quiet voice as he stood aside and waved them in. 'Thank you, Byson: that will be all.' Then he shut the door. 'All nice and snug, gentlemen. Now to get down to business.' He walked over to a table and picked up a long and very sharp implement. 'I really am going to enjoy this.'

'Look, are you going to order or aren't you?' The girl standing over them had mousy blonde hair drawn back in a ponytail, a rounded face, and a stroppy tone that was beginning to irritate Tegan.

'We're just trying to make our minds up,' she explained, well aware that, although the British Museum around the corner might be delighted by the handful of eighteenth-century French francs provided by the Doctor, McDonald's probably wouldn't be.

The girl stabbed a finger at the sign affixed to the wall above their heads. ' "Please purchase your food before taking your seat." In plain English, you buy your burger and then sit down. Savvy?'

'We won't be much longer,' Diva chipped in.

'Too right you won't, mate.' The girl pointed at the glass doors with her thumb. 'There's a menu in the window – make your minds up out there, okay?' When Diva and Tegan remained seated, her voice rose. 'You heard me: out!'

They stood up reluctantly. 'Thank you for your outstanding service,' Tegan peered at the girl's badge, 'Dorothy.'

'Don't mention it,' she replied cheerily, watching them walk towards the doors. As she turned round, she knocked into a tall man in a pin-stripe suit. 'Watch it, mate!'

'Why should I?' His tone was off-hand, but there was something terrifying behind his grey eyes. 'Now get out of my way, girl.'

Dorothy stepped back as the man left in something of a

hurry. She swallowed. There had been something odd about the man – and the two women, come to that. Something unreal.

'For Christ's sake, Dorry, will you give us a hand back here?'

'Sorry, Col.' Seconds later she had forgotten all about the odd trio and was wrestling with the complexities of large fries and a cheeseburger.

The Doctor peered at the brass-framed monitors through his glasses. 'Have you ascertained the origin of the Legion's attack?' he muttered over his shoulder.

Lassiter sat back in his chair and sighed. For the last two hours, he and the Doctor had analysed and re-analysed every last shred of information about the running of the Bucephalus Grid over the last day. And achieved precisely nothing. Everything – every reading, every statistic – was as boringly normal as possible. There was definitely no evidence that anything had happened to the Legion, apart from the fact that it was in the infirmary. 'A big fat zero. What about you?'

'Hmmm.' The Doctor rose and stepped over to Lassiter's station at the horseshoe-shaped console. 'Proof but no evidence,' he muttered, as if he had read Lassiter's mind. 'Perhaps it's time to hurl a few theories in the air and see which way they fall.'

'Such as?' He spun his chair round to face the Doctor.

'Such as the possibility that somewhere, out there, is a comparable set-up to the Crystal Bucephalus.'

' "Comparable set-up"?' He leapt to his feet. 'Do you realize what you're saying? No one in the galaxy could come close to matching all of this!' he shouted. 'Besides, you admitted that there wasn't any evidence.'

'Maybe not evidence, but inferences, Alex, inferences!' He reached past him and tapped away on the keyboard, bringing up a complex waveform. 'That is the anchor beam we activated. Do you notice anything different?'

Lassiter stared at the waveform and carried out a Fourier analysis in his head. And then he saw it in the ninth term. 'The beam was jammed,' he said incredulously. 'At the source. Here.'

'Exactly. But by whom?'

'Another Grid,' he murmured, a sheen of sweat breaking out on his forehead.

'Exactly. Maybe not an exact duplicate, but enough of a copy to be able to tap into the Bucephalus. Can you think of anybody capable of doing that?'

Lassiter shook his head. 'No.' He could think of someone; he just didn't want to.

The Doctor continued to press him. 'What about Hellenica Monroe? I thought that she was deeply involved in your initial researches?'

'Too deeply,' whispered Lassiter, the pain clear in his voice. 'No, she couldn't have. I didn't come up with the final innovation that I needed to build the Bucephalus until after we divorced. We were more than research partners, you see.'

The Doctor's voice was even more demanding. 'And what was your great discovery, Professor Lassiter? And why couldn't someone else, such as Professor Monroe, duplicate it?'

Lassiter moved over to the window set into one of the walls of the Suite, a one-way window invisible from the outside. Through a clever use of lenses, the vista encompassed the whole Mezzanine, showing the serried rows of Cubiculi, the cherubim and seraphim that frolicked on the ceiling, the diamond chandeliers – and the impressive horse that reared majestically, a reminder of an era of conquest, power and glory.

'You see that? Bucephalus. Alexander was given that horse by his father, and he tamed him, wild and wilful as he was. Like Time, eh, Doctor? Wild and wilful. So wild and wilful that the time gates that Hellenica and I theorized weren't stable; they collapsed in seconds. But I persevered, even after Hellenica left, and thanks to one of my research students, I finally overcame that obstacle. We devised a crystal matrix capable of absorbing the quantum aberrations – time spillage – and phasing them into harmless radiation. A green crystal.' He paused, spinning round from the window with a glorious fire in his eyes. 'Have you guessed yet?'

The Doctor joined him at the window. He pointed. 'That's it, isn't it? The heart of the grid? Your glorious centre-piece?'

Lassiter gave a wry smile. 'Got it in one, Doctor. I could have had a shapeless crystal lump sitting in the middle of this place, but I decided to take advantage of your financial backing. The most exclusive restaurant in the galaxy gets its name from thirty tons of adulterated dichronomide pentafluorate.' He stabbed a finger at the statue. 'Take a good look; you paid for it. The Crystal Bucephalus!'

The Doctor snorted. 'I'm glad to see that my money was well spent.' He didn't sound amused.

DeSalle's laboratory was in stark contrast to the antiseptic whitewash they had seen so far. The brick walls were black, and the only illumination was provided by a thin strip of some fluorescent material that ran around the walls like a picture rail. The room contained only the sparsest of furniture: a metal table, a leather chair and a large flat padded bench. It all made Tornqvist feel very uncomfortable. When one visited the Crystal Bucephalus, he decided, one did not expect to end up in the hands of a discredited scientist and her decidedly creepy sidekicks.

'I am Monsignor Hercule DeSalle,' said the small man, pursing his lips, 'generally regarded as the foremost psychovator in the Union.'

'Psychovator? What does that mean?' asked Turlough.

'Tell him, Sven. Or have you forgotten what the Lazarus Intent's own Guild of Pyschovators does for a living?' He smiled, revealing small, jagged teeth. 'I would explain, but I find this all adds to the air of menace and futility that I like to instil.'

Tedious little man. 'Psychovators are masters of all forms of interrogation techniques. They're commonly referred to as mind-rapists.'

'Charming. So we're going to be mind-probed?'

'He is,' said DeSalle, nodding at Tornqvist. 'You can watch. I find I work better with an audience.' He moved over to the table and picked up a gold wire circlet. 'This is the most sophisticated id-probe ever created. And all my own work.' He reached up and fitted the circlet around the Prelector's head. 'I try not to use anything I haven't had a hand in making.'

'I expect you enjoy a great deal of job satisfaction,' muttered Tornqvist as DeSalle adjusted the circlet.

'One learns to get one's pleasure where one can, Your Grace.' He stepped back. 'There: a perfect fit.'

'Why are you doing this?' Turlough stepped forward. 'What has he done?'

DeSalle was fitting a set of metal caps onto his fingers. Each cap came to a very sharp point. 'That is what I am trying to ascertain. My employer is rather anxious to learn what the Prelector is carrying around in that pious mind of his. So anxious, in fact, that he hired me, and I do not come cheap. Please, Your Grace?' He inclined his head towards the bench.

'I don't even know who your employer is,' Tornqvist protested as he lay down. Until this moment, he had been trying to reject what was going on as nothing more than a bizarre practical joke. DeSalle's masochistic glee had made that impossible.

'Oh, don't be so obtuse. Given the current fiscal position of the Union, there are only two powers in the galaxy which possess the resources to finance Matisse's work – or to pay me, for that matter: the Lazarus Intent and the Elective. And your lot didn't build it, did they?'

The Elective? But then that would mean . . . Tornqvist started to sit up. 'You work for Arrestis?' Panic which had been barely restrained began to overcome him.

'Worked,' pointed out Turlough. 'Arrestis was murdered a few hours ago in the Crystal Bucephalus.'

DeSalle shrugged. 'I wouldn't concern yourself with that, Your Grace: you can rest assured that the Elective is in good hands.' He cracked his knuckles and clicked the metal caps together. 'Now, if we might begin.'

'Are you going to hurt him?'

DeSalle scratched his chin. 'I pride myself in being as humane as possible. Unfortunately, the Prelectors of the Intent are a bit more stubborn than most: something to do with the mental disciplines they undergo in the seminaries. Breaking down those barriers could prove . . . uncomfortable.' He picked up a small light-harp from the bench and pressed a contact on its base. Strings of green materialized. He plucked. And Tornqvist screamed.

Lassiter shook his head as he studied the results of yet another diagnostic. Nothing. Despite the Doctor's insistence, despite the interference in the anchor beam, the scan showed nothing. 'I'm sorry, Doctor,' he called over his shoulder. 'That's the most intensive diagnostic I can run, short of dismantling the Grid. It still doesn't tell us anything. I can see the interference: I just can't trace the source.'

'Do you recognize this?' The Doctor typed for a second, bringing up an image on Lassiter's screen. 'I've been looking at the background radiation that was around at the time of the infarction. I decided to apply some clever filtering equations: removing background noise, that sort of thing,' he called over.

Lassiter examined the shape. 'It's an eccentric strophoid involute.' He snapped his fingers and pointed in one fluid movement. 'It's the involute of a Legion's navigation pulse!'

The Doctor raised an eyebrow. 'Really?'

'Legions navigate the Vortex by sending out signals and interpreting the feedback, rather like bats, I suppose.' He got the feeling that the Doctor already knew this, and didn't appreciate being made to feel like a clever child, showing off to the adults. He'd had enough of that when he *was* a clever child.

'So, the presence of the antiphase of the signal might cause a Legion to have a few problems, wouldn't you say?'

Lassiter stared at the hologram intensely, taking in the parabola that wrapped round itself at the focus. 'If this antiphase was aimed at a Legion signal of the same frequency . . .' He slapped his forehead. 'A Legion's navigation ganglions are right next to its matriculation net. If it were hit by an antiphase that cancelled out its navigation signal, it wouldn't be able to surface into the space-time continuum.'

'Exactly!' said the Doctor, rushing over to Lassiter and stabbing a finger at the screen. 'A perfect definition of an infarction. Is that evidence enough?'

'It could be coincidence.' But he knew it couldn't. A Legion's navigation signal was as unique as a fingerprint was to a human being. The chances of an accidental antiphase being of exactly the same frequency . . . Lassiter gave a panicked look. 'The frequencies are classified, encrypted into the Bucephalus webwork.' He stood up and took some deep breaths. 'There is someone out there, isn't there?'

He didn't like the Doctor's expression. 'What do you think?'

Lassiter looked around at the brass and crystal heart of the Crystal Bucephalus. The knowledge that others were watching, touching, controlling . . . He shuddered. 'I think we'd better talk to the Maitre D'.'

The Doctor patted him on the shoulder. 'Yes. I would hope that he'd be interested in the fact that the Bucephalus has rats in its kitchen. Don't you agree?'

Four

―――――

'Can't you see you're hurting him?' screamed Turlough. The Prelector's face was ashen and shiny
with sweat. His eyes were closed, but tears still managed
to squeeze through the lids and trickle down his temples.

'Of course I can see,' said DeSalle. 'That's why I wear
glasses.' He played another tune on the harp, plucking the
beams with the pointed thimbles and savoured the cries
that issued from Tornqvist. 'It's not my fault that he's
resisting the probe.' He plucked again.

Turlough found himself drawn to the holosphere that
had appeared in the air only seconds after the assault on
Tornqvist's mind had begun. The images were blurred and
confused: one moment he could see some rickety shanty
town; the next, he was on board a starship flown by
monks. He wasn't giving his secrets up without a fight.

'His childhood on Mirabilis, apparently,' commented
DeSalle. 'Such an unfortunate world. He was lucky to
be rescued by the Intent.' He plucked again, eliciting
another scream. 'But I'm not interested in Tornqvist's
formative years. My instructions are quite precise: 10,663
to the present day.'

'And what if you can't get the information?'

He grinned. 'Unless the Conclave of Prelates is in the
habit of giving seats to vegetables, his career in the clergy
will be finished.'

'You're sick, DeSalle.' Turlough sprang forward.

'And you're becoming a nuisance.' He was clutching a
small cube. 'One step closer and this will churn your brain
to the point where you'll need earplugs to stop your grey
matter from pouring out. Understood?'

He moved back, realizing that there was nothing he could do to help Tornqvist.

'Ah!' screeched DeSalle, looking up from the small harp. 'Now we're getting somewhere!' He nodded towards the holosphere. An image of a person was beginning to resolve with a great deal more clarity than before. Turlough immediately recognized it as Arrestis, dressed in a smart blue suit with a high collar. But the voice that issued from the sphere was definitely the Prelector's.

'No, Monsignor Arrestis. The Lazarus Intent does not need your sort of help.'

Turlough realized that they were seeing it from Tornqvist's point of view. Obviously.

'It might, if it isn't careful.'

'Threats, Arrestis? We don't need those either. I suggest you take yourself and your lack of ethics back to Hexdane where you belong.'

The sphere fogged and vanished.

'I've lost the signal,' sighed DeSalle, placing the deactivated harp on the table. 'Then again, I suppose I should have expected it. I learnt all about Lazarine training before I was expelled from their Guild of Psychovators.'

'Will you let him go now?'

He ignored him and spoke into his talkstick. 'DeSalle to Matisse.'

After a moment, Matisse's silky tones echoed around the dead weight of DeSalle's chamber. 'Yes, Hercule?'

'Tornqvist has had enough: I can't get any more out of him at the moment.' He smiled at Turlough. 'But I can't wait to try again.'

In an ever-changing world, thought Tegan, there were always some constants. The sun always rose, Australia always won the Ashes, and Oxford Street was always total chaos. London in the mid-eighties did nothing to dispel her convictions.

'This is terrible!' shouted Diva as a horde of exchange students threatened to knock her off the pavement into the path of a Number 17 bus. 'It's worse than the great Birastrop Stampedes!'

'This is London, Diva. It's always like this.' They were standing outside McDonald's, on the corner of Oxford Street and Tottenham Court Road. Above them, the towering shape of Centrepoint glittered in the summer sun. It was a glorious day. A glorious day to be chased through London by a shape-changing headcase. 'I think we'd better make a move, don't you? If the Suit is behind us . . .'

'But where? You're familiar with this zone: what do you suggest?'

Tegan was impressed by Diva's calm reaction to all of this, remembering her first trip in the TARDIS, and the blind terror she had felt. But then the memories of the Master began to surface, and Aunt Vanessa. *Focus on the job in hand, Tegan.* She looked around, trying to decide the best place to go. She carefully considered their four options: New Oxford Street – a good Chinese restaurant, but not much else; Tottenham Court Road – electronics shops; Charing Cross Road – well, they could hide in Foyles, but that was about it. No, their best bet was Oxford Street, with its wonderfully busy department stores. 'This way!' she shouted, realizing that Diva had been swept away by a gaggle of blue-haired old ladies wielding their John Lewis carrier bags like dangerous weapons.

Diva waded towards her with an aggrieved expression on her face. 'Why couldn't the Suit have sent us somewhere a little less hectic? Like World War Five, say.' She grabbed Tegan's arm, obviously determined not to be separated again. 'What's the plan, then?'

With Diva firmly attached, Tegan started pushing her way through the crowds. She quite fancied the idea of losing herself in Liberty. It was just a shame that she hadn't brought her credit card with her.

As she and Diva were immersed in the throng, a man in a pin-stripe suit stepped forward. He smiled as they tried to hide in the mass of people milling around. His tracking systems were more than a match for rucksack-bearing children and geriatrics. With amused determination, the Suit entered the fray.

'No. Out of the question. Totally out of the question.' The Maitre D' had predicted that the Doctor would try something like this. Lassiter's presence was more worrying.

'But we have proof!' exclaimed the Doctor. 'Proof that external forces have access to the Bucephalus.'

'Proof, or yet another product of your overworked imagination?' he boomed, standing up behind his desk. 'Perhaps these spies and assassins are yet another fancy you've plucked from the air.'

'But Sebastian, we can demonstrate this.'

'Conspiracy theories are all well and good, gentlemen, but not when they interfere with the running of this establishment. The Crystal Bucephalus has opened on time every single night since its inauguration, and I do not intend to alter that fact.'

'Why are you denying evidence that is before your very eyes?' yelled the Doctor. 'Or are you prepared to let these people continue their agenda of assassination?'

'I am not prepared to listen to half-cocked drivel! The Crystal Bucephalus is frequented by the highest echelons of galactic society. What possible reason would they have to act out this pantomime of carnage?'

The Maitre D' could feel the Doctor's anger like a furnace. He was quite prepared for it.

' "Highest echelons"? "Highest echelons"?' The Doctor's face was only inches from the Maitre D's as he leaned over the desk. 'The Union, a corrupt bunch of incompetents with an empire falling apart at the seams? The Elective, drug-runners and brothel-keepers? Only the Lazarus Intent has any saving graces, but who can be sure that they don't have some hidden agenda? I can't believe that you can stand there and say that you can't see any reason why any of those would want control of this place!'

The Maitre D' narrowed his eyes. Almost time to play his trump card. 'The Crystal Bucephalus will open as usual, in exactly,' he withdrew his watch from his waistcoat, 'seven hours and twelve minutes, to be precise.'

'Have you forgotten exactly who I am, Maitre D'?'

Time to play it. 'No, Doctor, because you wouldn't let me forget. But I have some bad news.'

'Bad news?'

'You might consider it to be so. You may own the Crystal Bucephalus, but I run it. You see, I've consulted the Judiciary.'

The Doctor frowned. 'Now why don't I like the sound of that?'

'The Judiciary is the supreme legal authority in the Union. As I said, you may own the Crystal Bucephalus, but your absence makes you a sleeping partner under Union law. It would appear that you have limited authority in the day-to-day running of this establishment. Whereas *I* have supreme authority.'

'You can't be serious?' demanded Lassiter.

'The law is the law. You now have seven hours and eleven minutes to unearth your conspiracy. I suggest you run off and solve your problems quickly before I decide to rescind even that amount of freedom. Good day to you.' He pointed towards the door.

As they stepped onto the Mezzanine, the Doctor turned to Lassiter. 'Somehow, I don't think that went particularly well, do you?'

The scientist tugged at his moustache. 'I'm sorry about that. Sebastian is quite obsessive about the Bucephalus.'

The Doctor sighed. 'Our options are limited and time is short. Just the way I like it.'

With a grunt, Byson heaved Tornqvist on to the bed before leaving the room. The series of electronic squeaks indicated that the heavy door was now locked.

Their quarters were a welcome relief from DeSalle's laboratory: the walls were painted a tasteful blue, with two comfortable-looking beds, a table and a couple of armchairs. The light was provided by four fluorescent tubes that ran from floor to ceiling at each corner of the room. A groan from the bed told Turlough that Tornqvist was waking up.

'Easy, Your Grace.'

The Prelector smiled weakly. 'Believe me, Monsignor Turlough, I haven't got the strength for anything else.' He sat up, rubbing the back of his neck. 'And let's dispense with all this formality: you can call me Sven.'

'And Turlough will do just fine. How are you feeling?'

'How do you think I feel?' he snapped, and closed his eyes in pain. 'That ghoul couldn't have tried any harder if he'd taken out my brain and dissected it.'

'He didn't get what he wanted, though.'

He raised an eyebrow. 'Didn't he, now? My psychic barriers must be stronger than I thought. Which means he'll be back.' He rubbed his eyes with the palms of his hands. 'Still, as Lazarus said to the Helemites when they chained him to the –' He stopped as the door to their room was unlocked and opened. Byson walked in, pushing a trolley. A collection of silver covered platters clustered on top, surrounded by various other oddments of silverware.

'Dinner,' growled Byson, pushing the trolley alongside the large table. He began to move the crockery and cutlery from trolley to table, but only succeeded in dropping a jug of what looked like gravy all over the floor. Byson stared at the brown stain with a hurt look on his face.

'Oh, move out of the way.' Tornqvist bustled in, and lifted the largest platter off the trolley. 'You're hardly silver service material, are you?'

'Sorry. I'm not particularly clever, you see.'

The Prelector gave him a penetrating stare. 'I wouldn't say that, Monsignor Byson. In fact, I'd say that you were a vital part of Professor Matisse's operation here, wouldn't you?'

Turlough was astonished to see that the giant's eyes were glazing over. He touched Tornqvist's arm, but he brushed him away.

'In fact, I doubt that Professor Matisse could continue

running the Exemplar if you weren't here. Don't you agree?'

Byson gave a slow nod. Suddenly, a loud chime issued from his talkstick.

'Garrett, it's Ladygay. Have you finished delivering the food to the Prelector and the brat yet?'

'I'm just leaving,' he muttered, shaking his head.

'Excellent. I have a little job for you. I'll see you in five minutes.'

He replaced the talkstick. 'Sorry, I've got to go.' With that, he left. The door issued yet another burble as it locked.

'What did you do?' asked Turlough. 'Some sort of hypnotism?'

Tornqvist grinned. 'Clever, wasn't it? It wasn't exactly hypnotism, more like empathic mind control, actually.'

'Mind control?'

'Perk of the job.' He held up the pendant that Turlough had noticed earlier. On closer examination, he recognized it as an infinity sign.

'Before you ask, it's called an Inf: the symbol of the Lazarus Intent. Because I sit on the Conclave of Prelates, this one has an empathic neuristor built into it. A few seconds more, and Byson would have been completely under . . .' He sighed. 'Never mind. Let's see what's on the menu tonight, shall we?' He lifted the first cover off. 'Rutan prawns with garlic mayonnaise, followed by . . .' Second cover. 'Ah, how delightful: dodo in what seems to be a hollandaise sauce. Shall we dine?'

'That's all I need!' yelled Lassiter, thumping the lectern. After the scene in the Maitre D's office, they had returned to the Grid Control Suite, as good a place as any to continue their investigations.

'Alex?' The Doctor looked up from the central control panel. 'You sound as if our problems have just multiplied.'

'That's putting it mildly. The Legions are threatening to go on strike unless I can guarantee their safety. They're already talking about requesting a shuntship from their home world.' Lassiter smoothed his moustache with the palm of his hand. 'I can do without that: without them, this place is useless.' Even as he said it, he felt guilty about the lie, but there was no point in involving the Doctor in the deceptions that lay behind the Crystal Bucephalus. 'I think I've calmed them down, but it's yet another thing to worry about.' He picked up a white mug with PROPERTY OF THE CRYSTAL BUCEPHALUS printed on the side.

The Doctor was standing by the central pillar, staring into its flickering interior. 'Has their been any word about Arrestis's death?'

Lassiter almost choked on his coffee. 'What?'

'It's been almost eight hours since he died: I'd have thought that the Elective would have been in touch by now.'

Lassiter suddenly realized that he had been so relieved by Arrestis's death that he hadn't thought of the inevitable consequences – inevitable consequences that didn't seem to be happening. 'There's been nothing. I know that Sebastian sent a squirtpacket to Hexdane offering his condolences, but I don't think we've heard anything back.' He grinned wryly. 'And I don't fancy asking him at the moment.'

'Quite,' laughed the Doctor, and then his expression changed to one of enquiry. 'The Maitre D' told me that Arrestis had been poisoned . . . by what exactly?'

'Pyletheric acid wiped round the neck of the bottle.'

'Pyletheric acid? snapped the Doctor. 'Are you sure?'

'Definitely, the stewards identified it immediately.' He couldn't work out why the Doctor seemed so agitated.

'I must see the body; I assume it's still here?'

Lassiter shrugged. 'I suppose so. They would have taken it to the infirmary.'

Clapping his hands, the Doctor made for the doors. 'Excellent. I'd like to take a look, if you don't mind.'

'I don't mind, but I'd hate to think what Sebastian would say about it.'

'Then we won't tell him, will we?'

* * *

76

Starting off with a leisurely browse through the Virgin Megastore – 'You mean people stored music on these?' was Diva's reaction upon seeing what Tegan called an LP – the two women had meandered their way along Oxford Street.

'This is amazing!' said Diva, looking at the racks of elegant clothing. No replicators, no tailoring drones; the clothes were simply *there*. It all seemed extremely impractical.

'It's Marks and Spencer, what else do you expect?' Tegan was holding up a white negligée. 'What do you think?'

'Very nice.' Diva still couldn't believe that people would buy clothing without having it tailored to suit their personal tastes. In this era, two people could be wearing exactly the same dress! Still, that was the purpose of the Crystal Bucephalus, a taste of simpler times. 'Actually, I was talking about the culture.'

'Culture? In the early eighties?' She laughed. 'You've got to be kidding. Things haven't improved since I was last here.' She replaced the negligée and started looking at a red and black one. 'Anyway, I thought you'd be used to all of this: with something like the Crystal Bucket, you must travel in time all the, er, time.'

Diva shook her head. 'Beswicks was my first visit to the Bucephalus. But I've travelled around the Union quite a bit – with my father in the Fleet, it came with the job – and I've never seen anything quite so, so alien as Ancient Earth. Not even the Paluthian Hives on Jesentral, and that's saying something. Their practices with small furry animals don't bear thinking about.'

'It's fun, though, isn't it?' Tegan was dragging her off towards shelves of shoes. And then she stopped. 'Don't look now, but we're being watched.'

'Where?' She started to turn round, but Tegan squeezed her arm.

'Over by the jackets: the man in the pin-stripe suit. But don't look.'

Out of instinct, she looked anyway. The man in question

77

was examining some jumpers. 'It's your imagination.'

Tegan shook her head. 'Trust me. That's the Suit. He's been in every shop we've visited so far. I thought it was my imagination, but it can't be – it has to be him.' She frowned. 'Either that, or an over-zealous store detective.'

'So what do we do?' Diva couldn't work out why she was panicking. If he had wanted to kill them, he could have done it back in the Bucephalus. Then she realized that the twentieth century was the perfect place to hide the bodies. 'How do we get out of here?'

'The side exit. Up Poland Street, across Oxford Street, and down Hanway Street.'

Diva shrugged. It was gibberish to her. 'I'll take your word for it.' And then followed as Tegan hurried towards the stairs.

The man in the pin-stripe suit emerged from behind the lambswool jumpers.

The infirmary was situated in one of the radial corridors that connected the Crystal Bucephalus to the encircling Emerald Syphax. The Doctor found it easily, and was surprised to see how small it was: obviously the Bucephalus didn't expect many cases of food poisoning. The main surgery was about ten feet square, with a standard medibed, and a limited amount of equipment. Four doors suggested recovery rooms; one of them was probably acting as a makeshift morgue, he decided. He noticed a black-haired oriental woman in a yellow smock leaning over a small light-harp on the other side of the room.

'Excuse me,' he called.

'Yes? Can I help you?' The nurse walked over. Her name badge identified her as Yukio Tsang.

'I'm the Doctor,' he said charmingly. 'I wondered if it might be possible to see Monsignor Arrestis's body?'

'His body?' She frowned. 'I'm not sure that it would be quite proper.' Her eyes darted over to one of the side rooms.

The Doctor stared straight into her eyes. 'I'm sure it

would be quite all right, Nurse Tsang. It wouldn't be any trouble, would it, Nurse Tsang?' He watched as her pupils dilated.

'It wouldn't be any trouble, Doctor,' she repeated almost tonelessly. 'I'm sure it would be quite all right.'

'I think you should check on the Legion. I think it's feeling a little peckish,' he urged.

'I think I should check on the Legion, Doctor. I think it's feeling a little peckish.' With that, she walked over to one of the doors and entered.

The moment she shut the door behind her, the Doctor dashed over to an equipment locker and produced a hairpin from within his silk jacket. Seconds later, the metal door swung open. In a flash, he grabbed a genetic analyser from its rack before closing the locker and darting over to the room indicated by Tsang's glance. With a furtive look behind, he pulled the door open and entered.

The lights were low and cold, antiseptic lights casting antiseptic shadows which transformed the room into a morgue. Laid out on the bed, Arrestis's body shone with the faint pinkish glow of a stasis field, his sleepy features frozen. Divested of his clothes, his compact body was well muscled and hairy, looking as much a thug in death as he had been in life.

The Doctor examined the analyser, a brick-shaped device with a three-inch probe at the end, and instantly figured out the controls. Stroking one of the membrane buttons, he touched the corpse with the probe and examined the readings. 'Of course!' He pinched the bridge of his nose. 'Accelerated degradation of the nucleotides.' The analyser showed exactly what the Doctor had suspected: replicative fading. 'For goodness' sake, man, your DNA is unravelling before your very eyes!' he shouted at the unresponsive body.

The Doctor cursed himself for not finding out the cause of death earlier. Ingestion of pyletheric acid was rarely fatal to human beings, but it had a rather more terminal effect on genetically accelerated clones, attaching itself to the unique tags in their genome and causing immediate respiratory failure. And if the body in front of him was a clone . . .

Shoving the genetic analyser beneath the bed, the Doctor made a swift exit.

'Magnificent, eh Turlough?' The Prelector leaned back in his chair and patted his stomach appreciatively. 'I'm sure that Lazarus must have felt like this after the Final Dinner, just before his denial and betrayal.'

'A comforting thought.' Turlough wiped his mouth on a napkin. 'Do you know, I can see why the Crystal Bucephalus is so popular. The ability to eat in the finest restaurants anywhere in history must be irresistible.'

Tornqvist sipped his wine. 'Absolutely. Before Matisse snatched me, I was the personal guest of König Wilhelm, First of the Wine Lords. A fascinating society, Turlough. For a thousand years, they had the best kept cellars in the galaxy; their wines were exported across the stars.'

'How long ago was this?'

'The trial of the Wine Lords ended about seven thousand years ago. A sad day for connoisseurs everywhere.' He put the glass down. 'They would not have approved of that,' he said.

Turlough was intrigued. Tornqvist had a compelling enthusiasm reminiscent of the Doctor. 'They were put on trial? Why?'

'Dreadful business. They'd been selling the '56 and claiming it was the '37. They were found guilty of infanticide and put under the prohibition. So endeth the Wine Lords.'

Turlough laughed. 'I don't think I've ever met a priest quite like you before. Have you really been waiting five thousand years for your saviour to return?'

'Well, not me personally!' said Tornqvist smiling. 'But yes, that's about the size of it. And we'll wait another five thousand if that's what it takes.' He took another sip of the wine and grimaced. 'Not a patch on the '69, I can tell you.'

'Was he real? This Lazarus person, then?'

'Definitely. Before he died, he wrote the Codex, a collection of parables and commandments that defined the religion. After he sacrificed himself on Sontara to end the war, his closest disciple, Saint Clavis, read out his final Intent: we were to carry on Lazarus's teachings and spread them across the galaxy. We would receive his blessing on one condition: as soon as time travel was developed, we would bring him back from the moment before his death to lead us to new heights of salvation.' He reached for the wine, but obviously thought better of it.

'Wasn't he hoping for rather a lot? I mean, not only would someone have to develop time travel, but his followers would have to be able to get their hands on it. All seems a bit risky to me.'

Tornqvist fingered his Inf. 'Geographically, the Lazarus Intent stretches from the Great Hole at the galactic centre to the most distant clusters in the Perseus Rift. Over the millennia since Lazarus's death, ours has become the dominant religion. Our converts are without number and from countless civilizations. Earth Reptiles have forsaken their lizard god, the Martians have turned their backs on Claatris, God of War, and, demographically, my brothers and sisters range from the lowliest of bond servants to members of the Presidium itself.' He changed his mind and drained his glass. 'Believe me, Turlough, if time travel is discovered, the Intent will be the first to hear about it.'

'Is that why you were in the Bucephalus, then?' Turlough leaned forward and gave him what he hoped was a penetrating stare. 'Because it's halfway to being a proper time machine?'

Tornqvist raised an eyebrow. 'You might think that –' He broke off as the door opened. 'Ah, Monsignor Byson!' he stated expansively, a trace of relief in his voice. 'A truly enchanting meal. What a pity that you and Professor Matisse couldn't have joined us at table.'

Byson moved over to clear the remains of the meal. 'Ladygay's a bit busy at the moment,' he grunted, as he

81

transferred the empty crockery to the trolley. 'She doesn't have much time for lunch.'

Tornqvist's voice had assumed the lilting tone that Turlough recognized as mind-control mode. 'What a terrible pity. A big lad like you needs his food.'

'Food.' Byson's voice was slurring.

'So why don't you stay here and nibble our left-overs, while Turlough and I take a doggy-bag to the Professor.'

'That sounds nice,' he mumbled.

'Excellent.' He beckoned to Turlough. 'We'll be off then.' With that, he dragged Turlough through the door and slammed it behind him.

'How long have we got before it wears off?' asked Turlough.

'About twenty minutes, usually. More if the subject is exceptionally receptive.' Tornqvist laughed. 'So we've got about three hours, I reckon.'

Turlough looked up and down the white-walled corridor. 'To achieve what, exactly?'

'I have no intention of subjecting myself to DeSalle's attentions again. We're going to force Matisse to send us back to the Crystal Bucephalus.'

'Easier said than done, Sven. We can't just burst into her control room.'

'On the contrary: that's exactly what we're going to do.' Tornqvist touched the Inf around his neck. 'Have a little faith.'

'Tell me about cloning.' The Doctor had stopped the steward on the outer ring of the Cubiculi.

It cocked its head for a moment. 'The term is unfamiliar, Doctor. Could you be more specific?'

The Doctor pinched the bridge of his nose. 'Cloning . . . er, eugenics, asexual reproduction of living organisms from genetic samples.'

'I will access the Union net.' There was a long pause, which gave the Doctor another chance to examine the clashing styles of the Bucephalus: the art deco of the walls against the bauhaus furnishings, coupled with the gothic splendour of the columns and arches that framed the statue. His displeasure at his investment was interrupted by the steward. 'I now have access. The last authorized research project into genetic experimentation began on Tersurus in the year 6198. It was fully funded by the Federation Scientific Executive.'

'And what happened to the project?' The Doctor had some very uneasy suspicions.

'A Sontaran stealth raid penetrated the frontier and destroyed the planet with an earthshock bomb in 6211.'

'So the Sontarans even bargained with the Cybermen to win their futile and bloody little war,' he muttered. 'What about the research team, were they all killed in the raid?'

'Given that Tersurus was atomized, it is the logical conclusion that all members of the research team were killed,' said the steward without a trace of irony.

'Quite. Have you the team roster?'

'Negative. That information was lost.'

'How?' Nasty little cogs were making nasty little turns in his mind. 'Surely that information wasn't atomized?'

'That information was lost three weeks before the destruction of Tersurus. A Sontaran strike attack on Io introduced a virus into the Federation DataCore. Before the virus was stopped, it destroyed all information about the Tersurus Institute.'

The Doctor frowned. 'Very convenient. But that was five thousand years ago. Surely there's been sufficient time to rediscover the science?' The cogs began to move.

'The teachings of the Lazarus Intent prohibit scientific research into genetic experimentation. Because of the influence of the Intent, Union regulations also prohibit such research.'

All cogs clicked another turn. Clones in the infirmary, areas of uncharted information . . . He patted the steward on the shoulder. 'Thank you for your time. I have an appointment to keep with Professor Lassiter.'

* * *

As Tegan and Diva shoved open the side exit, Poland Street was empty, apart from two men in leather jackets walking into the pub opposite.

'This way!' shouted Tegan, running down the road. After a breathtaking game of dodge the taxi across Oxford Street, she stopped to catch her breath and saw Mister Pin-stripe coming out of Poland Street. 'Keep on my tail, all right?' she yelled to Diva. With that she barged her way through the ever-present crowds, hoping that she was following her.

About a minute later, Tegan almost ran straight past the top of Hanway Street. It was a tiny road that connected Oxford Street to Tottenham Court Road, hardly noticed by the surging masses of people that passed by. She was hoping that they could lose their pursuer by cutting through to Tottenham Court Road. 'Over here!' she urged. Satisfied that Diva was behind her, she ran down Hanway Street.

And stopped.

In 1981, Hanway Street had led to Tottenham Court Road. In 1985 or thereabouts, the road was blocked by a combination of scaffolding, skips and piles of bricks.

They were trapped. And the Suit was right behind them.

Matisse stared at the hologram with a tinge of pride. Even though she knew every single filament of the quantum linkage that connected the Exemplar with the Bucephalus webwork, she still hadn't been convinced that this particular part of the plan would work. But the intricate pattern that hovered between the light-harp and the Archway was proof that she had complete control over Lassiter's oh-so-mighty achievement.

As she thought of Lassiter, she remembered their time together on Pluto. Frantic days of research and frantic nights of passion, as they pushed forward the frontiers of discovery in more ways than one. As she had worked out the necessary additives for the clathrates in the crystal matrix, he had designed the temporal projectors and bubble generator. Until that final night, that night when he was supposed to be guest of honour at the Emeritus Gala on Kentaurus.

Sitting at the light-harp, she had cracked all but the final code of his personal logs, uncovering a cornucopia of information that made it quite clear that Lassiter's earlier line of research had been rather more fruitful than the barren failure that he would have had everyone believe.

And then he had walked in. Heated words and shattered trust: he had accused her of wheedling her way into his affections to uncover his past, while she had pointed at the evidence that he had suppressed his discoveries. The argument escalated, until she finally let slip exactly who her paymaster was. She hadn't been prepared for the sheer violence of his reaction.

They parted company that night. She caught the next shuntliner to Hexdane, while Lassiter went into hiding on New Alexandria, retiring from academic life completely.

She shook her head; that was all in the past. She had achieved the Exemplar without Lassiter's help, and had tapped into his precious Bucephalus Grid without the slightest difficulty. Then again, the information she had managed to extract from his records had been more than useful.

The hologram told her all that she needed to know. At the centre of the image, two amber double hoops inclined at 45 degrees represented Grid Control, generating the time bubbles. The silver ring that encircled it was the Legion tank, with a thousand silver cables snaking out to a polyhedral shell whose vertices were golden dodecahedra indicating the Legions' propulsion of the bubbles within the Cubiculi. Enclosing the dodecahedra, was a torus made from millions of incandescent points of light: the multitude of possible time zones programmed into the Bucephalus Carte de Locales. Another thousand connections, delicate shining filaments, linked the Cubiculi to a selection of time zones. The Bucephalus never slept, even during its shutdown period, and those thin chains represented the default settings of the Grid.

Matisse gave a predatory smile. It was playtime. Her long fingers reached out to the light-harp as she began to play a melody of chaos.

'A vortex probe?' The Doctor peered at the schematics on the brass-framed monitor. 'What a good idea.'

Lassiter looked up and grinned. 'I hope so. When I designed the Grid, I obviously set up security protocols. I thought that they were unbreachable, but clearly they weren't. My probe should skirt around the boundaries of the Grid and sniff out unwelcome intruders. What do you think?'

The Doctor pursed his lips. 'Our opponents are very clever: they know exactly what is going on here and appear to be able to monitor our every move. Have you any idea who they might be?'

Lassiter tapped away on the brass keys for a second before answering. 'No, Doctor, I have no idea.'

'Tell me the truth, Alexhendri. The truth!' The Doctor punched the wooden lectern. 'You are protecting somebody, somebody who helped you design the technology that we see around us. Who is it, Professor Lassiter? Or do other people have to die first?'

Lassiter swallowed, realizing that the Doctor was turning his own argument against him. 'I don't really have a choice, do I? Her name is Matisse, Ladygay Matisse. After Hellenica and I divorced . . .' He broke off, his voice filling with emotion. 'After she went, this brilliant research student approached me. She wanted a career in temporal physics research, and, since I was professor of temporal studies at the Union Scientific Centroplex on Pluto, she came to me. We immediately struck it off, both professionally and personally. Not long after we teamed up, she discovered the correct mix of additives to dichronomide pentafluorate, and we were soon able to generate the first stable projection manifold.' Lassiter fell silent as the magnitude of the betrayal came back to him across the years. He looked up at the Doctor, his eyes glistening. 'It can only be Matisse. She's the only person in the galaxy who would have the faintest idea of how to duplicate my work here. But please, Doctor, don't ask me any more.'

Diva looked up at the mouldering façade, a tightness gripping her stomach. Halfway down the tiny road Tegan had called Hanway Street, two large metal containers blocked their progress. But it was the building to the left which had seized her attention. The flaking sign above the boarded-up window was still legible, ornate old-human lettering pathetically proclaiming 'Beswicks'. It just brought home the fragile nature of the universe.

'Over here!' Tegan had taken a position in front of the bricked-up doorway, a lump of wood in one hand. She was slapping it in the palm of the other. 'Here he comes.'

The man that Tegan had decided was the Suit was only twenty feet away: although the logical part of Diva's mind told her that this was probably a solid hologram projected by the actuator rod, she couldn't help but be disturbed by those horrible eyes.

The words tumbled out without thinking. 'Why did you kill Max?'

The Suit laughed. 'You really are obsessed, aren't you? Still, since you obviously think you know who I am, I'll give you another clue.'

The dark jacket and trousers blurred into the frighteningly familiar suit of battle armour, its blue mirrored sheen reflecting the greys and brick reds of Hanway Street as magenta abstracts. 'Is this better?'

'How's the probe going?' The Doctor was leaning over Lassiter's shoulder, interpreting the symbols that the scientist was entering through the keyboard.

'Very well, actually. I'll be able to drop it into the Vortex in about an hour.'

'Excellent. Have you considered a Higgs detector? If our mysterious friends are tapping in via a real world interface —'

'Professor!' The yell from the technician cut through

the conversation. 'Professor, can you come over here? I can see it, but I don't believe it.'

Lassiter jumped from his chair and ran over to the technician's station. As he stared at the monitors, his eyes widened in horror. Seconds later the Doctor was standing behind them.

'This can't be right, Professor. The topology of the Grid doesn't work like that.'

'Too right it can't!' Lassiter stood up and banged into the Doctor. Without even apologizing, he sprinted over to the main console. A few seconds and a few keystrokes later, the area between the console and the pillar flared up in the radiance of hidden holographic projectors.

'And what might that be?' asked the Doctor, transfixed by the glittering arrangement.

'A holographic representation of the entire Bucephalus Grid: Grid Control, Legion tank, Cubiculi and time zones.'

The Doctor put his glasses on and examined the hologram. 'If the filaments represent the flow of control, I take it that they're not meant to be unravelling?'

Lassiter turned from the console, cold sweat pouring down his face. 'No, Doctor, they're not. Don't ask me how, but the entire topology of the Grid is coming apart.'

Matisse threw back her head and let rip with a rich, bubbling laugh. 'So much for your precious Grid, Alexhendri!' She plucked an arpeggio. Within the illuminated splendour of the hologram, the strands of amber light from the dodecahedra were thrashing around like epileptic anemone fronds. One by one, they were disconnecting from the double-hoop of Grid Control and vanishing like burst bubbles. Furthermore, the thinner chains that linked the Cubiculi to the torus of time zones were blinking in and out of existence, whilst similar chains were materializing between the points of light. 'Let's see what you can come up with to get yourself out of this mess!'

Her triumph was cut short as the doors to her left were flung open. The Prelector and the boy were standing there. She didn't hesitate. 'Androids to the control centre! Immediately!'

Tornqvist gave a satisfied smile. 'Good evening, Professor Matisse. May we come in?' And then, over his shoulder, 'Turlough, lock the doors!'

Before Matisse could react, Turlough slammed the doors shut and scrambled the electronic lock with a good blow from his fist. The Prelector leapt at Matisse and pinned her against the wall, her arm twisted and locked behind her.

'You idiots! Let me go!' she screamed.

'Please don't struggle, Ladygay. The light-harp is so much more melodic when played with two hands.'

There was clear satisfaction in the Suit's voice as he addressed them. 'So, you guessed I was following you?'

'Given that clever suit of yours, you weren't exactly discreet,' quipped Tegan.

'Discreet? Why should I be discreet? I wanted you to run. The more you moved around, the more chance that someone back in the Bucephalus would notice you. You in particular, Diva.'

'Me?' The uneasy feeling in her stomach was increasing. How did he know her name? Unless . . .

'Of course, you stupid woman. I wanted to trap you in the past because I wanted to see to what lengths your beloved Lassiter would go to rescue you.'

'I don't understand,' said Tegan. 'What are you on about?'

'I want him to show his hand.' The Suit's gauntlets reached up to the domed helmet. As he unfastened the catches, he continued: 'A prize like you would be well worth risking everything for, don't you think? And it isn't just Lassiter: did you really think I didn't see through you from the very beginning?' He removed the helmet.

Diva gasped. Her legs began to fail her, and Tegan had to grab her to stop her from collapsing. 'Are you all right?'

'Max?' A dream and a nightmare danced in Diva's

mind as she stared at the Suit, his helmet removed. A thin face, with close-cropped wavy brown hair, full lips and heavy lidded eyes. He smiled, a cruel, powerful smile. 'Don't I even get a kiss?'

Diva was shaking her head. 'But you died, I saw you!'

He shrugged. 'So why am I standing here? But then again, you've probably never heard of a clone, have you?' He pulled a black rod from a concealed pocket in his battle armour. 'I'd love to stop and chat, but I'm in a bit of a hurry.' Blowing a kiss at Diva, he pressed the actuator button. 'See you around, dearest.' Nothing happened.

The light-harp chimed. Matisse struggled against Tornqvist's grip, but he was having none of it. 'Sorry, Professor, but I've got you exactly where I want you.'

'Damn you, Tornqvist, you don't know what you've done!'

'It's no good,' muttered Lassiter as he pulled himself out of the bronze cube that stood behind the crystal pillar. 'I've stopped any feedback – whatever happens is isolated from the main power couplings – but I can't stop the topological transform.' He typed a rapid sequence on a keyboard set into the cube and darted over to the main console to re-examine the readings. Almost in confirmation, he looked at the hologram, its furious activity still in progress, before wiping his hands on his trousers. 'I suppose we should be grateful that it happened now, during closedown.'

'Why's that?' asked the Doctor.

'Two things, really. Firstly, I don't know what the Legions would have made of it, and secondly, I'd hate to think what would happen to anybody who tried to use their actuators while the Grid topology rewrites itself.'

'Oh?'

'With the navigation paths no longer aligned, Grid Control can't get a firm grip on the bubbles.' He held out his hands in a gesture of impotence. 'They'd probably be flung into the Time Vortex, like the Prelector and your friend.' As the Doctor closed his eyes, Lassiter immediately regretted his words. A sudden shout from Ottway bellowed across the Suite.

'The Grid's not clear!'

'What?' Lassiter punched up a command. In response, one of the monitors resolved into the image of a darkened alleyway. Two women were clearly visible.

'Tegan!' exclaimed the Doctor.

Lassiter blinked. It couldn't be, but the image was too clear for mistakes. He swallowed. 'I must close down the recall system before they try to use their actuators.' Running past the hologram, which was now a brilliant gold torus with a dark star at its centre, he reached one of the lecterns and began typing.

'Let me go, you stupid fool!' Matisse was furious. Every second that she delayed retrieving Arrestis from the Grid was another second closer to the moment when the Grid became inaccessible to the Exemplar. And if one of those women tried to use their actuator rods in Arrestis's proximity . . .

'Not the most spectacular exit I've ever seen,' said Tegan.

'Shut it.' Arrestis examined his actuator carefully and tried again. Still nothing. His actuator was linked directly to the Exemplar: Matisse had been quite clear about what a Bucephalus actuator would do, once she had made her 'adjustments'.

'It seems like your little toy is broken, Max.' Diva moved closer. 'Never mind, perhaps ours still work.' She pulled out an actuator rod.

It took a few seconds for her words to sink in. And then, 'Don't touch it, you idiot!'

But she had already pressed the button.

'Oh no,' groaned Lassiter. 'There's an actuator powering up in the Grid.' He stabbed a finger at a porthole-like screen which showed the characteristic waveform of a time bubble.

'Have you managed to disable the recall systems?'

'I'm still trying to circumvent the safeguards,' he replied, urgently typing commands.

The Doctor thumped the console. 'For goodness sake, man, do something!'

As Arrestis tried to grab the actuator, a strong wind began to swirl around them, lifting empty crisp packets and other rubbish in a hectic dance. And then they were surrounded by flickering hoops of amber light that plucked at their clothes and hair.

Lassiter grabbed the sides of the lectern. 'It's too late: Grid Control has received the signal and is responding.'

They watched impotently as the Crystal Bucephalus reached back in time to retrieve its guests.

Within the hologram, a final orgasm of connections and reconnections took place, amber cables and silver filaments thrashing around in a whirling vortex. Then all activity ceased.

Matisse gasped as a more discordant tone sounded from the harp. 'It's too late,' she murmured. 'Far too late.'

The Doctor looked from the lectern to the monitor and back again. As Tegan and the other woman were consumed by the hoops, the screen went black.

Lassiter touched his arm. 'I'm so sorry, Doctor,' he said quietly. 'There wasn't anything I could do.'

Tegan opened her mouth to scream, but nothing happened. Whether it was because she couldn't make a noise, or because she was being drowned out by the modulated chimes that seemed to vibrate around her, she didn't know and didn't care. The only thoughts that filled her mind were of the agonizing pain as she was ripped apart, atom by atom.

Five

Turlough jumped back from the door as a deafening series of thumps resulted in an explosion of blue sparks from the locking plate. 'The doors aren't going to hold much longer!' he yelled.

'Call off your metal men, Matisse, or else.'

'Or else what, Your Grace? You'll kill me?' She squirmed in his grip. 'Hardly the act of a pious man.'

His answer was lost as the doors to the control room were thrown open. The two androids stomped through, one grabbing Turlough, while the other bore down on the Prelector.

'I'd let me go, if I were you,' said Matisse smugly. 'Or my "metal man" will rip your friend's head off.'

Reluctantly, he released her, and was immediately seized by the android. Matisse put her hands on her hips and gave a thin smile. 'Sorry to spoil your party, gentlemen, but you've well and truly spoilt mine.' She leaned down and strummed the harp. Nothing: the Exemplar had lost contact with the Grid. Which was actually just what she had intended, but with Arrestis on this side of the Archway, not the other.

'Things not going according to plan?' said Turlough sarcastically.

Her eyes burnt into him. 'I've warned you once: do I have to warn you again?' She shook her head. 'No, you're not worth it; you've taken up enough of my time as it is.' She touched another strand, causing a holosphere to descend to eye level. The image within showed Byson, fast asleep in the cell.

'The legendary mental abilities of the Lazarus Intent – I

93

should have watched you a little more carefully.' She flicked a hand at the androids. 'Take them away.' As they reached the doors, she suddenly remembered something. 'And Your Grace: don't try any more of your head games. From now on, the only contact you'll have will be with androids, and I doubt that they will be quite as receptive to your charms.' She stepped forward and tore the Inf from around his neck. 'Still, better safe than sorry, don't you think?'

The Doctor turned away from the lectern, his head lowered. First Turlough, now Tegan. All he wanted to do now was find the TARDIS and set the coordinates for as far away from this benighted place as possible. Quiet little voices were whispering constant admonishments in his mind, tiny daggers of guilt: if you'd been a good little Time Lord and shut the Bucephalus down as you were supposed to, none of this would have happened. This is what comes of not following orders, of breaking the rules.

'Doctor.' Lassiter's voice was quiet.

'I'm sorry?' he said quietly. 'Did you say something?'

'I understand how you must feel.' More than he could possibly imagine, he thought coldly. The only reason that he could carry on was by locking the pain away in a box deep within his mind. He knew that one day he would have to deal with it. But not yet.

The Doctor's reply was frigid, without a trace of compassion. 'Do you really, Professor Lassiter?' he snapped. 'Your genius has attracted some unwarranted attention, and that has cost the lives of my two friends.'

'If you would let me finish,' said Lassiter in measured tones, 'I was going to say that I would also understand if you wanted to leave.'

He shook his head gravely, dangerously. 'No, I don't think so. This is just the beginning. The potential for destruction that this technology represents is too great a threat for me to just walk away.'

Lassiter ignored the dig. 'I'd still appreciate your help.'

He wasn't prepared for the menace in the Doctor's voice. 'And besides, I'd like to meet the people responsible for this carnage. Wouldn't you?'

Blackness brightened to a misty red as the pain subsided. Earth to Tegan. Earth to Tegan, respond please. Slowly, painfully, her surroundings resolved from the blur. Her first impression was of stone: stone walls, a high stone ceiling. And smoke, not cigarette smoke, but the fragrance of burning wood. Stone and smoke. Tegan suddenly recognized the place – or rather, the type of place – she had materialized in. And why shouldn't she: it had only been a couple of days since she had last been in one. It was the hall of a medieval castle.

The hall was almost twice the size of Sir Ranulf's, but just as cold: the flambeaux affixed to the walls gave out a lot of smoky light, but precious little heat. Huge columns supported the ceiling at all four corners. The walls were decorated with large but simple paintings and beautifully woven rugs. Whereas Sir Ranulf's table had been set against the walls, here it was in the very centre of the hall, with about a hundred people standing or sitting around it, all talking in loud voices. Lots of smaller tables, also covered in food, stood by the walls, with yet more people gathered around them. A group of musicians played a quiet but tuneful refrain.

Thankfully, one of the pillars hid Tegan and Diva. Tegan glanced round and saw her friend sitting against the wall, her clothes, like Tegan's, once again transformed. Thankfully the rough woollen dresses were warm, even if they were uncomfortable. The silk headgear was a bit much though: Tegan felt like a nun.

'Diva!' she hissed. 'Are you awake?'

She managed a faint smile. 'Does your head hurt as much as mine does? We must have been bounced around the Vortex like . . .' She caught Tegan's puzzled look and stopped. 'Where are we?'

Tegan nodded at the tables, where everyone was tucking into the feast with obvious gusto. Thankfully, they hadn't been spotted. Yet. 'We're still on Earth, thirteenth century or so. This is a medieval banquet.'

Diva blew through her lips. 'I don't see how that could have happened. When I used the actuator, it should have sent us back to the Bucephalus, not another time zone.' She shook the actuator. 'It must be broken.'

'Great. So we're trapped in the thirteenth century! At least I would have been at home in 1985.' Ignoring Diva's confused expression, she continued. 'We'll just have to sit it out until the people at the Bucket notice we're missing.' A sudden thought struck her. 'Talking of missing people, where's your boyfriend?'

'Don't call him that!' Diva snapped, her ferocity surprising Tegan. 'I was his employee, nothing more, nothing less. Understand?'

'Fine, fine.' Tegan put up her hands in mock surrender. 'But where is he? He's already demonstrated that he can look like anybody.'

'I still don't understand how he can still be alive.'

Tegan remembered Arrestis's words, just before they'd all been knocked for six. 'I don't think he ever died. Not the real one, that is.'

'What do you mean? Of course he died. I was there when it happened.' She shuddered at the memory.

'No, you were there when someone you thought was Arrestis was murdered. I think someone murdered a clone.'

'Max used that word. What's a clone?'

Tegan tried to dredge up everything she knew about cloning, which was hardly PhD material. 'Well, a clone is –' She stopped as a rough hand was clamped about her arm.

'I don't think we need to go any further.' The now familiar voice belonged to a fat, florid-faced man in a red woollen tabard, tights and a pair of thigh-length leather boots. A black cloak completed the ensemble.

'Max?' hissed Diva.

'Full marks for observation.' He looked around the hall. 'I suppose it's a bit more . . . ethnic than our last location, but it'll have to do. At least we might get something to eat.'

'We should try to get away,' said Tegan. 'If we use the actuators again –'

'I don't think so. If you two experienced half of what I did coming here, you'll know to keep your fingers well away from them.'

'So what do we do, then?' she demanded. She had taken a real dislike to Arrestis: his threatening behaviour notwithstanding, the man was a grade A male chauvinist pig.

'Can't you get it through your pretty little head? The Crystal Bucephalus has been sabotaged – by me, I might add. One unfortunate aspect is that I wasn't supposed to be here when it happened.' He shrugged. 'The only way we'll get out of here is if Lassiter drags us out. So, since we're here for the long haul, I suggest we grab a bite to eat.' He nodded towards one of the smaller tables, where a huge side of beef and fresh bread waited invitingly.

'I just hope it tastes better than it did the last time I was in this century,' quipped Tegan. And then she remembered that the feast at Sir Ranulf's was the last time she'd had anything to eat, thanks to the Bucephalus yanking them away from France. 'Scratch that! I'll eat anything!'

'Well, that's the Navigus rebooted. Thankfully it shut down before any serious damage occurred. I'd hate to think what it would have done if the Legions had been hooked up to the Grid.' He stepped back from the eight-foot high silver cube in the corner of the Legion tank and placed his ganymede driver in the inside pocket of his waistcoat.

'I thought you said that you couldn't duplicate the Legions' functions?' The Doctor was confused. The Navigus was another of Lassiter's technological achievements that belied his stated limitations.

Lassiter shrugged. 'Not all of them. But even Legions need a break. Unfortunately, the Bucephalus can't be shut down.'

'Why not? I would have thought that was quite a simple operation.'

He nodded. 'Oh, it is. Except that the statue needs a minimum amount of time spillage throughput; without that, the crystal matrix starts to denature. And I'd hate to be around if that ever happened.'

'So the Grid goes on standby?' The Doctor peered at one of the monitors: it showed a schematic of the power-feeds snaking about the complex like coloured spaghetti.

'Exactly. At the end of each shift, the Legions link each Cubiculo with a default setting, and the Navigus locks that setting with a permanent vortex chain.'

The Doctor bit his lip. 'Let me see if I've understood this correctly. Even when the Bucephalus is closed and the Legions are off duty, transit is still possible between the Floor and the time zones.'

'As long as it's one of the default locations, obviously.'

'So Tegan and this other woman must have just wandered into one of the Cubiculi. I can't say I'm impressed with your security, Alex.'

'Now wait a minute. Before you start hurling accusations at me . . .' He broke off and started staring at the Doctor's jacket, at the silver embroidery buried in the blue silk. 'They're still alive!' he shouted, punching the air.

The Doctor spun round. 'Alive?' The inklings of a smile crossed his face. 'But how can you possibly know?' He suppressed any feelings of elation. He needed proof.

Lassiter ran over to the plantation of stone pillars and brought up the hologram of the Grid. It was still a shining golden ring around a black sphere. 'There is currently no contact between the Grid Control Suite and what's left of the Grid. Whatever Matisse did, it certainly messed things up.' He beckoned the Doctor over. 'You see the way that the time zone annulus looks denser?' The Doctor nodded. 'Well, the last diagnostic explains that. Somehow – and don't ask me to explain it because I can't – she's created some sort of self-sustaining logical linkage between the time zones.'

'Is that possible?' He knew it was, but the techniques were purely the province of the Time Lords. They had no place in a decaying technical infrastructure like the Union.

Lassiter smoothed his moustache. 'If you'd asked me an hour ago, I'd have said no, but now . . . There's one logical path that connects all one million and thirty-seven thousand, eight hundred and forty-one zones in the Carte de Locales.'

Obviously not the province of the Time Lords any more. The Doctor really did want to meet this Matisse. 'That's what I call a solution to the travelling salesman problem. So, if Tegan or her associate are still in the Grid . . .' He turned round. 'You said that they were still alive. I'm afraid I don't follow your logic.'

'That's the clever bit.' Lassiter was virtually wobbling with excitement. 'I was convinced that activating a gate would be fatal: with the navigation paths out of alignment, I couldn't see any way that the Navigus could correctly handle a signal from an actuator. But I was wrong: the Grid is now a topologically closed system. There isn't any access to the Vortex.'

Realization dawned on the Doctor. 'I take it that the actuators simply generate time bubbles around anachronistic elements?'

'Exactly! When the time bubble materialized around them, Tegan and . . . and the woman would have been propelled to the next zone in the path.'

The Doctor grinned, patting the scientist on the shoulder. 'And when did you work all of this out?'

Lassiter grinned back and pointed at the snake motif woven in silver on the Doctor's jacket. 'I don't suppose that you've ever heard of Kekulé, have you?' The Doctor feigned ignorance, so he continued.

'Kekulé dreamt of a snake swallowing its own tail, oh, about nine thousand years ago. From that dream, he calculated the molecular structure of benzene.'

'Really?' The Doctor remembered crouching beside a bed whispering to the restless scientist for hours. 'Thank you for the history lesson, Alex, but what has that to do with Tegan's current predicament?'

'Your jacket: snakes winding round and around . . .'

The Doctor looked down at the serpentine motif. He had been so touched when Professor Litefoot had given it to him. 'Very ingenious: let's hope that you go down in the history books – for the right reasons, of course.'

Tegan, Diva and Arrestis had seated themselves at the table, well away from the noisy throng of the others.

'Isn't this nice?' said Arrestis, tearing a hunk of bread from the loaf. 'Traditional food, traditional surroundings, almost enough to make you grateful to Lassiter, isn't it, Diva?' He swigged from a silver goblet. 'I'm going to get some more of this.' He stood up and looked around for some more wine.

'This isn't right,' said Tegan quietly, holding a chicken leg up to the light. 'There's something odd about all of this.'

'You identified the time zone,' said Diva. 'Perhaps you made a mistake.'

Tegan had been surreptitiously examining the clothing worn by the others and comparing it to her own. If what Diva had said was correct, the Crystal Bucephalus cast solid illusions around them, disguising them and helping them blend in. Arrestis had taken it one stage further, presumably using his battle armour to change his entire physical appearance. But the illusion should have been perfect.

'Of course!' she yelled. 'Why are we sitting in the thirteenth century wearing synthetic fibres?' She clutched at her dress. 'This isn't wool, it's some sort of nylon stuff.' She looked around the hall, thankful that the other guests hadn't taken any notice of her outburst. 'We're in the present day. I mean, the twentieth century. This must be a reconstruction of a medieval banquet.' Although they hadn't really caught on in Australia, Tegan remembered reading a piece about them in *Time Out* when she was in London. 'I suppose you could call it a twentieth-century version of the Crystal Bucephalus.'

Diva turned to the main table. 'This is bizarre,' she mused. 'Why would anyone from the Bucephalus want to go to a reconstruction when they could have the real thing?'

'I don't know,' muttered Tegan. 'I just think we ought to be discreet, that's all.' And then she heard a shout. Looking round, she saw Arrestis at the main table, arguing with a moustached man in a green tabard and a clashing blue cloak. 'Great,' she hissed. 'That's just what we need.'

Arrestis was clutching a stone pitcher, trying to prevent the man from taking it. As the argument escalated, others were turning round and moving closer.

Tegan grabbed Diva's arm. 'Come on, I think he could do with some help.' She virtually dragged her over to the main table.

'What's going on?' asked Diva.

'This idiot claims that I've stolen his wine.' He held the pitcher up. 'I don't see your name on it,' he sneered.

The man looked at him with narrowed eyes. 'Who are you? Which party are you with?'

'I'm with these two,' he answered, turning to the women for support. 'Aren't I?'

'Which party?' insisted the man. His hand slipped inside his cloak.

'Look,' said Tegan, trying to sound reassuring. 'We don't mean any trouble . . .'

The man transformed.

Tegan was transfixed. 'Man' wasn't really the right word any more. *It* was eight feet tall, its skin grey and granite-like as if it was made of rock. Tiny red eyes burned underneath heavy brows that resembled a miniature precipice. The clothing had vanished. Immediately Tegan realized why her clothing had been synthetic: it had matched the aliens' – and theirs was some sort of illusion.

'This is a private party.' Unsurprisingly, its voice sounded like gravel being shaken.

'What is it?' whispered Tegan.

'Search me,' said Arrestis. He addressed the alien. 'Look, there's obviously been some sort of a mix-up. We'll just leave you to it.'

'That is unacceptable. This is a matter for the justices.' It snapped two of its three fingers. Tegan stepped back as the medieval group rippled and swam in front of her. Seconds later the transformation was complete. Instead of a hundred men and women, a hundred creatures made of various shades of rock surrounded her. Three of them, two sandy yellow and one brick red, came forward to stand next to the grey one, who was growling into some sort of communicator.

' "Grab a bite to eat", Arrestis?' snapped Tegan. 'What a brilliant idea!'

'Just leave it, woman.' He threw his arms open. 'There really must be a solution to this.'

'There is,' rasped the red one. 'The justices. Gate-crashing a private party carries the death sentence on Marmidon.'

'Death sentence?' echoed Tegan. 'You really take your parties seriously, don't you?' She glanced at Diva. 'We've got to get out of here!'

'The Great Rock of the Cosmos decreed that parties must be sacred,' rattled one of the sandstone ones. 'Transgressing Its laws demands the ultimate penalty: dissolution in acid.'

'Acid?' Tegan's reaction was interrupted by the sound of stone on stone reverberating from the doorway. Three more Marmidons, all of them orange, stood there, wearing dull black armour. With guns. Great big guns.

'Grab your actuator,' barked Arrestis, dismissing his period costume and changing into his battle armour. 'We've got to get out of here.'

The justices stepped into the hall. One of them caught sight of Tegan, Diva and Arrestis and pointed a stumpy finger at them. 'Blasphemers,' it rattled.

'You said it was dangerous to make another jump,' said Tegan.

'And they're not?' He pointed at the justices with their

vicious-looking guns. 'Just do it!'

Diva reached inside the solid hologram of her dress and retrieved the black rod. 'Here goes.' As Arrestis pulled Tegan closer, she pressed the button.

The lead justice raised its rifle and fired. The energy bolt passed through the fading amber hoops and hit the stone behind, disintegrating a section three feet across. The justice stared at the damage for a second, before giving a grating shrug.

And then it never happened, as time gently righted itself.

'It was worth a try, wasn't it?' Tornqvist sank into the chair.

'I suppose so.' Turlough smiled, remembering the look of panic on Matisse's face when they'd burst in. 'I can't be certain, but I get the feeling that we've put one hell of a spanner in her works.'

The Prelector scratched his beard, a curiously cat-like gesture. 'Mmm, I thought that as well. Let's hope it's serious, eh?'

'And where did you learn an arm-lock like that?' asked Turlough. 'More religious training?'

Tornqvist grinned. 'Ooh, definitely not. My colleagues in the Conclave would be horrified if they knew. No, I was brought up on Mirabilis.' He studied Turlough's face. 'I see that doesn't mean anything to you.'

'Should it?'

'I thought everyone knew. Oh, never mind. Care for a little history lesson?' Without waiting for an answer, he continued. 'Mirabilis was part of the Federation. When the civil war started, it sided with the rebel forces, those not loyal to the Emperor.'

'Emperor?' asked Turlough. 'I thought the Federation was a democracy?'

'You are in the dark, aren't you? No, the Chen dynasty put an end to that. Anyway, the final, decisive battle that overthrew the Emperor took place in the Mirabilis system. The Federation won, but the Imperial Fleet took one last shot at Mirabilis: it was caught by an atmospheric plasma burst.' He closed his eyes. 'Folk stories, and records in the Union webwork, say that Mirabilis was a beautiful planet, without pollution, without overcrowding. After the plasma burst, overcrowding was the least of our problems.'

Turlough remembered reading about the effects of plasma damage on the biosphere of Qo'noS. Nasty business. 'I can imagine,' he muttered.

The Prelector gave a dry, cold laugh. 'After the hurricanes and tidal waves came the volcanoes and earthquakes. Ninety per cent of the population died, and the few who survived probably wished they hadn't.'

'Couldn't the Federation help? Send in a terraforming team or something?'

'The Federation turned its back on us — too busy sticking Chen's head on a spike.'

Turlough looked horrified. 'And that's your home planet?'

'For a thousand years, we eked out a living from the poisoned soil and the mutated flora and fauna. Gangs of children roamed the shanty towns, stealing and killing just to survive.' Tornqvist blinked rapidly. 'And that was me. I was only twelve, but I'd already killed ten people to keep myself alive. The Intent rescued me from that nightmare. I was taken to a Lazarine seminary and educated. Eventually I went into the priesthood, and . . .' He reached for his Inf, remembering where it was as soon as his fingers clutched empty space. 'And here I am. And that's why I hate people like Matisse and Arrestis. They just take and take. The Intent is based on fellowship, mutual respect, love. That bastard Arrestis, with his concubines and servants, he could never understand the Lazarus Intent, or why it was founded.'

'Ah, Legion, thank you for coming,' said Lassiter as the doors to the tank were opened. A hairy black ovoid hovered in the doorway, both there and not there.

Its choir-like voice echoed around the stone walls of

the Legion tank in fluting harmonies. 'My pleasure, Professor. I hope that my particular talents can be of use.'

'I'm sure they will.' Lassiter guided it towards the pit.

It stopped and manifested a crown of phosphorescent blue stars like a halo. 'My race has paid the penalty for its crimes: eight millennia of imprisonment beneath the Time Lords' interdict, incapable of traversing the Vortex, was more than sufficient punishment.' Neither the Legion nor the Professor noticed the Doctor staring at the floor in embarrassment. 'I cannot believe that someone could bear a grudge against us for all this time.'

'I don't think the grudge is against you,' said the Doctor. 'Is it, Alex?'

'I am ready.' The Legion had taken its place in the pit, and was already connected to the solid block in the middle by cables. Instantaneously. The Doctor was impressed: he hadn't even seen the Legion's temporal sleight of hand.

Lassiter was leaning over one of the pillars, typing into the stone keyboard.

'What precisely do you hope to achieve?' asked the Doctor, trying to make sense of the commands being entered.

Lassiter ran his fingers through his short hair. 'I'm hoping that the Legion can reach out through the Vortex and detect the zone annulus.'

'And then?'

'Once the link is established, I'm sure that a full complement of Legions will be able to unravel this mess.' He flicked a sequence of pebbles on the pillar. 'You now have access to the Grid, Legion.'

Aaah, freedom!

The Legion extended its tendrils in nine perpendicular directions, bathing in the radiance of the time winds. The Time Lords had known exactly what they were doing when they imprisoned the Legion's race: that barrier that cruelly prevented their movement through time. But the race had learnt its lesson, and one of their rewards after the Time Lords had unlocked their jail was service to Lassiter and his Crystal Bucephalus. Lassiter had shown the Legions that their limited spatio-temporal abilities could be amplified by its tank, giving them access to the endless tracts of the Vortex.

His gift was welcomed by a people desperate for a chance to make amends; at least, that was what he thought. If Lassiter had any idea of the feelings of infinity and eternity that the Legion tank gave them, that moment of apotheosis; he had created the ultimate Legion drug. After millennia of incarceration by the Time Lords, such freedom was a precious commodity. For a transcendent moment, however, the Legion experienced an eight-dimensional surge of bitterness: whatever the Time Lords' motives, he held no love for the ancient race. One day, the Legions would have their revenge.

Remembering its task, it began searching for the patterns of time, space, matter and energy that signified the errant zone annulus. It extended its sensory polyps, seeding the Vortex with pulses of attenuated time spillage, then interpreted the feedback. Measureless moments later, it detected a region of the Vortex that displayed the precise conditions it was looking for. Plunging into the heady flows of the Vortex, it was delighted to see that its senses had been correct: laid out before him like some celestial crown, Lassiter's annulus coruscated in the darkness.

A tendril snaked out, intersecting the annulus in a seven-dimensional hypervolume. The Legion confirmed that Lassiter's guess was correct: all the zones were chained together, millions of them into a self-contained pocket of the Vortex. As it explored the phenomenon, it noted idly that there was a slight anomaly in the chain: one of the zones was linked to two others, which then converged once more. Only the random laws of chance would decide which of the paths a traveller would take.

The Legion continued its journey through the annulus.

* * *

Tegan felt sick. Even before she opened her eyes, she knew that she was floating in zero gravity; when she opened them, she was able to queasily confirm it. Fifty feet above her hung a silver wall, while pink emptiness occupied every other direction. 'What the hell is going on!' she yelled, trying to turn round and immediately realizing her mistake: she began spinning, silver and pink circling round her in a dizzying roundabout.

'Tegan,' came an admonishing voice, as a hand grabbed her arm and stopped her rotation. 'Don't be so childish.'

'Childish? It's not my fault someone forgot which way is down, is it?' As she stopped her retort, she realized that Diva wasn't in the same predicament: she was lying on her stomach on a wide, flat disk, reaching out to hold Tegan's arm. And they were both naked, which gave her a grudging admiration for the image inducers: it was sweltering under the three purple suns, and she could feel the heat on her skin, even though she was really wearing a billowing silk dress. Fighting against her conflicting senses and somersaulting stomach, she looked up. 'What sort of a madhouse are we in now?' Diva pulled her up on to the platform. Tegan sighed as she felt gravity cut in.

'We're on Diadem,' stated Diva. 'The most relaxing planet in the galaxy.'

Now that her sense of direction had returned, Tegan could examine her surroundings. The silver wall was the ground, an endless vista of silver sand. The pink sky held even more surprises: countless orange globes hovered at regular intervals, their surfaces rippling in the soft, cinnamon-scented breeze.

'What is going on here?' Manoeuvring into a sitting position, she pointed at a nearby globe where two turtle things were diving around. 'Is that water?'

Diva nodded and sat up, dangling her legs off the edge of the disk. 'This planet was legendary: localized pockets of zero-gravity, water spheres with invigorating properties . . . legendary.' She gave a wistful smile.

'Have you been here before?' Tegan had to agree that it did look very inviting, and at least there weren't any bad-tempered rock people shooting at them. Nor old grannies with shopping bags, come to that.

She nodded. 'My father brought me here when I was little.'

Tegan was puzzled. 'I thought the Crystal Bucket sent people back to the past? What's the point of using it to go somewhere that you can get to by hopping on a spaceship?'

She looked downcast. 'The Union discovered that Diadem was rich in jethryk and trisilicate. They raped it for its mineral deposits.'

Tegan couldn't believe what she was hearing. 'That's horrible? A beautiful place like this, torn apart by greed.' It was clear that human nature didn't change.

'Jethryk is vital for power, and the galaxy's entire technology is based on trisilicate. You can't fight the argument: what's one pleasure planet against the survival of the Union?' It was clear, however, that she didn't agree with the logic.

'If the Union's like that, I'm glad I don't have to live there.' Tegan immediately realized her mistake, but Diva hadn't noticed. She was lost in her thoughts.

'I tried to persuade Max to come here, but he insisted on Beswicks.'

'Of course!' Tegan knew that she had forgotten something. 'What happened to him?' She looked around at the floating platforms, but they were unoccupied. 'He's not here.' She frowned. 'Unless he's invisible?'

'He's not here.' Diva pointed at the rims of the platforms: they were all yellow, apart from the one next to the globe with the turtles in it. 'That one is occupied: the rim is mauve. The others are free.'

'But that shroud-thing of his —'

'Can't disguise his weight. He's not here.' Tegan couldn't help noticing the relief in her voice. 'We can relax.'

'Relax?' She was shocked. 'Arrestis is still alive, goodness knows what's going on back at the Bucket, and you say relax?'

Diva threw her arms open. 'This is Diadem: calm,

peaceful, wonderful! What else can we do? Obviously the zones are all linked together in some kind of Vortex chain.' She tailed off and pointed at the orange globe about fifty feet from their platform. 'Fancy a swim?' Without waiting for an answer, she propelled herself into the air. 'Come on,' she urged. 'You'll love it.'

As Tegan inched gingerly to the edge, she tried to quiet her concerns. Diva knew a hell of a lot more about time travel than she had any right to.

'Jump!' prompted Diva.

As she fell into weightlessness and swam after Monroe, her protesting stomach overrode her concerns.

'Look at this!' shouted Lassiter. He was pointing at a monitor in the pillar top, a marble-edged screen displaying a burning torus which rotated about a fiery spindle. A white star stood out from the green backdrop.

The Doctor crossed the distance between the pit and Lassiter's station in seconds. He peered at the monitor. 'The Legion has located the annulus?'

Lassiter poked the screen. 'Annulus, Legion; Legion, annulus. What do you think?'

'Interesting.' The Legion's poly-vortex sensory array was detecting something quite odd in the zone annulus, a scintillating point of orange light shaped into a fluctuating diamond that burnt like a star. From the radiation output, it was as if another Grid was tapping in to the Bucephalus. The Legion manoeuvred itself to get a better look.

'Just a bit closer,' whispered Matisse, as her fingers stroked the photon strands . . .

The Legion extended a frond into the orange diamond . . .

Matisse gave a determined pluck . . .

And a burst of radiation vomited from the star, bathing the Legion in acid incandescence. With a scream that was carried on the time winds, it sprang back into reality, back into the pit.

Both Lassiter and the Doctor took an involuntary step back from the monitor as the radiation surge blanked out the screen. 'What was that?' whispered Lassiter. Simulteneously, they glanced at the pit and saw the Legion thrashing about in obvious agony.

'Quickly!' yelled the Doctor, but Lassiter didn't need any prompting. They leapt into the pit, but were much too late. In front of them, the Legion's cerebral polyp exploded and assorted tendrils, fronds and tentacles hit the floor with a sickening plop.

The Doctor performed a rapid examination of the body. 'I'm sorry, Alex, it's dead.' He held up a limp tentacle. 'I think we'd better examine what happened to it, don't you?'

Lassiter gave a nervous laugh. 'I guess I'm not going to win employer of the year, am I?'

Flexing her fingers, Matisse stood from the light-harp. 'Now, unless my sums are hopelessly wrong, twenty minus two leaves eighteen. I do believe that leaves you just a little short-staffed, don't you? Get out of that.' She glanced at the hovering ring of holospheres. Suddenly, her eyes were drawn to one of the globes. Plucking a chord, she watched as the globe swooped down to eye-level.

'For the love of Lazarus!' she screamed. At that moment, Byson entered the control room.

'Ladygay, are you all right?'

She gripped the arms of her chair. 'I'm fine, but I've just located our errant time-travellers.'

'The boss man?' he growled.

'Yes, and the two women — alive and well, if chronologically displaced.'

'But if they're all alive, why are you looking so upset?'

She sighed. 'Because that inquisitive Legion has somehow changed the rules. Their reality quotients have increased to zero point seven.'

Byson scratched his chin. 'Sorry, Ladygay, I don't follow.'

'No, of course you don't. In simpler terms, they're now real enough to divert the course of history.' She shook her head. 'And for once, I have to admit that this is beyond even my talents. We'll have to hope that Alexhendri can rise to the occasion. For once.' She began to compose an urgent communiqué.

'It gets worse, doesn't it?' Lassiter was slumped in a chair. Everything was unravelling, and he knew exactly who to blame. He should have realized that she would surface eventually.

The Doctor patted him on the shoulder. 'I regret the death of the Legion as much as you do, but we do have a link between the Bucephalus Grid and the zone annulus.'

Lassiter threw off his hand. 'Which is about as much use as a chocolate teapot.'

'I'm sorry?'

'Professor Alexhendri Bartholemew Lassiter's ABC of the Crystal Bucephalus, Volume One. The Legion tank needs twenty Legions to function at optimum levels, and a minimum of nineteen to function at all. And, unless you have some inability to count, we now only have eighteen Legions capable of manning the tank.'

The Doctor steepled his fingers and sucked through his teeth. 'Oh, I see. But can't you get replacement personnel?'

'Not in time to open the Bucephalus, no.'

'Why not? Reticence on the part of the Legions?'

'Not until now, no,' he snapped, irritated by the unintended slight on the Bucephalus. 'They're queueing up to get a job here. No, it's the distance. It'll take at least six days to get replacements.'

The Doctor raised his eyebrows, as if he were carrying out a quick mental calculation. 'Why the delay?'

Lassiter shot him a puzzled look. 'Delay? There isn't any delay, that's how long it takes. New Alexandria is on the edge of the Capricorn Tract.'

'Even so . . .' The Doctor's eyes widened. 'The Capricorn Tract? Well I never.'

'Sorry?'

'I'm not too far from my place of birth. Anyway, at shuntspeed fifty, it shouldn't take more than a day, surely?'

Lassiter laughed. 'Shuntspeed fifty? What sort of ships have you been travelling on recently? They just don't go that fast any more. Things are rough out there, Doctor: widespread technological failure, insufficient funds or knowledge to replace the worn out equipment . . .' He shrugged. 'I suppose I'll have to try to persuade Sebastian to keep the Bucephalus closed for another three days.' But he knew what the reaction would be.

The Doctor sat down. 'Well, that's it then, isn't it?' He straightened his jacket. 'The Grid stays shut until the replacement Legions turn up.'

Lassiter sighed. 'Quite. And I am not looking forward to telling Sebastian.' His eyes caught the monitor. Actually, every monitor. Every single screen in the Legion tank was displaying the same message.

'Doctor!' He pointed at the nearest screen.

'"RQ=0.7". Reality quotient?' The Doctor stroked his chin. 'I don't understand.'

'It's Matisse.' She really had got it in for him. In a very big way. 'Tegan and M . . . and the other woman are able to change history. We've got to get them out!' He realized that the Doctor wasn't looking at him.

He was staring at the Legion tank, at the place where the technicians had only just removed the dead Legion's remains. There were few races in the cosmos with the time sensitivity necessary for the operation of the Bucephalus. Legions, of course; Tharils, Chronovores, their cousins, the Eternals, the Transient Beings and, of course, the Time Lords. The Doctor was torn: should he tell him the truth, and face the inevitable consequences? But Tegan could now shatter the web of time. Deciding that he had ignored his responsibilities for too long, he knew it was time to come clean.

He gave a nervous cough. 'Could you reconfigure the Grid with eighteen Legions and a Time Lord?'

Lassiter frowned. 'Probably. But where would I find –' He looked at the Doctor with a bemused expression. 'You *are* joking?' Bemusement turned to awakening anger. 'You mean –'

The Doctor pouted. 'Sorry, Alex, but it's true. I'm a Time Lord. A very desperate Time Lord.'

Six

'You bastard!' Lassiter stood up from his chair, his eyes blazing. 'I suppose you think this is all a big game, don't you?' Mister High-and-Mighty Time Lord, wading in to have a laugh with the plebs and their tinker-toy technology! What are you going to do when you get bored, eh, Doctor? Destroy this place and rip all knowledge of it out of my mind?'

'I sincerely hope such measures will not be necessary.'

He shivered as if the temperature in the tank had dropped by ten degrees. He could do it, he realized. The Doctor could tear out that information without breaking a sweat. 'So why are you here?'

'Alex,' he said, some measure of reassurance in his voice. 'I'm here in a completely informal capacity. In fact, the Time Lords would be extremely angry if they learnt that I had done nothing to shut the Crystal Bucephalus down.'

'You mean you're not going to close the place?'

The Doctor shrugged, but his answer was evasive. 'Our first priority is to rescue Tegan and the others before they damage the web of time.'

Lassiter leant on the console. 'It's the one thing I've been afraid of, you know: the Time Lords.' He knew that that wasn't exactly the truth, but under the circumstances . . . 'For centuries, everyone had assumed that your lot had retired from the galactic arena. I mean, for five thousand years, since that business with the Dalek Civil War, no one had heard a thing. And then, eight years ago, a message was received throughout the Union. They were releasing the Legions from their temporal prison.'

'And you thought that they'd try to stop you? Why? I mean, the Bucephalus is nothing more than a highly advanced temporal projector. "My lot" only act if someone happens upon the means to disrupt history. And you're nowhere near that sort of technology. Are you?'

As Lassiter realized that the Doctor's final words had been a question and not a statement, he started stroking at his moustache furiously. 'I don't see what you're getting at.'

'Don't you, Alex, don't you really? Then perhaps I should be a little clearer. I don't believe that the Crystal Bucephalus is the crowning glory of your academic career at all. In fact, I think that this sparkling travesty is a deliberate technological dead-end.' He waved his arms about the Legion tank. 'With this equipment, it wouldn't take too much of a leap to start encroaching on the Time Lords' secrets. If you did that, they might be forced to act, and the Legions are a shining example of the punishments that my people are capable of inflicting.'

Lassiter swallowed. Seeing New Alexandria sealed within a temporal field for eternity was not a prospect he relished. 'Are you serious about getting hooked up to the tank?'

'Can you think of another way?'

'But it's not designed for a Time Lord's physiognomy; it's not designed for anybody apart from the Legions.'

The Doctor rubbed his hands together. 'Then we'll have to improvise, won't we?'

Turlough banged the door with his fist. 'How much longer is she going to keep us locked up like this?' It had been hours since Matisse's androids had locked them back in their cell.

Tornqvist opened his eyes. 'Sorry, I must have fallen asleep; too much excitement, I suppose.'

'You haven't missed much,' said Turlough. 'I just wish I knew what she was up to. Why is she keeping us here?'

The Prelector stretched with a yawn. 'Eschewing false modesty, it's me she wants. Or rather, her paymaster wants.' He stood up. 'Damn that man!'

'What man?'

'The head of the Elective. The poisonous little dwarf whose blood money finances Matisse's work. Arrestis.'

'But Arrestis is dead,' Turlough replied, straightforwardly, matter of fact. He wasn't prepared for the reaction.

'Dead? Dead?' Tornqvist started laughing in a most unclerical way. 'Well, I've always said that Lazarus pays debts without money.' He frowned. 'How do you know?'

'He was murdered a few hours before we were brought here. He and his girlfriend were having dinner in the twentieth century when someone poisoned him.'

'They murdered him in the Crystal Bucephalus? Someone's got a lot of nerve. Still, that's one less lost soul that the Lazarus Intent has to watch out for.' He scratched his chin. 'Do you know what happened to his . . . friend?'

Turlough shook his head. 'I'm afraid not. So, who is Matisse working for?'

Tornqvist shrugged. 'I doubt that the Elective would remain ungoverned for long. I can think of quite a few equally loathsome specimens who would take control: Dillon, Kimberly, even Samsys of Draconia.' He snapped his fingers. 'Do you know, this reminds me of the parable of Cletus and Brock in the temple of the Acronids of Theese.'

Turlough sighed. Since being incarcerated with the Prelector, he'd heard enough parables, fables and other assorted religious homilies to last him a lifetime. More than a lifetime. 'Enough, Sven; I feel like you've quoted the whole of the Codex to me already!'

Tornqvist smiled sheepishly. 'I'm sorry. In situations like this, I find my faith one of the few things I can draw strength from.'

'The Intent means a lot to you, doesn't it?'

'What sort of a question's that?' asked Tornqvist, staring at him. 'I'd hardly have become a Prelector of the Lazarus

Intent without believing, would I?' He stood up. 'The Lazarus Intent has helped countless millions in the galaxy. As technology decays and economies collapse, faith in the Intent is the only thing that keeps people going, as they wait for the salvation that Lazarus promises upon his return.'

Turlough narrowed his eyes. 'So what happens then?'

'When?'

'When Lazarus finally does return. Will your boss – the Benefactor, isn't it? – simply hand over control?'

Tornqvist's gaze grew suddenly distant. 'Of course. If Lazarus sets foot on Clavidence, the Benefactor will relinquish Saint Clavis's Chair.'

Turlough was immediately suspicious. Given Tornqvist's avowed faith, why had he used the word 'if'?

'Is everyone ready?' Lassiter looked at the pit: eighteen Legions and one Time Lord plugged in to the pit coordinator block. He had had to make a few adaptations, given that the Doctor lacked the necessary bionic implants needed to interface with the Grid: the Doctor was now wearing a skull cap, its micro-needles penetrating his cerebral cortex, performing the same functions as the cables that linked the Legions.

A tremolo chorus of assent replied to his question, but Lassiter couldn't help noticing that the Legions seemed a little more subdued than normal, making none of the piccolo-like chit-chat that usually preceded their immersion in the tank. Perhaps it was the recent death of one of their fellows, or maybe the presence of one of their legendary gaolers was a little unsettling.

'I think I've got the hang of this,' said the Doctor.

'Great. Remember: we're not powering up the entire Grid. Just latch on to the connection established earlier. From there, I want you to unravel the zone annulus and reweave it into the pattern that I've programmed into your sensory nets. Doctor, you're just there to make the numbers up, but be ready to help out if any of the Legions request assistance.'

He moved over the clusters of panels. 'Any questions?'

'How long should this take?' asked the Doctor.

'Hopefully not long. Although I should warn you: it's going to play merry hell with your nervous system, I'm afraid.'

'It's going to hurt. That's what you're saying, isn't it, Alex?'

'That's about the size of it,' answered Lassiter regretfully. 'Anyway, no time like the present, is there?' Cracking his knuckles, he flicked a few pebbles on one of the pillars. A deep throbbing rose from the pit, its frequency increasing rapidly to a screech before passing out of human hearing.

The Doctor grimaced.

'I wonder how you've managed that?' Matisse beckoned Byson over. 'He's found a replacement for the dead Legion.'

'But you said they wouldn't be able to get there in time.'

'Quite; time-sensitives are hardly thick on the ground. Let's take a closer look.' Although the Legion's actions had meant that the Exemplar had lost any control over bubble creation, the tap into the Bucephalus webwork was still in place. She brought up the profiles of the Legion tank's personnel. And raised an eyebrow. 'Where did you find *him*?' she hissed.

'Him? Not a Legion?'

'Most definitely not. Our Professor Lassiter has found himself a Time Lord, of all things.'

'Aren't they all dead or something?'

'So we all thought, until the Legion message. But why is there one at the Bucephalus? Perhaps they've come to shut Lassiter's little operation down.' She shook her head. 'No; if that were the case, why would he be helping Lassiter? Still, the most important thing is to try to access that oh-so-brilliant mind while we have the chance. With the knowledge of time technology housed within that Time Lord cranium, I could dispense with the Exemplar

118

completely.' And get the respect that I deserve, she thought bitterly.

She positioned herself before the harp. Time for a mind probe.

Tegan floated at the centre of the globe, breathing in the warm orange water and peering at the three suns through the haze of refraction. 'This is marvellous!' she exclaimed, her voice deep and resonant through the liquid. 'What did you call this stuff?' she asked, waving her arms through the orange and watching the turbulence subside.

'Super-oxygenated water,' came the reply. 'Takes a little getting used to, but the result is worth it.'

'How long do you think we're going to be stuck here? It's relaxing, but it doesn't seem right.' If the truth be known, Tegan was beginning to feel guilty about lazing about on Diadem. Who knew what sort of trouble the Doctor and Turlough were getting into without her? 'Why haven't we been picked up yet?'

'It's obvious that the Grid malfunctions have caused some sort of a realignment of the zone ann–' Diva tailed off and started looking around the globe, at the suns, at anything but Tegan.

'Come again?' Tegan's suspicions were well and truly aroused.

'Sorry?' she asked innocently.

'Look, Diva.' She twisted round and gently grabbed Diva's arm. 'This bimbo act's all well and good, but it's beginning to get a bit tedious.'

'Bimbo act? Why are you being so rude to me?' She even sounded hurt.

'Okay, okay, that was a bit much. But for someone who claimed to be Arrestis's bit of stuff, you know a hell of a lot about the Crystal Bucephalus.'

'I saw a documentary,' Diva protested.

Tegan laughed. 'A documentary? About the most exclusive restaurant in the galaxy? I don't think so, somehow. And then there's what Arrestis said when we were in London: something about having seen through you.' She stared at her. 'Don't you think you'd better come clean?'

Diva sighed. 'You're right. After what we've been through, you've got a right to know the truth.'

'That's it!' Lassiter watched the read-outs and hologram with satisfaction. The zone annulus was unravelling: the filaments that currently connected the multitude of time zones were being rewoven into a new design with the now illuminated Grid Control Suite symbol at the centre. He looked at the Doctor. His face was clearly strained, sweat beading on his forehead. 'Hold on, Doctor,' he whispered. 'Not long now.'

Fascinating, absolutely fascinating, decided the Doctor. Although his nervous system felt like it was on fire, he couldn't help but be impressed. He was familiar with the Time Vortex, but seeing it through the TARDIS scanner, or swimming through it when connected to a TARDIS's Vortex shields, were nothing compared to being immersed in it. With his senses augmented by the Legion tank, he could actually see chronon-anti-chronon pair annihilation: time meeting anti-time. And there was a standing Higgs wave, dancing a pirouette that defined reality! It was as if Picasso had been asked to interpret a book on theoretical physics.

A sharp dagger of pain made him wince, but it wasn't related to the Legion tank: this pain was on a psychic level, and he was surprised to realize that someone was trying to probe his mind. Under normal circumstances, Time Lords were capable of resisting all but the most sophisticated of mind-ripping techniques – but circumstances were far from normal. With tremendous effort, he concentrated on the lattices of time spillage that formed and reformed in tiny crystal eddies around him, and tried to lend some strength to the eighteen Legions.

'Nothing!' The probe wasn't registering anything. 'Perhaps the legendary iron will of the Time Lords isn't a myth at all.' Matisse cracked her knuckles. 'Let's see how you cope with this.' She hurled her arms outwards. 'Maximum power!' she yelled.

'Got them!' Two traces were clearly registering on one of the monitors. Without a moment's thought, Lassiter powered up the recall systems. In response, the Cubiculo in the corner of the tank lit up.

'I should have told you earlier, but, well, I wasn't sure what you'd say.' Diva's manner had subtly changed: her poise was more confident, more dominant, and her voice had acquired a deeper, more forceful timbre.

'Well, you won't know unless you tell me,' Tegan urged.

'All right . . .' She broke off as amber hoops of light formed around them. 'The Grid! He's found us.'

Within moments the globe was empty, the surface rippling in tiny orange waves.

The strain was becoming unbearable. The mind probe was more powerful than ever, boring into the Doctor's brain with unceasing agony. But he didn't dare risk channelling any more psionic energy from the task at hand to shore up his mental shields. He was suddenly aware that the women had been found, a surge of force that ran through him. He could even feel the bubbles, swirling through the Vortex to the safety of the Bucephalus. He reached out to touch the bubbles . . .

. . . and the mind probe hit with unexpected violence. Involuntarily, he forgot all about the Grid and slammed down an impenetrable mental shield. He forgot that the Legion tank needed the participation of nineteen operators.

Matisse jumped back in her chair as the feedback from the Time Lord's brain blew her probe. 'Damn!' she spat. 'I was almost there.'

* * *

The Doctor tried to reintegrate himself into the brother-hood of Legions, but something seemed to be stopping him. It was almost as if the Legions themselves were setting up some sort of psychic barricade. But why would they do that?

He reached out to the nearest presence with a gentle, helpful touch.

'Our revenge, Doctor.'

A backlash of mental energy seared into his mind, driving out the glittering Vortex and replacing it with insensate blackness and alluring cold.

Tegan found herself surrounded by a cloying dark noth-ingness, a sponge that seemed to suck her vitality away. She could make out vague shapes in the void, but they vanished when she concentrated on them, like figures seen out of the corner of her eye. She called out for Diva, but her words were swallowed up instantly. And then she began to panic, soundlessly and impotently.

'Oh no, not again.' Lassiter realized with frantic horror that it was an action replay of the events leading up to the death of the Prelector. He risked a glance at the Doctor, and was shocked to see that he was unconscious. His hands moved frantically over the controls in a desperate attempt to re-establish control over the bubbles, but it was too late. They were stuck halfway, jammed in the Vortex just beyond the reach of the Grid. Within minutes, the envelopes of reality would dissolve around them. Tegan and Diva would then bask in the time winds for as long as it took for their bodies to decay into dust.

'Can't I trust you to do anything right, Alexhendri?' Matisse glanced across the ring of holospheres. The women were stuck, their bubbles perilously close to disintegration. 'Well, as I've always said, if you want a job doing properly . . .' With a glissando, she activated the Archway.

* * *

'They've, they've gone.' Lassiter stared at the readings in disbelief. There was no evidence that the bubbles had dissolved, nothing. They had just vanished. Double-checking what had happened at the precise moment that the bubbles had vanished, he found it: the energy profile that he and the Doctor had detected earlier, the last time Matisse had interfered. Then he remembered the Doctor. Leaping into the tank, he disconnected the unconscious form. The Legions were extending their sensory polyps in the Doctor's direction.

'Is he injured?' one of them chimed.

Lassiter felt for a pulse, but could find only one. He started applying cardiac massage to the Doctor's left heart.

'Welcome to the Exemplar, ladies.' The woman looked slightly arabic, with dusky skin and beautiful black hair. Her outfit, a black and gold silk kaftan, looked totally out of place in the clinical white-tiled room. She was staring at Tegan. 'And who might you be?'

'Tegan. Tegan Jovanka.' She glanced at her body and was relieved to see that both she and Diva were not only dry, but were wearing their original clothes as well, albeit ripped, torn and dirty. Tegan felt very underdressed compared to their elegant host.

'Charmed to make your acquaintance, Signora Jovanka. I'm Professor Ladygay Matisse, and this,' she pointed at a huge man with a goatee beard, 'is Garrett Byson.' She squeezed Tegan's hand. 'I'm sorry it took so long to retrieve you; I'm sure the company must have been almost unendurable.'

'I should have guessed that Max would have needed a hard-faced bitch like you to pull off a stunt like this,' hissed Diva, and Tegan almost recoiled from the sheer hatred in her voice.

'Temper, temper,' said Matisse. 'I saved your lives, remember?'

'There must be something in it for you. Scientific research always came a poor second in your book.' She gave a dry smile. 'Probably because you weren't particularly good at it.'

Matisse pouted. 'Jealous, are we? Well, there'll be time for such pleasantries later.' She beckoned Byson over. 'I think it's time our guests were shown a little of our hospitality.'

Diva frowned at Byson. 'Still hanging around with your ape, Ladygay?'

Matisse shot her a look of pure venom. 'Better an ape than a monkey, Hellenica.'

'I hear that you've been having problems, Alex?' The Maitre D' stood in the centre of the Legion tank, his hands on his hips.

Lassiter glanced up from the bank of controls. 'I didn't hear you come in. Or knock for that matter.'

'Don't prevaricate. What's going on?'

Lassiter strode up to him and looked him in the face. 'You want to know what's going on? Very well, then I'll tell you. The Doctor is unconscious down in the infirmary, having suffered some form of psychic attack while plugged into the tank. We're a Legion short of full tank operation. And to cap it all, an external force has kidnapped the Doctor's companion and Arrestis's mistress.'

The Maitre D's eyes narrowed. 'Are you trying to tell me that the Bucephalus may not open on time?'

Lassiter's tone was one of total exasperation. 'A snowball would stand a better chance in hell than this place opening on time. And anyway, why would you want to open now? Three people have died, and Matisse has got her talons into the very heart of this place.'

The Maitre D' looked surprised. 'Matisse? Your Matisse?'

'How many Matisses do you know? This isn't funny.'

'Nor is the fact that this establishment is supposed to be open in three hours' time.'

'Open? Would you seriously open this place knowing that she's involved?'

'I don't care if the devil himself has booked a Cubiculo,

I want this place open on time. Do you understand what it would mean to my reputation if the Bucephalus weren't to open this evening? *Our* reputation?'

'But more people might die,' Lassiter implored. 'Do you really want their deaths on your conscience?'

'They're insured, aren't they? And a full scale attack by the Union fleet couldn't breach the perimeter defences, let alone reach New Alexandria. The galaxy needs the Crystal Bucephalus, you know that! Without it, the Union would grind to a shuddering halt.'

Lassiter sat down. 'You don't know what you're asking.'

His reply was quiet. 'Alex: Arrestis is dead.'

'I know.'

'So you don't have to worry about him any more, do you?'

'I suppose you're right.' He got up and ran a finger along the surface of the pillar console. With Arrestis dead, he no longer had to continue living with the fear that had driven him into exile on New Alexandria. Even Matisse's operation would presumably fall apart when the next CEO of the Elective decided that it was no longer viable. 'There is a way that I could get the place up and running . . .'

'You'll do it? Alex, that would be wonderful!' The Maitre D' was positively bubbling with excitement.

'I'll need about four hours. Five to be certain.'

'You can have four and a half. How's that?'

He sighed. 'All I can say is that I'll do my best.'

The Maitre D' put his arm around his shoulders. 'I'm extremely grateful, you know that.'

Lassiter looked up. 'What are brothers for?'

Byson had escorted Tegan and Hellenica Monroe – the Australian was having difficulty getting used to her real name – through the whitewashed corridors until they reached a particular black door. He tapped a small block against the entry panel and the door swung open. 'Go in,' he growled.

'Tegan!'

'Hellenica!'

Turlough and a man in a black and scarlet suit stood from their chairs, and both ran over to the respective women. While Tegan gave Turlough a warm hug, the man held out his left hand and Monroe knelt and kissed his ring.

'What the hell are you doing here?' asked Tegan. 'And where is here?'

Turlough shrugged. 'It's a long story. This planet is owned by the Elective — have you heard of them?'

'Heard of them? I've spent the last ten hours with Arrestis's girlfriend. And been terrorized by the boss man himself.'

Silence fell over the suite. The tubby man turned to Tegan. 'Signora, I'm Prelector Sven Tornqvist, Prelate of the Lazarus Intent. Are you saying that Arrestis is still alive? Turlough told us that he had been murdered in the Bucephalus.'

'Well, he was. Sort of. From what I can gather, he sent a clone to accompany Diva, sorry, Hellenica, to the Bucephalus.' Tegan shrugged. 'Sorry if it's confusing.'

'Clone? What might that be?' It was obviously an unfamiliar term to the Prelector.

Tegan looked at Turlough and gave a 'what planet are they on?' look.

'A clone,' explained Turlough, 'is a duplicate of a person grown from a genetic sample.'

Tornqvist's eyes widened in horror. 'Such research is strictly forbidden by the Lazarus Intent! Does that man have no ethics?'

Tegan sat on one of the beds. 'Would one of you care to explain what the hell you've been up to?' She looked at Monroe. 'I mean, one minute you're Arrestis's mistress, the next minute you're working for the Lazarus Intent.'

'Hellenica's mission was to meet with Professor Lassiter, creator of the Crystal Bucephalus, and persuade him to make certain . . . discoveries available to the Lazarus Intent.'

'But why Arrestis? Why couldn't she have accompanied you, Sven?' asked Turlough.

'Many of the guests in the Bucephalus are of the faith. As a Prelector, I have a certain, er, image. Being seen in the company of an attractive woman just wouldn't do.'

'But why Arrestis?' repeated Tegan.

'Because he is the most dangerous man in the galaxy.' Tegan immediately noticed the tone in the Prelector's voice. Fear. 'We also wanted Hellenica to keep an eye on him.'

'I'll save you the bother of asking the other question,' said Monroe. 'I was chosen because the Crystal Bucephalus is based on research by Professors Lassiter and Monroe. He's my ex-husband.'

Tegan sighed and gave Turlough an exasperated look. 'It's like a soap opera.'

'Although I don't get the reference, I think I know what you mean,' said the Prelector. 'Unfortunately, there's one more fact you ought to know. Ladygay Matisse is also a past romantic liaison of Lassiter's. You could say that there's a lot of bad blood around.'

'So, apart from the fact that everyone is everyone else's ex, you went out with Arrestis simply to get access to the Bucephalus?' Tegan snapped. 'That's nothing short of prostitution! Sounds to me like the Lazarus Intent is no better than Arrestis and his cronies.'

Monroe shook her head. 'You're wrong, Tegan. The Lazarus Intent's ideals are diametrically opposite those of the Elective. We want to help people.' She held a hand out to the Prelector. 'The Intent rescued Sven from the hell pits of Mirabilis. The Elective would have sucked the planet of its resources and then exported the inhabitants to work in the jethryk mines. That's the difference.'

'Okay,' sighed Tegan. 'So you're the good guys.'

After a few seconds of disorientation, Maximillian Arrestis had recognized his surroundings. A bar. There were some universal constants, and a seedy dive was one of them. Within minutes, he'd managed to pick the pocket of one of the more inebriated drinkers, and was now enjoying yet another scotch, courtesy of the purloined wallet.

And now he was drunk. Not totally drunk, but the sort of drunk where you know you're slurring your words but hope that no one else notices. He leant back against the bar and examined his surroundings. The place was dark, with black walls and a black ceiling, and it stank of cigarette smoke and alcohol. Just the way Arrestis liked it. Some people sat at irregularly placed round tables, looking furtive, while others leant against the bar like Arrestis.

Why had he got drunk? he asked himself, then decided that it was all Matisse's fault. She was supposed to pull him out before she pulled her clever tricks with the Grid. So why was he stuck in some backstreet dive? He'd visited backstreet dives on countless planets before, and had a good time: he just didn't enjoy being stranded in one. He drained his scotch and slammed the tumbler onto the bar. 'Another. A double.'

The barman, an effeminate teenager with blond hair, took the glass. 'Ice?'

'Straight,' he answered. 'Just get a move on!'

The barman scowled. 'There's no need to be so rude.'

Arrestis leaned across the bar and grabbed him by the throat. 'I'm the most powerful man in the galaxy. You don't . . .' Squeeze. 'Talk back . . .' Squeeze. 'To me.' He let the gasping barman fall to the floor. 'Just pour.'

He felt a vice-like grip on his shoulder.

'I think you'd better leave, don't you?' The man was dressed in the same sort of suit that Arrestis's clone had worn in Beswicks. He was very big and very nasty, with a shaved head and a blond beard.

Arrestis narrowed his eyes. 'Make me!' He reached into the solid hologram of red sweatshirt and jeans and pulled out a disruptor.

Tegan paced up and down between the door and the furthest wall. 'I'm sick of being caged up here. There must be something we can do?' It seemed years since she had persuaded the Doctor to make a slight detour from the Eye of Orion.

'Please, Doctor?'

The Time Lord raised his eyes heavenwards. 'There's a fully stocked food machine here in the TARDIS, Tegan. And if that isn't enough, I'm sure that there's a kitchen somewhere around. Unless I jettisoned it.'

'That's not the point, and you know it!' she interrupted. 'I want to be pampered. I want waiters calling me madame and pulling my chair out.'

The Doctor examined the console. 'You've just eaten with English royalty. Sort of.'

'Greasy food served by dirty, foul-smelling peasants . . .'

Spinning round from the console, he held his hands up in surrender. 'All right, all right. What do you fancy?'

'French cuisine. I haven't had a decent French meal since I went to Paris as an exchange student.'

'France, eh? Ah yes!' The Doctor snapped his fingers. 'I know an exquisite little place, just outside Paris. Built on the ruins of an old Abbey.' His hands flew over the console with breathtaking speed. 'They do the best bouillabaisse in the galaxy.'

'Wonderful! Thanks, Doc. I'm going to slip into something suitable.'

The Doctor frowned. 'Actually, I've always wondered how they keep the fish fresh all that way from the docks . . .' But no one was listening: the console room was empty. 'Ah, right. I suppose I'd better get changed.'

'Face it, Tegan,' replied Turlough, shaking her from her daydream. 'There's nothing we can do. Sven and I tried to escape using his mind control device, but Matisse has stopped us having any contact with anything but androids.'

'Androids?' Monroe looked up from her book. 'Standard design?' This last sentence was aimed at Tornqvist.

He nodded. 'I suppose so. They don't look much different to the ones on Clavidence. No one's got the technology to rethink them, nowadays.'

'Brilliant,' said Monroe, placing her book on the table.

Tegan idly took note of the title: *The Codex of Lazarus*. 'Now, how many gate actuators can we rustle up?'

'What?' Tegan was puzzled.

'Gate actuators? Come on, come on.' Monroe's commanding tone was light years away from her Diva persona. Tornqvist reached into his jacket as Monroe rifled through her handbag. Tegan and Turlough exchanged bemused glances. 'Two. Well, I suppose it might work.' Monroe picked one up in each hand and seemed to weigh them.

'Would you mind explaining what you're up to?' She was beginning to think that she preferred Diva to Hellenica.

Monroe smiled. 'All right, here we go. Matisse's androids are probably like ninety-nine per cent of the androids in the Union: all based on the Syzgerny-Durok model, designed two thousand years ago.'

'Is this important?' whined Turlough.

'Yes, so shut up. After the great cybernetic massacres of the eighty-fifth century, people were afraid to have sentient androids serving them. The S-D model was intended to prevent androids from possessing free will; they're all connected to a coordinating webwork.' Catching Tegan's blank look, she elaborated. 'The androids in a closed system, such as here or the Bucephalus, are linked to a single, artificial intelligence, with a whole battery of constraints and safeguards to prevent free will, so there's no chance of rebellion.'

'So what's that got to do with a couple of actuator rods?' asked Tegan.

'The androids are all part of a hyperspatial token ring network. All communications between them and the webwork pass through hyperspace. Which is a subset of the Time Vortex —'

'And the rods propel us through the Time Vortex!' Tegan grinned, pleased that she had picked up something from Monroe's earlier slips of the tongue.

'Exactly. I think I should be able to rig up something from these two rods that can isolate the android from the webwork. The next time an android comes in here, it'll find itself quite literally brainless.'

Turlough grinned broadly. 'Someone on your level, Tegan.'

'Speak for yourself.'

Tornqvist held up his hands. 'Please! Hellenica has a lot of work to do, and we don't know when the next android will turn up.'

With that, Monroe reached into her handbag and extracted a thin, flexible rod.

'Time scientist and electronics expert,' said Tegan. 'Is there no end to your talents?'

Monroe looked up from her work. 'Yes, Tegan, there is. That's the problem.' She started rewiring the actuator rod.

'Damn!' Lassiter pulled his hand back from the base of one of the pillars as one of the quarkblocks shorted out.

'Problems?'

He looked round to see the Maitre D' standing there.

'Don't you ever sleep, Sebastian?'

The general manager smiled. 'I had to see the Major-domo of the Syphax. I've only just finished.'

'The Majordomo?' Lassiter grinned. 'He's almost as much a windbag as you are. I'm surprised you managed to escape.'

After a wounding raised eyebrow, he continued. 'Since the opening of the Bucephalus is to be delayed, I thought it wise to inform him that he'll have to keep the guests occupied for a few hours.'

'And then you thought you'd come and check up on me.' Lassiter slapped the top of the pillar. 'Well, you'll be pleased to know that we're right on schedule. So, why don't you go back to your office and grab a catnap?'

'Are you sure?'

Lassiter laughed. 'Of course I'm sure; I wouldn't say it if I wasn't. Now, bugger off and let me finish this.' He jerked his head backwards at the Navigus cube.

The Maitre D' tutted. 'Such language, Professor Lassiter.'

'Go on, get some rest. I promise you that this will all be up and running in time for you to start bossing the guests about.'

Matisse rubbed her eyes. It had been a long day, and Arrestis still wasn't out of the Grid. Damn Lassiter. Why did he have to shut down the Legion tank, and not activate that half-hearted station-keeping device of his? Although she could override the Bucephalus control systems and use the Exemplar to reach into the Vortex and grab time bubbles, there was absolutely nothing she could do now that Lassiter had taken the Legion tank out of the loop: there was no way to actually generate a bubble in the first place. That was Lassiter's little secret, and no amount of digging through the Bucephalus web-work could reveal the answers. She decided to see what Arrestis was up to and activated one of the holospheres.

She froze. He was standing in a bar of some sort, a disruptor pistol in his hand, aiming it at the three people surrounding him.

'Blast you, Arrestis!' The fool had no idea that his actions could now influence history. Waving a disruptor around; it would be just her luck if he shot somebody really important.

Then again, there was very little information about what would happen under these circumstances, practical information. For that sort of research, one would need true time travel, and the vaunted Lords of Gallifrey were hardly going to hold symposia on the subject. What did exist were the posited theories of Ethra and Teelis, and their idle – and most probably alcohol-induced – musings on temporal embolisms and paradox wavefronts. What happened next made their musings all the more important.

'Just get away from me!' Two more bouncers – Arrestis remembered the term from a particularly riotous visit to Ancient Earth via the Bucephalus – had joined the first one and were standing round him. They obviously didn't recognize a standard issue Union disruptor. 'I'm warning you: one step closer and you're history.'

One of them, a large black man, turned to the first bouncer. 'Doesn't look like any gun I've ever seen.'

'Too right; looks like something out of *Star Trek*,' muttered the third, an older man with grey hair.

'I think he's bluffing,' said the one called Roy, and suddenly rushed forward. He was extremely surprised when his chest vanished.

What Arrestis didn't realize was that Roy Jarvis would – without his interference – eventually have had a great-great-grandson. And two hundred years later, Commander David Jarvis would have sat on the bridge of the Colonial warship *Dauntless*, in the middle of the battle of Cassius, where he would disregard orders and fire the decisive volley that would end the Dalek blockade of the Solar System. But Roy Jarvis was dead. Time would have to take care of that. History would have to be rearranged.

Matisse watched, not wanting to believe, as the readings within the holosphere went haywire. The universe was in embolism.

Seven

M ax scanned the bar. Their shock at the man's death would only last a few more moments, and then his actions would sink in. Then standing at the bar, disruptor or no disruptor, would not be the safest place in the galaxy, even in disguised battle armour.

As he edged towards the door, the black bouncer glanced up from Roy's body and noticed. Max reacted instinctively, and the bouncer went to pieces. Tiny little sub-atomic pieces.

Lassiter stood from his crouch and wiped his hands on his trousers: his work on the Navigus was almost complete. The silver cube was now rather less regular than before: odd growths and encrustations abounded over the engraved surface. As the Doctor had openly suspected, the Navigus had contained virtually everything necessary to replace the Legions. All Lassiter had needed to do was to rewire a few exitonic pathways, reroute the odd quarkblock linkage, and drag one of the containers of esoteric components from the vault beneath the floor of the Legion tank. He took his talkstick from its hip holster.

'Lassiter to Ottway.' He was glad that Carl Ottway was on duty; his grasp of the technical aspects of the Grid was second only to Lassiter's. 'I'm ready to begin preliminary tests on this new equipment.' Not that Ottway or any of the other technical staff had the faintest idea what was really going on in the tank. 'I'm hooking it up to the Grid architecture now. Bring up the power feeds in one minute.'

Replacing his talkstick, he reached over and closed the access panels to the Navigus, before trotting over to the cluster of pillars. As much as he prided himself on his own genius, he would have felt a lot happier if the Doctor had been helping, instead of being comatose in the infirmary. Still, the less the Time Lord knew, the better, as far as Lassiter was concerned.

Moments later he stood back from the pillars and watched as, right on schedule, a wave of tell-tales swept across the pillar tops. He turned to check on the Navigus: as he had hoped, the external circuitry was glowing with a pearly radiance, while the additional blocks of components glittered and sparkled. He checked one of the pillars to confirm that the Navigus was duplicating the abilities of the Legion tank, and was pleased to see that all readings were within a fraction of a per cent of those of the Legions.

It would do until more Legions arrived from their home world. And then the Navigus would be stripped back to basics, permanently.

'For the love of Lazarus,' mouthed Matisse, staring at the impossible tableau. Arrestis was still sweeping his gun around in that insufferably arrogant manner of his, but the others were paying him no attention as they milled around the incomplete corpses sprawled on the floor. From the readings she was monitoring, Ethra and Teelis would soon have all the empirical research they needed. She could feel the sweat on her forehead and as it trickled behind her ears she contemplated the consequences: history being rewritten, until neither the Bucephalus nor the Exemplar existed. The inevitable paradox – who would have then sent Arrestis back in time in the first place? – could be left to the physicists and philosophers who remained in the altered reality.

A twang from the light-harp snapped her attention up to a holosphere. The information it contained was too good to be true. 'Alexhendri, I could hug you!' With almost inhuman speed, she played the light-harp, a fugue of desperation and last chances. Her face was set with determination as she felt her way into Lassiter's glory.

'Sounds like one of them is coming,' said Turlough, his ear to the door. Tegan decided that eavesdropping was a perfect use of his talents.

Tornqvist leaned over Monroe's shoulder. 'How's it going?'

Monroe was still making adjustments to her invention. The two rods were now bound together end to end by twisted optic fibres that had been ripped out of the inner workings of the lights. The long tube ended in a glass cube that had once powered the toilet's autoflush. Tegan had enjoyed smashing up the bathroom; it had been better than just sitting around.

Monroe closed a tiny panel and looked up. 'Done. This should do it.' As she spoke, a faint electronic warbling noise came from the door. 'Is this it?'

'Well it's not the Avon lady,' said Tegan dryly.

The door opened to allow seven feet of shining metal in human form to enter, pushing a trolley. 'Food,' it announced in a low, synthetic voice.

'Give it to him, Diva!' yelled Tegan. But Monroe was already aiming the device with her left hand, and squeezing the fibre optic contact in the other.

The android froze, its iridescent plates locked in place. Turlough ventured forward and tapped it. It remained motionless. 'I think you did it.'

'Yes!' shouted Tornqvist, punching the air. 'Let's get the hell out of here.'

Tegan decided to ignore this unclerical exclamation, and followed the others through the door.

Lassiter frowned. His years of familiarity with the Grid made him especially sensitive to the slightest changes in operation, subconscious triggers that suggested that something was, well, different. He examined the read-outs on the pillars and frowned, refusing to believe what his instruments were telling him.

'Ottway?'

'Yes, Professor?'

'Is everything okay over there?' He tried to keep the worry out of his voice.

'Seems to be. All readings are textbook. Then again, you did write the textbook.'

Indeed, thought Lassiter. But someone else was leafing through its pages. His instruments showed that a time bubble was being generated, but no such instructions had been given from the Bucephalus. He moved over to another pillar and began entering commands. There was no way he was going to let Matisse get another one over on him. Not after what she'd done.

As she fired up the Bucephalus Grid by remote control, Matisse realized that there was a good chance that Lassiter was well aware of her interference, and probably not very happy. But he'd be a damned sight less happy if a temporal embolic wavefront came knocking at his door. She made a few final adjustments, and prayed that the article penned by Ethra and Teelis in the March 9978 issue of *Abstract Meanderings in Theoretical Physics* actually did hold water, and wasn't just the witterings of a couple of drunken old Earth Reptiles who hadn't had anything better to do.

'Let's see what you make of that, then.' Lassiter finished his adjustments with a flourish. Deep within the Grid, half-forgotten subroutines began to stir, defensive programs that he'd written years ago, mainly out of boredom. But he had always been wary of someone attempting to hack into the Crystal Bucephalus.

True, the Bucephalus webwork was protected by the standard barrage of anti-incursion netware, more than sufficient against the technology that existed beyond the confines of New Alexandria. But Matisse was a genius, head and shoulders above the rest of the fading scientific community. An interloper of her calibre demanded special treatment.

* * *

To an observer, the Doctor appeared unconscious. Within his mind, however, it was quite a different story. Something was bothering him, something he was supposed to remember. The area in question lay buried like a treasure chest under the sands of memory, and he was trying to decide which particular spade to use to dig it up. Over the centuries, he'd picked up a vast armoury of such diagnostic techniques, ranging from the id–ego balancing tenets taught by his hermit on the hill to the skills of the Mind monks of Darron.

Methodically, he dug the sand away from the chest until it was revealed. And then he began to unlock it, a telepathic key to a psychic lock, feeling the tumblers match and turn. There! He lifted the lid, and a single name flew out like a startled bat.

Tegan.

Without a second's hesitation, the Doctor broke his trance and leapt from the bed. It was time to get a few answers.

Everything was set. Unbeknown to Arrestis, a potential time bubble now surrounded him. All it would take was a single pluck of the harp, and the bubble would manifest itself, yanking him away from his self-inflicted carnage. Unfortunately, it wasn't as simple as that.

By her calculations, she had approximately twelve minutes before the damage to history erupted in a temporal embolism that would hurtle up the time lines, devouring the past and excreting a new reality in its wake. However, she still had work to do before she could recover Arrestis: the time bubble had to be adjusted, fine-tuned, so that it not only encapsulated Arrestis now – now, in a Blinovitch sort of way – but his preceding fifteen minutes of bloodshed as well.

With a practised flourish, she began playing the harp, shaping the bubble, moulding it backwards.

Matisse pulled her hands back from the harp as if they had been burnt. Somehow, her command pathways were locked. A quick check in one of the holospheres confirmed her theory: her gateway into the Bucephalus webwork was now a *cordon sanitaire* of defensive viruses which were destroying every attempt by the Exemplar to gain access.

She stared into the holosphere, half hoping that she could somehow influence Lassiter. His understandable preventative measures might very well have signed the galaxy's death warrant.

At the sound of footsteps on the stone floor, Lassiter looked round from the Navigus. He broke into a broad grin as he recognized the figure in the blue jacket. 'Doctor! How are you feeling?'

'I've felt better. Where's Tegan?'

The scientist began to feel a little uncomfortable. 'Tegan? Well, I . . .'

'Don't waste my time, man. What's happened to her?'

Lassiter waved his hands about. 'The bubbles . . . the Grid lost control of them –'

'And?' The tone of command in the Doctor's voice was like an irresistible force, and Lassiter wasn't quite the immovable object.

'And I have good reason to believe that they were "rescued" by Matisse,' he said bitterly.

'So she's alive. The first good news all day,' he said pointedly. 'So how do we get her back?'

'It's not as simple as that. We can't just get in touch with Matisse and say, "Can we have our friends back?" Anyway, I've just caught her trying to destroy the Grid by tapping into the webwork.'

'Destroy the Grid?' The Doctor ran a finger through the pearl web on the Navigus's surface, leaving a rapidly fading trail of lights like tiny fireflies. 'Think about it logically. She has a technological base comparable to the Grid, she has the financial backing of the Elective and she obviously has a direct tap into this operation. If Matisse wanted to bring this place crashing down around you, she'd have done it long ago. Agreed?'

Lassiter couldn't fault his logic. 'I suppose so. But she's

definitely up to something,' he insisted.

The Doctor was looking at the pillar tops. 'Yes, I can see that. I can also see that you've decided to show your hand.'

'Sorry?'

He pointed at the cube. 'The Navigus. According to your instruments, it's now capable of performing all the tasks that the Legions have traditionally handled.'

'It's all coming down as soon as their replacements arrive. It's a favour. To the Maitre D'.'

'Quite a favour, but I can sense you're not at all comfortable about this open display of your genius.'

Lassiter decided to change tack. 'What about Matisse? As soon as the Navigus came on-line she forced it to activate a time bubble, and was powering up the recall systems.'

'Really? You seem rather calm about it.'

'Some time ago I wrote a few defensive programs, just in case I ever encountered someone who could fight me on my own level.' He grinned like a child. 'They take up rather a lot of the webwork's resources, so I hadn't bothered to activate them – until now, leaving poor old Ladygay like the proverbial monkey with its hand in the cookie jar.'

'She can't get out until she lets go.' The Doctor looked more carefully at the readings. 'Alex, don't you think we'd better find out exactly what cookies Matisse has her fingers round? I mean, why would she be generating a bubble?'

Lassiter looked horror-struck. 'Unless she was trying to retrieve someone from the Grid, someone we overlooked!'

The Doctor nodded. 'Exactly. Someone trapped in the past, with a reality quotient of 0.7.'

'For the love of Lazarus, what have I done?'

The Doctor touched him on the arm. 'I don't know, but I think it's time we found out, don't you?'

It was useless. In less than six minutes, according to Ethra and Teelis, the damage would be permanent, and she was sitting there with a frozen light-harp and a half-formed time bubble. There was no other choice: she'd have to swallow her pride and principles, and contact Lassiter. And with his little programs prowling about, she'd have to do it the hard way. She started to compose a squirt-packet to New Alexandria – and stopped as a scale issued from the light-harp. Someone was trying to communicate with her, through her link with the Bucephalus webwork.

'Ladygay Matisse,' she stated curiously. 'I presume that's you, Alexhendri?'

'It's been a long time, Ladygay.' His voice made something quite disturbing stir deep within her. Feelings that she would have sworn had never existed in the first place.

'Not long enough. What do you think you're doing?'

'Trying to stop your interference. What are you doing?'

Before she could answer, another voice took over. 'Professor Matisse, I'm the Doctor.'

'Alexhendri's pet Time Lord, I presume. If you've come to shut us all down, you're not exactly doing a very good job of it, are you?'

'Please, Professor. All I want to know is what you were doing in the Grid in the first place. I thought you'd already retrieved the misplaced travellers?'

'Doctor, tell Alexhendri to lower his defences. He doesn't know what he's doing.'

'Nor do I,' said the Doctor in exasperation. 'Who is in the Grid?'

'An Elective agent. An Elective agent with a reality quotient of 0.7 who's already murdered three people. We're four minutes away from an embolism. A great big embolism that will wipe out history!'

The Doctor turned to Lassiter. 'Unlock your defences.'

'But –'

'Do it! If you don't, you can wave goodbye to the Bucephalus. You can wave goodbye to the entire Union, for that matter,' he said breathlessly.

For a second, Lassiter froze. Then he fell on the pillar

consoles, his hands moving at an unbelievable speed. 'Try it now, Ladygay: you've got control,' he said bitterly.

Matisse didn't hesitate. An elegant harmony issued from the light-harp as she finished off her temporal artistry. She was operating at the borders of abstract physics. That bumbling pair of alcoholic Earth Reptiles had theorized that it took twenty minutes of absolute, Blinovitch, time for alterations in history to become permanent: almost like paint drying. She had only a couple of minutes to excise Arrestis's bad behaviour from history before the embolism began. And then all hell breaking loose would be an understatement.

Arrestis was now surrounded by eight bodies, all missing various limbs, heads and other assorted body parts. He felt no guilt over the carnage: given the nature of the Bucephalus, this was nothing more than a game. He remembered the historical documentation about cyber-space and virtual reality, a passing fad that everyone had rapidly got bored of. This was much more fun.

The bubble was now extended across a small but perfectly formed region of the space-time continuum. With deft plucks, she manifested the bubble.

Four men in dark blue uniforms leapt at Arrestis, knocking the disruptor from his hand. Fists and boots overpowered him within seconds, allowing the few people remaining in the bar to breathe a communal sigh of relief. They weren't prepared for the shining yellow hoops that encircled the mêlée, shining with a strange light that was both there and not there. And then . . .

The azure radiance faded, leaving a blue battle suit that reflected the white of the Archway. Arrestis removed his domed helmet and sneered. 'You took your time, didn't you? Thankfully the armour stopped me getting too battered about.' He stepped forward and placed the helmet on the table.

'I'm sorry for the inconvenience, but at least you're still alive,' said Matisse. 'A few more minutes and there wouldn't have been an Exemplar for you to return to.' She ignored his look of confusion. 'Anyway, welcome back.'

'So, that's that,' sighed Lassiter. 'Matisse has rescued her agent, withdrawn from the Grid, and I'm quite prepared to expend the resources necessary to keep her out. I'll pop over to Grid Control and ensure that the defence programming is watertight.'

'Excellent,' said the Doctor. 'All we have to do now is rescue Tegan and the other woman.'

For a second, Lassiter wrestled with his conscience, before deciding that he had a right to know. It was time to be honest. 'The other woman, Doctor: she's Hellenica Monroe.'

He sighed, running a hand through his hair. 'How long have you known?' There was a trace of irritation in his voice.

'Since I saw her in the twentieth century.'

'And you didn't say anything? Considering what you've said about your past relationship with her, I find that very difficult to understand.'

Lassiter shook his head rapidly. 'That was all a long time ago. Hellenica's history.'

'Why do I find that even more difficult to believe? If there's one thing I've learnt about humans, it's that they tend to put great store by interpersonal relationships.' If Lassiter hadn't known better, he would have sworn that he could detect regret in the Doctor's voice. 'Even so, she is still a prisoner of Matisse, and so is Tegan. I've already lost one companion since arriving here: I intend to do everything in my power to ensure that I don't lose a second. Is that clear?'

'Of course.' Lassiter looked over at the Navigus. 'I might be able to tap into her little operation, the same way that she poked into ours. Although I did promise

Sebastian that I'd have the Bucephalus up and running so that it can open on time.'

The Doctor raised his eyes heavenwards. 'I don't believe it. After everything that's happened, the Maitre D' is still concerned about his reputation.' For a second, it looked as if he was about to launch into another outburst, but he simply tutted. 'Very well. I have other business to attend to.'

'Such as?'

'Can you program a Cubiculo for the eighteenth century? Earth? France?'

Lassiter frowned. 'Isn't that where you were dining when all of this started?'

'Exactly. I want to ensure that this embolism was properly aborted. And the equipment here –' he gestured to the Navigus, but clearly meant the entire Bucephalus, 'isn't quite sensitive enough.'

'Your TARDIS,' said Lassiter.

'What?'

Lassiter winked. 'You're a Time Lord, aren't you? You must have turned up on Ancient Earth in something; you certainly didn't use the Bucephalus.'

The Doctor stuck his bottom lip out. 'Quite. Yes, Alex, I want my TARDIS back. Can you arrange a Cubiculo?'

'Of course.' He paused. 'So you'll be bringing the TARDIS here?' He couldn't hide his enthusiasm.

'Er, yes,' he replied with a frown. 'Although I do have reservations about mixing and matching time technologies: the statue might set up some resonances in the TARDIS's own crystalline . . . but that's another problem. Are you sure that Matisse's access to the Grid is blocked? I'd hate to find myself prey to her whims.'

'Absolutely sure,' Lassiter snapped, a little more forcefully than he had intended. 'She had two points of access: one was through the Grid – one of the zones, as our late Legion found to its cost – and I've excised that particular zone from the topology. The other was a tap into the Bucephalus webwork, and my counter-intrusion

144

measures have put paid to that. She's clever, but there's no way that she can get through what I've set up. Does that satisfy you?'

'Perfectly. When I return from France, we're off on a little trip.'

'Trip?' Lassiter had a fairly good idea where they would be going but said nothing, busying himself over the stone console.

The Doctor gave a predatory smile. 'Oh yes. It's time this particular Doctor made a house call on Professor Ladygay Matisse.'

'How long do you think you'll be?' he muttered without looking up.

'I could be glib and tell you that I'll be back five minutes ago, but I don't want to take chances with either the Bucephalus or the TARDIS. I'll have to play it by ear: a standard materialization would get buffeted about by the turbulence the Bucephalus causes in the Vortex, and I'd probably end up in Matisse's lap without trying.' He stroked his chin. 'By the way, what are the coordinates of New Alexandria? I'll need them to pilot the TARDIS.'

'Of course.' Lassiter tapped a couple of pebbles and pointed to a monitor. 'Et voilà!'

The Doctor looked at the string of numbers in silence, before looking around the room with a strange expression. For a long moment, he said nothing, before muttering, 'Ah, quite.' But he had a very odd expression on his face.

'It'll take a couple of minutes to stabilize the gate.'

The Doctor shrugged. 'Time seems to be something we have in abundance.'

Arrestis strode towards the door, his expression angry. He hadn't been impressed by Matisse's explanations. 'Thank you for filling me in on what's been happening. I'm off to get changed.'

A sudden warbling noise issued from the light-harp. 'Hang on a second.' Matisse strode over to the light-harp and sat down.

'For Lazarus's sake, what now? I want to get out of this bloody armour!'

'Lassiter's activated a Cubiculo: 1791, Earth, Ancient France.'

'That's where you snatched the Doctor, isn't it?' He rubbed his now stubbly chin. 'What's he up to?'

'He's probably sent the Doctor to get his TARDIS back,' she replied in a matter-of-fact way, before she realized that this was one particular fact she had forgotten to tell Arrestis.

'TARDIS? As in Time Lords?' He sounded worried. 'Where do they fit in?'

She sucked through her teeth. 'I don't know how to tell you this, but, well, the Doctor's a Time Lord.'

He stared at her in horror. 'A Time Lord? Oh, great. That's all I need, those bloody high-and-mighty protectors of the time lanes poking their noses in.'

She refused to take the blame. 'May I remind you, Monsignor Arrestis, that it was your idea to involve the Doctor? Getting me to invoke the recall systems as soon as the webwork detected his brain patterns in the Grid?'

'That was before you told me that he was a bit more than a galactic entrepreneur,' he snapped. 'I might as well have asked the director of taxes to have a look over the Elective's books.' He didn't laugh. 'I wanted the Doctor present for the same reason I stranded Diva in the past: I thought that upping the stakes, especially after my supposed death, would force Lassiter to show his hand. Given your overwhelming inability to do anything correctly, it seems I was wrong.'

She deliberately ignored the slight. Insults were Arrestis's favourite method of communication. 'What do you want to do about the Doctor?'

'Kill him. A squad of androids can head him off before he reaches his TARDIS.' Arrestis seemed to relish that option.

'No, no, no, Maximillian. Remember, we're dealing with a reality quotient of 0.5.'

'We bumped off my clone without a hitch.'

'Because the wine and your clone had the same reality quotient. Being a Time Lord, the Doctor has a special relationship with time; your androids would be useless. And besides, I'd rather not bring the wrath of the Time Lords down on us: remember what they did to the Legions.' And then it hit her. The one option she'd overlooked. 'Of course! Outside the Grid.'

'Outside?' he repeated. 'Can you do that?'

She smiled. 'The Grid uses the Carte de Locales, the list of all possible time zones. Using my . . . other route into the Bucephalus, I can add more zones to the Carte de Locales without him suspecting a thing. And once the Doctor arrives in the new zone I'll remove it. Lassiter will be none the wiser.'

'I hope you're right. Where are you going to send him?'

She raised an eyebrow. 'Oh, don't worry about that. I have somewhere perfect in mind. Have you ever heard of Pella Satyrnis?' She straddled the light-harp and began strumming. 'He's just about to enter the gate.' Her smile broadened. 'I'm going to enjoy doing this. Zone added . . . redirection applied.' She stood up and gave Arrestis a cruel smile. 'Zone removed. The Doctor is now missing in action.'

'Let's hope that's the end of him.' He clapped his hands together. 'The Bucephalus is up and running; the Doctor is missing, presumed dead; and we're on the verge of cracking Lassiter's discovery once and for all. What could possibly go wrong?'

The doors to the control centre flew open, revealing Tornqvist, Monroe, Tegan and Turlough. Matisse turned to her three androids. She was shocked to see that they weren't moving.

Tornqvist widened his eyes. 'Arrestis. What an unpleasant surprise.'

'That's odd.' Lassiter double-checked the granite monitor. The Doctor's signal seemed to have disappeared. 'Ottway?'

'Carl's off duty, Professor. Kruust here.'

'Kruust: anything odd going on?' Kruust was an Earth Reptile; technically competent but prone to going all wobbly at the first sign of trouble.

Kruust sounded puzzled. 'Odd? Odd as in wrong? No, Professor, everything's running smoothly. Better than smoothly – you must have given the Legions a pay rise.'

He forced a laugh. 'Okay, Lassiter out.' But the Doctor had definitely vanished, with no sign of him in Ancient France. Lassiter instructed the webwork to run a sweep of every site in the Carte de Locales. It could just be an equipment malfunction, but he had a bad feeling about it.

'Are we to disappoint our guests, or will there be rejoicing as the Crystal Bucephalus opens its doors?' The Maitre D' was striding into the Legion tank.

Lassiter frowned. 'Seabstian, oh, she's ready to open. Now, if you want.'

The general manager checked his pocket watch. 'Oh no, Alex, we still have one minute left.' He came forward and slapped him on the shoulder. 'I knew you wouldn't let me down.'

'Wait a moment, you don't understand.'

'Understand what?'

'The Doctor.' He held his hands open. 'He's vanished. Vanished from the Grid.'

The Maitre D' sneered most unpleasantly. 'Good riddance to bad rubbish, I say.' He tugged on his waistcoat. 'Let's put all that trouble with the Doctor and his friends behind us.' He smiled, almost beatifically, and rubbed his hands. 'The Crystal Bucephalus is now open for business, and all our problems are over, Alex.'

Lassiter looked at the monitors and displays, trying to counteract the feelings of dread that were shooting up his spine. 'Oh no, Sebastian. I've got the most horrible feeling that they've only just begun.'

The Doctor fell out of the Time Vortex, his body wracked with excruciating pain. It wasn't supposed to be like that! For a brief moment, he was able to take in the faint twin suns peering through the pinkish sky, the grey stone cones that stood to the left and right. Then he felt the cold: definitely below the tolerances of even a Time Lord, especially one who'd just been ripped out of the Vortex. Within seconds his mind cut out, his body admitting defeat to both the forces that had ravaged his body in the Vortex and the sub-zero temperatures. He collapsed on to the cold pavement with only his limpness preventing serious injury.

Within minutes, his blue jacket and silk pantaloons had been covered by the ceaselessly falling snow.

The Main Course

Eight

'Get these people out of here!' shouted Arrestis. And then he saw that the androids weren't moving, their pearly skins now a dull grey. 'Ladygay! Where the hell is that ape of yours?'

She grabbed her talkstick. 'Byson to the control centre immediately!' Then, to the prisoners, 'What do you think you're playing at?'

Tornqvist stepped forward. 'We've had rather too much of your hospitality, if you don't mind. We're leaving here. Now.'

'I hardly think so. The Exemplar is under my control, and you leave when I say so. I suggest that you return to your room before things get unpleasant.' She looked between them to the doors. 'Ah, Garrett.'

Tornqvist spun on one foot and kicked Byson in the groin. The giant collapsed with a scream and lay unconscious in the doorway. 'You were saying?' He pointed towards the Archway. 'Hellenica: can you operate this?'

She shot a look of hatred at Matisse. 'I must admit, I am a little rusty with the light-harp; such ancient technology.' She walked over to the harp. Matisse moved forward to stop her, but both Tegan and Tornqvist ran from the doorway. Tegan elbowed Matisse in the stomach, knocking her to the floor, while Tornqvist threw his arm around Arrestis's neck and moved behind him. Even though Arrestis was protected by his battle armour, his neck was bare and vulnerable.

'If you make a move to stop her, I'll break his neck,' he barked. 'Understood?' Matisse struggled to sit up but said nothing. She couldn't understand how the situation could have got so out of hand so quickly. She had had no warning that they had escaped: presumably they had cut the android from the webwork, which wouldn't have been noticed because it would have assumed that the android was off-line.

Arrestis struggled to look at Tornqvist. 'You're quite violent for a minister of Lazarus, aren't you?'

'Where you're concerned, I'd quite happily break your neck. You ordered DeSalle to rape my mind: can you imagine what that felt like? A complete stranger opening my memories for all to see?'

'You should have complied,' he replied. 'It would have been so much easier.'

'That's it!' shouted Monroe. 'I've managed to link to the Bucephalus Grid.' The Archway was now alight with blue fire. 'You first, Turlough.'

Turlough, who had been keeping out of the action until now, moved from the doorway towards the Archway. 'Back to the Bucephalus? About time.' Two androids appeared behind him.

'Grab them!' Matisse yelled.

Monroe suddenly panicked. 'I've dropped the inhibitor!'

'Hellenica, Turlough — get away!' ordered Tornqvist, moving towards the doors using Arrestis as a shield. 'You too, Tegan!' Monroe and Turlough ran through the Archway, vanishing in mid-stride. But the androids stood between Tegan and the Prelector's escape route. She ran over.

'What now?'

'We're going to have to take our chances here. When I say run, run.' They were now standing directly in front of the doors. 'Run!' He threw Arrestis sprawling into the centre of the room before following Tegan.

Matisse shook her head. 'That didn't go very well, did it?' She picked up her talkstick which had fallen to the floor when Tegan had winded her. 'Two prisoners are loose in the complex. They are to be apprehended; do not kill them.'

'I'd quite happily gut Tornqvist,' said Arrestis, rubbing his throat. 'And Diva's probably running into Lassiter's arms as we speak, telling him everything.' He grabbed Matisse's arm. 'This is not the result I would have liked.'

She broke free and straddled the light-harp, bringing a holosphere down to hover in front of her. Then she laughed. 'It seems that Hellenica is more than capable of messing things up on her own.'

'What do you mean?'

She stood from the harp. 'The Exemplar locked into the Grid, but the signal was scrambled. Wherever they've gone, it definitely isn't New Alexandria.'

Monroe opened her eyes, but everything was still a multi-coloured blur. The only real sensation was that of Turlough's hand gripping hers. 'Are you all right? I wasn't sure that I'd set the coordinates properly.' The blur started to resolve as her surroundings came into focus. But it wasn't what she had expected. The ceiling was low and crossed with dark wooden beams, the plain yellow walls decorated with what she could only assume were contemporary religious icons: images of a man attached to a wooden cross. It made her think of her own saviour and her hand flew to the Inf about her neck.

'Er, Hellenica?' Turlough sounded agitated.

'What?'

'I think we've got a problem.' He gestured towards the ten or so tables that surrounded them. Guests in the same manner of clothing that Turlough and Tegan were wearing were looking up from their meals with looks of shock and disbelief on their faces. 'We've just materialized out of nowhere in the middle of a restaurant in eighteenth-century France.'

'So? Visiting historical eating places is the *raison d'être* of the Crystal Bucephalus. What are you worried about?'

'This restaurant is built upon the ruins of an Abbey that was burnt to the ground a hundred years ago — burnt down by the villagers who suspected the nuns of witchcraft.' He inclined his head towards the guests. 'I doubt that their opinions have changed all that much.'

She realized the seriousness of the situation, just as an elderly woman in a huge black dress screamed. That seemed to be the cue for the rest of them. A man in a tall white wig and a silver jacket stood up and thrust an accusing finger straight at them. 'One hundred years have passed since the servants of Satan were cast into the pit. And now they return: Lillith and Azazel return to mock us!' Some of the less terrified guests joined in the accusations, shouting incomprehensible abuse at them. The woman picked up her glass and hurled it at Monroe. It missed, but wine and shards of glass hit her leg. Egged on by this, others started picking up crockery, cutlery and glassware, while a man in a similar jacket to Turlough's reached up and grabbed a torch from the wall. His next words shocked Monroe.

'Burn them!' The chant was soon taken up by the rest of the guests. 'Burn them! Burn them! *Burn them!*'

'Come on!' urged Turlough. 'We've got to get out of here. Now!' He pointed towards the door. Even as he did so, a shrew-faced little man stepped in front of it. Turlough didn't hesitate. He bulldozed the man out of the way, sending the Frenchman flying into the lap of the woman in the black dress who let out yet another scream.

They emerged into the balmy night air. For a second, Turlough seemed to be taking his bearings, before pointing towards some woodland to their left. 'This way. They'll be after us any second.'

'Where to?' shouted Monroe as she ran after him. She could see a group of people with torches milling out of the restaurant.

'The TARDIS – it's only a couple of minutes away.'

'TARDIS?' Her eyes widened. 'As in Time Lord?'

'Yes! Now get a move on!' He plunged into the wood, and she followed.

And ten guests with blazing torches followed her.

In the ten minutes since they had escaped from the control

centre, Tegan and Tornqvist had narrowly avoided three parties of androids. They were currently running down yet another white corridor.

'This is stupid, Your Grace. We don't have the faintest idea where we are. We don't even know the layout of this place. Have you got a plan, or are you hoping for a bit of divine intervention?' she said breathlessly.

In contrast, the Prelector wasn't even breathing heavily. She could only guess that he was a hell of a lot fitter than he looked. 'Half plan, half prayer. It's a technique that has stood me in good stead over the years, I assure you. And call me Sven; "Your Grace" makes me feel as if I'm in my dotage.' Reaching a crossroads, he pointed left.

'Would you care to reveal the plan bit, then?'

'I'm after some evidence, but this is hardly the place for a discussion on tactics.'

'Tactics?' she repeated. 'So all this running hasn't been random at all?'

He grinned, showing his overbite. 'Well, yes, it has, but I thought you'd feel better if you thought I knew what was going on.' They turned another corner. And both stopped dead.

They must have reached the outer edges of the complex, because they had entered a wide curving corridor that presumably encircled the entire base. But that wasn't the half of it, thought Tegan. The outermost wall of the corridor was made of glass, offering a perfect view of the planet on which Matisse had built her Exemplar.

'It's beautiful,' she whispered. Through the window, the surface of the planet stretched away to the horizon, great plains of blue and black that scintillated and sparkled in the sunlight, with occasional pools of green liquid which bubbled with escaping gas. Then she looked up and corrected herself: the light wasn't coming from a star at all. Hanging overhead, a huge globe with red and yellow bands shone dimly through the thick turquoise atmosphere. It was a planet like Jupiter, and the base was obviously on one of the moons.

'And quite deadly,' added Tornqvist. 'At a guess, I'd say

we were looking out on to the surface of a rather inhospitable moon, possibly Tanthane. The Elective is supposed to have a base there, but Intent Intelligence hasn't been able to prove it.' He pointed to the nearest pool. 'Hazarding another guess, those pools are liquid nitrogen. I can't see us escaping by leaving the base, can you?'

Tegan remembered an experiment in chemistry class, years ago. The teacher had stuck a red rose into a flask of liquid nitrogen for a second. Taking it out, he dropped the rose to the floor, where it had shattered into hundreds of tiny red fragments. It wasn't a fate that she would choose. 'What now?'

'Since we're on the outer edges of the complex, it might make it a bit easier to explore. This is a big base, far too big for Matisse alone. I want to know what else is going on here.'

'Fine. Just so long as you don't decide to go for a swim in the nitrogen lakes.' She followed Tornqvist round the curving corridor.

'How far now?' Hellenica was finding it increasingly difficult to make headway through the wood, especially since Turlough's passage through the branches inevitably sent them springing back towards her.

'The TARDIS should be in the next clearing,' he yelled. 'Just keep moving.'

'What do you think I'm trying to do?' she screamed, as another twig hit her in the face. She looked over her shoulder and could see the glow of the torches about a hundred yards behind. She tried to block out their incessant chanting. 'They're definitely getting closer.' Suddenly she fell forward as the dense tangle of branches and twigs gave way to a small clearing.

'At last,' sighed Turlough and pointed ahead. A large blue box sat amongst the greenery, a box with regular indentations on its sides and translucent windows. 'The TARDIS.'

'That's it? That's a TARDIS? The pinnacle of time

technology reduced to a wooden shack with a lamp on top?'

He smiled. 'It was the last time I looked.'

Hoping that this wasn't some strange delusion on Turlough's part, she followed him over to what looked like the door. He started banging. 'Kamelion, it's Turlough. Open the doors.' The natives were right behind them, pushing through the woods and demanding that they be burnt. He thumped even harder. 'Kamelion!'

Was he making it up? she thought. Would the final fate of Hellenica Monroe be as the victim of a crowd of bloodthirsty religious maniacs on Ancient Earth?

'Please, Kamelion.' A rock bounced off the blue doors, causing Monroe to jump aside. 'Open the door, you cybernetic imbecile!' The crowd was only feet away – and then the doors opened. Turlough rushed through, grabbing her hand and dragging her after him.

'So, this is a TARDIS?' As Turlough shut the doors, she took in the white walls with their regular pattern of roundels, and the hexagonal central console with its central glass pillar. She was faintly disappointed by the less than impressive display of Time Lord technology.

'What took you so long?' Turlough was shouting at the other occupant of the TARDIS, a dull silver android with a roughly human face and an exposed brain pan which revealed simplistic circuitry. 'We could have been killed out there.'

'I was in the Cloister Room. It took time for the TARDIS to forward your request to me,' it answered in a rich, fruity voice.

This didn't appear to satisfy him. 'The Cloister Room? What were you doing skulking about there?'

'I do not skulk. I was following the Doctor's instructions to avail myself of the TARDIS's facilities.' The android even sounded hurt by the accusation. 'I am pleased to see that neither of you appear harmed.'

'No thanks to you,' he retorted. 'Anyway, allow me to introduce Hellenica Monroe.'

She took the proffered hand and shook it. 'So, you're

an android.' She turned to Turlough and whispered behind her hand. 'And a pretty primitive one at that. Solid state circuitry, indeed?' She was shocked when Kamelion answered her.

'Appearances can be deceptive, Hellenica. Would you like a demonstration of my gifts?'

'Go on, Kamelion, show our doubting friend what you're capable of.'

For a second, the android was motionless. And then its body was surrounded by a whirling vortex of blue light which momentarily flared before fading. Monroe swallowed. Max was standing in front of her, wearing the dinner suit he had worn in Beswicks. 'Hi, Diva. Missed me?'

'What? I don't . . .'

'I'm not called Kamelion for nothing,' said the *faux* Max, melting back into the silver android.

'As you can see, it's a shapechanger. The Doctor decided to bring him on board.' The tone of his voice suggested that Turlough didn't approve of the Doctor's decision. 'Anyway, that's the introductions over and done with. I suppose we'd better get out of here and back to the Bucephalus.' He suddenly looked down at his green jacket: it was filthy, with rips and tears from their run through the woods. Monroe realized that her own attire was in just as bad a state.

'Actually,' he sighed, 'I think a change of clothes wouldn't go amiss. Some of us can't just conjure up a new outfit. Can we, Kamelion?'

Tegan was bored. Even the marvellous views of the surface were beginning to pall. 'It might help if you told me what we were looking for,' she said.

'What might help?'

'The complete and utter mind-numbing boredom.' She flung her arms out. 'I'm worried about the Doctor, I'm worried about Diva – for goodness sake, I'm even worried about Turlough! And we're on a sight-seeing tour. What the hell are we looking for?'

'As I said, Tegan, I want information. Arrestis is up to something here, and I want to know what it is. If you're bored, I suggest we have a look in here.' He pointed at the inner wall. There was a door. 'At last,' he muttered. 'A way back in.'

The door was like every other door Tegan had seen in the base: black, riveted metal with a locking plate next to it. 'So how do we open it?'

Tornqvist reached into his scarlet and black jacket and pulled out a thin wire with a slight thickening at the end. 'Genuine gambit picklock.'

'You came prepared?' Tegan was amazed: priests with skills at streetfighting and lock-picking were something new.

He shrugged. 'I never go anywhere without it.'

Tegan suddenly realized something. 'Why didn't you use it to get out of the cell?'

'There wasn't a locking plate inside the cell.' He touched the picklock to the plate and waited a second before pushing the door open.

'What if there's someone in there?' she hissed.

'It's a bit late now, isn't it?' He waved his hand at the open doorway. 'After you.'

There was no way that she was going in first, Tegan decided. No way at all. 'Age before beauty,' she said, a laugh in her voice. 'Or should that be pearls before swine?'

He paused in the doorway. 'You didn't tell me that you were familiar with the Codex.'

Tegan remembered the book that Monroe had been reading. 'I'm not,' she protested. 'It's from the Bible.'

'The Bible?' He sounded puzzled. 'What's that?'

'Never mind.' She urged him into the room and followed, examining the interior. There was a faint illumination, but Tegan couldn't identify the source.

She and Tornqvist were in a square chamber about twenty feet across. But the room was completely empty apart from a simple chair in the centre. What shocked Tegan were the pictures on the walls: they made her feel sick. There was no denying the artistry, the talent, that had created such pictures, but it was what they showed that turned her stomach. All four walls were covered in murals, each one made up of a number of smaller images in radically different styles. The only similarity was that each picture showed a particular life form in the advanced stages of torture. Most of the aliens were unfamiliar to Tegan, although she did recognize the disembowelled Cyberman and the Terileptil with its hands chopped off, as well as the three-eyed thing she'd seen earlier with what looked like electrodes attached to its . . . She put her hand over her mouth. 'It's – it's disgusting.'

Even in the pale light, she could see that all the colour had drained from the Prelector's face. He was transfixed by the fourth wall which consisted of a single image, that of a creature with light brown skin and a domed head. Tegan couldn't even begin to describe the atrocities it was undergoing, more for fear of throwing up than anything else.

'What is it?'

Tornqvist answered in hushed tones. 'A Sontaran: one of the creatures who killed our Lord Lazarus. I can understand a member of the Intent having reason to dislike them, but this?' He closed his eyes. 'This is the product of a very sick mind.'

'Can we leave? I'm not feeling particularly well.'

'I can't say I blame you.' He placed his hand on the back of the chair. 'I just wonder what sort of person would enjoy sitting in a room like this.'

'So DeSalle didn't get anything?' asked Arrestis, walking into the control centre. He had changed into a grey jumper, black trousers, and a thick brown leather jacket with a fur collar.

Matisse turned from her work: with a portable light-harp, she was preparing the next stage of her assault on the Bucephalus. Her access through the new route was both stable and secure; that was of paramount importance. Even if he detected it, there was nothing Lassiter could do, short of disconnecting the dimensional stabilizers while the Grid was up and running. And if he did that, the resulting carnage would be far, far worse than anything she was planning. She suddenly realized that Arrestis was expecting an answer.

'I'm afraid not. Tornqvist's psychic defences were too strong.'

'DeSalle should have realized that – the man's a Prelector, for Lazarus's sake!'

'Calm down, Maximillian.' She gestured to a cafetière on an adjacent table. 'Help yourself to a cup.'

As he poured, she said, 'Anyway, I've reviewed what DeSalle did manage to extract. If it's any consolation, I don't think he does know anything.' She plucked a harmony of beams and examined the results in the small holosphere at the base of the harp. 'Don't forget, he's still in the complex: when the androids pick him up, I'll let our resident mind-rapist have another go.'

Arrestis threw himself into a nearby chair and sipped his coffee. 'How soon before you have another go at Lassiter?'

She checked her watch. 'The Bucephalus has been open for forty-five minutes; it should just about be full by now.'

'Is that important?'

She smiled. 'Most definitely. The more people in the Bucephalus, the more galactic dignitaries we can hold to ransom.' She strummed the harp, downloading her work into the main webwork. 'In fact, I'm ready now.' She moved to the main light-harp and sat down. Cradling her hands, she cracked her knuckles before placing her hands on either side of the harp. Then she ran her fingers through the photon strands, willing the virus into existence. Through the harp she could feel it, a complex pattern of malevolent logic that was spiralling through the Exemplar/Bucephalus interface like a trained assassin. She craned her neck to look at Arrestis. 'It's in.'

'How long before anything happens?'

She shrugged and poured herself a coffee. 'It's hard to

say. First of all, I've designed the virus to strike at random, and secondly, it has to infiltrate the webwork's command nexus. Still, I don't see that being too much of a problem. Alexhendri's been so determined to guard the Bucephalus from outside attack, he's left the internal systems wide open.'

Arrestis peered at her through the steam from his coffee, his half-asleep eyes as penetrating as ever. 'But will it work? Your last two attempts weren't exactly successful.'

'The Doctor isn't around to hold his hand this time. Alexhendri won't know what's hit him.'

Monroe watched with professional interest as Turlough circled the console, flicking a switch here and pressing a key there. The android followed behind like an obedient dog, whispering clues and pointing a long silver finger at the console. After an indeterminate time in what Turlough called the wardrobe room, Monroe had chosen white trousers, a white blouse and a green jacket, while he was dressed in black trousers, with a black jacket over a white shirt. A striped tie completed the outfit. 'Are we ready to leave?' she asked.

'I'm not sure.' He turned to the android. 'Well, Kamelion?'

'The idiosyncratic nature of the Doctor's vessel makes certainties impossible. The only TARDISes with which I am familiar, apart from the Master's, are the primitive Type Twenties which the Ooolatrii captured during the Celestial Wars, but their fixed interfaces mean that . . .'

'Yes, yes, yes, Kamelion. Are the coordinates set for the Crystal Bucephalus?' he said with exasperation.

The android frowned. 'However, might I point out that the coordinates of New Alexandria are the same as – '

'No, you may not point out. Answer the question!' he shouted.

Kamelion sounded resigned. 'As far as I can tell, this TARDIS is set to materialize on New Alexandria.'

'Right, then.' He tentatively reached out for an insignificant blue button and pressed it.

Monroe had heard about the Time Lords when she was a little girl. Masters of the Universe, they traversed the continuum in their timeships, fabulous machines with infinite interiors and the ability to effortlessly slip from world to world, era to era. She wasn't prepared for the deafening roar that issued from the console, nor the sickening way that the floor lurched away.

'Turlough!' she screamed as she hit the wall. 'What's going on?' She rolled out of the way as Kamelion crashed into the toppling hatstand.

Turlough was grabbing the hexagonal base of the console as the floor listed at forty-five degrees. He looked faintly perturbed. 'I think I might have miscalculated.'

Nine

Eight-thirty, and the restaurant was already full. But then, the Tempus Fugit was always full. Patrons in their best finery sat at the tables or in the private booths, while discreet waiters ferried the *haute*-est of *haute cuisine* from the kitchen. The unobtrusive lamps mounted on the carpeted walls showed off the sheer opulence to its best advantage: the whole place glittered, and everything that didn't glitter simply glowed.

The Maitre D' of the Tempus Fugit, dressed in a striking grey suit as befitted his position, stepped forward to greet the new arrivals. He knelt down to shake their paws. 'Pfifl, Laklis; how wonderful to see you both.'

The two Hroth nodded their heads vigorously, their pink ears flapping. They resembled nothing more than white, furry coffee tables, with flat but curiously dog-like faces. 'We wouldn't miss this place's fifth birthday for the world, would we, Laklis?' Pfifl angled himself towards his mate and rubbed his nose in her fur.

'Behave yourself!' Laklis admonished, the area around her little black nose turning faintly green with embarrassment. 'You know we always love coming here.' Her muzzle darkened even further. 'But five years! We're so proud of you.'

It was the Maitre D's turn to look embarrassed. 'I've reserved the best booth in the restaurant for you — Benefactor's booth. Shall I lead the way?'

Laklis bared her teeth in the Hroth version of a smile. 'That would be wonderful, Doctor.'

'I wonder if there's another way out?' Tornqvist was

examining the door that he and Tegan had used to enter the wretched room. Once closed, the door had matched the walls perfectly, becoming part of a Draconian hanging upside down with its throat cut. If his suspicions were correct, this room was only the start of it.

'Why? Are you hoping to find more of this?' Her expression made it quite clear that the whole thing was making her quite ill. Even looking at the ceiling hadn't helped, with its perfectly painted tableau of a Martian Grand Marshal having acid poured into his armour.

'Definitely not. But I get the feeling I'm on the right track.' He walked over to the opposite wall and started feeling it with his outstretched palms. 'Ah!' Faint grooves in the Sontaran tableau indicated the door he was after. Another few seconds of searching and he located the locking plate. 'Over here.'

Tegan, who had been sitting in the chair with her eyes closed, came over to the newly opened door. 'I'm warning you, Sven: another room like this and I'm going to chunder.'

'I think I get your meaning. No, this one looks a little more . . . by the Scars of Saint Clavis!' he exclaimed, beckoning Tegan through the door before closing it.

This room was considerably less gruesome — and far more familiar. The left and right walls were painted with scenes from the Codex. On the left was the Final Dinner, with Lazarus — his face blank, an anonymity demanded by the second commandment — surrounded by Logan, Clavis, and the rest of his twelve disciples, looking on with devoted expressions. Naturally, their number included Issasis the Draconian, who would betray him, and Untaxyr the Martian, who would deny him; their actions had led to certain factions of the Intent declaring that reptilian races were the devil's spawn, but Tornqvist didn't sympathize with that particular interpretation of the Intent, doubting that Lazarus would have approved of it.

He turned to the opposite wall, and was impressed by an absolutely magnificent representation of Lazarus's Sacrifice. A blank-faced Lazarus stood in prayer, defiant

167

against a belligerent-looking Sontaran in blood-red armour. The ultimate peacemaker versus the ultimate warrior, mused Tornqvist as he reached for his Inf, only to remember with irritation that Matisse had taken it.

An altar stood directly in front of them, the plain stone slab favoured by the Minimalist faction of the Intent. He knelt down before it in supplication — and then noticed what was lying on top of it. He reached out and grabbed it, examining it carefully. Although Tornqvist always referred to himself as a Prelector, the truth was slightly different. He was actually Prelector Magnus et Dominus, a title he shared with only two others in the Intent, and one that meant he was second only to the Benefactor himself. It also meant that there was very little about the history of the Lazarus Intent that he didn't know, and the item in his hands simply reinforced his worst fears. Shoving it into his jacket, he stood up and gestured to another door behind the altar.

'I've seen enough. Let's move on.'

'Would you care to let me in on it?' said Tegan. He could tell that she was annoyed, but he couldn't share his suspicions with anyone, even this forthright young woman.

'Not yet.' He touched his picklock to the plate and pushed the door open.

Lassiter closed his eyes. He'd been awake for over thirty-six hours, and he could think of nothing else but sleep. The Crystal Bucephalus was running smoothly once again and Sebastian was out amongst the guests, distributing his unique brand of largesse to the visiting dignitaries, none of whom knew that anything had ever been wrong. But something was still awry: Hellenica and the Doctor were still missing, and he couldn't shake the feeling that he hadn't seen the last of Matisse's interference.

He yawned and ran his fingers through his cropped hair. Perhaps there was something he could do. He looked over to the bank of lecterns to the left of the Grid Control Suite. 'Kruust?'

The Earth Reptile looked up from his lectern with an inquisitive expression on his scaly green face. His third eye blinked slowly. 'Yes, Professor?'

'You can take your break now. I'll take over.'

'You, Professor?' he asked in his wobbly voice.

Lassiter's exhaustion pushed his irritation to the surface. 'Yes, Technician Kruust. I did build the bloody place, didn't I? I'm sure I can cope for an hour or so.'

Kruust's voice wobbled even more. 'Of course, Professor.' Thick reptilian hands reached up for his Inf.

'Great,' Lassiter interrupted. 'Come back in a couple of hours.' He watched impatiently as Kruust plodded out of the double doors.

As soon as the stewards closed the doors, Lassiter went over to the horseshoe-shaped main console. He was rather at a loss as to where to begin. In an ideal world, he would have enlisted Kruust, Ottway and the rest of his army of technicians and taken the Bucephalus apart quark-block by quark-block. But this was reality, and there was no way that Sebastian would allow him the three weeks' downtime necessary to do that. His investigations would have to take place while the Bucephalus was up and running, and that required a certain ingenuity.

With a practised play on the console, he instigated a tertiary systems diagnostic, stepping back as a wave of lights flashed across the controls, reflecting off the brass and making the crystal glitter. Lassiter smiled, his gaze wandering over the brass-framed screens. And then he stopped smiling as one of the screens grabbed his attention. It was the screen dedicated to monitoring the status of the Time Vortex surrounding New Alexandria.

The monitor usually showed the globe of the planet at the bottom of a curved cone of isochrones, the rings increasing in diameter and distance apart until the lines of equal temporal stress merged into the rolling green plane of the Vortex. In fact, he couldn't remember ever seeing it vary – until now. A tiny point of disturbance was bouncing from isochrone to isochrone, causing the rings to shudder and distort. Something with an extremely high temporal potential was heading towards New Alexandria, and only one object could do that. He pulled on one of the levers and zoomed the display in on the disturbance, breaking into a broad grin as he recognized it. The Doctor's last words as he had stepped in the Cubiculo had been 'Look out for a large blue box.'

The display showed just that, bouncing its way towards the Crystal Bucephalus like a stone being skipped across a lake. Perhaps things were finally looking up.

'For Lazarus's sake, Turlough, can't you do something?' The TARDIS floor was now listing at about sixty degrees, while the cacophony from the console was becoming unbearable, a straining groan that was getting worse with every second.

'Such as what?' He had finally managed to reach the pedestal beneath the console, but yet another jolt sent him sliding back with a thud, hitting the wall that was currently behaving more like a floor. 'I don't even know why it's acting like this,' he cried, bouncing up and down as another tremor hit the TARDIS. 'Kamelion, can you reach the console?'

The android turned its face towards him. 'If either of you can supply a suitable mental image . . .'

The TARDIS seized that moment to right itself, hurling them to the floor — the real floor. Out of the corner of her eye, she could have sworn that the android had momentarily transformed into a large rubber ball. She wondered what Turlough had been thinking about.

'What happened?' She scrambled to her feet and scanned the dials and monitors, trying to concentrate — not that easy considering the bump on her head. 'The TARDIS is a time machine. The Grid is a time machine.' She thumped the console, eliciting a rather aggrieved bleep in return. 'Of course!'

Turlough raised an eyebrow. 'If you could share your discovery?'

She laughed. 'I'm sorry, but it's so obvious. The

TARDIS travels through the Vortex, doesn't it?' He nodded. 'Well, I imagine that the Vortex around New Alexandria is quite churned up with all that time transference going on. The TARDIS hit a rough patch and was thrown about a bit.'

It was Turlough's turn to laugh. 'You mean we hit some turbulence?'

'Exactly. I'd hazard a guess that the TARDIS hit this turbulence, rattled about a bit, and then bounced out. I imagine it'll be plain sailing from now on.'

The TARDIS shuddered.

'You were saying?' said Turlough dryly.

'Coffee, Ladygay?' Byson could see that Matisse was busy at her harp, but it was late at night and she hadn't eaten for hours. He was worried about her.

She turned in surprise. She looked exhausted, with dark bags under her eyes, but he had known her his whole life, and seeing her staying up for days on end was nothing new. Still, he didn't like to see her get too tired.

'Thank you, Garrett. I kept meaning to get myself a cup, but I couldn't drag myself away.' She reached out and took the mug. She sipped the coffee and smiled appreciatively.

'What are you doing?' he asked, hoping she would explain it in simple terms. Normally, though, she just told him to go away. He sometimes got the feeling that she would rather he wasn't around.

'The time has come to inflict some serious damage on Professor Lassiter,' she said.

'Why?' he asked, sitting down and drinking his coffee. 'I thought you wanted his secrets?'

'I do. I just want to cause enough trouble so that he has to come begging to me for help. And then we can bargain.'

Something was bothering him. He didn't want to say anything — he remembered the other times that he'd mentioned it — but he couldn't help himself. 'Why do you hate him so much? I mean, he is —'

She slammed her mug on the table next to her. 'I don't want to be reminded of that! Thanks to him, I was forced to run away to Hexdane, to cease my research!' She slammed a fist into her open palm. 'When people talk about temporal theory, who do they think of? Blinovitch, Findecker, Ethra and Teelis, Lassiter and Monroe! Not Matisse, oh no. How could I research when Alexhendri went around blackening my name?'

'But he didn't, Ladygay. You told me that when you left, he started up the Crystal Bu . . . Bu . . .'

'Bucephalus, you moron!' She closed her eyes. 'I'm sorry, Garrett. I didn't mean that. But no one has ever hurt me the way that Lassiter did. I never meant to let him get inside . . .' She slumped into her chair. 'You do understand, don't you?'

He shook his head. He only cared for one person, and she was standing in front of him. 'Are you ashamed of me? Do you hate me?'

She lifted her head, revealing tears welling in her eyes. 'Of course I don't. I love you; how could I do otherwise?'

He pouted. 'I'm not very bright, am I? I let the Prelector get away.'

She reached out her hand and grabbed his huge hairy paws. 'I have loved you since you were born. I'm just not a very good mother. Especially when I have a son who is nine years old and nearly seven feet tall.' She stood up and hugged him, dwarfed by his massive frame. 'I love you, Garrett. I always have and I always will.' She stared at his bearded face. 'I just wish my feelings weren't so confused.'

'What a touching scene.' Arrestis was leaning against the doorframe, his arms folded. There was a cynical smile on his face. 'I always worried that placing you with Lassiter would have this effect. Who'd have thought it: a love triangle between the three greatest temporal physicists in this era.' He looked at Byson. 'And then you have a child. What a pity that you spent so much time near high-energy sources that you gave birth to a mutant, a mutant with the body of a thirty-year-old and the mind of a retard. So tragic.'

Byson hadn't understood much of that, but he knew that Arrestis was being nasty. Arrestis was always being nasty: to him, to the people in white coats behind the glass walls, and especially to Matisse.

She narrowed her eyes. 'I wouldn't expect you to understand or show the slightest trace of compassion. If I hadn't spent so much time trying to duplicate Alexhendri's work, Garrett would be normal!' She pointed an accusing, damning finger at Arrestis. 'You just use people; the whole Union is just a playpen to you, isn't it? People for muscle, for brains, for sexual gratification: you can satisfy all your inadequacies, can't you?'

Arrestis sprinted from the doorway and grabbed her wrist in his hand. 'I own this base, I own this planet – and I own you!' She tried to wriggle free but failed. 'I have more power than anyone in the galaxy. If I treat people like chess pieces, it's because I can afford to.' He stopped as he was lifted two feet off the floor.

'Leave her alone. I won't let you hurt her.' Byson glared at him. 'If you hurt her, I'll hurt you.' He let him drop to the floor.

Arrestis looked from Matisse to Byson and back again before getting to his feet. His face was red. 'Never again. Understood?' With that he strode from the control centre.

She grabbed Byson's hand. 'I have never been so proud of you, Garrett: please remember that. But Monsignor Arrestis is going to be very angry about this, so I think you'd better go to your room.'

For a second he wondered whether he should protest: why was he being sent to his room if he'd done a good thing? But he decided to obey his mother.

'Yes, Ladygay.'

She watched as he left the control centre before slumping into a chair with her head in her hands. 'For the love of Lazarus,' she mumbled. 'What am I going to do now?'

* * *

'What is this supposed to be?' Tegan was relieved that the room wasn't a sadist's boudoir or a shrine for some religious nutcase, but it was just as disturbing in its own way. It had an *atmosphere*.

Tornqvist shrugged. 'This really is a journey of discovery, isn't it? DeSalle would have a field day.' He gestured towards the centre of the room.

'It's the galaxy, isn't it?' Floating in the centre of the room, a ten-foot-wide hologram of the Milky Way provided the only light, billions of stars in curving arms rotating around a brilliant dense core. Tegan recognized it from a number of previous encounters, ranging from a children's book of astronomy to the image on the TARDIS's scanner when the Master had sent her and Nyssa back to Event One, the creation of the galaxy itself.

'Yes, but it's more than that.' He pointed at the areas of the hologram which were coloured. 'That blue chunk is the Union, while the green section bordering it is the Draconian Republic. There you have the Cyberlord Hegemony, the radioactive remains of the Sontaran Empire. He's mapped out the political regions of the entire galaxy.'

Tegan grabbed his arm. 'Who, Sven, who? Who are we looking for?'

He pointed at the map. 'Look closer, Tegan. Look at all the red dots. What do they represent, eh?'

She examined the hologram more carefully. Thousands of red points were scattered amongst the political entities, their positions following no discernible pattern. 'Search me.' She grabbed his arm, turning him round to face her. 'For God's sake, tell me what's going on around here! A torture room, a miniature church, and now a map of the galaxy. This is more like an adventure game than a spying mission!'

He stroked his beard. 'After we failed to escape, I decided to make the best of a bad job, to see what the Elective was up to. Having discovered that this was Tanthane, I was even more eager to have a snoop around.'

'What have you discovered? What's the significance of all this?' Tegan was determined to get at least one straight answer out of the Prelector. He suddenly grasped her hands in his and gave her a deep, doleful stare.

'Believe me, Tegan, I can't. Not now; or at least, not yet. There's too much at stake.' She could have sworn he glanced at the map. 'It's time to get back to the Bucephalus, I'm afraid.'

Tegan looked at him curiously. 'Afraid of what?'

He closed his eyes. 'My soul, Tegan, my immortal soul.' With that he walked straight through the hologram, curdling the stars and gas clouds. After his admission, she decided not to press him for information. At least, not for a while.

Turlough sensed the build-up to materialization, recognizing the particular patterns of light on the console instruments that indicated that the TARDIS was about to land. He just hoped that they had set the coordinates correctly.

'At last.' Monroe watched as the Time Rotor slowed. 'I must admit to being a little worried about all of this. I'm hardly Alex's favourite person.'

He shook his head. 'Matisse hates Lassiter, Lassiter hates you, and Arrestis seems to hate everybody. What a charming spirit of coexistence the Lazarus Intent has fostered.'

'The Intent has nothing to do with this, Turlough!' He jumped back, surprised by the vehemence of her outburst. 'Well, not in that way. This is a purely personal matter.'

'He is your ex-husband: I suppose you're entitled to a little animosity.' Turlough remembered Tubby Nelson at Brendon. His parents had split up in an extremely public manner, with articles in the gossip columns and journalists hanging round the school. The Brigadier had soon put paid to them.

'It's not like that. I know how badly I hurt him. I haven't spoken to him for nearly eleven years and I don't know how he's going to react, especially with all this

175

business with Matisse going on. I imagine he's feeling rather vulnerable at the moment.' A chime from the console interrupted her.

Two stewards passed the marble base of the statue en route to Cubiculo 667. The party of Cyberlords in 312 were negotiating a treaty with the Thal contingent, and their stewards had passed the token gift of the rare mineral tarranium to the Bucephalus's stewards to give to their opposite number in 667. Moments later, the trumpeting strains of a Type Forty time capsule in rematerialization mode echoed off the vast bulk of Alexander the Great's warhorse. Had the stewards been a little less diligent in the delivery of their charge, they would have seen the statue flare with its internal green light, as the ambient time spillage was converted into visible light by the crystal. But they weren't, and they didn't. Nor did they see the mathematical representation of a twentieth-century police box fade into existence next to the base, its roof light flashing in time with the statue.

'Have we arrived in the right place?' asked Matisse.

'According to the instruments, we've materialized at the coordinates Kamelion and I set before we left Earth,' said Turlough. 'Still, I suppose it wouldn't do any harm to check.' He reached out and touched a button on the console. A hum accompanied the scanner shield opening to reveal a landscape of wooden booths and marble flooring. 'I'd say that that looks like the Bucephalus, wouldn't you?' Turlough pressed the door control, and watched as the roundelled doors opened.

She frowned. 'I didn't notice when we ran into here, but that,' she pointed towards the black void beyond the doors, 'looks like the interface between a Cubiculo and one of Alex's time bubbles.' A strange look crossed her face, a combination of anger and pride. 'Does that mean that he's that close to TARDIS technology? Is that why the Doctor stepped in?'

'I doubt it. He doesn't do that sort of thing. Besides, we

didn't exactly turn up in the Bucephalus by choice.'

'But he's a Time Lord, Turlough.'

Turlough gave her a broad grin. 'He may be a Time Lord, but that doesn't mean he shares their beliefs. I suspect that we were brought here to take the blame for Arrestis's clone's death, not as part of some plan to shut the Bucephalus down.' But Turlough wasn't as sure as he made out. Although he'd seen the Doctor commit acts of almost unspeakable nobility, he had to admit that he wasn't sure what really motivated his mysterious Time Lord friend.

Monroe looked through the open doors. 'I'll take your word for it. Let's find Alex.'

Turlough walked up to the doors and gestured her over. As she reached the threshold, he turned to Kamelion. 'You stay here. I don't trust you.'

Kamelion cocked his head in a curiously steward-like gesture. 'I was looking forward to seeing Professor Lassiter's achievements.'

'And you can drop the hurt-little-robot routine,' Turlough snapped. 'You're staying here and that's final.' Ignoring the wounded look that Kamelion assumed, he walked out of the TARDIS.

Talkot slammed the metal beaker on to the table with an echo that attracted the attention of a couple of eight-foot tall spiders ten feet away. His drinking companion gave him a critical stare with a pair of rapidly extruded optic filaments.

'Should you be drinking in your condition?' It was a rhetorical question: a Legion's grasp of past, present and future was a view that its three-dimensional acquaintances could never share. Although its attention was focused on this ongoing moment of his friend, multi-dimensional senses could see Talkot as an egg, as a hatchling, as a mother.

'You really are a killjoy, Legion.' A reptilian claw waved precariously towards one of its tendrils, and the Legion instinctively withdrew that section of itself from the present and emerged it about ten minutes ago.

'A joke, Talkot. I know that your sons will crack through their shells without a blemish. They will be the pride of Chelonia.' The Legion reached out with a newly formed proboscis and sucked at its ale.

'Sons?' The Chelonian craned his neck forward. 'Sons?' Talkot's eyes glinted with pride.

'Naturally. A Chelonian of your bloodline will always breed true.' The Legion chuckled, its laugh ending before it had even begun. 'I'm sure they will all inherit their mother's skills at floral engineering.'

'I don't like time,' Talkot slurred, seemingly unaware of his *non sequitur*, his head theatening to retreat back into his carapace. 'I mean . . .' He paused suddenly, his skin turning a darker shade of green in embarrassment.

'Do go on.'

'I feel a bit stupid, actually. Your race are masters of time.'

'Not at all.' The Legion shook two dimensions of a furry appendage, and did something extremely clever in about two minutes' time. 'My people have an experience of reality and temporality unique in the galaxy, I agree. But mastery over time? If that were true, we would not have lost our empire to the Time Lords. Even now, many of my race are still paying their debt to society: there are many reasons why I serve Lassiter, but philanthropy is not one of them. I digress; if I have understood you, you are nervous about time travel.'

The scaly head oscillated. 'Exactly. Consider our current locale.' Talkot waved a claw around in a slightly uncoordinated motion.

The Legion spent a good ten minutes examining the bar. They had travelled back to the glorious blood and thunder days of Pluvikerr, Throneworld of the Gubbage Cones. Their present drinking establishment was a typical example of its period, a huge silvered dome covering a stone arena scattered with tables, chairs and a central bar, packed with belligerent examples of the mercenary corps that the Gubbage Cones had gathered during their brief tenure as lords of the galaxy, seventy thousand years ago. The silicon Excalbians mingled with the feathered people of Velopssi around the Mirebeast fighting pit, whilst androids from Exo III jostled with the Lamp People of Badefex for a place at the bar. With another glance, it could see the military bearing of an Ice Lord contrasting with the slovenly Ogron warrior in the queue for the toilet. All in all, it was a perfectly good night in one of the roughest bars in the galaxy.

A second after Talkot had spoken, the Legion answered. 'Our locale is exquisite. Your humour is not. What's really bothering you?'

Talkot leaned forward almost conspiratorially. 'What if we alter something? We might return to our own time, only to discover that an act on our part here wiped out one of our races in prehistory!'

The Legion quivered in sympathy. 'I can understand your worries, Talkot.' It paused to sip from its newly filled beaker. Allowing the ale to intoxicate it ten minutes later, it continued. 'The theories of Professor Lassiter have made it impossible for that to happen.'

'Who?'

'A Human temporal scientist. He wrote the papers that made the Crystal Bucephalus possible. To assuage my own worries – given my own special relationship with time – I studied his findings. He theorized that alterations caused by guests to the Bucephalus do not carry sufficient weight to become part of the past.'

'I don't follow,' said Talkot, holding his beaker in front of him. The Legion leapt forward by three minutes and saw the Chelonian vomit. It returned to Talkot's present, determined to make it quick.

'When guests are projected back in time, they are not as real as their surroundings. Does that make more sense?'

Talkot smiled lopsidedly, his thin green lips glistening with spittle. 'If it's good enough for you, Legion, it's good enough for me. I just wanted to be certain that we'd have a Crystal Buck . . . Bucky . . . Bucket phallus . . .'

'Bucephalus?'

'That's the place. One of those, to go back to.' He reached for the next beaker of ale. The Legion wrapped a black tentacle around Talkot's hand and prevented him from grasping the beaker. 'Don't worry about it. I assure you, the Bucephalus will be there when we return.'

'Useless!' Lassiter threw the Laserson probe at the nearest wall of the Grid Control Suite, where it bounced of the wooden panelling with an unsatisfying thud. For the last thirty minutes he had explored every pathway, every sub-routine, every piece of hardware, software, firmware, wetware. Nothing, a big fat zero. Whatever means of access Matisse had used to divert the Doctor, it wasn't showing up on any of his scans – but that was only to be expected. The scans and diagnostics were inferior to his anti-incursion viruses, and she had side-stepped those without breaking a sweat. Or had she?

Sinking back into his chair, he decided to approach the problem from a different angle. What if she hadn't had anything to do with the Doctor's disappearance? He remembered the Doctor's concerns, about how his Time Lord masters would have wanted him to shut down the Bucephalus. Perhaps they'd abducted him: taking him back to Gallifrey to face the consequences of his inactions. He stroked his moustache thoughtfully: yes, that would be it. He'd been assuming it was Matisse when she couldn't possibly have had anything to do with it. He was getting paranoid in his old age.

Perhaps Sebastian was right. Arrestis was dead – he had nothing to worry about any more. For ten years he'd hidden on New Alexandria, protected by his stewards, the ground-based defences, the perimeter satellites, and he hadn't had a holiday in all that time. He broke into a grin. 'Webwork?'

'Yes, Professor Lassiter?' Cultured tones filled the Grid Control Suite.

'I fancy a break from all this, a holiday. Can you suggest a location?'

'Please specify the type of location you require: do you

wish to use the Crystal Bucephalus, or would you rather remain in this time zone?'

Lassiter thought about this. The Bucephalus offered over a million options, but none of them was real: a cornucopia of restaurants, theatres, hotels, brothels, all of them shadowy half-lives that offered nothing but fun without responsibility. Where was the challenge in that? He stood up and walked over to the edge of the pit. No, he wanted a real holiday, somewhere where he could eat real meals, meet real people, form lasting friendships, escape from the bloody great prison that he'd built around himself.

'Not the Bucephalus. Somewhere relaxing, interesting, exciting. He clapped his hands together. 'Show me a few places that fit the bill.'

A hologram column materialized in front of him, a vision of sandy beaches and inviting pink skies, with strange bird-like creatures with three wings wheeling in front of the twin red suns. 'This is the equatorial region of the planet Calica. Average temperature is ninety degrees, and the cuisine is generally regarded to be exquisite. The most popular holiday pastime is underwater exploration under controlled conditions –'

'No, I hate the idea of just lazing around or swimming under computer control. I get bored too easily. What about an adventure holiday?' He wanted somewhere where he could try himself to his limits – indeed, rediscover those limits. A decade hiding behind the perimeter defences around New Alexandria, terrified that Arrestis would come looking for him, had definitely dulled his edges.

The column changed, revealing blue snowcapped mountains under a sky filled with deep green clouds. 'This is Alcruz Six, renowned for its mountaineering and skiing.'

Lassiter knew that the webwork was tapping into his personality profile, trying to match a location with his recorded likes and dislikes. What a pity that he'd deliberately falsified the profile. Well, he didn't want a computer knowing his innermost secrets, did he? 'No, too cold and wet. What about –'

'Professor, there is a serious problem in the Grid. Does this have priority over your previous instructions?'

'Too right it does!' He sprinted over to the horse-shoe-shaped console and speed-read the instruments. And began to feel sick. 'Contact Ottway and Kruust. And Linder and Brown. Get them here straight away.'

'Understood.'

Lassiter grunted at the controls, at a complete loss to understand what was going on. Everything was normal apart from the gate stability readings. The read-outs suggested that it was down to seventy-five per cent, right across the board. Seventy-five per cent: the gates became unstable at forty-eight, with gate collapse a certainty. Then there were the random fluctuations which would strike at gates between seventy and forty-nine: these were inevitable with such widespread systems failure. All thoughts of a holiday evaporated as his mind went into overdrive. His previous reasoning about the Doctor's absence were obviously wrong: Matisse had to be responsible for both the Doctor's disappearance and this, this sabotage. His software defences had been insufficient, and now she was about to hold the entire Bucephalus to ransom.

'Get Sebby here right away!' he yelled, as he began to introduce a stabilizing routine into the Grid, praying that it would be enough. But he knew that it wouldn't be. Matisse had attacked the system nucleus of the Crystal Bucephalus, and anything he did would be a temporary respite at most. Then he heard the webwork again.

'Please restate your request.'

He froze in anger. Pointless anger, he knew. But it was a release.

'Contact Sebastian Lassiter, you stupid machine! The Maitre D'! Tell him to come to Grid Control immediately.'

The webwork didn't react to his fury. 'Should I give a reason?' it answered calmly.

'If he needs a reason, tell him that fifteen hundred people are about to die.' He corrected himself: he knew what would appeal to his brother. 'Strike that. Tell him that the Crystal Bucephalus is about to become the scene of the greatest disaster in history. Tell him that he'd better get his fat backside over here immediately, or else New Alexandria will be the centre of a very, very nasty war. Okay?'

'Understood, Professor.'

He studied the console and the impossible readouts, as gate stability fell to seventy-two per cent, realizing that his prophecy was, in all probability, quite true. Unless he could solve the problem, the battlefleets of a hundred civilizations would converge on the Bucephalus. And its destruction would be the bloody precursor to galactic war.

Ten

Having shown Pfifl and Laklis to their booth – Benefactor's, with its mosaic floor, antique marble feeding slab, and authentic eighth-dynasty paw-knitted wall-rugs – the Doctor returned to his office, nodding at the mixture of Hroth and human guests who frequented his establishment as he went.

'They've arrived then?' The Tempus Fugit's assistant manager, Raphael, looked up from the accounts. He was thin and boyish-looking, with a flamboyant taste in clothing. 'Your foster parents?'

The Doctor raised an eyebrow. 'Don't mock, Raph. Pfifl and Laklis have been very good to me over the years.' He sat down in his chair and placed his feet on the table. 'If it hadn't been for them, I would have died of exposure when I first arrived here.'

'That old story,' sighed Raphael. 'I can't wait for your autobiography.'

Ignoring his assistant's cynicism, the Doctor thought back to his arrival on the arctic planet of Pella Satyrnis. Unconscious in the snow, he had been dragged back by Pfifl and Laklis to their stone domicile, where they had nursed him for days until he finally awoke. It hadn't taken him long to work out what had happened: Pella Satyrnis wasn't part of the Grid.

Call it intuition, call it a Time Lord gift, but the Doctor realized that he was isolated from Lassiter's sensors, and therefore stranded on the world of the Hroth at the turn of the sixty-third century. Logically, he inferred that Pella Satyrnis had not produced a restaurant of the calibre necessary for inclusion in the Carte de Locales.

Rather than wait for a suitable establishment to be created – he might have been a Time Lord, but he didn't fancy using up a few regenerations in the hope that the Hroth improved their culinary skills – and not willing to travel from star system to star system searching for a restaurant that was part of the Grid, the Doctor did the only sensible thing.

He started a restaurant of his own. Deciding that his centuries of experience – dining in the best eateries in the galaxy, being taught to cook by the greatest chefs in existence – made him an ideal candidate, he paid a visit to the local branch of the First Galactic Bank . . .

The Doctor finally reached the front of the queue. 'I'd like to open a local account, please.'

'An account?' The clerk looked extremely dubious, but the Doctor decided that his homespun clothing, a shapeless brown jumper and ill-fitting grey trousers, courtesy of Laklis's skills as a seamstress, was probably to blame.

'Yes. I'd like to transfer some funds from my central account on Iapetus to here, and then make a cash withdrawal.'

The clerk raised a doubtful eyebrow. 'And how much were you thinking of transferring?'

'Let's say about, ooh, twenty million credits?'

'Twenty million!' The Doctor noticed that he was pressing a button, undoubtedly an alarm.

'If you would care to check?' He picked up the small retinal scanner and placed it to his eye.

The clerk's expression changed from doubt to incredulity. 'This is more than some planetary reserves . . .' he muttered, before looking up to see two security guards standing behind the Doctor. He addressed the fat balding one. 'Ah, Vincent. Could you escort this gentleman to the manager's office?'

The Doctor gave a superior smile and followed the guard.

'Oi!'

The clerk looked from left to right before dropping his gaze by a few feet. A Hroth with a runny nose was crouching there, panting.

'Name, please?'

'Garruss,' barked the Hroth. 'I'd like to speak to the manager about an overdraft.'

The Doctor sipped at his coffee as he checked the evening's progress on the bank of monitors. After five years, the Tempus Fugit was a phenomenal success, with guests travelling from all over the quadrant to sample the legendary cuisine. It hadn't been easy, he thought wryly: being able to eat or cook good food was no guarantee of business acumen, and there had been times when he longed to be fighting Daleks or saving the Earth from alien invasion. But, looking back, he decided that the five years he had spent building up the Tempus Fugit had quite possibly been the most enjoyable of his long life.

'It's here!' yelled Raphael. 'About bloody time, too.'

The Doctor turned to the screen indicated and felt a slight flutter in his hearts. It was standing next to a party of avian Kobaldians, its goat-shaped head inclined to one side. A Bucephalus steward, its image inducement penetrated by the Tempus Fugit's advanced sensors.

'So this is it, then, Doc, the end result of all your hard work: a weird-looking android.'

With a faint sinking feeling, the Doctor realized that he was right. After five years of the day-to-day routine of the catering business, he was now free to leave, to return to the crisis in the Bucephalus.

He wasn't actually sure whether he wanted to go.

The rear door from the map room led to another plain white corridor, the end of which was lost in the distance. Tegan began to realize exactly how big the base was. 'Thank God that's over,' she said thankfully. 'I was beginning to wonder what the interior designer from hell would come up with next.'

Tornqvist looked up the corridor. After his earlier

outburst, he was strangely calm, like the weather before an almighty thunder-storm. Tegan hoped that she was well under cover when that happened. 'This seems to be heading in the right direction.' He started walking.

Catching up, she decided to unload something that had been worrying her since he had told her of his plan to return to the Bucephalus. 'Why should Matisse send us back? We didn't exactly part on good terms, did we?'

His reply was muted. 'I think I can persuade her. Once I tell her my suspicions, she'll be only too willing to send us back. Unless she already knows, in which case her punishment will come from a much higher court.'

'I see. So you're going to tell her, but not me. That really stinks, Sven!' she yelled. 'After all we've been through –' She stopped as she spotted what was ahead. On one side of the corridor, the brickwork gave way to glass. Forgetting her complaint, she pulled him against the wall. 'How are we going to get past that?'

He frowned. 'More importantly, what lies behind it? I suggest we try the horizontal approach.' He got down on the floor and began crawling along the floor.

With a shrug, she copied him, pulling up her tattered gown to stop herself from tripping up. 'This is ridiculous,' she hissed, inching across the floor like a huge bundle of red rags.

'Better than getting spotted.' He paused for a moment. 'Actually, I'm surprised that we haven't been apprehended yet. I can't help feeling that we're deliberately being ignored.' Before Tegan could question him on this, they were beneath the window. Without a word, they both raised their heads above the two feet of brickwork and looked through the glass.

The room beyond was about one hundred feet square. Rows of benches stood against the left and right walls, their surfaces covered with portable light-harps, hovering holospheres and lots of glassware. Around sixty people were hard at work, all of them wearing white jumpsuits. Nobody noticed the two spectators. 'Oh, great. A laboratory. I can't say I'm impressed,' she observed. 'Unless the

Elective has decided to get into the beer industry, but I wouldn't be too keen on pink lager.' The objects of her derision stood against the farthest wall, huge cylindrical tanks full of pink liquid adding the only splash of colour in the antiseptic white room. Objects floated within the tanks, but they were too far away for her to identify. 'More evidence?' she said sarcastically.

Tornqvist shook his head. 'I've got enough of that to damn me forever. This is wholly irrelevant. I suggest we make our way to the end of this corridor and find Professor Matisse.'

Tegan said nothing. Something had happened to Tornqvist: he'd seen something or realized something and now he was as tight as a clam. She decided to let it be. If the Prelector's plan worked out, they'd soon be back in the Bucephalus, and then the Doctor could sort it all out.

'Explain your hysterical message.' The Maitre D' was not happy. He'd been in Cubiculo 498, enjoying coffee and liqueurs with Senator Xavier on Risa when his brother's request had arrived. 'I do not appreciate being summoned.' He stood in the doorway of the Grid Control Suite, the two stewards waiting with cybernetic patience for him to move so they could close the doors.

Lassiter turned his chair round to face him. 'I'm sorry, Sebastian, but I assure you it is urgent.' He gave the control panel a quick glance. 'Matisse has sabotaged the Grid, and I mean sabotaged. Grid stablility is falling apart. If things continue the same way, we have about ten minutes before random gate collapse starts happening. Do you know what that will mean?'

'You're the time scientist.'

He rose from his chair. 'It means that your precious guests will get picked off one by one, their atoms torn apart by the time winds and spread through the Vortex. Wholesale murder.'

'An exaggeration, surely?' The doors were closed as he stepped forward.

'No, Sebby, no exaggeration,' he snapped, prodding him

188

in the chest. 'This place is falling apart around our ears! "In the Crystal Bucephalus, the decisions that govern the future of the galaxy are being made in its past." Remember that?' He pointed through the window towards the Cubiculi. 'This place is full of senators and prelectors, kings and emperors. If they die, New Alexandria will be the fuse that lights an intergalactic war!'

'You want me to close the Bucephalus? Evacuate it?' He shook his head forcefully. 'It's impossible, Alex. Can't you solve the problem?'

'No,' Lassiter replied. 'I can't just "solve the problem". Matisse has got this place just where she wants it.'

'How can you be sure that she's responsible?'

'Who else could it be?' He clenched his fists. 'I just wish I knew how she introduced it.'

'It?' The Maitre D's technical knowledge was limited to the little he had picked up from Lassiter over the years.

'A virus. The diagnostics have detected evidence of one in the webwork. An extremely nasty virus. Not only is this virus undetectable – apart from seeing where it's been – but it's immune to all eighteen thousand standard techniques, as well as about three thousand that aren't quite in the public domain. I haven't got time to analyse this one. We've got to shut this place down.'

'Close the Bucephalus?' The Maitre D' could feel his heart pounding. 'That's impossible. Never –'

' "– has the Crystal Bucephalus closed in its entire history," ' Lassiter completed. 'Yes, I've heard that one before as well. But this time it's different. If we don't get everyone back here, people will die. Lots of very important people.'

'Do it.' There was no hesitation. Balancing the reputation of himself and the Bucephalus against his own conscience, there was no question as to the outcome. 'Recall them, Alex. We'll come up with a cover story later.'

Lassiter gave a deep sigh. 'Thank you, Sebastian.' He sat down over his console, his hands playing over the brass and crystal. 'Recall program initiated.' Lassiter tapped in

189

about fifty keystrokes, constantly monitoring the screens. And then he thumped the console, causing the wooden structure to vibrate in protest.

The Maitre D' could tell that something was wrong. Terribly wrong. 'Is there a problem?'

Lassiter leapt from his chair. 'That's an understatement. Matisse's virus must have infiltrated the command nexus: the recall program has been disabled.'

'Disabled? What are you saying?'

'She must have put one hell of a lot of effort into creating this virus.' He shook his head. 'It's over, Sebby. There's nothing I can do to save this place. People are going to die, and I'm here, helpless.'

The Maitre D' grabbed him by the jumper. 'Helpless? Helpless? Do something!'

Lassiter wriggled free. 'I'll use every trick in the book. But once I've done it, this place is closed, understand?' He glared at the Maitre D'. 'Permanently.'

'I understand.' He tugged on his waistcoat. He'd persuade Lassiter to reverse that decision later. 'I will brief the stewards for the evacuation –' A shrill tone from one of the control panels interrupted him. Automatically locating the source, he noted with a queasy feeling that a bank of lights was flashing in red. Blood red.

'The Chelonian Emissary,' muttered Lassiter, the strength drained from his voice. Before the Maitre D' could say anything, he shook his head.

Talkot stopped his discourse about the difficulties of arranging roses as the Legion expanded in all directions, including those undetectable to most life-forms. 'Legion?'

It was the Legion's turn to feel sick. Something was heading towards them, a tidal wave of uncertainty and improbability rushing along the Navigus's synthetic time-chains.

Talkot was momentarily aware of simultaneously vomiting and seeing a group of belligerent Ogri shuffling towards them, before every last aspect and facet of his future – eggs, sons, place on the Chelonian Floral Council – were dispersed by the time winds.

Matisse heard the doors opening but didn't turn round. She sat over the light-harp, watching the readings from the first gate collapse and half-expecting to receive another call from Lassiter.

'Ladygay?' He sounded cold, distant.

She still refused to look round. 'Yes, Monsignor Arrestis?'

'I want to be there when Lassiter realizes it's all over. I want you to get me to the Bucephalus.'

This time she did turn round, rising from her chair as she did so. 'You want to do what?' She pointed over her shoulder towards the Archway. 'The entire gate system is unstable; there's no saying what would happen if I tried to access the Grid.'

He stepped forward and grabbed her round the throat. 'Not so tough without your son around, are you, Matisse? Not so free and easy with the insults, either.' He threw her to the floor. 'Open a gate to the Bucephalus – and make sure it's safe.'

She scrambled to her feet and tried to look defiant. 'You need me.'

He pointed a silver ovoid at her. 'Do you know what this is?' She shook her head, betraying her nervousness. 'It's a *jablecta*, the sacred weapon of the Tharil Antonine Killers. It dissolves the internal organs.'

'Why are you threatening me? Without me this is nothing.' She looked around the control room. 'There isn't anyone else in the Union who could duplicate my work.' But she couldn't help feeling that her bargaining position seemed rather weak at gunpoint.

He grinned unpleasantly. 'That's where you're wrong. You see, I've been thinking. You based your work on Lassiter's own researches, the only information that you were able to steal during your brief partnership.' She bit her bottom lip but said nothing. 'Why shouldn't I use Lassiter himself?'

191

'You're mad!' she spat. 'Lassiter hates you. Why should he help?'

'Because of Diva,' he said simply. 'He loves her. If she asks him to help me, he will. Eventually.'

Her eyes widened in amazement. She couldn't believe what he was saying. 'Monroe? Why the hell should she help you? You told me that she only acted as your whore to get access to the Bucephalus. She's a Lazarine spy, for Lazarus's sake!'

'Exactly. And I know how to appeal to her piety. But to get to the point, Ladygay: I don't need you any more. Get me to the Bucephalus, and you can go. The next shuntship is due in a week. You and your gorilla can settle down on one of the Elective paradise planets. It's not as if you haven't been well provided for.' He even sounded reasonable about it.

Matisse froze. The Exemplar was far more than a shadow of the Bucephalus, far more than a means to an end for Arrestis. She'd been approached by Arrestis eleven years ago when she had been an undergraduate at the Academia Scholastica on Vulcan. He had appealed to her deepest desire for scientific glory, and she had obeyed him. She had seduced Lassiter, only to find herself equally attracted to him, and her final betrayal had been as much a betrayal of herself as it had been of him. Once back on Hexdane, she had again agreed to help Arrestis with yet another betrayal of Lassiter, only to discover that she was pregnant. She carried Garrett, she gave birth to and nursed Garrett, and all the time she designed and built the Exemplar. Sometimes Matisse wondered which one was her real child: Garrett Byson, or the Exemplar.

As Lassiter had built up the Crystal Bucephalus, she had been only a few steps behind, tying the two time machines together with an intimacy which would have horrified her former partner. Unable to duplicate the engine which created the time bubbles, she wrote complex programs which would enable her to activate the Bucephalus from a distance: the Exemplar was nothing more than a vastly expensive remote control unit, a threat that had hovered over Lassiter for nearly a decade without his knowing.

However, in signing up with Arrestis, she had signed away her name in the history book. As she had told Byson earlier, the future would remember Lassiter and Monroe as the architects of the Bucephalus. Her contribution, the all important crystal matrix that stabilized their theoretical gates, would be ignored, overshadowed. A decision made years ago had consigned her to the dustbin of scientific achievement, and the Exemplar was to have been her way of reversing that, her route to true glory. She would have forced Lassiter to recognize her contribution, to have publicly admitted that dichronium pentafluorate was her discovery. Now it was over. Arrestis, the man that she had trusted, obeyed, forced herself to submit to, was discarding her like a child throws away a toy because it finds a more exciting one. Worse still, the more exciting one was Lassiter, the man she loved, the man she hated.

'You bastard!' she screamed, leaping at him. 'I've given up everything for you and you think you can just shrug me off?' Arrestis fell to the floor as she hit him, his *jablecta* sliding off along the floor.

'What are you doing?' he shouted, as Matisse tried to claw at his face. He grabbed both her wrists and forced her off him. With a final shove, he threw her on to the floor. As she lay there, he stood up and looked for his weapon.

'Why?' Matisse was crying, crying for all the lost opportunities that her bondage to Arrestis had caused. 'Why have you forsaken me?'

He picked up his *jablecta* and smiled at her. 'It's over. You're no good to me now; you're a dead weight.'

'I won't activate the gate. You'll never get to the Bucephalus.' He still needed her, he still needed her knowledge. He wouldn't leave her with her ambitions half-fulfilled.

'Really? Sometimes, Ladygay, you overestimate your own importance.' He shoved the *jablecta* in his jacket pocket and straddled the light-harp. Matisse sat up and stared, but said nothing. She knew that Arrestis didn't have the first idea how to operate the Exemplar, even as he started tentatively plucking the photon-strands.

The Archway lit up.

'How?' The Exemplar was hers, her creation. How could he have activated it?

He must have read her mind. 'I've been learning. I haven't really needed you for quite some time now. Your son's behaviour was the final straw.' He stood up. 'I'm going now. I don't expect to find you here when I come back.'

'No!' she screamed. Another hour, and her unwitting spies might have uncovered something in the sealed-off portion of the base that she could use against him.

'You can't do this,' she pleaded. 'Without me you're nothing!'

Arrestis reached the threshold of the Archway, its blue light flickering off his face. 'Believe me, Ladygay: I've been something for quite some time now.' He stepped into the actinic glare and vanished.

Matisse ran to the light-harp and sat down. But she didn't reach out and abort the transmission. She simply slumped in the chair and cried. It was over. In five short minutes, Arrestis had taken her dreams and hopes and crushed them without a thought. For the first time in her life, she felt powerless, with no tricks up her sleeve, no clever bits of information to use as leverage.

Then she blinked away the tears and stared at the Archway with unbridled anger. It wasn't over. With deft plucks, she replayed something she had detected earlier.

Within the holosphere that hovered in front of her eyes, an object took shape, a tumbling blue box that rode the waves of time. A TARDIS. She would give Arrestis time to involve himself with Lassiter, then she and Byson would follow him to the Bucephalus. What she had in mind would make the Exemplar look like a glorified party trick.

It had been hard to say goodbye to Pfifl and Laklis.

Raphael had been closer to the truth than he realized when he had called them the Doctor's foster parents: since his unwilling arrival on Pella Satyrnis, they had been his friends, his confidants, and the closest thing to a family he had had for longer than he cared to admit.

As he closed the door of Benefactor's booth, leaving a pair of extremely emotional Hroth behind him, the Doctor caught sight of his reflection in one of the windows: cricketing trousers, white shirt, pullover and long beige jacket, a gift from a regular guest who happened to be a Kolpashan tailor. He frowned. It had been a long time.

Feeling slightly depressed, he returned to his office, where Raphael was sitting in one of the armchairs, reading.

'Hardly light reading, is it?' he said, holding the book-player up. '*Tersurus Genetic Institute: Collected Papers 6209–6210.* It's hard to work out who the bad guy is.'

'Mmm,' said the Doctor, remembering the hologram of the research team he had seen in the book. 'Some friends of mind are having exactly the same problem.' He reached into his jacket and pulled out an envelope. 'Here, Raph, this is for you.'

Raphael tore it open and read the contents rapidly before looking up with an extremely shocked expression. 'You're giving it to me? The Tempus Fugit?'

The Doctor nodded. 'This place has to go down in history,' he said, opening the wall safe and grabbing a foot-long black rod. 'Just because the steward is here, it doesn't mean that our fame has been assured. If I leave and the place goes to pot, it might never become part of the Grid – and that could cause some very unpleasant time paradoxes and get me into serious trouble.'

'Aye aye, Doc,' quipped Raphael, jumping to his feet. 'Your wish is my command.'

The Doctor gave him a hard stare. 'I mean it, Raph.'

His tone became serious. 'So do I. This place means everything to me, you know that. I'm hardly going to let it fall apart just because you've left, am I?'

'And one more thing: Benefactor's is reserved for Pfifl,

Laklis and their descendants in perpetuity – all meals on the house.'

Raphael shrugged. 'If you say so, Doc.' He reached out to shake the Doctor's hand. 'Best of luck.'

He squeezed it firmly. 'Thank you. I get the feeling I'm going to need it.' With that, he grasped the actuator rod. Nothing happened.

'Oh,' said the Doctor. 'Perhaps you won't be changing the menu yet, after all.'

The Legion tank was now a scene of intense activity. With the assistance of his four technicians, Lassiter had once again opened up the vault that lay beneath the stone floor and removed more of the metal crates that had been there, undisturbed, since the Bucephalus had opened. The crates contained equipment that he would always have denied could exist – until now. Complex egg-shaped circuitry nodules, datacubes containing rerouting programs, delicate assemblies that channelled unimaginable forces through their gossamer-like webs; the technology that the Doctor had immediately suspected Lassiter could create. With the buried equipment, he could convert the Crystal Bucephalus from a temporal projector into a time machine capable of permanent interaction with the past. Two days ago he would rather have died than even admit such technology existed, but Arrestis's death had made matters a lot easier. For a brief moment, he mentally patted himself on the back for having had the foresight – and the courage – to keep it all in the first place.

Even so, he thought, as he watched Kruust and Linder feeding cables of golden bladamite tubing from the Navigus to the Legion tank, it would serve its purpose and no more. Once this particular operation was over, the entire Grid was going to be taken apart and its constituent parts hurled on to the surface of the neutron star that New Alexandria orbited.

'Professor?' Ottway was running a hand through his bright red hair as he stood over a foot-high cylinder that he had been trying to attach to one of the pillars. 'I can't seem to synchronize the couplings.'

Lassiter sighed. He was expecting a lot from his people: none of them had ever seen technology like it, but he had given them instructions to hook it all up to the Grid in as little time as possible. Reaching into his waistcoat, he pulled out his slightly dented Laserson probe and trotted over to help. A strident alarm made him freeze. Somewhere in the past, another gate was collapsing.

'Are you sure you know where we're going?' Monroe was not impressed by Turlough's orienteering skills. Since they had left the TARDIS, they had succeeded in circumnavigating the Mezzanine twice. At least that's what it seemed like. They were currently standing outside the Maitre D's office. The Maitre D' himself was nowhere to be seen.

'You were the one who reckoned we'd have no difficulty in finding a steward,' he retorted. ' "Don't worry, Turlough: once we leave the TARDIS, there'll be stewards crawling all over the place." ' He swept his arm around the Mezzanine, taking in the wooden Cubiculi, the ornate statuary, and the avenue of grey pillars. And the complete lack of stewards.

'Right,' she said, clapping her hands together. 'Let's start again, shall we? And this time, no short cuts through the Cubiculi; we'll follow the wall round until we come across a steward, or a door. Or something that looks promising. Agreed?'

Turlough shrugged. 'Your wish is my command, Professor Monroe.' With that, they started off once again.

Neither of them noticed the figure that detached itself from the shadows and followed them at a discreet distance.

Kamelion closed the scanner and gave an almost human sigh. Although the Doctor had welcomed him aboard the TARDIS, his other companions had made their dislike of him obvious. But Kamelion was unsure as to the correct course to take. Since his construction as a weapon of war during the invasion of Xeriphas, he had never been in a position where trust and friendship had been important. When his masters had retreated from the planet – and he still had no idea why they had withdrawn – he had closed down his consciousness and entered a period of non-existence, the duration of which he was unsure. And then he had been forcefully awakened by a new Master, one who promised absolute power in return for total obedience. Kamelion, who did not desire power and who had been designed for total obedience, was only too happy to assist the black-garbed stranger.

After helping him repair the damage to his TARDIS, Kamelion had travelled with the Master for quite some time, impersonating various life-forms on a number of different worlds. As his experiences grew, his programming began to evolve. He started to feel unease about his association with the Master, an unease that developed into a desire to escape his thrall. But two things prevented that: his prime directive to obey the strongest mind in the vicinity, and the stubby black weapon which the Master wielded. Although Kamelion was capable of forms that could withstand the heart of a star and remain unscathed, the tissue compression eliminator used energies that could permanently disrupt the block transfer computations that gave him existence.

The Master had lured the Doctor into his trap. Kamelion could remember the Master's vindictive cackling as he plucked the other TARDIS from its flight in preparation for a humiliating defeat. But the defeat had been the Master's, as Kamelion found willing association with the Doctor preferable to bondage and slavery.

He wondered whether he should continue his exploration of the TARDIS, but thought better of it. Despite Tegan and Turlough's distrust, Kamelion was now fully capable of independent thought, and felt sure that his unique abilities would prove a definite asset to the crew of the TARDIS. He reached for the door control – and paused. His current appearance had been suggested by the Master as some sort of perverted conceit on the Time

198

Lord's part, but it was no more his true form than any of the countless shapes he could assume. In truth, as a set of solidified mathematical equations, he had no real form. Deciding that a primitive android was as good a form as any, he opened the door and stepped out on to the Mezzanine.

And was overwhelmed by a personality so strong, so single-minded, that it virtually shone in Kamelion's mind. The delicate engrams of independent thought were washed away by a desire to serve, to obey.

He stared at the short man with sleepy eyes who was standing in front of him and gave his answer to the unasked question.

'Yes, master?'

'Please, Sven; it's like walking around with an open grave.'

'Your trite wit is becoming a bit tiresome, Signora Jovanka,' he retorted.

Tegan stopped and stared at him. From a jolly bundle of fun, he had turned into a right pain. 'For Christ's sake, what's bugging you?' All right, so she had decided to ease off, but his behaviour was really getting to her.

'Who's Christ?' he asked curiously. 'I've heard you use the name before.'

She shook her head. 'In my time, he's a saviour . . . in the same way that Lazarus is yours.'

'I sincerely hope not,' he muttered.

'You've seen something, haven't you? Please, Sven – tell me.'

He closed his eyes and placed his hands on her shoulders. 'This Christ . . . how would you feel if you discovered something about him that was totally at odds with your belief?'

'Is that it? One of the rooms has shaken your faith?' Tegan's view of religion had once been very jaundiced, but two things had changed her mind. Seeing the innocent members of Victor Lang's New Light organization burning and screaming as they fell victim to vampires had made her realize that faith was a tangible, measurable thing that people could rely on. And she had discovered her own reserves of faith after her soul had been raped by the Mara, a deep, unyielding faith in herself – and in the Doctor.

She examined the man standing in front of her, definitely the most faith-filled person she had ever met. The very foundation of Tornqvist's life was falling apart as she watched, and she didn't have the faintest idea why, or what to do about it.

'It's more than that, more than just my faith,' he said, as if he had been reading her mind. 'Look, I'm not ready for this yet. Let's find Matisse and get out of here.' He gave her an imploring look. 'Please?'

The end of the corridor was now only a few hundred yards away and Tegan could see that it ended in a plain, white wall. Leaving Tornqvist behind, she ran the final distance and stopped: there was no visible exit. She beckoned Tornqvist over with rapid gestures.

'I should have expected something like this,' he muttered. 'Everything was going too well.' He ran his hands over the brickwork and frowned. 'Hang on.' He gave her a grim smile. 'I recognize this sort of door. We use them in the Benefactor's Residence on Clavidence. Legend has it that they were designed by Lazarus himself.'

'You mean there's a door here?'

'Oh yes; it's just disguised by an image inducer. Give it the correct set of syllables and it should open.'

Tegan's eyes widened. 'So we've got to stand here hurling words at it? Great. Wake me up in about a hundred years.'

The Prelector rubbed his hands together nervously. 'I – I think I can open it.' He stepped back and cleared his throat. 'In the beginning was the word.'

The brickwork evaporated, revealing an open doorway.

'How did you know?' asked Tegan, beginning to feel as if she was reading the end of a book, but the first half was missing.

He shrugged. 'It's the first line of the first book of the

Codex.' He stepped through the doorway — and groaned in shock as he sank to the floor on his knees.

Tegan dashed in and grabbed him, then looked up and saw.

The room was filled with glass tubes which ran from floor to ceiling — thousands of them. Each one was about three feet wide, and filled with the same pink liquid that they had seen in the laboratory. Something floated in each one. Tegan had to force herself not to retch: in many ways, this was worse than the torture room.

The tubes contained body parts. With a single glance, she could see arms, legs, internal organs, even genitalia. But that wasn't the worst of it: that floated in a tube about ten feet away. She froze, unable to believe what she was seeing. As if hypnotized, she walked up to the tube and stared through the glass. Sightless, lifeless eyes stared back at her from the head of Maximillian Arrestis.

Eleven

'Cycling complete.' Lassiter looked up at the crystal column, a faint smile of pride crossing his face as he watched the fluorescence burn brighter within the central core. Brief flickers reflected off the polished gold of the bladamite tubing and the brass support cradle as the generators deep below the surface of New Alexandria were called upon to double their output, then double it again. He checked the horseshoe-shaped console, analysing the dials and monitors until he was sure that his earlier calculations, calculations glued together with a large helping of guesswork and prayer, were holding up.

He glanced out of the window in the Grid Control Suite, over the tops of the Cubiculi and towards the horse, the true crystal Bucephalus. Only a trained eye would have noticed the increase in its internal illumination, but Lassiter had such an eye. A two hundred per cent increase in time spillage, manifesting itself as a few more candelas of light. If only it were that simple, he thought. With the situation so critical, he had seen only one way out. Matisse's virus was causing the time gates to collapse randomly – they'd already lost a Legion, the Chelonian Emissary to the Union, four Thals and a Terileptil – and the critical point hadn't been reached yet.

Given Matisse's previous actions, Lassiter guessed that she was trying to force him to come running to her for help, and the cost would be exactly what he had now created. He refused to go begging to her: he knew what she had in mind, and his enhancements to the Grid would render her sabotage impotent. Once he sent the reality pulse through the Navigus, the patrons would suddenly achieve a reality quotient of one. Fifteen hundred or so unauthorized time travellers, beyond the reach of collapsing bubbles and the time winds; all quite capable of altering history.

Lassiter couldn't help shuddering at the thought. But once they were real, they were immune to Matisse's virus, and the recall program he had written could bring them all back to the Bucephalus. He suddenly remembered that he ought to check with the Maitre D', and grabbed his talkstick. 'Lassiter to the Maitre D': how's it going?'

His brother's plummy tones came over the talkstick. 'I have stewards placed by every Cubiculo. We're ready.'

Lassiter frowned. 'We don't have that many stewards in the Bucephalus.' The human factors people had decided that they would never need more than seven hundred stewards, but then again, they had never foreseen a wholesale evacuation of the Grid. Who had?

'We do now. I requisitioned three hundred stewards from the Majordomo.' There was a veiled sense of amusement in his voice.

'I bet that was a fight worth watching, Sebastian.'

'Indeed,' he laughed. 'Anyway, we're ready. Maitre D' out.'

Lassiter couldn't help chuckling. His brother would never change. He leaned over the console and activated the reality pulse. Through the window behind him, the statue glowed even brighter. He counted down from ten to one, sufficient time for the pulse to take effect, then set the recall algorithm going. In a few minutes, all the patrons would be back – and then he would be leaving New Alexandria for ever.

He heard the sound of a scuffle outside the doors, and turned from the console, unsure of what was going on. Who would want to come in here?

Then the doors flew open, and he saw who was responsible. His stomach churned and his next breath was snatched from his throat. It wasn't possible . . .

She smiled, obviously aware of the reaction her presence was causing. 'Hello, Alex.'

The words spilled out almost by instinct. 'Hello, Hellenica.'

All of the stewards were in place, their numbers swelled by the bizarre androids from the Emerald Syphax: bejewelled frog-featured humanoids with sinister whispery voices. They gave the Maitre D' the creeps.

He checked his watch. If Lassiter's calculations were correct, the patrons should be coming through any time now. Naturally, they would be distressed — only the rich, the famous and the powerful frequented the Bucephalus, and they tended to have such delicate sensibilities — and if he could smooth a few ruffled feathers, then so much the better. He suddenly noticed something awry.

'Why is Cubiculo 553 unattended? Where's the steward?' He hated disorganization, especially where the occupants of 553 were concerned. He always found Alpha Centaurians so excitable, and the thought of four of them twittering away was more than he could bear. He turned to the steward attending 552. One of the frog ones. 'Well?'

'The steward will arrive in seventeen seconds,' it replied in its whispering voice.

'Excellent.' He tugged his waistcoat. 'Then we're ready for anything the fates choose to send us.'

'Really, Sebastian?' The shape emerged from the shadows. 'Are you ready for me?'

The Maitre D' felt his heart skip a beat as he recognized the smaller man. 'But you died . . . I saw the body,' he whispered. Miracles held no place in his ordered life.

Arrestis gave a chilling smile. 'I got better.'

Despite the shock, the Maitre D' grabbed the tattered remnants of his composure together. 'What do you want?'

'Want? Well, quite a few people have wondered about that over the years.' He reached into his jacket and pulled out the blunt shape of a *jablecta*. The Maitre D' was only too aware of its capabilities. 'But my current aim is your brother, and you're going to take me to him.'

'He isn't here,' he stuttered. 'He's taken a leave of absence after all the trouble.'

'Really? Forgive me if I don't believe you. If you value your limited abilities,' he waggled the gun, 'you'll take me to him.'

The Maitre D' decided that he had already surpassed the boundaries of his bravery. He pointed across the Mezzanine. 'When I last spoke to him, he was in the Legion tank.' He glanced nervously at Arrestis, but he didn't react.

'Come on, Kamelion.' He snapped his fingers at a steward that had been lingering behind. 'Lead the way, then.'

How Arrestis had control over a steward and why he had given it a name were two questions that he chose not to ask. Identifying the most convoluted route to the Legion tank, he set off.

They were standing outside the room full of body parts. Tornqvist was white, having deposited the meagre contents of his stomach over the floor, while Tegan was trying desperately hard not to follow suit. 'How are you feeling?' she asked gently.

He smiled tentatively and rubbed his stomach. 'I've felt better.'

'I'm glad about that, Your Grace,' said a woman's voice.

'Matisse?' Tegan cried. The voice was coming over some sort of public address system.

'I'm so glad you still remember me, Signora Jovanka. I've decided that I've missed your company, so I'd be grateful if you would join me for refreshments in my control centre.' As she spoke, another door shrugged off its camouflage and materialized on their right. One of Matisse's huge androids stood just inside.

'If you would follow your guide?'

'Well, Sven?'

He closed his eyes, obviously still recovering. 'What choice do we have? I don't doubt that dear old Ladygay has been following our every move, allowing us to remain untroubled – until now.'

'But why?'

'Because,' came the disembodied voice, 'I was as eager to investigate my paymaster's private apartments as you clearly have been.'

'Arrestis?' Tegan's opinion of the crime lord plummeted to the point where she would have needed a step-ladder to reach the gutter. 'All these sicko rooms are his?'

'Fascinating,' said Matisse. 'I can't wait to hear more.'

They stepped through the door. She nudged him. 'Did you know this belonged to Arrestis?'

He said nothing, but Tegan couldn't help but notice that his knuckles were even whiter than his face as he clutched something silver in an unbreakable grip.

'How are you?' Monroe's words were innocuous, but just hearing her voice brought all the memories, thoughts and emotions rushing back. In the eleven years since she had quite literally walked out of his life, not a single day had passed when Lassiter hadn't remembered some aspect of their life together. For the first four months, the pain of his loss had disrupted every corner of his existence. There were the forgotten weeks spent drunk, first in the Faculty bar, and then, when his superiors had given him quite clear warnings, in the seedy, no-questions-asked dives on the outskirts of Megalopolis Six. There were the other women, all of whom had possessed some minute fraction of her looks or personality, but whose attractions had rapidly paled as his guilt took over. There were the attacks on his closest friends, blaming them for not being there for him, even though he had violently resisted their help. Eventually – and he still didn't know where he'd found the strength to do it – he had pulled himself back. The pain was still there, as penetrating and chronic as always, but he had succeeded in building up enough defences to face the world again.

Half a year later, the divorce still freshly entered into

the Union webwork, he had been introduced to a brilliant research student from the Vulcan Academia Scholastica: dignified, attentive, the perfect partner in scientific discovery. But Matisse had offered so much of what he so desperately needed. She became Monroe.

'I'm fine,' he muttered. 'And you?' Brief words that were meant to convey every last nuance of the hurt, the betrayal, the desire, the hole in his life that had festered and bloomed within him over the last eleven years. He smiled as she walked over to him, her smell tearing at his senses and dragging yet more memories from that now unlocked vault. She turned her head to look at him, to speak to him.

'You bastard!' She slapped him across the face. 'After all this time! I was even beginning to wonder whether I'd been mistaken: perhaps you never did discover proper time travel; perhaps I just wanted to believe it was true!' She thumped the console, possibly less violently than she had him. 'But it's all here – all of it! Look at the readings. The Bucephalus has a direct link to the past – reality quotients of one all over the place. You knew all the time, didn't you?' She tried to slap him again, but Lassiter grabbed her wrist.

'You don't understand. I couldn't tell you –'

'Why not?' she screamed, pulling her arm free. 'You know what the Intent means to me. You know what lies at the heart of the Intent. And yet you denied me the chance to fulfil Lazarus's will. Why, Alex?'

He leant on the console with both hands. 'Do you have any idea what you did to me?' he murmured. 'Do you?' He spun round to face her. Everything that he had always wanted to say to her when he saw her again came out like an erupting volcano. 'I came back from my last lecture and you weren't there. You took enough of your belongings to make it clear that you'd gone, but left enough to rub it all in. You didn't even bother to make sure I was all right, did you? Whether I was hurt, upset . . . ready to kill myself!' He could feel the tears welling up. It didn't matter. Eleven years of pain, and he wasn't about to stop now. 'I checked the communications log, Hellenica. I saw all the calls you made to those Lazarine friends of yours, all those calls arranging your escape. You set off for Clavidence without a second thought!'

'It wasn't like that.' She reached out for him, but he was beyond even her ability to calm him down.

'Wasn't it? Wasn't it?'

'I couldn't live with you any more, Alex. How could I?' Even she was crying. 'It was over!'

'Over? A red envelope on the shelf?' The words still burnt in his mind. ' "I'm really sorry that I've left this way?" How does that sound? What about "I just hope that someday you'll forgive me and that I haven't damaged your life too much"?'

'I meant it!'

'I'm sure you did!' The tears were running down his face, but he didn't care. He grabbed her shoulders. 'You tore my soul apart!'

'Really? Didn't take you long to shack up with that bitch, did it?'

He froze. 'You weren't there.'

'A brilliant excuse, Alex,' she sneered.

'I still love you.'

'How moving.' The familiar voice caused Lassiter to reach for the console for support. 'And Diva; what a pleasant reunion.' Arrestis stepped over the threshold.

Lassiter stared at him. Seeing Monroe again had been something he had both desired and dreaded. Seeing Arrestis was simply a nightmare come true. 'What do you want?' he whispered.

'Asking the totally obvious seems to be a Lassiter family trait. I hope that lying isn't.' Arrestis clicked his fingers over his shoulder, and a steward thrust the Maitre D' forward into the room. There was a bright red welt across his face.

Lassiter took deep breaths to prevent the panic from overwhelming him. Sabotaging the Grid was one thing, but hurting his family? 'Sebby: are you all right?'

The Maitre D' made a valiant attempt to look indignant. 'I tried to keep him away —'

Arrestis raised his hand to silence him. 'Not very successfully. Now, I've come a long way and I'm not in the mood to wait any longer. You're coming with me.'

Lassiter stepped forward, shaking his head. Somehow he had always known that it would come to this: the direct attack by Arrestis. All of his running away, his hiding, had only made it easier for the man in front of him to track him down. Setting up a restaurant that catered to the highest echelons of the galaxy, only to chart Arrestis's inexorable rise to those very heights. It was almost as if he had subconsciously choreographed the entire confrontation. Now it was there, laid out in front of him, and Lassiter, who had rehearsed the scenario countless times over the years, almost as many times as he had dreamt of the reunion with Monroe, suddenly found that he wasn't afraid. If anything, he was relieved.

'No. After all you've done, after all you're capable of, if you want time travel, I suggest you carry on supporting Matisse. Although she's got as much chance of succeeding as Sebastian has.'

'That's not an option any more: she's no longer on the pay-roll.'

'That just about sums you up,' sneered Lassiter. ' "On the pay-roll." That's all people are to you –'

'Oh shut up, for Lazarus's sake! I've just had to put up with the same speech from Matisse. After all the trouble she and her retard son have caused me, I'm beginning to think that I should have come after you in the first place.'

Son? 'You can't make me,' he said defiantly.

Arrestis smiled. 'Who's got the gun? Anyway, it's time for one of those tired clichés. Here's one reason.' He walked over and grabbed Monroe, placing the *jablecta* to her temple. Then he snapped his fingers again. To Lassiter's disbelief, the steward's hand transformed into a disruptor aimed at the Maitre D'. 'And there's another. Do I make myself clear?'

Lassiter's eyes narrowed. 'You wouldn't dare.' He stood his ground. Arrestis was many, many things, but he wasn't inhuman.

'Fine. Have it your own way.' He nodded to the steward. Who blew the Maitre D's head off.

'Do try the champagne.' Matisse proffered two glasses. 'I'm very interested in hearing what you've seen.'

'You let us wander about? Just like that?'

Matisse gracefully seated herself and sipped from her flute. 'Yes, Signora Jovanka, just like that. I needed to know what Arrestis was hiding.' She put the glass down. 'I could monitor your location; I just had no idea what he kept in those rooms.'

'Your worst nightmares.' Tegan shook her head. 'He's warped.'

Matisse looked at Tornqvist. 'Well, Your Grace? What is your opinion?'

He held up the item he had found in the shrine. 'Do you recognize this?' He knew that she wouldn't, but he wasn't ready to admit what he suspected.

'It's an Inf. So?'

'So, Ladygay, it's a rather special Inf, made of an alloy of metals that hasn't been used for the last five thousand years.'

He laughed. 'An antique. I'm sure the famous museum on Clavidence would be more than happy to display it.'

He didn't want to tell her. He wanted her to come to the right conclusion without his help. If another person believed him, he might not be so condemned. 'This Inf is of a particular design, of a certain metal,' he insisted. 'Only two of this design were ever made. One was owned by Saint Clavis, and is now round the Benefactor's neck. The other –'

Matisse leapt from her chair. 'But you mean –'

'That's it!' Tegan slammed her glass on the table where it shattered, the champagne trickling on to the tiled floor. 'I'm sick to death of all this. Will you tell me what the hell is going on? I've just been on a tour through some basket case's personal chamber of horrors, accompanied by a priest who keeps going on about some dark secret that he couldn't possibly share. Then we turn up here, you flash

210

some piece of jewellery about, and now she's in on it!' She turned to Matisse – but she was on the other side of the control centre on the threshold of the Archway, the blue radiance silhouetting her.

'Where are you going?' Tornqvist demanded, already knowing the answer. The last thing he wanted was for her to go blundering in.

'I'm getting out of here. After what you've told me, I want to get as far away from Maximillian Arrestis as is humanly possible.' And then she smiled. 'Although humans won't have an awful lot to do with it.'

'What are you talking about?' asked Tegan.

'I'm off to the Bucephalus to pick up something that your dear departed Doctor has no further need for. And don't bother trying to follow me: as soon as I pass through the Archway, the Exemplar will disconnect from the Bucephalus Grid. If you're on your best behaviour when I return, I might be persuaded to drop you off.' With that, she turned into the light and vanished.

'That's all we need,' said Tornqvist. 'The phrase "loose cannon" comes to mind.'

'I think that might be the least of our problems.' Tegan pointed at the light-harp. All the strands had vanished, and the holospheres, now flashing red, were sinking to the floor.

'So? She's disconnected it all from the Bucephalus; everything's shutting down.' Which meant they were trapped ten thousand light years from New Alexandria. He gripped the Inf even tighter.

Tegan frowned. 'That's not it. Don't ask me why, but something's wrong.'

Deep within the Exemplar's webwork, a surge of power washed over the command pathways, triggering systems that Matisse had intended would never be used again.

'Will it work this time?' Raphael had found it very difficult to hide his amusement when the Doctor's first attempt to escape had failed so unspectacularly. 'That 'doesn't exactly look very state of the art.'

'Appearances can be deceptive,' the Doctor retorted. The actuator's casing lay discarded to one side, while its internal circuitry had been reworked into a small tetrahedron. 'Despite its admittedly haphazard construction, this happens to be a micro-dematerialization circuit. When activated, it should lock on to the Grid's temporal field and trigger the recall systems, pulling me back.'

'You hope.'

'Do you always have to be so negative?'

His assistant laughed. 'You always claimed that I was the perfect antidote to your natural optimism, Doctor.'

'Did I? Well . . .' He stood up and straightened his jumper. 'No time like the present, is there? Goodbye, Raph. And good luck.'

'It strikes me that you're the one who needs the luck. After five years, are you sure you can remember what's going on back at the Bucephalus?'

'Of course I can.' He reached out and flicked the tiny switch on the side of the tetrahedron. A faint grinding, warbling noise began to echo around him.

As the Doctor slowly faded from existence with a cheery wave, Raphael couldn't help noticing the expression on his face. It was doubt.

Matisse stepped out of the Cubiculo − and immediately withdrew as a steward walked by, escorting a bewildered and extremely agitated Alpha Centauran.

'What is happening?' it squealed, rapidly blinking its single eye. 'Why was my meal cut short?'

'There are technical difficulties with the Crystal Bucephalus,' hissed the steward, its frog-like head thrust forward. 'All guests are being evacuated to the Emerald Syphax.' It escorted the twittering alien away.

Technical difficulties? What a wonderful euphemism. Matisse came out of the Cubiculo and looked around. Even though she had been studying the specifications of the Bucephalus for nearly ten years, this was her first visit to Lassiter's crowning glory. Despite her feelings towards the man, she couldn't help but be impressed by his invention. The place dripped wealth, and there was simply no contest between the heady mixture of white marble and dark gothic, and the ascetic charms of the Exemplar. Besides, the Bucephalus *worked*. Realizing that she was in shadow, Matisse looked up and a smile formed: the horse. For a moment she was able to forget that it was actually nothing more than fifty feet of adulterated dichronomide pentafluorate acting as a dimensional stabilizer, and she could appreciate the fine lines of the flaring nostrils, the beautifully carved flanks. She walked over to the black base of the statue, deciding that the centre of the floor made a good point from which to orientate herself.

Then she saw it. An incongruous blue box – the Doctor's TARDIS.

The rapidly assembled plan unfolded in her mind. With the Doctor's machine, she would have immediate access to all of the deeper mysteries of time. She didn't doubt that the contents of every last paper written by Lassiter and Monroe would be in the TARDIS data banks, classified as elementary learning for kindergarten Time Lords. Years of servitude to Arrestis, years of being overshadowed by Lassiter's achievements . . . within the TARDIS lay the true route to her eternal glory, her place in the history books.

She strode up to the double doors and looked at the lock. Could she open it? She placed a hand on the right door, and was surprised when it creaked open. With a shiver of anticipation, Matisse stepped into the TARDIS.

The doors to the control centre were thrown open with a bang. Byson stood in the doorway, a look of confusion on his face. 'Where's Ladygay?' he asked, a note of panic in his voice.

Tegan glanced at Tornqvist. The Prelector was slumped in a chair, mumbling to himself. She smiled at the giant and beckoned him in. 'Ladygay's gone to the Crystal Bucephalus; she'll be back soon.' Tegan couldn't really see Matisse piloting the TARDIS, but then she remembered how she herself had managed to move it outside the Urbankan ship and shuddered. If she had been able to operate it, Matisse would have no problems.

'Has she gone to see my father?'

'What?'

Tornqvist looked up from his reverie. 'Garrett here is Matisse's son by dear old Lassiter,' he muttered.

Tegan sneered. 'You are joking? Her son? But he's about —' A loud bang erupted from the rear of the control centre. 'What the hell is going on around here?' she shouted.

'I would guess that something's burning,' said a curiously familiar voice from behind her.

'Doctor?' Tegan span round. And saw him. 'Doctor!' She was a little puzzled to see that he was once again wearing his cricketing outfit, but decided to let it pass. What counted was that he was there.

'In the flesh, so to speak.' He walked into the centre of the room and started examining the unstrung harp and the collection of holospheres that had dropped to the floor like discarded Christmas tree ornaments. 'It looks like I've arrived just in time. I take it this is Professor Matisse's little operation?'

Tornqvist stood up and proffered his hand. 'It was. I'm Sven Tornqvist. And you?'

'I'm the Doctor.'

'*The* Doctor? Tegan's Doctor?'

The Time Lord raised an eyebrow. 'I suppose you could put it that way.' He turned round to Tegan. 'Tegan, is Professor Matisse still around?' He was fiddling about with the base of the harp with what looked like a hairpin.

'No, she vanished through that arch thing about five minutes ago.' Something was bothering Tegan. And then she realized what it was. 'How did you get here?'

An odd look appeared in his eyes. 'By quite a roundabout way, as a matter of fact.' He returned his attention to the harp and made a decisive twist: the holospheres rose uncertainly from the floor and assumed their circular formation, while the harp restrung itself.

'No, I mean *how*. Matisse disconnected the Exemplar from the Crystal Bucephalus.' She smiled at her technical knowledge.

'What?' The Doctor looked back at the holosphere ring. 'That can't be possible. It's generating a massive temporal field throughout the Bucephalus's Carte de Locales.'

'She did it just before she left,' she protested. 'To stop us following her.'

He started plucking at the harp, examining the holospheres. 'Fascinating. It appears that Professor Matisse has made something of a miscalculation.' He turned round.

'Miscalculation? Why don't I like the sound of that?'

'Because it's somewhat of a fatal miscalculation. Although I don't have time for a complete examination, I'd hazard a guess that there's been some sort of feedback from the Bucephalus.' He steepled his hands and sucked his fingertips. 'Rather like tearing a tooth out without the benefit of anaesthetic.'

'Is that bad?' asked Byson.

The Doctor's eyebrows shot up. 'You could say that. There's a catastrophic build-up in the Exemplar's power core.' He looked around the white room. 'And that means an extremely big bang.'

Tegan swallowed. 'Shouldn't we try to get out of here?'

'Yes, Tegan, we should,' he said with the faintest trace of panic. 'Unless, of course, we want to learn about black holes from the inside?'

'Well, Professor Lassiter?' Arrestis had seated himself in one of the leather chairs next to the control console, maintaining his grip on Monroe's neck. 'Does that make you more amenable to my offer?'

His voice was barely a whisper as he replied. 'You bastard. He wouldn't have hurt you.' He couldn't help looking at the decapitated body. 'He wouldn't have hurt you!' The tears brimmed in his eyes. For all his bluster, the Maitre D' had a heart of gold, and the Bucephalus had meant everything to him: he had been the real driving

215

force behind it, persuading Lassiter that it would make the perfect hiding place. Now he lay there, a victim to the one person the Bucephalus was designed to protect them all from.

'Well?' There was no evidence that Arrestis felt anything approaching guilt, just that nauseatingly smug expression.

'All right!' he cried. 'I'll come with you. Just let Hellenica go.' He didn't know how he was coping with his brother's death: if Monroe was hurt . . .

Arrestis released his armlock around her neck. 'What possible use would time travel be to you, Max?' she asked, rubbing her throat.

'Ah, delightful Diva deigns to speak.' Arrestis stroked the console. 'What possible use? As spies go, you weren't particularly successful, were you? I expect you've been a grave disappointment to your masters on Clavidence.'

Monroe laughed mirthlessly. 'I needed you to get me to New Alexandria.' She sighed. 'I don't suppose it matters now. It was the only way to get to Alex. To persuade him to hand over time travel to the Lazarus Intent.'

'It's a bit too late for that, Hellenica.' All the horror, the hatred, the pain and the hopelessness was eclipsed by a desperate need to tell. 'Isn't it, Maximillian?' Or was it a confession? 'For the last eleven years, I've lived in fear. Not fear of the Time Lords, no. Something much worse.'

'What are you jabbering on about?' moaned Arrestis, but Lassiter could see sweat the beading on his forehead.

'I've lived in fear of you, Arrestis. Of who you are, of what you are. I built all of this to protect me from you: stewards and perimeter defences and restricted access – this entire marble prison!' He shook his head. 'But you were so clever, weren't you? You became exactly the sort of patron this place courts. As you came here more and more often, I got more and more frightened, but I convinced myself that I was still safe in this art deco womb. And then you died, lying there on the floor with your face twisted in fear, and I laughed. I laughed! Because I was free, free of you!' He swallowed. 'But that wasn't good enough for you, was it? I should have guessed that you'd come back from the dead. I mean, it's what you're good at, isn't it?'

Monroe stepped over to him and clasped his arm. 'Calm down, Alex. What are you talking about?'

He broke free of her grip. 'Don't you understand? I did it for you! I would have done anything for you!'

'Then why did you suppress your research?' she hissed. 'You knew what my faith meant to me — why didn't you give me time travel and let me fulfil the Intent?'

'The Intent?' Lassiter laughed, almost on the verge of hysteria. 'You don't get it, do you? Of course I developed time travel. Look around you. This is a fully functional time machine, for Lazarus's sake!'

'Then why —'

He grabbed her wrists with his hands. 'Eleven years ago I managed to stabilize and focus a time gate.'

'That's enough, Lassiter.' Arrestis was pointing the *jablecta* at him. But it didn't matter; nothing mattered any more. Monroe had a right to know after all this time and all this hurt.

'It was quite easy; the location isn't exactly undocumented.' Part of him got a great deal of pleasure out of her expression. It was about time she shared the blame and the guilt.

'What are you saying?'

'I did what you wanted, Hellenica. I fulfilled the Lazarus Intent.' He let go of her arms and pointed at Arrestis. 'Show me your golden age of peace and prosperity, then. Show me the dawn of enlightenment, of universal salvation!' he yelled. 'Because I fulfilled the Intent! I saved Lazarus from death!'

Monroe stared at Arrestis, her face a mixture of disbelief — and something else, an indefinable quality that unnerved Lassiter, even as he found himself continuing.

'That's right, take a good look. The man responsible for every brothel and drug den, every illegal racket and bent operation from here to the Perseus Rift. Maximillian Arrestis, the man we've all been waiting for. The Heir to Saint Clavis's Chair, Lord of All Prelates, the One True Messiah.'

'Arrestis is Lazarus. I brought him back.'

Twelve

'Fascinating, absolutely fascinating.' Matisse examined the interior with a professional eye. She wasn't totally unfamiliar with the workings of the legendary TARDIS machines – as soon as she had spotted the Doctor's vessel in the Vortex, she had brought up all the available information on the wrecked TARDIS discovered in the Terran asteroid belt twenty years ago – but to actually be within one, in the dimensionally transcendental pocket of reality that comprised its interior . . . she was closer to being overwhelmed than she could remember.

She reached out a crimson-nailed finger and touched the hexagonal console, almost to prove that it was real. Despite the primitive appearance of the controls, she was well aware of the mighty forces that lay underneath.

'These should be the helmic regulators.' She stroked two large black rings on each side of the nearest panel before moving on. 'And this should be the vortex primer.' Suddenly aware that the two great doors were still open, she looked around for a way to close it. 'Ah,' she whispered, catching sight of a large lever surmounted by a big red ball. 'The door control.' Slamming the lever down, she wasn't prepared for the deep concussing boom that echoed around the console room.

Feeling the first faint stirrings of panic, she hastily looked around, suddenly realizing that the doors were closing – and were closed before she could reach them. And then the central column, which the detached scientist part of her identified as the time rotor, began to rise and fall, accompanied by a raucous trumpeting.

She backed up against one of the roundelled walls, hypnotized by the activity of the console and unwilling to face up to what she had done. But there was no way back and no way out: she'd set the TARDIS in motion.

An extremely disturbing image appeared in her mind: an isochronal map of the Time Vortex surrounding New Alexandria: closely packed circles surrounding the planet, circles that represented its position at the bottom of a space-time well. She'd watched this TARDIS's hazardous journey from Ancient France, and that was downhill as far as the gradient of the Vortex was concerned. Attempting to leave New Alexandria would mean actively opposing the contours of the Vortex . . .

She sighed. 'I hope the Time Lords built their TARDISes well.' And then she remembered the wreck in the asteroid belt. And shuddered.

'Can't you stabilize it?' Tornqvist was peering over the Doctor's shoulder as he sat astride the light-harp.

With a final strum and a sigh of irritation, the Doctor stood up. 'I'm afraid not. According to all of this, the feedback has knocked out the failsafes – not particularly adequate failsafes anyway, if I might make so bold,' he said breathlessly. 'We have about fifteen minutes before the power core goes critical.' He turned to Byson. 'How many people are on this base?'

He started counting on his fingers.

'Roughly?' he snapped.

'We saw about fifty or sixty people in some sort of a laboratory,' offered Tornqvist. 'But this is a big base; there could be hundreds more.' Including a certain Professor DeSalle, he thought, trying to suppress a most un-Lazarine relish towards the psychovator's death.

'Any signs of a spaceport, long-range matter transmitter, anything like that?' The Doctor's eyes were studying the control centre like a bird of prey.

'We didn't see anything like that. Then again, we didn't exactly visit the choicest spots,' said Tegan dryly.

The Doctor seemed oblivious to her complaint. 'There

has to be some way off this world. It can't be completely cut off.'

Tornqvist frowned. 'In the current financial climate, even the Elective can't afford to have shuntships languishing on remote bases. And Tanthane – this planet – is far beyond the boundaries of the Union.'

'You mean we're sitting on top of a great big bomb and all we can do is sit here?' Tegan slammed the table. 'You've got to do something, Doctor!'

'Tegan, I am well aware of the severity of our current situation, but panicking won't help, will it?'

'Nor will standing there being so damned calm about it!' she yelled back.

'How big will the explosion be?' Tornqvist decided to inject a little rationality into the proceedings, then realized immediately how morbid the question sounded.

'In order to generate the tremendous amounts of power needed to reach into the Time Vortex, Lassiter used the most energetic reaction currently known: collapsar pair annihilation. I don't doubt that Matisse uses a variant of the same.'

'Collapsar?' repeated Tegan and the Prelector in union.

'Collapsar. Point singularity? Black hole?'

She understood. 'You are joking?'

'Tegan: I rarely joke about the primal forces of the cosmos. When the core goes critical I would imagine that it will consume this entire star system.'

'Even better! We can't do anything by halves, can we? A tiny little bang isn't enough, is it?'

'Stop it, Tegan,' bellowed the Doctor. Tornqvist was impressed. Plainly, the way to shut Tegan up was to out-shout her. The Doctor turned to Byson. 'Is there any form of transportation off this planet?'

'We wait for the shuntship to arrive. It turns up every two months with supplies. The next one is in a couple of weeks.'

'Sadly, we don't have a couple of weeks; we only just have a couple of minutes.' He started patting his pockets. 'Our only hope is to use the tools we have to hand.'

'Like what?' asked Tegan.

'Like this barely functional time machine.' The Doctor had already removed a plate from the side of the Archway and was poking about inside. He paused to take out his glasses. 'You know, it's times like this when I really miss my sonic screwdriver. I should have sued the Terileptils for criminal damage.'

Monroe stood there, transfixed. 'Lazarus?' Lassiter could see that the disbelief was waning. But the other emotion . . .

Arrestis smiled broadly and gave her a theatrical bow. 'Professor Maximillian James Antonius Arrestis at your service, my lady.' He threw back his head and laughed. 'Five thousand years, and nobody ever discovered Lazarus's real name. There's faith for you.'

'Another professor,' said Turlough archly. 'I'm beginning to feel hopelessly underqualified.'

'Now do you understand? I brought your saviour back for you. So how does it feel to worship the biggest bastard in history? Then again, it shouldn't be too much of a problem: it didn't take much persuasion for you to become a whore in the pay of the Lazarus Intent, did it?'

She didn't seem to have heard him. 'You did it for me?'

He nodded sadly. 'Eleven years ago. I rigged up the Vortex scoop and reached back to the Sontaran Throneworld – and that emerged.' He gave Arrestis a look of disdain.

'Thus fulfilling the final request of Lazarus to his people.' Arrestis grinned. 'My publicity people did one hell of a good job, didn't they?'

'Publicity people?' said Turlough. 'What are you trying to say?'

'He's saying that the Lazarus Intent was created to further the ambitions of a greedy little geneticist, Turlough.'

'What happened next?' Monroe's quiet voice drew everyone's attention. 'After you came back?'

Arrestis clapped his hands together. 'Your ex-husband is rather more perceptive than you give him credit. It didn't take him long to realize that Lazarus wasn't quite the saint that history would have everyone believe.'

'Catching you trying to download my files was rather a giveaway,' said Lassiter dryly.

'At that point I decided that discretion was the better part of valour: I caught the next shuntliner out of Pluto, and ended up on Hexdane.'

'Where you became the head of the Elective,' added Turlough. 'It must have been quite a comedown – god-head to godfather in one easy move.'

'One easy move? If only. It took me two years to work my way up to being the head of the Elective: then again, the ability to be in two places at once was a considerable help.'

'Genetic engineering?' asked Turlough.

'What do you think? I was the premier geneticist of my time. There are thousands of Arrestises lurking round the Union – and beyond.'

'Did you hear that, Hellenica? Wear one out, and you can grab another.' Lassiter ignored her reaction and looked at Arrestis. 'Don't you get an inferiority complex?'

He sat down in one of the heavy Victorian chairs, toying with his *jablecta*. 'Not really. Not only do they have a limited lifespan, but I retarded their intelligence. There may be thousands of me scattered around the galaxy, but there's only one Lazarus.'

'So why do you want time travel?' Turlough moved forward. 'The Lazarus Intent wanted it to bring you back, but you're here now. What use could you possibly have with it?'

'As the companion of a Time Lord, I would have thought that you'd have known the answer to that one.' Arrestis held his hand out, palm upwards. 'Absolute mastery over this galaxy, now and forever.' He clenched his fist, as if the galaxy had been floating there and was now in his grasp. 'I'm a power-hungry megalomaniac who controls the Elective and will soon sit on Saint Clavis's

Chair as rightful ruler of the Lazarus Intent. *Saint Clavis*!' He chuckled. 'If only dear old Simon could hear that! Simon Clavis – drug addict, pervert and all round dirtbag – canonized!' He glanced at Turlough. 'I'm sorry, I digress. I'm still level-headed enough to realize that the control of time and space is a bit beyond even an army of clones. But it will make a useful tool to control the here and now. And, of course, I need to protect a certain period of time.'

Turlough snapped his fingers in realization. 'You can't afford to have anyone interfering in your earlier life, can you? That would really upset things if someone reached back to before the time Professor Lassiter rescued you, wouldn't it?'

'Very astute. Your initial research project, Alex, will be to find a way to shield the moment of my "death" from other prying eyes.' He broke off as he realized that someone was standing next to him.

Monroe moved in front of Arrestis. He tightened his grip on the *jablecta*, but said nothing. He just stared.

She knelt down in front of him.

'As it was written, so it shall be spoken. The family of the Lazarus Intent opens its arms, its hearts, its homes to the glorious return of our Lord and Saviour from beyond the vale of death. We kneel before the everlasting and eternal might, power and sovereignty of he who has come back to lead mankind to a new age of understanding, peace and harmony. From the depths of our souls and the heights of our passion, we embrace the return of our one true Lord, Lazarus.' Monroe's head sank down and she remained in place, abasing herself before her messiah.

Arrestis clapped. 'Well quoted, Diva. I even remember the night I wrote that: my PR people spent ages making it sound pompous enough.' He looked at the others standing around. 'Didn't sound too over the top, did it, gentlemen?'

Monroe stood up. 'Well, that's the official part over and done with: the Rite of Acceptance, as written in the Codex.' She shook her head. 'I can't believe that I was the one who delivered it.'

'Well you did, and that's that.' Arrestis looked over at Lassiter. 'How long will it take you to download everything you need?'

Lassiter decided that stalling tactics were in order. 'About two hours. But I need to bring a few other things with me.'

'Like what?'

'Key components: bits of the Navigus, the entire command nexus . . .'

'Irrelevant. My people can duplicate everything you need. You've got twenty minutes.'

'There is one thing you can't duplicate.' He was sure that Arrestis wasn't going to buy it, but it was worth a chance. 'The dimensional stabilizer.'

'You don't mean . . .?'

'I'm afraid I do. We need to take the Bucephalus statue. However good your people are, I doubt that they'll be able to recreate the crystal matrix.' He glanced out of the window at the dominating emerald horse.

'Really?' Arrestis's tone made it clear that Lassiter's plan had been shot down in flames. 'Unless I'm very much mistaken, wasn't it a certain Ladygay Matisse who developed your "crystal matrix" in the first place?'

'But you've sacked her,' said Turlough.

'I've also cloned her and copied her mind. A nice, obedient little Ladygay is waiting for me in stasis on Hexdane.'

Lassiter sighed. Another point to Arrestis. 'All right. I'll start downloading.'

'There's a good boy.' He snapped his fingers as if he had just remembered something. 'By the way, you won't be lonely on Hexdane.' The smile was chilling. 'I've decided to open my doors to your little playmates.'

Lassiter wasn't prepared for Monroe's reaction. 'My Lord Lazarus: that would be a pleasure and an honour.' That indefinable quality – Lassiter finally realized it was faith.

* * *

225

The once-steady lighting in the console room was now dipping and flickering as if something was interfering with the power supply. The rise and fall of the glass column was jerky and erratic, with unpleasant electrical noises accompanying each movement.

'Damned machine!' Matisse slammed her fist on the white panel, and jumped back as what sounded like a scream of pain issued from the console. She examined the walls: three of them were identical, white and roundelled. Of the other three, one was dominated by the huge double doors, another had a smaller door, presumably into the limitless interior of the ship, and the third contained a shuttered viewscreen.

She looked around for a way to open it. After her last experience with the console, she was loath to experiment, but a mixture of scientific curiosity and the beginnings of panic was a strong motivation. Scanning the control surfaces, she noticed two large disks, two panels round from the take-off lever. Remembering the blueprints she had seen, she guessed that they were the telepathic circuits.

Although she would never have described herself as telepathic, her psi-rating was higher than average. Deciding it was worth a try, she placed her hands over the disks and concentrated, focusing on an image of an open viewscreen showing an isochronal map of the TARDIS's location. She refined the image in her mind, feeling the colours, the shapes . . .

Her mind touched the bottomless, boundless entity that was the TARDIS. For a brief, agonizing second, her consciousness was bounced around that of the TARDIS, an infinitesimal speck that was all but lost in the ageless, timeless vessel. She became privy to the ship's innermost hopes, fears and desires; saw stars forming from clouds of gas before collapsing into black holes in a scream of X-rays; experienced civilizations evolving from the primordial slurry, growing into sentience, and then dying in a terrifying combination of atomic war, plague, even sheer apathy; she agonized with the TARDIS as it reached out to help its master, friend and colleague through yet another transformation.

But Matisse's mind, however brilliant, was only finite. With blessed relief, she escaped from the wonders that the TARDIS would show her, denied herself the secrets of the universe, and slumped over the console.

Behind her, the scanner shutters slid open, revealing an isochronal map of the Time Vortex. Matisse was unfortunately unable to register the blatant fact that the TARDIS had run aground in the Vortex. She was also incapable of realizing that her disconnection of the Exemplar from the Crystal Bucephalus had had a rather undesired effect.

The once stable equilibrium between her time machine and the Bucephalus was now a decidedly unstable one. As waves of time spillage churned up the Vortex like a tidal wave, the only thing maintaining any semblance of balance between the two systems was the TARDIS.

Matisse still didn't wake up when one of the panels began to crackle and smoke.

'That's it,' said the Doctor. 'I've done everything I can to stabilize the core.'

Tegan had heard that tone before. 'We're going to die, aren't we?'

He ran a hand through his blond hair and sighed. 'Ever the optmist, Tegan.'

'If you say "brave heart" to me once more, I'll hit you,' she snapped.

'Yes, well,' he flustered. 'I was hoping that I could re-establish the link between the Exemplar and the Grid, but Matisse did her job only too well.'

Tornqvist frowned. 'But you came through it, after it had been disconnected.'

'Not exactly. It seems that Professor Lassiter has been making some pretty radical changes over on New Alexandria, and Matisse has been trying to keep up. She'd altered her own recall systems, and when I sent out a strong enough signal, the Exemplar locked on to it, despite being disconnected from the Grid. A very ingenious woman.'

'And a very alive one, unlike us. How long have we got?'

'About eight minutes, Tegan. Then this whole place will become the seething nucleus of a black hole.' A sudden frenzy overcame him; he started reaching into his pockets, obviously looking for something.

'What is it?'

'Hush, Tegan. I'm trying to concentrate.' He plucked a truncated tetrahedron from within his beige jacket. 'Monsignor Byson?'

'Monsignor Doctor?'

'Is this complex airtight?'

Byson frowned, and then sucked his thumb, clearly trying to remember. 'Ladygay did say that the control centre could be sealed off in case something went wrong with the, um, the jellytic lavs.'

'I think you mean the genetic labs.' He clapped Byson on the shoulder, a bit of a reach, even for the tall Time Lord. 'Excellent! Tegan, Your Grace: make sure that all exits to the control room are sealed off. All except that one.' He pointed to the main doors.

'Why? What are you planning?' Tegan tried to hide her apprehension: the Doctor's solutions tended to be more dangerous than the initial problem. And then he chewed his bottom lip. Yep, thought Tegan, this is going to be good.

'I need to get the Exemplar away from Tanthane, and the only safe place for the sort of explosion this place is going to cause is going to be the Time Vortex.'

'The Time Vortex?' Tornqvist's eyes suddenly widened. 'You mean . . .?'

The Doctor threw his arms open. 'I'm going to give Professor Matisse what she always wanted. I'm going to turn the Exemplar into a TARDIS and take it away from all this.'

Tegan didn't say anything. She just swallowed. Hard.

* * *

228

'How much longer?' asked Arrestis. He was still holding the *jablecta*.

Lassiter looked up from his lectern. 'As your spies have probably told you, there's quite a lot of information held within the webwork.'

'And most of it carefully under lock and key, eh, Alex?' Monroe's voice betrayed a touch of bitterness.

'You've got what you want, Hellenica. Can't you leave it?' The time for arguments was past. All of his worst case scenarios had come true and were standing around him. Lassiter was surprised how well he was coping.

'You could have told me all of this a decade ago –'

'Professors, please!' Turlough's voice cut across the argument. 'I'm sure that Arrestis doesn't really want to listen to yet another of your interminable post-marital rows.'

'Thanks; I couldn't have put it better myself,' said Arrestis. He was clearly getting impatient.

'Give me another five minutes: I'll have it all then, including the command nexus.' He continued working at the console.

'Professor?' It was Turlough.

'Yes?' replied Lassiter absently. The last few data streams were trickling from the nexus into the datacube.

'I think you'd better have a look at this.' He was pointing at one of the brass-framed monitors on the far side of the console.

There was something in the boy's voice that made Lassiter willing to forget the threat of Arrestis's *jablecta* and trot over to him. One glance at the readouts confirmed Turlough's worries. 'Hellenica?' He wanted a second opinion, even if it was hers. 'What do you make of this?' He pointed at a most peculiar waveform.

She studied it for a second before replying. 'I don't understand.' She turned to him, her voice accusatory. 'This place was balanced, wasn't it? You did balance the temporal potential of all the gates against the dimensional stabilizer?'

'What do you think I am, an incompetent bungler?' he

growled. 'Of course the Grid is balanced. Do you think it would have stayed in operation for nine years if it wasn't? I built nearly two hundred per cent of buffer into the systems: I could have increased the number of Cubiculi by one thousand eight hundred and the crystal matrix of the horse would have held.'

Turlough was tracing the line of the wave. 'No, that's not it.'

'By the scars of Saint Clavis!' Lassiter immediately realized what the problem was. 'You're right: the system is unbalanced.'

'That's what I said,' argued Monroe.

'Would you care to explain this technobabble?' Arrestis was standing behind them.

'Each of the Cubiculi generates time spillage, a waste product caused by penetrating the Time Vortex,' Lassiter stated. 'It's that which causes a non-balanced gate to collapse.'

'As Alex and I found out a decade ago,' interrupted Monroe.

'Yes, thank you, Hellenica.' She was not going to let it rest. 'To stabilize a gate, the spillage needs to be bled off and converted into something harmless, like photons of visible light. The Grid uses that.' He nodded towards the window.

'The crystal Bucephalus? The horse?' said Turlough.

'Exactly. Adulterated dichronomide pentafluorate – the green crystal – is able to absorb time spillage and release it as light.'

'So what's the problem?' said Arrestis, the frustration showing in his voice.

Lassiter sighed with irritation. 'Naturally, there is a maximum amount of spillage the statue can take. There is also a minimum amount, necessary to keep the crystal matrix of the statue from breaking down. When I built this place, I balanced everything against those two limits. Somehow they've changed: the Grid is no longer balanced.'

'Meaning?'

Lassiter shrugged. 'Meaning, boom!'

'Matisse!' Monroe grabbed his arm. 'Don't you see?'

It suddenly became clear: no wonder Matisse had been able to infiltrate the Bucephalus. She'd been there at the very beginning! 'Of course!' He turned to Arrestis. 'How long ago did Matisse set up her version of the Bucephalus?'

'Do you really expect me to –'

'Answer me, damn it!'

'Nine years ago.'

Lassiter slapped his forehead with his open palm. 'Then that's it. What a conceit that must have been for her.' He turned to Monroe. 'I thought I'd locked her out of the Bucephalus systems, but she still managed to introduce a virus. Because she had access through the one route I would never have expected.' He stared at the proud green horse.

'She was tapping into the crystal Bucephalus itself.'

'Are we going somewhere?' Garrett Byson sat in the chair, his expression clearly indicating that he didn't have the faintest idea what was going on.

Tornqvist dragged a chair over and sat down opposite. 'From what I can gather, the Doctor is trying to remove the Exemplar from Tanthane.'

'How?'

'He's going to turn this room into a time machine.' There, that should be simple enough. 'Then this will all vanish . . .'

'And blow up.'

'And blow up.' The Prelector leapt up. This was a point that had managed to evade him. He hurried over to the Archway, where the Doctor was sitting cross-legged on the floor, myriad components scattered about him in an untidy circle. The Doctor looked up as he approached.

'I haven't got the time or the materials to build a timer or a remote control, Your Grace.' The Doctor had obviously heard. 'You, Byson and Tegan should leave.

Probably about now, come to think about it.' He leapt to his feet and smoothed down his jacket with his palms. 'The power core will go critical in about three minutes, so I'd hurry if I were you.'

'We're not leaving you, Doctor!' shouted Tegan, but the Prelector began dragging her towards the exit.

Tornqvist gave the Doctor what he hoped was a brave smile. 'May the grace of Lazarus be with you always.'

He was rather shocked – but not altogether surprised – by the Doctor's response. 'I sincerely hope not, Your Grace.'

They were halfway to the door before Tornqvist realized that Byson wasn't with them: he was standing behind the Doctor, holding a small box that was attached to the disembowelled Archway by a thin red cable. A small box with a single button.

'No!' he screamed.

The Doctor turned, but it all seemed to happen in slow motion. As he reached for the box, Byson pressed the button.

An ungodly grating, roaring noise filled the control room, its savage tones modulating and ululating as it reached a crescendo. Tornqvist suddenly remembered the doors, and was relieved to see Tegan slamming them shut and thumping the locking plate.

At least they were airtight.

The oceans of the Time Vortex were becalmed around Tanthane, gentle waves of fundamental forces and exotic particles so different in appearance from the seething maelstrom around New Alexandria as to bely their being the same thing. Then their faint ebb and flow was disturbed by the materialization of an object foreign to them: a tiny white-bricked block, linked to a black sphere like a convict's ball and chain.

'Two minutes; I can't hold back the core any longer than that.' The Doctor was frantically poking at one of the holes in the Archway. 'Hopefully things will be a little

232

easier now we're in the Vortex.'

Tegan glanced round from the corner where she was trying to comfort an extremely distressed Byson who had now started crying. 'What's going to be easier? We're stranded in the Time Vortex riding a very large bomb, and we're going to die. What could be easier than that?' The words came out before she realized, and she grimaced as Byson started sobbing again.

'Escape, Tegan. Adrenalin has an extremely efficacious effect on the synapses. I think I can see how to tap into the Crystal Bucephalus,' he called over his shoulder, before yanking his hand out of the gap with a yelp.

'The Bucephalus?' Tornqvist felt better already. Somehow the Doctor imbued trust, even in a jaded old cynic like him. 'You can get us back?'

'If I can lock on to the Grid. It shouldn't be so difficult now. The Grid has a permanent analogue moored in the Vortex.' He smiled, before running over to the light-harp. Leaning over, he played it like a virtuoso, repeatedly glancing up at the holospheres that hovered above his head. 'Yes, that feels right.'

'The Bucephalus?' asked Tegan.

'What else? There's a very strong signal at the coordinates of New Alexandria. I would think the laws of probability would back me up, don't you?'

'I've waited long enough.' Arrestis waggled the *jablecta*. 'Grab the datacube; we're off.'

'How do you intend to leave New Alexandria?' said Lassiter. 'This planet has more defences than Maradnias itself. If an Elective ship comes within half a light year of here, the perimeter satellites will blast it out of the heavens.'

'I'm sure they would – if I was waiting for a ship. But there's a nice ten-seater pleasure yacht waiting in the Emerald Syphax's docking bay. We'll just be another party of evacuated guests.'

Monroe's eyes widened in realization. 'Do you mean the *Imperator*?'

'Quite. The Elective shipyards have souped her up a bit: shuntspeed forty should get us to Hexdane quickly enough, don't you think?'

Lassiter whistled through his teeth. 'That's fast.' The fastest ship he'd ever travelled on, the one which had brought him to New Alexandria, had only managed half of that.

'Not fast enough, my lord.' Monroe raised her hand. 'I can get you there a bit faster than that. Or rather, Alexhendri can.'

Arrestis furrowed his brows. 'And how the hell can he do that? I didn't realize he was a shuntdrive specialist as well.'

Lassiter stood back as she beckoned Arrestis over to the console.

'All we need do is set the coordinates for Hexdane, and open a time gate.' Her hands were poised over the keyboard that would add a location to the Bucephalus's Carte de Locales. Lassiter had to admit a grudging admiration for her abilities: eleven years, and she could still remember his prototype blueprints and designs.

'What use is that?' he demanded. 'Why would I want to be sent back to Hexdane's past as a ghost?'

'What counts as the past, my lord? A thousand years? A century? A year?' Her voice grew quieter. 'A second?'

'But I'd still be unreal,' Arrestis snapped.

Monroe shook her head. 'You're forgetting the one thing this business has all been about. Alex's improvements mean that the Bucephalus can now transport people through time properly. Not only is it a true time machine, it's the most powerful matter transmitter in the Union.'

Arrestis gave a broad grin. 'Of course! I'm a genius and I didn't even know it. Given the state of the Union's transport system, people will be willing to pay anything to buy this!' He smiled at Monroe. 'Do it.'

Lassiter ran his thumb and forefinger through his moustache. Arrestis and Monroe seemed to have the whole thing sewn up. Everything he'd worked for, his entire life's work, being pawed over by a hypocritical messiah and a fawning acolyte whose faith was more important than trust, pride — even love.

She stepped back from the console. 'There we are: Hexdane is now part of the Grid.'

The control room was vibrating, a shudder sufficient to set Tegan's teeth on edge. 'What's going on?'

'Only another few seconds, Tegan.' The Doctor was attaching a thin grey wire from the light-harp to the Archway. 'There!' He stepped back, bowing and holding his arm out as if to summon them through the brilliant blue doorway.

'Is it safe?' asked Tornqvist.

'It's a damn sight safer than staying here, Sven.' Tegan pulled the Prelector over to the Archway. 'Doctor?'

'You three get through. I'll follow.' The vibration was now unbearable: Matisse's remaining champagne flutes suddenly became a pile of glittering glass shards on the tiled floor, knocked from the table and shattering before they hit the ground.

'Now, Tegan!'

She ran into the brilliant blue opening, dragging the Prelector and Byson behind her.

It's over. You can wake up now.

Matisse wasn't sure whether it had been her subconscious or the TARDIS that had spoken to her, but the effect was the same: she opened her eyes and saw only off-white panelling — the TARDIS console. She pulled herself upright, unable to remember how she'd ended up in that position. The last thing she could recollect was looking for the viewscreen control.

She sighed, then felt the shuddering. The TARDIS was obviously still in trouble, and she had no idea how to sort things out; it wasn't the sort of situation she was used to finding herself in. Catching sight of the single door that led into the interior of the Doctor's vessel, she decided on a course of action: she would seek scanctuary in the bowels of the TARDIS. If the Time Lords were so wonderful, there should be some kind of an escape capsule.

As she touched the door handle – more of a steel grip than a handle – she was startled by a sudden noise, a sound reminiscent of the TARDIS's dematerialization.

To her surprise, a section of the wall lit up in a strangely familiar arch shape, magnificent blue in contrast to the plain white of the console room. Then a person appeared, falling through the Archway – of course, Archway! – and skidded to a halt. It was that wretched Jovanka woman, followed by Tornqvist and her son.

'Garrett!' she exclaimed.

'Ladygay!' He squeezed her in a breathtaking bear-hug. 'Where are we?' Before she could answer, Tegan's shout cut her off.

'It's gone!'

The arch had vanished, leaving only the familiar roundels. 'What are you talking about?'

Tegan stared at her, a look of horror in her eyes. 'The Doctor, he was right behind us.'

'So he's still on Tanthane?' said Matisse.

'You don't understand!' Tegan yelled. 'The Exemplar went critical, thanks to you. We only just got away.' She glanced back at the roundelled but archless wall. 'The Doctor was still in the control room when the whole thing blew up!'

Matisse tried to understand what the woman was saying, but her concentration was interrupted by yet another disturbance. It was a bell, its deep tocsin reverberating around the console room.

'The Cloister Bell,' whispered Tegan.

'What?'

Tegan clenched her hands into fists and shook them. 'The Cloister Bell: it's the TARDIS's way of saying it's about to blow up!'

Thirteen

'**O**ne bona fide time gate, set for Hexdane,' said Monroe proudly. The plain Cubiculo in the corner of the Grid Control Suite was radiating azure light from its open door. 'The coordinates are stable at both ends, and the time differential is only one-point-six nanoseconds, virtually contemporal.'

'I'm impressed.' Arrestis looked over to the doorway, where Kamelion, still disguised as a steward, stood guard. 'Kamelion?'

'Yes?' The android came over, morphing into his original form as he did so.

'We're about to go through the time gate. I'll go second, you follow up the rear.' Arrestis inspected his prisoners. Each would have a role in his next venture, as he absorbed the Lazarus Intent into the Elective and effectively seized control of the Union. For a moment, his imagination took over, as he looked forward to crushing the non-human empires that polluted the galaxy: the Chelonians, the Draconians, those repulsive Alpha Centaurians. With Lassiter's discoveries and his unparalleled knowledge of genetic engineering, he would introduce an ethnic cleansing programme that would ensure the human ascendancy. His dreams of glory were shattered by a strident bleep from the console. 'What the hell's that?'

Monroe turned to him, panic in her eyes. 'We're losing the gate!'

Arrestis pointed the *jablecta* at Lassiter. 'Help her!'

Lassiter moved to her side and tapped one of the monitors. 'A massive disturbance in the Time Vortex.' He checked the location and gave a faint smile. Earlier,

237

Arrestis had let slip the location of the Exemplar. 'Around Tanthane.'

'Tanthane?' Arrestis immediately thought of Matisse. What had she done? 'Check in, Diva.'

Monroe shrugged. 'That's what the instruments say, my lord. The Vortex in the immediate vicinity of Tanthane is virtually boiling. Unfortunately, that lies directly between here and Hexdane.'

'So the gate's out of the question?'

Lassiter nodded. 'Go through that,' Lassiter nodded towards the flickering Cubiculo, 'and you'll end up on Hexdane in pieces.' He smiled. 'Although you're welcome to try it.'

'Very amusing.' Arrestis glared at Monroe. 'Thank you for your brilliant idea, Diva.'

'Who's idea was it to duplicate the Bucephalus on Tanthane? It's not her fault that Matisse blew herself up, is it?'

Arrestis realized what Lassiter was saying. 'You mean that the Exemplar has blown up? Ladygay?' It hurt; it hurt a damned sight more than he'd either wanted or expected.

'Unless Matisse can survive an explosion that can rip the Time Vortex apart,' Lassiter sneered. 'Then again, that hard-hearted bitch could probably fly through a quasar and come out the other side.'

Arrestis wasn't amused. 'Obviously I brought out her better side.'

'If that's the case, I don't think I want to see her bad side.' He shrugged. 'The time gate's down; if you want to get out of here, I suggest you use your yacht.'

'Can't you stop that damned bell!' shouted Matisse, trying to make herself heard over the irritating chimes.

'Not unless you get the TARDIS out of danger,' Tegan snapped.

She decided to drop the subject. 'What happened to the Exemplar? You said it blew up.'

'Too right it did,' said Tegan. 'The Doctor sacrificed his

life to save us. All that crap you spouted about disconnecting your Exemplar from the Crystal Bucephalus, all you did was destroy the place – and the Doctor with it.'

Matisse sneered. 'You're talking nonsense, girl; trying to frighten me . . .'

'It's true, Ladygay.' Byson came forward. 'As soon as you went through the arch, things started to blow up. The Doctor turned the control room into a time machine and then I accidentally started it and then –'

'Be quiet, for Lazarus's sake!' she bellowed. 'Even my own son turns against me!' She steadied herself against the console as the floor bucked again, accompanied by another toll from the Cloister Bell.

'What's the pattern on the screen mean?' Byson was pointing over Matisse's shoulder. She spun round and saw that the scanner was displaying the isochronal map that had almost cost her her mind. The sight did nothing to reassure her. The TARDIS was at the centre of a raging storm of time spillage. Looking further afield, she swallowed. Instead of the regular patterns of the Exemplar, chaos had taken their place. Tegan had obviously been correct: the Exemplar had detonated – and ripped the Time Vortex apart in the process.

'What does it mean?' asked Tegan. 'Then again, what the hell is it?'

Matisse raised a carefully drawn eyebrow. 'Hell is quite a good description, Signora Jovanka.'

'Call me Tegan. Please?'

Matisse noted the information and carried on regardless. 'The destruction of the Exemplar has caused a massive disturbance in the Time Vortex. We are feeling the effects of that disturbance.'

'But the TARDIS is designed to travel through the Vortex.'

'Ocean-going yachts are designed to sail the seas, but how many sink in storms and hurricanes? That's the position we're in. The TARDIS had stalled in the Vortex, in the path of an unstoppable wavefront of unimaginable power.'

Byson was squinting at the control console, entertained by the flashing lights and little patterns on the monitor. But he'd obviously been listening, since he looked up and spoke. 'Does that mean we're going to blow up as well?'

'Unless we can move the TARDIS, yes.' Then it struck her. She stabbed a finger at Tegan. 'You travel with the Doctor. Can you pilot it?'

She looked horrified. 'I – I thought I'd piloted the TARDIS to Castrovalva, but that turned out to be Adric's doing, and I managed to take off once . . .' She looked crestfallen. 'But the TARDIS got stuck in outer space.'

'You mean that you travel with a Time Lord and have never learnt to operate this vessel? Have you no curiosity, girl?'

Tornqvist leapt to Tegan's defence. 'You're the temporal scientist, Matisse – do something!' He was interrupted by the detonation that erupted from the console. The panel was torn apart, leaving a smoking ruin of charred circuitry burning with acrid blue flames.

Matisse gave him one of her most charming smiles. 'You're the Prelector, Tornqvist – pray.'

'I don't like this,' muttered Lassiter. 'I don't like this at all.' He peered at the output on one of the monitors, waiting to see the results of a more detailed analysis of the Vortex. 'I wonder what happened to the Exemplar? And what about Matisse?' He didn't feel strong enough to contemplate the death of someone else he cared for.

Monroe was staring out of the window at the horse. 'Whatever it was, it's seriously disrupted my lord's plans.'

Lassiter beckoned her over to the console. 'Before your piety overwhelms you, I think you'd better take a look at this.' He pointed at the monitor. 'The results of the analysis are just coming through.'

They both watched as the image built up layer by layer, the detail becoming clearer and more terrifying by the second.

'Good grief!' hissed Monroe. 'What sort of force could

240

do that to the Time Vortex? Earbrass theorized that –'

Lassiter grabbed her with surprising force. 'Words, Hellenica, equations and words. We're the first people to actually see a . . .' Let Hellenica say the words. He wasn't going to tempt fate.

She obviously recognized it as well as he did. She went white. 'A Vortex rupture?'

Lassiter nodded. 'And that's not all.'

'Will you shut up and get a move on, for Lazarus's sake!' yelled Arrestis, smiling as he realized what he had just said. 'Eleven years in this time period and I've started taking my own name in vain. Oh, I'm going to have fun with the Lazarus Intent. Anyway, the *Imperator*'s waiting.'

'Forget that. Something's going on. I need to sort out exactly what it is.' Lassiter began tapping into a keyboard.

Arrestis glared. 'We haven't got time for that; I've already indulged your scientific curiosity long enough.'

His voice was defiant. 'Listen to me. This could be serious, very serious. You must give us another five minutes. Please?'

'Since you ask so nicely, no. Get your backsides over here. We're leaving.'

'For Lazarus's sake . . .' Lassiter trailed off, realizing what he'd said. But Hellenica was in there, backing him up.

'My lord: unless we can ascertain exactly what is going on, we cannot be certain that we can get away anyway.' That was a good argument: shuntspace was related to the Vortex. If one was behaving oddly, it was a fair bet that the other one was as well.

He relented. 'Okay. Do what you have to. But if you take too long, I'll ask Kamelion to morph into something really unpleasant. Understood?'

'Perfectly.' Lassiter returned to the console, Monroe close behind. 'I think we'd better take a closer look, don't you?' He tapped the keys; seconds later, a holographic image materialized above the floor between the console and the crystal column.

'That shows the portion of the Vortex containing

'both us and the remains of the Exemplar,' he said, pointing.

The green surface had two distinguishing features. One was a veritable fountain, as a flume shot up from the surface and then cascaded back down, causing the continuum to bubble and boil: the Vortex rupture. The other was the site of the Crystal Bucephalus, and that was what was worrying Lassiter. The last time he had looked, New Alexandria had been at the centre of regular, concentric waves of mild time spillage, the tolerated overflow that escaped the statue. Now it was chaos, with time spillage pouring from New Alexandria, gushing in torrents that washed outwards in a circular tidal wave.

'Where the hell is all that coming from?' he whispered, staring at the display.

'Isn't it obvious?' said Monroe. She pulled her dress up and vaulted over the console, wading into the hologram. 'Can you get this thing to show the convection currents of the Vortex substrate?'

Of course he could do it, thought Lassiter. But why? He instructed the webwork to show the ocean beneath the surface of the Vortex, and gasped at the result. The Vortex rupture, a geyser of time spillage, was a lot more active than he had initially assumed. It was erupting downwards as well, an inverted mushroom of motion in the usual calm substrate that underpinned the Vortex. And a stream of that super-heated substrate, branching off the main body, shot back up to the surface — immediately beneath New Alexandria.

Monroe ran her hand through the visualized stream. 'Here's the problem, Alex. The Vortex rupture has created an undercurrent that's pumping straight into the Grid. The statue can't cope with it all.'

'But why should the undercurrent . . .' Then he realized. 'Matisse! Of course, her tap into the Bucephalus; not only has she unbalanced the Grid, but the tap set up a line of least resistance in the substrate — a line that this undercurrent followed.' He slammed his fist on the console. 'Thank you, Ladygay. Sending us a wave of time spillage after making sure that the systems couldn't cope with it.'

Arrestis appeared by his shoulder. 'That's enough theorizing, Lassiter. Can we get away?'

'Well . . .'

'Diva?'

'Yes, my lord. Although the Vortex is unstable, shuntspace isn't affected. We can set off for Hexdane immediately.' Lassiter frowned: shuntspace was becoming more turbulent by the second. Why was Monroe lying to her saviour?

'Excellent. We're off to the docking bay.'

Lassiter stepped forward. 'I need to set the spillage buffers.'

'What?'

'The spillage buffers. They're something I put together when I designed this place, but I never expected that I'd actually have to use them.'

'What do they do?'

'They're an emergency feature: they should absorb all this excess spillage. If I don't activate them, there's a pretty good chance that the spillage will feed back and blow this place to kingdom come.'

'What do I care?'

Monroe had returned from the hologram. 'The evacuated ships aren't far enough away. If New Alexandria is destroyed, they'll be caught in the explosion.' She gave Arrestis an imploring look. 'I doubt that the patrons' governments will be very happy.'

Arrestis considered this for a moment. 'Can you do it from here?'

Lassiter shook his head. 'No; I need to get to the Legion tank.'

'Okay,' he said grudgingly. 'You've got ten minutes. Kamelion?'

The android turned its head. 'Yes, Monsignor Arrestis?'

'If he causes any trouble, maim him.' Arrestis slapped his hands together. 'We're all off to the *Imperator*. Meet us there.'

'Yes, Monsignor Arrestis.' Lassiter was sure he could hear an insolent note creeping into the android's silky voice. Perhaps it was becoming immune to Arrestis's influence? He sincerely hoped so.

The entire party moved over to the huge silver doors.

'So what's Hexdane like?' Lassiter heard Turlough asking Monroe.

'Arguably the greatest concentration of wealth in the Union.'

'Great: from one luxurious prison to another.'

Lassiter smiled as he and Kamelion turned towards the Legion tank, leaving Arrestis and the others to make their way to the docking bay.

The tolling of the Cloister Bell was becoming intolerable, each chime overlapping the other to generate a resonating background roar that did nothing to improve the situation – or their temperaments.

Matisse was staring at one of the undamaged parts of the console, hazarding an occasional flick of a switch or press of a button, but nothing she had done had made the slightest difference to the situation they were in. 'Damn!' She went to thump the console but thought better of it, pulling her fist back and clenching it even harder.

'Obviously no luck?' asked Tornqvist.

'Obviously,' Matisse echoed scornfully. 'I have the most unpleasant feeling that nothing I do is going to make the slightest difference.'

Tegan tried to swallow her panic. She wasn't very successful. 'How long before . . . anything happens?'

'That's hard to say. According to that,' she pointed at the screen, 'the TARDIS is soaking up time spillage like a sponge, but even this magnificent vessel must have its limits.' Her eyes widened as if she had suddenly remembered something. 'Escape pods!' She grabbed Tegan's arm rather harder than she would have liked. 'Where are the escape pods? There must be escape pods?'

'Calm down!' shouted Tegan. 'Please!' She prised her hand away. 'If the TARDIS does have escape pods, I've never seen them.' She recalled the terrifying incident a week or so ago, when Nyssa's bedroom had started to dissolve. There had been no mention of escape pods then, and if there had ever been a time they needed them . . . if there had ever been a time they needed either Nyssa or Adric, come to that. She would even have welcomed Turlough, she decided. She looked down at the console, and found herself staring into the smoking hole left by the recent explosion. Something dark and nasty was in there, barely restrained. She pulled her eyes away.

'That doesn't look good. In fact, it's going to blow!' she heard Matisse saying, but her words didn't register – until Matisse grabbed her and Tornqvist and threw them to the floor. 'Garrett!' she screeched. 'Get down!' Byson dropped on to the floor.

The noise that followed was one that Tegan hoped never to hear again as long as she lived. It wasn't the sound of the explosion, united with a blinding fireball that consumed the control console. It was a scream, a scream of deep and unendurable pain that reached out from the console and pleaded, begged, beseeched her to help it. It was a cry that issued from beyond time, beyond space, and yet from within Tegan's own mind. It was the TARDIS dying.

As the reverberations died down, Tegan lifted her head from the floor and looked round. And had to do a double take. The glass column was missing; in fact, most of the console was gone, only a few twisted pieces of metal and plastic and scattered shards of glass surrounding the burnt and blackened pedestal that remained.

'That's that then.' She was surprised at how calm her voice sounded.

A creak sounded out, followed by the rending of metal and the snapping of ceramics.

'The ceiling's coming down!' Tornqvist pulled open the door to the interior and frantically waved the others through. 'Get out of here!'

Tegan was the last out. The final thing she saw before the roundelled door shut it out was the white ceiling cracking and breaking into three large slabs which dropped to the floor, the mysterious hexagonal device that had hung from the ceiling hitting the remains of the console with a deafening concussion. Now I'll never know what it does, she thought. The whole horrific scenario was illuminated by the flames that simultaneously erupted through every single roundel. As far as Tegan was concerned, it looked like a vision of hell.

'Any ideas?' She suddenly realized that the Prelector was talking to her.

'Er . . .' But where could they go? The only parts of the TARDIS she had visited were the bedroom annexe, the ill-fated Zero Room – then she remembered the Cloisters. Something about that calm, introspective environment convinced her that they'd be safe there. Indeed, she had often visited the stone chambers late at night, when she needed to mull over the experiences her new lifestyle had subjected her to. Especially when the Mara . . . She forced the image away. 'There is somewhere. I get the feeling that it's quite a way from the centre of the TARDIS.' Tegan managed a superior smile at her deduction: just as the weight of the TARDIS had seemed to bear down on her near the Zero Room, the atmosphere in the Cloister Room had always seemed rarified, as if the grey rock walls were set into a mountain that overlooked the console room far below.

'Then you had better take us there,' Tornqvist looked back at the closed door as another dull thud shook it in its frame, 'and quickly.'

The four of them set off down the corridor at a brisk pace, as Tegan tried to remember the correct route. The trouble was, she had never set off looking for the Cloister Room before, she just sort of ended up there. She stopped the group at a crossroads, and stared down each corridor. 'I'm sure this wasn't here before!' she muttered.

'Admit it: you're lost,' complained Matisse. 'You have no idea where we're going.'

Tegan spun round and grabbed her by the collar of her jumper. 'Listen, Ladygay bloody Matisse! I am sick and tired of your continual, holier-than-thou attitude! If it hadn't been for you, the Exemplar would never have blown up! But no, that wasn't enough for you, was it? No, you had to hijack the TARDIS and get us into this mess!'

With great difficulty, Tornqvist pulled the two women apart. 'Look, I don't care who's fault this is, our priority is to get to safety.'

'I suppose so,' muttered Tegan, taking deep breaths to calm herself down.

'If you want to go somewhere, the TARDIS makes sure you get there,' stated Byson as if it was obvious. And to Tegan, it was. It explained how she had always found the Cloister Room in the past.

The others turned round in unison. 'How did you know that?' asked Matisse.

'It told me,' he replied innocently.

She decided to leave the debriefing till later. 'We should go.'

'This way.' Tegan pointed down the left-hand corridor. 'I think this one –'

The floor bucked as if an earthquake had begun. Behind them, at the distant start of the corridor, a wall of flame had sprung up, a wall that was rapidly churning towards them like a fiery tidal wave.

Tegan looked left and right in rapid succession, trying to decide which option to take. Unfortunately, the decision was made for her. Both corridors vanished, to be replaced by unbroken roundelled walls. With perfect timing, the TARDIS had reconfigured its interior. There was only one option left.

'Run!' she yelled.

The Grid Control Suite was silent. The unholy energies that powered the Crystal Bucephalus, that lit up the Grid's towering time rotor which in turn lit up the room, were only detectable as a mild ionization in the air. With the evacuation of the staff and patrons, there was no one there to observe the Cubiculo in the corner of the wood-panelled suite suddenly flare into life.

No one saw the door open to reveal a tall figure with long blond hair, wearing a pair of striped trousers, a white cricketing jumper and a beige frock coat. And no one was there to help him as he staggered out and fell to the parquet floor.

'Why did you do it?' asked Turlough as the party left the Mezzanine through a huge pair of double doors.

'Do what?' Arrestis muttered absently. They had entered a wide corridor lined with thick beige carpet. Masterpieces hung on the walls, but he wasn't particularly impressed: he had most of the originals back on Hexdane, and those he didn't have were probably in the vaults on Clavidence, so those were his too. Technically.

'Set up the Lazarus Intent,' prompted Turlough. 'It must have taken a lot of time and effort.'

He smiled. 'Money and power, why else?' Why else indeed, he pondered. Immortality and the human ascendancy were also pretty good reasons, but he doubted Turlough would understand that. He was probably one of these bleeding heart liberals who didn't mind sharing the galaxy with reptiles.

'But it seems a pretty complicated way of getting rich,' said Turlough. 'Couldn't you have started a business or something?'

His smile became a laugh. 'A business? What the hell do you think the Lazarus Intent was, eh? I had a team of professionals working for over three years preparing the groundwork. Public relations, seeding the newsnets with my parables and miracles. I predicted disasters – which I arranged, of course – and healed the sick. Then I wrote the Codex, basing most of it on some ancient religious tract that everyone else in the galaxy had long forgotten. I even got the name from it.' He shrugged. 'It was either Lazarus or Jesus Christ, and I decided that Lazarus had a better ring.'

Turlough shook his head. 'I still don't understand. What was so important about the intent part of it?'

Arrestis stopped and stared at him. 'Isn't it obvious? For

eight years, I reaped the rewards of being the new messiah. I had everything and everyone –' he glanced at Monroe '– I wanted. But I was playing for higher and higher stakes. Eventually, I started mixing in very dangerous circles, trading defence secrets with the Sontarans, the Rutans, even the Cybermen.'

Turlough whistled through his teeth. 'High stakes indeed.'

He nodded. 'And I wasn't prepared to pay the price of losing, but the Forbes lab hadn't quite perfected their consciousness transfer program, so I couldn't rely on the immortality I have now.' He slapped his chest proudly. 'This is my fifth body since I arrived in this era. Anyway, eventually I hit upon the time travel angle. I had a pretty good idea that it would be developed eventually; I just didn't realize that it would take five thousand years.'

'We were ever vigilant, my lord,' said Monroe devotedly.

'Indeed: "And the Lazarines shall wait and watch for the doors of time to open," *Magnificat, Act 1, Verse 12*,' he quoted. 'As it turned out, my mission to Sontara was unsuccessful. The Imperator wasn't willing to honour his side of the bargain, and shot me. Lassiter reached back seconds before that and rescued me – and the rest is history.'

Turlough gave a wry smile. 'There's nothing like thinking big, is there?'

Lassiter strode through the open doors of the Legion tank, remembering the moment when he had first brought the Grid on line. He and Ottway had watched proudly as the Legions had reached out into the Vortex, establishing the Grid and marking the technical inauguration of the most exclusive restaurant in the galaxy – the Lassiters' dream. Now Sebby was dead, and he was the prisoner of the ultimate egomaniac. He shuddered. 'This won't take long,' he muttered to Kamelion.

'Time is irrelevant to me, Professor Lassiter. I was designed to serve.'

As he pondered the stone pillars that controlled this particular portion of the Grid, Lassiter also pondered Kamelion's words, convinced that he had missed something important. Returning his attention to the controls, he activated deeply-buried systems that he had hoped would never be needed. With the dimensional stabilizer unbalanced, there was no way for the Bucephalus to safely channel the time spillage being pumped out by the Exemplar. Furthermore, the nature of the Time Vortex was such that the spillage couldn't dissipate quickly enough, leaving it to churn and boil, and eventually, inevitably, feed back into the Grid. There wouldn't be a lot left after the collapsar annihilator was bathed in those sorts of energies.

The spillage buffers were his answer to the once-hypothetical problem of such a situation: a specially attenuated domain of the Vortex which would surround New Alexandria and bleed off the spillage, scattering and diluting it so that it wouldn't cause any problems. He brought up the specs in his mind: at maximum attenuation, the buffers would be more than capable of handling the amounts that Matisse's monumental miscalculation was spewing out.

'There!' he announced theatrically, well aware that his only audience was an indifferent robot. 'Of course!' he yelled, spinning round to face Kamelion.

'Kamelion: morph into me,' he ordered.

For a second nothing happened, and he began to worry that his guess was wrong. Then a cloud of sparkles obscured the cybernetic body before clearing. The tubby figure with cropped hair, ponytail and moustache smiled at him.

'Is that what I look like?' Lassiter mused. 'I ought to lose a little weight.' But it had worked. The android obviously responded to the strongest mind in the vicinity – and Arrestis, with his usual arrogance, had assumed that he could maintain control from a distance. Lassiter bit his bottom lip. That arrogance was going to cost him dearly.

'Keep that form and get back to the *Imperator*. As soon

as you see Arrestis, kill him.' He shivered, half-expecting to be struck down by a thunderbolt.

'Understood. Have you a preferred method of murder?' he said, endowing Lassiter's voice with his own conceited tones.

'No. Just do it. The sooner that bastard is gone, the better. If he leaves here with me, the Union – the whole galaxy – is finished.' Disguised as Lassiter, Kamelion could strike before Arrestis could regain control.

'I can fully appreciate that, Professor. Arrestis's death is best for all concerned.' The false Lassiter turned and paused, before adding: 'All apart from Monsignor Arrestis, that is.'

Lassiter watched as he walked off through the doors. For a second, he considered ordering Kamelion to destroy himself afterwards, to avenge his brother's death. But Kamelion had only been a puppet, a toy. The true murderer was Arrestis. His death would be vengeance enough.

Whenever asked his religious persuasion, Lassiter always said 'Lazarus Intent'. In that case, his orders amounted to deicide, but it was something he should have done a long, long time ago.

The wall of flame was only feet behind them, and Tornqvist could feel the heat singeing the back of his neck. Even though he prided himself on his physical fitness, he knew he couldn't run much further.

'In here!' screamed Tegan, throwing open the first door they came to and diving through. Byson was the last in; he slammed the door shut and leant against it, panting.

'Will the door hold?' shouted Matisse.

'We must pray it does,' replied Tornqvist. 'As Saint Clavis said when the Peloris besieged the Minarets of Khnum –'

He stopped in mid-parable as the whistling, crackling noise from the corridor reached a crescendo, and touched his Inf, mouthing a silent prayer. He wasn't ready to die: his confession, his dreadful, blasphemous confession, had not yet been taken, and without that final act of faith, he was condemned. He closed his eyes and prepared for the journey to his very own hell.

'It's okay, Sven.' Tegan was tugging at his sleeve. 'It's passed.' Even as she spoke, a deafening explosion reverberated from some distance away. 'I think we got away with it that time.'

He forced himself to smile at her, but he didn't feel relieved. His death was inevitable, and so were the eternal consequences. 'Where are we?' he said softly.

Matisse was scanning their surroundings like a bird of prey. 'Wonderful, another corridor,' she groaned. 'Is it much further, Tegan?'

'I – I don't know. Your son's the expert.'

'The TARDIS isn't very well,' said Byson. 'It's very sorry, but it can't be as helpful as it normally is.'

'That's the second time you've said something like that, Garrett. Are you in communication with the TARDIS?' asked Matisse.

He looked nonplussed. 'Of course I am. Aren't you?'

'I think your son should lead the way, don't you?' suggested the Prelector. 'If he can hear this ship, perhaps he can lead us to safety.'

'A good idea.' Tegan frowned. 'The Doctor always referred to the TARDIS as if it was alive, but, well, I never really took much notice.'

'Well, I suggest we take a bit of notice now. Garrett: where do we go?' Matisse patted him on the forearm in reassurance.

He shut his eyes for a second, cocking his head as he did so. It reminded Tornqvist of a steward contacting the webwork. After a lengthy pause, he looked up. 'The next door on the right. If we go through that room, it'll lead us towards . . . towards somewhere not so dangerous.' He smiled. 'Was that all right?'

Matisse smiled warmly, and Tornqvist was shocked to detect evidence of maternal feelings in the woman. Perhaps there was hope for her yet.

'Come along, then.' Matisse grabbed her son's arm, and

the two of them made their way down the corridor, followed by Tegan and the Prelector.

After about thirty seconds, Byson pointed at an unremarkable white door complete with roundel and steel grip. 'In here,' he said, pulling it open.

They all stared. Even Tornqvist's jaw dropped.

The room appeared to have no ceiling. If it did have one, it was so far above them as to be invisible. But that was not what had drawn their attention. The room's most impressive feature — features — were its walls. Two of them that formed a corridor that extended to a vanishing point possibly miles away. The walls were bookshelves, bookshelves miles high and miles long, containing enough books for a thousand civilizations. Thin brass ladders ran up the shelves at regular intervals.

Matisse turned to the others. 'I could stay here for ever,' she whispered, overawed. 'The library of the Time Lords.'

'Nice idea, Ladygay, but the TARDIS is about to go castors up,' Tegan pointed out. 'Byson has told us that we need to go through here, not spend our time browsing.'

'Hold on; this isn't an ordinary library.' Matisse was pointing to one of the shelves. Tornqvist followed her indication, and was fascinated to see a new book materializing between two others, making a tiny TARDIS noise. The books on either side didn't seem to move; it was as if the room itself had extended to fit the new addition. A miracle worthy of Lazarus, he mused, but was forced to step back to allow Matisse to snatch it from the shelf almost before it had solidified. Tornqvist was fascinated to note that the leather was already covered in a fine layer of dust.

'The Search for the Double Nexus — the Collected Works of Ernst Findecker: 4912–5010,' Matisse read from the spine. 'Required reading at the Academia Scholastica. How not to make a time machine.' Matisse tried to open the book, only to discover that the whole thing was a fake: the case opened to reveal a single cube resting on a velvet cushion that filled the interior. 'What magnificent artifice: archaic books containing out-dated trionic lattices —'

'Ladygay.' Byson tugged at her sleeve. 'The TARDIS says that we should hurry. It can't hold out for much longer.'

'If only I hadn't started this blasted machine! I could have explored this library . . .' She trailed off. 'You're right.'

The four of them assumed a brisk pace between the imposing walls of words. 'Garrett?' asked Tornqvist.

'Yes, Your Grace?' He turned without breaking step.

'Do you know where the TARDIS wants us to go?'

He frowned before replying. 'It says that this is a short-cut to a faraway place where we'll be safest.'

'Safest?' That didn't sound particularly safe.

'I think the TARDIS is pretty sure it's going to die.'

That makes two of us, thought Tornqvist. Divine retribution for both time machines and blaspheming prelectors. Lost in his despair, he didn't notice Matisse lagging behind.

Lassiter spent the walk from the Legion tank with the irrational conviction that Arrestis or Kamelion was about to jump out from behind a Cubiculo. But he finally reached the Grid Control Suite without incident. If everything had gone according to plan, the patrons were shunting away from New Alexandria as fast as their ships could take them. He sincerely hoped so: what he was about to do should disable the Grid permanently, but it might also blow the place sky-high. He carried on working out the commands necessary to complete his task.

But when he entered the Suite, his calculations and algorithms evaporated as he saw the prone figure slumped by the Cubiculo. He recognized the Doctor immediately. He ran over and checked for a pulse. Thankfully, he was merely unconscious, his twin hearts beating strongly.

'Doctor, wake up!' He slapped the Time Lord around the face, gently at first, but soon he found himself beginning to vent his pent-up anger on him. 'You've got to wake up! Arrestis can't be far behind —' As he reached out to administer another slap, the Doctor's hand grabbed his arm in a steel grip.

'That's quite enough of that, if you don't mind.' The Doctor looked at him as if he was trying to remember who he was. 'Ah yes, Professer Lassiter.' He sprang to his feet. 'Alex.'

Lassiter was slightly puzzled by the change of clothes, but decided to say nothing. 'Are you all right?'

He patted himself. 'Everything seems to be in the right place. The last thing I remember is being in the Exemplar.' Something obviously hit him. 'Tegan and the others! Where are they?'

'Hellenica's here, so is Arrestis. But Tegan –'

'But the Exemplar locked on to the signal.' His tone changed to one of inquiry. 'Where's my TARDIS?'

Lassiter had completely forgotten about the box skipping through the Vortex. 'I saw it earlier: it was heading for the Bucephalus.' He was having trouble following the Doctor's train of thought. What did the TARDIS have to do with anything?

The Doctor slapped himself across the forehead. 'Prince of fools!' he shouted.

'What is it?'

'I'm an imbecile. I stupidly assumed that the signal that the Exemplar had locked on to was the Bucephalus. But if the TARDIS was in the Vortex, *between* the Exemplar and the Bucephalus . . .' He frowned. 'Can you magnify that?' He pointed towards the hologram of the Vortex that still hovered in front of the pillar. Still confused, Lassiter moved over to the console and brought up an even more detailed picture of the Vortex.

They both froze when they saw it, their training in the temporal arts allowing them to experience the true horror of the holographic image. The time spillage from the Exemplar was still flowing into the unbalanced Grid. That was to be expected. But the Grid wasn't bleeding it off to the spillage buffers as Lassiter had planned: the swirling patterns around New Alexandria were a clear and worrying indication that the spillage was still increasing.

'If I'm not very much mistaken, the build-up of time spillage is well above the capacity of the Bucephalus: 3.1 on the Bocca scale and rising.'

Lassiter gave him an extremely supercilious look. 'I'm well aware of the Bucephalus's capabilities, Doctor, but why isn't the spillage being vented to the buffers?' It looked as if the deeper green of the spillage was being drawn to a spot half-way between the Bucephalus, a spot where it seemed to darken even further.

The Doctor stepped forward and extended a finger towards the hologram, pointing at the spot. 'Magnify this,' he ordered.

Lassiter complied, stepping back from the console to observe the results.

The time spillage wasn't being vented to the buffers because it wasn't reaching them. Instead, it was being drawn to a tiny double cube which appeared to be soaking it up like a temporal sponge. A blue double cube with panelled doors.

'The TARDIS,' whispered the Doctor.

As if on cue, all eight windows shattered outwards, great gouts of plasma streaming into the Vortex. At the same time, the pulsing white light on the roof exploded in a rapidly expanding fireball. The Doctor grimaced as if he were wracked by pain.

'So there you have it,' Lassiter heard himself saying. 'Your TARDIS is attracting all the excess spillage, bottling it up like a champagne cork.'

The Doctor's pale face grew even paler. 'Even the TARDIS has its limits, Alex. Unfortunately for the Crystal Bucephalus, those limits are orders of magnitude greater than those of the Grid.

'When the pressure gets too much, the TARDIS will explode. And the combination of that with the instantaneous release of pent-up spillage will not only destroy New Alexandria, but most of this galaxy as well.'

Fourteen

'The whole galaxy?' Lassiter was quiet as his mind whirled around the Doctor's words.

'At least,' said the Doctor. His tone was cold and logical. 'The entire fabric of the Vortex will be torn apart. Without the Vortex, the space-time continuum loses its support. The galaxy will simply drop out of reality.'

Lassiter was desperately trying to hold back the panic. 'What can we do about it? Can we get to your TARDIS?'

The Doctor shook his head. 'Trying to establish a gate would be both foolhardy and potentially suicidal, Professor. The Vortex is too unstable.'

The truth hit him. 'For Lazarus's sake, Doctor, do something!'

The Doctor grabbed him by his waistcoat, his calm facade disintegrating utterly. 'It's because of Lazarus that we're in this mess!' he shouted.

'You knew?'

'Isn't it obvious?' The Doctor released Lassiter and put his hands together, interlacing his fingers, building up his barriers once again. 'Professor Arrestis and his genetic research? I was stranded in the sixty-third century for five years, Alex, a time period before the Sontarans conveniently blew up the Tersurus Institute. I managed to get hold of their research papers. I recognized Arrestis in a hologram of the research team.'

Lassiter suddenly remembered. 'He's got Hellenica and Turlough. They're waiting for me and Kamelion to turn up.'

'Turlough?' The Doctor sighed with relief. 'He's still

alive . . .' He pouted. 'Kamelion? What's he doing out and about?'

'You know about the android?'

'A little. But he was supposed to stay in the TARDIS.'

Lassiter gulped. He'd assumed that the android was one of Arrestis's toys. He didn't feel so comfortable knowing that he'd turned one of the Doctor's companions into an assassin. 'I've sent him to kill Arrestis.'

'You've done what?' The Doctor stared at him in horror. 'But that's the worst thing you could have done!'

Arrestis sighed with impatience. Where the hell was Lassiter? He passed a few moments looking around the docking bay. When the *Imperator* had landed, the enormous, featureless hangar had been packed with shuntships from a multitude of civilizations. Now the place was empty, proof that the evacuation of the Bucephalus was complete. Empty, save for the single ship that he was standing in front of: the *Imperator*, one hundred feet of burnished chrome shaped in a flattened cylinder with a sharpened prow.

'Ah, Professor!' Lassiter was striding towards him, his face impassive. 'I was beginning to think you didn't love me anymore.'

The temporal scientist said nothing, and simply kept walking. As he reached the open door of the yacht, Arrestis stepped aside to let him pass.

And Lassiter vanished in a fountain of glitter, his body growing and rearranging into an eight-foot tall creature that combined all of Arrestis's greatest fears. It was a reptile, and his hatred of all cold-blooded life erupted as he was confronted by an amalgam of all he loathed about them: soulless, scaly abominations that sought to replace humanity with their inhuman existence. By denouncing his Draconian and Martian disciples in the Codex, he had hoped that the Intent would have done the job for him, but that hadn't happened – they were everywhere, in the Union, in the Elective, even in the Intent. Now one of them was looming over him.

It lunged towards him with foot-long talons, grasping his neck, raking his skin. Fetid breath assaulted his senses, and he fought to stop vomiting at the same time as he gasped for air. Just before his mind was completely overwhelmed, he realized.

'Kamelion!' he screamed. 'Freeze!' Just as he thought he was going to choke, the huge reptile stopped. And then it shrank, the scales lightening to blue-silver, the lizard leer becoming a mask of near-humanity.

Arrestis never thought that he'd be pleased to see an android, but Kamelion was virtually a friendly face. He waited for his breathing to return to normal before speaking. 'I take it Lassiter sent you here?'

'Who else? He is the only person left on New Alexandria apart from the occupants of your yacht. Not forgetting —'

'Yes, yes. Where is he?'

'I believe he was returning to the Grid Control Suite. From what I could ascertain from his mental patterns, he was attempting to dismantle the Bucephalus Grid.'

Arrestis growled. 'Won't that idiot ever learn? Even if he tears this place apart atom by atom, all the knowledge is still inside that bloated head of his. And if he won't cooperate willingly . . .' Arrestis savoured the vision of Lassiter as a drooling imbecile, his intelligence sitting in a vat of cyber-nucleic proteins: perhaps he should have done that in the first place. 'It was a stupid idea to let you wander off with him anyway.' Arrestis finally realized where he had heard about Kamelions before. 'I never understood why you were designed like that in the first place.'

'Because,' said Kamelion in his superior manner, 'the domination radius of one of my creator's minds is eight point four light years. About a hundred trillion times greater than yours.'

Arrestis raised an eyebrow. 'But I'm the messiah of a religion worshipped by eight quadrillion people. Slightly more than your makers ever achieved.' He pointed to the *Imperator*. 'Get them out. We're going on a little journey.'

'Might I suggest I assume a more threatening form?'

Arrestis shrugged. 'As long as it isn't reptilian.'

'The Sculti would be a wise choice.' Kamelion surrounded himself with a cloud of light before reforming. Arrestis had never heard of the Sculti, and he wasn't impressed. 'That's supposed to be threatening?' he laughed. Although the creature was a seven-foot-tall humanoid, its arms, legs and torso were only an inch wide, with a vestigial head without features, and it was salmon pink all over.

It held up one of its hands; four eight-inch fingers writhed like snakes. 'The Sculti generate a bio-electric energy field which is capable of disrupting the neural flow of the human brain. Death is instantaneous.'

'I suppose that's threatening enough. Go and get the others.'

They'd been walking through the library for ten minutes, but the other end didn't seem any nearer, and the background roar was growing ever closer, a drone that was increasingly punctuated by distant explosions. Matisse kept calm by remembering where she was: the ultimate repository of all knowledge.

'There's still no guarantee that we'll be safe when we get to the other side.' Tornqvist's cynicism was fermenting into pure, unadulterated pessimism.

'Look!' Tegan pointed ahead. An end, a doorway, was now clearly visible, as if the TARDIS was desperately trying to alter its internal dimensions to help them.

Matisse remembered the way the crossroads had vanished, and decided it was more likely to be another random rearrangement. Thankfully, no one noticed that she was hanging back, surreptitiously pocketing books with titles such as *The Symbiotic Nucleus: Rassilon's Triumph* and *The Triple Helix: The Inheritance of Rassilon*. Books that encapsulated the majesty and wisdom of Gallifrey. Books that would give her the scientific glory that she craved.

The others had increased their pace towards the door that lay ahead. Suddenly the floor began to vibrate, its frequency increasing rapidly. Tegan grabbed on to the nearest bookshelf to steady herself, but Byson and the Prelector weren't so fortunate: both of them lost their footing and fell backwards. Matisse, who had been reaching up for another book, hooked her arm round one of the brass ladders to steady herself; she refused to give up on the book.

'Things are getting serious,' said Tegan.

The Prelector was helping Byson to his feet. 'This place isn't going to last much longer. Time to make a run for it.'

Matisse was still dawdling behind, still snatching books. *Build Your Own TARDIS* was unmissable.

They reached the door. Tegan tugged at it, but it failed to open. 'It's locked!' she yelled.

'I sincerely hope not.' Tornqvist added his weight, tugging at the steel grip, but stood aside for Byson.

'Let me.' Grabbing the grip in his huge hand, he yanked: the door flew open, revealing a large empty room. Tegan gripped Tornqvist's arm and pulled him through. Byson followed.

Matisse's gaze alighted on a burgundy-bound volume on the next shelf up, one whose gold letters proclaimed it as *A Basic Primer in Block Transfer Computation, by Lady Jennikatrakaleyna*. She climbed a few rungs up the ladder and leaned over, but the book resisted her grip.

'For Christ's sake, Matisse, leave it!' yelled Tegan. 'We've got to get out of here.'

'A few more seconds . . .' The book was finally coming free.

The library flipped over as the TARDIS reconfigured itself. The shelves that she had been climbing up were now the ceiling. Matisse wrapped her ankles around the ladder, trying to keep horizontal, but, as she concentrated on that, the book fell from her grip and dropped to the floor. She instinctively watched its descent. The other set of shelves had become the floor, but the reconfiguration meant that it was now hundreds of feet below, and she shuddered as she heard the book's impact. If she lost her

261

grip on the ladder, she wouldn't stand a chance. She swallowed, aware of the perspiration dripping from her forehead.

Tegan was leaning through the door, the top of which was five feet below the new ceiling, twenty feet away. 'Hang on!' she called out.

'What do you think I'm doing?' Matisse replied, aware that the fear was obvious in her voice. She increased her grip on the ladder. 'You've got to help me!'

Tegan turned to Tornqvist. 'What do you suggest?'

He touched Arrestis's Inf around his throat. 'We pray that Matisse can climb.'

The Doctor gazed at the Grid's time rotor, its brilliant core brighter than ever. 'We haven't got much time. Have you got any suggestions?'

Lassiter shrugged. 'I did have a plan to dismantle the Grid. I had hoped that disconnecting the temporal substructure would help matters.'

The Doctor rubbed his chin. 'So you thought that by removing New Alexandria's time field, the spillage would disperse. Nice idea: unfortunately, the time field is governed by Erkulon's Eighth Precept. By the time the field dissipates, this planet and most of this constellation will have become a large number of free-floating quarks on the time winds.'

Lassiter scowled. 'I had worked that one out.' He pointed an accusing finger. 'You're the Time Lord. You get us out of it.'

'Might I remind you, Professor Lassiter, that you built this place. I do not take kindly to being dragged in to sort things out when they get beyond your capacity to control.' His voice was rising. 'Thanks to you and your tangled love life, one of my companions is being held hostage by a thug with delusions of godhead, another is his assassin, while the other – and my TARDIS – are stranded in the Time Vortex on the brink of destruction. And you expect to abdicate your responsibility to me?'

Lassiter's reply was arctic. 'Who paid for all of this in

the first place? Whose ultimate responsibility is the Crystal Bucephalus anyway?'

'The Doctor's, I hope.' Arrestis was leaning against the doorframe, tapping his *jablecta* against his palm. Monroe stood next to him, devotion written all over her face. Behind them, Turlough looked seriously annoyed, as a Sculti, presumably Kamelion, held a foot-long pink finger to his temple. Lassiter was well aware of what a Sculti finger was capable of.

'I should have killed you myself,' Lassiter muttered.

'You're welcome to try.' He moved into the Grid Control Suite. 'It doesn't look like you've done much dismantling.'

'I haven't.' A deep boom distracted him. Instinctively he looked out of the window and realized that the noise had been thunder. Lightning was playing around the statue, brilliant arcs striking the horse like electric arrows. A full-scale thunderstorm was in progress in the domed ceiling of the Crystal Bucephalus. It was even trying to rain.

'Ionization around the statue, my lord,' said Monroe. 'I think we ought to get out of here while we still can.'

'Not without our friend here.' He gave Lassiter a quizzical look. 'Well, Alex? Are you ready to leave?'

'Look at the hologram. If you don't understand it, I'm sure your disciple can interpret,' he said bitterly, indicating Monroe. 'When this place goes, it'll take most of the galaxy with it; that includes Hexdane *and* Clavidence. You won't be much use as head of the Elective or Heir to Saint Clavis's Chair then, will you?'

A flash of panic appeared in Arrestis's eyes. 'Stop it.'

Lassiter's voice simply dripped incredulity. 'Stop it? What the hell do you think I'm trying to do? The Crystal Bucephalus is now the biggest bomb in history: do you really think I want to be on top of it?' He stormed up to Arrestis and grabbed him by the jacket. 'Five thousand years ago, you created a religion which has evolved into the only thing which is holding this galaxy together, Arrestis. A religion based on fellowship, on respect; on love. And here's the mythical Lazarus: a two-bit thug whose idea of a relationship lies between the sheets. All you want to do is suck whatever you can out of five millennia of faith. Forget about the quadrillions of people who live their lives around the return of Lazarus: just come back and take everything they've got!'

'Who brought me back then, Alex? Who fulfilled the Lazarus Intent?'

Lassiter's anger was unquenchable. 'Don't you dare try to blame it on me. Thanks to your desire for immortality and Matisse's hatred of me, this place is about to destroy everything. That's the true Lazarus Intent.'

Arrestis stabbed a finger at the Doctor. 'Oh no, Alex, I can't take all the blame. He built this place. His money lies behind it. Blood money.'

'Me?' The Doctor looked surprised that he was being drawn into the argument.

'Yes you! A dilettante Time Lord who decides to have a bit of fun. Well, look where your fun has got us all. I thought your lot had laws against this sort of thing?'

The Doctor walked forward and grabbed Arrestis by the throat, lifting him off the ground. He managed to grunt for Kamelion, but a single look from the Doctor froze the android in place. Turlough took advantage of the fact and moved out of reach.

'I am a Time Lord, yes; and I have broken their laws, a transgression that my peers tried and sentenced me for. But I have served that sentence, Arrestis. You are an abomination to me, a creature that betrays his fellow man for the lure of power.' Lassiter could see the fire in his eyes. 'I've lived a long time, Arrestis, and I've faced tyrants and dictators that would leave you in the nursery. But I still remember the words of my tutor, Borusa: "Power over others detracts from yourself. Absolute power over others means you have no power over yourself." I have been offered absolute power, Arrestis, more power than you could possibly imagine.' He dropped him to the floor where he collapsed, rubbing his throat and trying to breathe. 'I rejected that power, but you: your aims are obvious. You want control of the galaxy.' The Doctor snapped his fingers. 'And, of course, protection around Sontara, circa 6211. Am I right?'

Arrestis leapt to his feet, *jablecta* in his hand. 'Time Lord or not, no one treats me like that!'

He fired.

Matisse's arms were trembling with the strain of hanging on to the ladder. 'I can't hold on much longer.' Tegan couldn't help feeling sorry for her; she obviously wasn't used to being in a situation over which she had no control.

Tornqvist was leaning as far into the library as he could, with Byson's arm round his waist to prevent him from falling. 'Let go of the ladder with your ankles, then start swinging. You should build up enough momentum to be able to reach the next ladder. I can reach you from there.'

'I'm a temporal scientist, not a gymnast!' she exclaimed.

'It's your only hope,' Tegan pointed out. 'For all we know, the library could disappear completely any second.'

'All right.' She tightened her hands around the ladder and moved her ankles from their lock around the lower rungs. She grunted in pain as she tried to maintain her grip, swaying slightly as she hung there.

'Start swinging,' Tornqvist instructed, moving even further into the library and reaching out his hand.

Matisse moved backwards and forwards in faster and faster arcs.

'Now!'

She let go with her right hand and propelled herself towards the next ladder. For a second, Tegan was afraid that she wasn't going to make it, but she sighed in relief as Matisse grasped the ladder with white knuckles.

'Try to reach my hand, Ladygay,' said Tornqvist reassuringly. 'I won't let you fall.'

'I'm glad to hear it,' she said nervously. She gripped the rung even tighter with her left hand, and tentatively unclenched the other. She groaned, but didn't slip.

'Now reach out.' Tornqvist's arm was at full stretch, but his fingers were still inches away from Matisse. 'Further!'

'I . . . can't . . .' she gasped.

And then the library simply fell away, and Byson had to drag Tornqvist back from the glittering blue void that now lay beyond the doorway to stop him falling in. Tegan recognized the void from her escape from Ruath's TAR-DIS – the Time Vortex. The TARDIS was coming apart at the seams, and this was part of the stitching. She touched the Prelector's sleeve. 'Ladygay?' she whispered.

He shook his head slowly, and stared through the doorway. The huge bulk of the library had dwindled into the sparkling azure distance. Then it was gone.

Byson was sitting on the floor, transfixed by the void. He looked up, his eyes wet with tears. 'Ladygay's gone, isn't she?'

Tornqvist laid his hand on Byson's shoulder. 'I'm afraid so.'

Byson swallowed and stood up. 'We have to hurry. There isn't very long.'

Tegan narrowed her eyes. 'It may have escaped your notice, gentlemen, but this room doesn't appear to have any exits.'

The room was about thirty feet square, with the ubiquitously roundelled walls. The only distinguishing feature was a thick white pillar with a sloping hexagonal base that stood in the exact centre. 'Garrett: have you any idea where we're supposed to go now?' Tornqvist looked extremely nervous. Clearly he shared Tegan's worries: had they escaped through the library and lost Matisse, only to be trapped in a room with no doors?

Byson sucked a finger and frowned. 'Ermmm . . .'

A frighteningly close detonation shook the floor, forcing Tornqvist to grab the pillar for support. 'Could you hurry things along a bit? That sounded nearer than I would have preferred.'

'Too right,' added Tegan. 'We can't have long left.'

'Over there.' Byson pointed to the wall that faced the ill-fated library.

As far as Tegan was concerned, it was nothing but a blank wall, but Byson was already dragging her over. Tornqvist trotted along behind. The three of them reached the solid wall of roundels.

'Yes?' said Tegan impatiently. 'Open sesame or what?'

Byson screwed his face up in concentration. The entire wall dematerialized. Not for the first time since their escape from the console room, Tegan and Tornqvist gasped.

'Not very clever, Arrestis. The *jablecta* is a beautifully vicious weapon, but certain forms of radiation do have a tendency to temporarily scramble its delicate circuitry.' The Doctor gave him a superior smile. 'For example, did you ever wonder why the Antonine rescue raid on Scultiis in 9381 failed? I believe it had something to do with the ambient radiation produced by its inhabitants. When the raiding party attacked the village where the hostages were being held, they discovered that their *jablectas* were nothing more than useless lumps of metal. Rather unfortunate, don't you think?'

'You cybernetic judas!' Arrestis spun round and grabbed the false Sculti by its pipecleaner neck. 'You knew that would happen. That's why you suggested this form, isn't it?'

'It is a dangerous habit to finger armed disruptors in the pocket of one's jacket, *Monsignor* Arrestis.' A salmon-pink hand shot out and grabbed the disruptor that he was reaching for inside his jacket. Although it was Kamelion's voice, Lassiter was convinced that the words were coming from, well, elsewhere.

The Doctor stepped forward. 'This posturing is all getting rather pointless, isn't it?' A deep rumble of thunder counterpointed the flash of lightning from the Mezzanine. 'I suggest we try to sort this situation out before the unthinkable happens.'

Arrestis sighed. It was clear that he knew when to give up. Unarmed and overpowered, he did the only sensible thing. He made a run for it.

'Kamelion!' barked the Doctor, but Lassiter got the impression that the true orders were given in quite another way.

The android shimmered and expanded, forming the grey mushroom shape of a Gubbage Cone with tentacles flailing in all directions, including that of the fleeing crime boss. Arrestis tripped and hit the marble floor.

Turlough was closest. 'He's unconscious.' He prised the *jablecta* from Arrestis's limp grip and began to slip it into his jacket pocket. Then he caught the Doctor's disapproving glance, and handed it over without a word.

'Keep an eye on him,' Lassiter ordered. The next words hurt. A lot. 'And on her.' He pointed at Monroe. 'She can't be trusted.'

The Doctor was leaning over the console. Lassiter was intrigued to see that he wasn't intently studying the readouts; instead, he seemed to be staring at the time rotor.

'Doctor?'

'What?' He looked surprised. 'What were you saying?'

'How long have we got before the TARDIS is –'

'Destroyed?' His words were icy cold. 'According to your sensors, spillage has reached 8.1 Bocca in the vicinity of the TARDIS. Her design parameters give 7 as the ultimate limit.'

'So why hasn't she blown up?' It was Monroe, using very little tact.

The Doctor raised an eyebrow. 'My TARDIS is a little more sophisticated than most others of her ilk and she's doing a very good job of resisting the spillage. Unfortunately . . .' He sucked through his teeth. 'Unfortunately, even she has her limits. We can't have more than another fifteen minutes.' He suddenly placed a hand on his chest. 'She's not going meekly, though. Definitely raging against the dying of the light,' he gasped.

'So let's get a move on.' Monroe moved over to the console. 'Alex?'

Lassiter ignored the twisting knife of emotion. Maybe she couldn't be trusted; but he needed her, and still loved her. 'Well, Hellenica, Doctor? A gaggle of time scientists: if anybody can do something, it's us.' He cracked his knuckles. 'Let's get to work.'

'I never realized.' Tegan stepped on to the balcony, a balcony which overlooked a sight that brought home the sheer size of the TARDIS. The view stretched for miles in all directions, so far that the distant reaches were lost. She looked back at the door they had come through, but it had vanished. And then she realized that it wasn't a balcony — it was a circular platform hundreds of feet above — above what? She no longer felt that she was inside: from the platform, the TARDIS looked like a city, with huge Corinthian columns that must have been hundreds of feet in diameter thrusting up from between the massive white domes. The featureless domes, thousands of them, were interlinked by snaking white corridors, and she could only assume that she was looking at some sort of representation of the TARDIS interior. It reminded her of some ancient film she had watched as a child, the city of Atlantis before it fell. She tried to banish the idea. Following the upward direction of the columns, Tegan strained her neck to see where they went. But they all vanished thousands of feet above in a boiling mass of grey and black cloud.

'This is unbelievable,' murmured Tornqvist.

'This isn't the safe place you mentioned, by any chance?' Tegan asked Byson.

Byson rubbed his beard. 'The TARDIS says it is.'

'Great!' said Tegan. 'We're stuck on a parapet over-looking the TARDIS's death-throes —' She broke off as one of the domes exploded, the resultant fireball soaring into the air in an incandescent mushroom cloud. The pillar that stood next to the now-gutted dome slowly toppled over, smashing into a line of more domes and shattering them like eggs. But they did not go quietly: simultaneously, all eight of them detonated like a string of titanic hand grenades, the shock vibrating the platform on which Byson, Tornqvist and Tegan stood. All three of them dropped to the white floor, their hands over their ears.

As the aftershocks abated, Tornqvist raised his head and looked at Byson.

'So, Garrett: this is the safest part of the TARDIS?'

He sniffed. 'It's the last place that will be destroyed, Your Grace.'

Tegan tried to hold back her panic. 'A ringside view of a TARDIS dying. All my birthdays have come at once.'

Another dome burst into flames.

Fifteen

'What about trying to regenerate the crystal matrix?' asked Monroe, staring through the window at the rearing horse as it scintillated with the reflections of a dozen lightning bolts. A faint mist was rising as the rainfall from the thundercloud evaporated off the crystal surface.

'Not possible,' said Lassiter. 'Once the pentafluorate denatures, it's useless. The Crystal Bucephalus is nothing more than a fifty-foot paperweight.'

'Not quite. There's still a lot of spillage throughput.' The Doctor pointed at one of the brass dials on the control panel. 'Look.'

Monroe peered at the dial and confirmed that the Grid systems were registering a considerable amount of spillage being converted into harmless electro-magnetic energy. 'I don't think the horse denatured quite as much as you thought it did.'

Lassiter assumed an expression of childlike amazement, and, for a second, Monroe was reminded of their honeymoon on the idyllic shores of Lake Tianca. A groan interrupted her reverie. Arrestis was regaining consciousness, sitting in one of the burgundy leather chairs under Kamelion's close scrutiny.

'I should have checked this when I first suspected the imbalance,' said Lassiter as he pouted at the results, the pout suddenly turning into a broad grin. 'Decrystallization began, and then stopped again. The whole left flank is denatured, but the rest is unaffected. That's why the throughput is interrupted,' he yelled. Monroe remembered that sort of enthusiasm; those glory, glory days.

271

'Although only twenty per cent is useless, it's interrupting the flow. If we could excise the flank . . .' Lassiter scratched his moustache. 'What do you think, Doctor?'

The Time Lord shook his head. 'Dichronimide pentafluoride cleaves too easily. The first incision would shatter the entire statue.'

'And then we might as well nail ourselves into our coffins and be done with it – the spillage would vent directly into the generators.' He gave a low growl. 'We're running out of time. From the look of these readings, we can't even get a ship into shuntspace any more.' He slammed the console. 'We must be able to do something!'

'I agree,' said the Doctor, staunching his outburst. 'Standing here, surrounded by the most advanced time machine in the galaxy. Of course! I knew I'd forgotten something!' It was the Doctor's turn to shout. 'The Crystal Bucephalus isn't a time machine at all, is it?'

'I don't –'

'Of course you do, Alex, of course you do. Before you added all these bells and whistles, the Bucephalus was nothing more than a temporal projector.' He paused. 'I want you to disconnect the Navigus.'

Lassiter's jaw dropped. 'Disconnect it?'

'The improvements, yes.' He closed his eyes. 'You have eight minutes.'

'Eight . . .' Lassiter began to argue, but obviously thought better of it. He set off for the doors at a run.

'Diva,' snapped Arrestis. 'Before Lassiter can throw a spanner in the works, I want you to activate a time gate. A *real* time gate.'

'Don't be ridiculous,' countered the Doctor. 'The Time Vortex is in no fit state to be penetrated.'

Arrestis ignored him. 'Thanks to Lassiter's delaying tactics, I haven't got a hope in hell of getting the *Imperator* off this damned planet.'

'And I doubt that all this time spillage is conducive to Forbes radiation,' muttered the Doctor.

'Trust you to realize that,' he sneered. 'Okay, Doctor,

you've made your point. I just don't fancy my consciousness being scrambled before it reaches the next clone.'

'Sounds like an improvement,' murmured Turlough.

Arrestis turned to Monroe. 'Well, Diva? I am your
Lord and Saviour.'

'Very well, my lord.' She turned to the Doctor. 'Help
me establish the gate,' she ordered.

The Doctor shook his head. 'You heard what I said,
Hellenica. We cannot establish a gate – the Vortex is too
unstable.'

'You're a Time Lord. You must have a few tricks up
your sleeve.' She bent down and pulled a thin wand from
her boot. 'Don't you?' She aimed the bore laser at his
chest. 'I doubt even a Time Lord could survive a hole in
the hearts.'

The Doctor narrowed his eyes. 'When you put it like
that . . .' He leant over the console. 'If we ramp up the
frequency, we should be able to penetrate the Vortex at a
level well below the surface turbulence. Although there is
still almost a ten per cent chance of premature gate
collapse.' He began typing into the brass keyboard.

'Which means a ninety per cent chance of success; odds
I'm prepared to take, Doctor.' Arrestis smiled at Monroe.
'Do this for me, Diva, and you'll be the first saint to be
canonized after I take Saint Clavis's Chair.'

Monroe looked downwards in respect. 'My lord
honours me.'

'Yes, I know. I'll expect you and Lassiter on Hexdane
within two days. Understood?' Arrestis stood from the
chair.

'I live to serve you, my lord.' She joined the Doctor at
the console. 'I'll enter the coordinates.'

Arrestis stepped over to the console and snatched
Lassiter's datacube from its port. 'I might need this. Now,
get a move on.'

'I really can't guarantee the gate's integrity for more
than three seconds,' protested the Doctor. 'So I suggest
you make yourself ready, Lord Lazarus.' The sarcasm was
clear.

'Thank you for your concern.' He walked over to the Cubiculo in the corner of the Suite.

'Think nothing of it. I save the lives of false prophets every day.'

'I'd canonize you, Doctor, but then it would be difficult for me to order my followers – all my followers – to hunt you down like a dog,' he sneered. 'As soon as I reach Hexdane, I'm going to issue orders to ensure that you are killed on sight. I'd order Diva to do it, but I get the feeling that you're all going to be a little busy for the foreseeable future. If you do manage to save the day, I'd advise you to avoid this time zone, and the years that follow. I'll make sure you burn in hell – my own particular hell – for the trouble you've caused me.'

The Doctor didn't react. 'What if I collapse the gate? Or mis-set the coordinates? I'm sure that even the vaunted Lazarus couldn't rise again from the core of a supernova.'

'True, Doctor: that pushes even my cloning expertise to the limit. But Diva will make sure you don't do anything like that, won't you, my dear?'

Monroe gave a shocked look. 'I would protect your life with my own, my lord.'

'As I thought. Activate the gate.'

Monroe pressed the button. Behind Arrestis, the Cubiculo lit up in a flare of blue-white radiance. With a cheery wave, he jumped through.

'He's made it.' She looked up from the console. 'Max is back where he belongs.'

The Doctor stared at her curiously. 'Do you intend following him? With Lassiter?'

Monroe smiled, but it was a smile of triumph and relief. 'You must be joking.'

'I don't understand.'

'You will.' Monroe waved at the console. 'Alex should be shutting down the Navigus just about now.' Deep inside, a thousand mixed emotions were churning and boiling, but the Crystal Bucephalus – and the fate of the galaxy – took priority. Considering what she'd done, it was the least she could do.

'Excellent.' The Doctor turned to the others. 'Turlough? Kamelion? I have a little job for you.'

'How much longer do you think we've got?' Tegan had just seen another clutch of domes ignite, bringing three more pillars crashing to the ground.

'I'm having trouble talking to the TARDIS,' muttered Byson. 'It's very ill.'

'We're going to die.' Tornqvist's voice was cold, inevitable. 'This is it.' He looked at Tegan. 'Will you accept my confession, Tegan?' he implored. 'I can't face my God without it.'

She looked at him in disbelief. 'You really are the life and soul of the party, aren't you?'

'I'm serious. Confessing on the death-bed prevents secrets going to the grave. It's a fundamental part of the Lazarus Intent.'

'Okay; it's just that I don't feel very, well, confessional, that's all.' She tried to sympathize with the Prelector, but wasn't exactly sure how.

He grabbed her by the shoulders. 'Please, listen to me!'

'All right, Sven. Confess.'

Tornqvist looked as if every word he was about to utter was going to burn him. 'You have to understand . . .' He knelt on the floor and clutched at the Inf around his neck. 'There is a truth behind the Lazarus Intent, but it isn't his return. Since Lazarus's death, the Intent has grown into an organization that brings hope to the Union. It makes people value themselves and their fellow life-forms, it treasures all aspects of life.' He pointed a thumb at himself. 'Look at me! A street urchin from Mirabilis, a vicious little brat who'd already killed ten people. The Intent showed me that there was a better way, a way that didn't depend on power and subjugation. That's the real Lazarus Intent!'

'What are you trying to say?' said Tegan.

'The Lazarus Intent is now more powerful than the Union. It's a fellowship that will survive the fall of the Union in the same way it survived the fall of the

Federation. But it's all founded on a corrupt saviour who died on Sontara.'

Tegan interrupted. 'His intent was that you'd bring him back – or forwards, rather. Save him from his sacrifice. Surely that lies at the heart of your religion?'

'No, Tegan.' The Prelector was pale, trembling as if he was in shock. 'Not any more. Once, the ultimate goal of any member of the Intent was to rescue Lazarus from his death. But then, after a thousand years or so, the Prelate realized that the worst thing that could happen to the Intent would be his return.'

'So it's all a lie.' Tegan felt something sink within her.

'Not at all. The drive to create a religion worthy of the Codex of Lazarus built everything the Intent stands for. But there's a catch: how could our messiah live up to the promises he made?' He clutched the Inf even tighter. 'Especially a messiah whose predilections lean more towards organized crime than universal fellowship.'

'Arrestis is Lazarus, isn't he?' said Tegan softly. The great secret that Tornqvist had been carrying, and it was now so obvious. She could have kicked herself.

'All the evidence points that way. I just didn't know how to tell you. You're right: that shallow, self-centred, ignoble bastard is the saviour that the Lazarus Intent is waiting for. Arrestis knew that I was close. That's why he arranged to have me kidnapped. He just wasn't prepared for Hellenica.'

'Diva?' Tegan sounded puzzled.

'Exactly.' Tornqvist stopped as yet another explosion rocked their platform.

'You mean Hellenica knew all about Arrestis? That he was her saviour? And yet she pretended to be his mistress?'

Shaking his head, Tornqvist continued. 'Not at all. She courted Arrestis to gain access to the Crystal Bucephalus, and hence Lassiter. We selected her because of her previous relationship with Lassiter. Her role was to convince her erstwhile husband to return with her to Clavidence.'

'Why? If Arrestis is already here . . .' Tegan was confused. She closed her eyes as a blinding flare lit up the horizon. This is definitely the end, she decided. And I'm taking confession from a priest?

'Indeed, and that has brought the Union perilously close to full scale war. Assuming Arrestis was Lazarus, we hoped that we could dispose of him.'

Tegan couldn't believe what she was hearing. 'Dispose of him? This is your saviour you're talking about!' shouted Tegan.

'For Lazarus's sake, can't a Prelector confess in peace?' he sighed. 'Even if Arrestis was . . . removed, there would still be the problem of a future party trying to reach back to Sontara and rescue him again. We wanted Lassiter to shield Sontara so that any future time travel experiments would be incapable of fulfilling the Intent.'

Tegan suddenly saw the problem. 'But Arrestis is with Lassiter and Monroe. What's the betting that that particular pair of people have unmasked him?'

Tornqvist made a praying gesture with his hands. 'Hellenica's faith is deep; I don't know what she will do when she discovers the truth.'

A sound like the tearing of heaven hit them, and she realized that that wasn't such a bad analogy. About a mile away from their parapet, a massive gash in space had opened up, a lenticular rip in the fabric of the TARDIS. The edges flickered in reds and golds as if they were on fire, but it was what it contained that sent icy daggers into her: the roiling blue miasma of the Time Vortex. The TARDIS had been holed.

Lassiter appeared in the doorway as Turlough and Kamelion departed at a run. 'Where are they off to?' he asked breathlessly, his face red with exertion.

'A little bit of wanton destruction.' The Doctor waved at the console. 'I'd appreciate it if you could inspect my wiring, Alex. I'm afraid it's been quite some time since I last had the chance to play with the Bucephalus.'

'Of course.' Lassiter was puzzled: he'd hardly call a day

'quite some time'. Still, time was the Doctor's province. 'But what did you mean by "wanton destruction"?'

Monroe smiled. 'What he means, Alex dear, is that Turlough and Kamelion have gone to destroy the statue.'

'What?' It meant the final end of his dream, but all his dreams had turned into nightmares anyway. He looked at Monroe and caught her eye: the warmth in her look made him hope that maybe a nightmare was about to become a dream. He suddenly realized that the Doctor was talking to him.

'The partial denaturalization gave me the idea.' The Doctor had brought up a hologram of the horse: the left flank was a duller green than the rest. 'The denatured portion is jamming the spillage throughput.'

'Well, yes.' Something he should have noticed earlier.

'And the entire statue is attracting the convection wave of spillage. It's diverting some of it from the TARDIS.'

'I thought that's what you wanted?' said Lassiter.

'The current level of spillage that's pouring through will destroy the TARDIS in . . .' He shut his eyes for a second. 'Oh, about six minutes.'

'So what will destroying the statue do? I'm sure the TARDIS is going to love the full brunt of the spillage being directed at it.'

The Doctor gave a telling smile. 'Yes, and that's the plan. Without the moderating influence of the Bucephalus, the TARDIS will be hit by all the time spillage that's going. Like a champagne cork.'

Lassiter realized what he was getting at. 'It'll be knocked out of the Vortex!'

'*She*'ll be knocked out of the Vortex,' he corrected. 'But yes, you've got the general idea. I reckon there's about another thirty seconds –'

Lassiter grabbed his jacket. 'Until all hell breaks loose! Your clever little tactic might save the TARDIS, but the spillage will hit the generators! And then we'll destroy this section of the galaxy!'

Monroe's hands dropped on to his shoulders, gently massaging. 'Calm down, Alex. I know that patience isn't your greatest virtue, but please, hear the Doctor out.'

The Time Lord nodded. 'Thank you, Hellenica. As I was saying, without your improvements, this place is nothing more than a temporal projector. Check the wiring, if you will?'

The gash was growing larger, a rapacious maw that was eating away at the domes and pillars like a cancer.

'We can't give up now!' Tegan turned to Tornqvist, now staring blankly into the inferno. 'Prayer factor nine, Your Grace?'

The Prelector smiled emptily. 'This is the face of hell. My punishment for attempting to slay my saviour.'

'Get real!' Tegan pointed at the rift. 'This is physics, Sven, not divine retribution. If we die, it's because the TARDIS was in the wrong place at the wrong time, not because God was angry with you! Arrestis is evil! Do you really think he cares less about all the good that's been done in his name? The whole concept of the Intent is his idea of immortality!'

'And we've pandered to it,' said Tornqvist dejectedly.

'No!' Tegan twisted him round to face her. 'The Intent is a force for good! Just because it was some bastard's passport to glory doesn't take away from the basic truth: the Intent has helped people! Remember Mirabilis?'

Tornqvist sighed. 'How could I forget? You've restored my faith.'

'Rubbish,' said Tegan. 'I just polished it up a bit.'

'Ready?' Turlough weighed Arrestis's disruptor in his hand. They were standing in the shadow of the statue. A fine drizzle filled the air from the miniature thunderstorm that rumbled above the proud horse-head.

'Of course, Turlough. Although I must admit to being a trifle insulted by the Doctor's insistence that you accompany me.' He was insulted, but not particularly surprised. He was more surprised that the Doctor had allowed him out of his sight. Having been so convinced that he had overridden his creators' programming, he had immediately fallen under Arrestis's influence. Then Lassiter had tried to use him as an assassin. He doubted that the Doctor would permit him to remain in the TARDIS after this fiasco.

'It's because you can't be trusted.' Kamelion could detect the hostility in Turlough's thought patterns.

'I did disable Arrestis's *jablecta*.' In an extremely clever manner, he thought proudly; even the Doctor had been impressed.

'You also ran out on Hellenica and me, and murdered the Maitre D',' he snapped. 'You really are a nasty piece of work. The Doctor told me that Xeraphas was a lifeless ball of rock – he should have dumped you back there. At least you wouldn't have caused any more trouble.'

'Very well, Monsignor Turlough.'

'Cut the obsequiousness; it doesn't become you.'

'On the contrary, I think it suits me rather well, Junior Ensign Vislor Turlough, VTEC 9/12/44.'

'And you can get out of my mind, while you're at it!' He sighted the disruptor. 'Anyway, what was it the Doctor said about the statue?'

Kamelion transformed into the Doctor. 'The crystal matrix of dichronomide pentafluoride is such that a directed energy burst at any point will cause the entire statue to shatter.' He pointed at the nearest flank, which was a much deeper green. 'But avoid that flank: that's where Professor Matisse's actions have denatured the matrix.'

'Very clever,' sneered Turlough. 'Can I trust you to shield me when that happens?'

Kamelion returned to his android form. 'If your mind was stronger, you could be assured of that fact,' he added. There was no point in letting Turlough have all the best insults, was there? 'Suffice it to say, I will protect you from injury.'

'Fine.' Turlough aimed the disruptor at the head and squeezed the trigger.

And nothing happened. He shook the two-foot-long grey cylinder in front of the android's face. 'Why isn't it working?'

Kamelion was impassive as he answered. 'I suspect that the radiation generated by my Sculti form has discharged its sarium krellide power cells.'

'And you didn't say anything? How are we going to destroy this statue?' Turlough looked at Kamelion with narrowed eyes. 'When you transform, you do change shape, don't you? It isn't just an illusion?'

'Certainly not. I am an extremely complex block transfer computation, capable of infinite form and variety.'

He gave a calculating smile. 'I want you to grow to fifty feet tall and smash the statue. Understood?'

Kamelion nodded his assent and triggered his transformation, feeling the equations solve themselves and solidify. He was immediately shrouded by a pillar of shimmering light which expanded and extended until it was as high as the green statue.

'Is this acceptable?' He boomed at the tiny Turlough down below.

'Perfectly!' shouted Turlough. 'Just do it!'

Kamelion struck the statue across the glittering mane with a silver forearm.

Fifty feet of exquisitely carved green crystal, fashioned in the form of Alexander the Great's loyal and trusting warhorse, fundamental component of the Bucephalus Grid, shattered. Or rather exploded, as the time spillage escaped the lattice that had imprisoned it with a sound like heaven breaking; Kamelion was pretty sure that that piece of imagery came from Turlough, who was currently falling to the floor with his arms over his head. Countless shards of burning green crystal cascaded outwards, raining over the Mezzanine in a shower of tinkling fragments which ignited tiny fires on the roofs of the Cubiculi. Remembering his instructions, he immediately fell on all fours over Turlough, a fifty foot metallic shield off which the diamond-sharp nuggets bounced with a machine-gun of sharp rat-a-tats.

Once the barrage had ended, Kamelion rose from his squat and shrank to his default appearance. Turlough stood up and put his hands on his hips and surveyed the Mezzanine and Kamelion did likewise. The thunderstorm was rapidly abating, but it had succeeded in extinguishing a few of the hundreds of fires which the burning pentafluorate had caused. The marble floor was covered in dull lumps of green rock: Kamelion walked over to a couple of lumps and kicked them aside, noting that the marble was slightly scorched. 'Was that satisfactory, Turlough?'

He looked at the black marble base: a pyramid of smoking green chips was all that remained of the crystal Bucephalus. 'I think you could say that.'

Kamelion formed his lips into a silver smile. But he knew that it would take more than that to convince Turlough and the others of his good intentions. Especially with that dark cackling voice that echoed in his mind.

'That's it!' Lassiter threw his arms open to embrace the console. All the readings were off the scale, accompanied by a cacophony of shrieks and bells and alarms. 'You've blown every failsafe in the Bucephalus.' He couldn't help looking out of the window: the destruction of the statue had been heartbreaking. Spectacular, but heartbreaking.

The Doctor rubbed his hands together. 'Excellent. I reckon we have two minutes until the feedback breaches the containment field around the collapsar annihilator.' He walked over to the console and began typing at one of the brass keyboards.

'At most,' added Monroe, glancing up from an access port. 'How long before the spillage hits the TARDIS?'

The Doctor closed his eyes. 'About ten seconds, I would think. Ah, Turlough, Kamelion!' He smiled at them as they came into the room. 'Just in time for the penultimate act, I think.' He gestured at the hologramatic display of the Vortex. 'Watch and learn.'

The small blue box rotated silently in its dark green cloud, seemingly oblivious to the jet black battering ram forcing its way through the Vortex towards it.

Lassiter was close enough to the Doctor to hear what he muttered.

'Kill or cure, old girl, kill or cure.'

The maw was now an abyss, the fluttering azure radiance of the Vortex casting its light over Tegan, Byson and Tornqvist. Despite Tegan's earlier protestations, it really did feel like the gateway to hell was gaping down over them. 'Brave heart, Tegan,' she whispered.

'What was that?' asked Tornqvist, his eyes never wavering from the tear in reality.

'Oh, something the Doctor always used to say.' She sighed.

'You say that as if you think he's dead,' he replied quietly.

'Well isn't he?' she snapped. 'He was trapped in Matisse's Exemplar when it blew up, for goodness' sake!'

Byson interrupted her. 'The Doctor's still alive. The TARDIS can feel him.'

'He's alive!' Suddenly Tegan felt the glimmerings of hope inside her.

And then it hit like the wrath of God.

One moment they'd been standing before the end of everything; the next, they were knocked to the floor as if some invisible hand had swatted them. And the noise! A scream of retribution swept through the ruins of the TARDIS, a sound that touched Tegan deep inside in the same way as the destruction of the console had. Only then it had been a cry of pain; now it was a triumphant whoop of victory. Victory? As she felt the platform tipping, she couldn't reconcile the TARDIS's celebration with the fact that they were about to be thrown hundreds of feet to their deaths. What was going on?

It stopped as dramatically as it had started. The noise and the wind and the light and everything just . . . stopped. Tegan looked up and somehow knew that it was all over. The abyss was gone, with no sign that it had ever existed, and for a second she wondered if she had imagined all of it. Then she saw again the burnt out domes and the crumbled sections of pillar, a landscape of ruin and desolation. Somehow she didn't think the

Doctor was going to be very impressed.

'It's over.' Byson clambered to his feet, blinking rapidly. Tegan guessed that he had felt the TARDIS's emotional outburst most deeply of all.

'The voice of God,' muttered Tornqvist. 'He heard us and sent deliverance.'

'Somehow I think it had more to do with physics than faith,' muttered Tegan, but as she spoke, a crack of thunder echoed from above. It could have been an aftershock, but she couldn't be sure. 'Although I'm sure your prayers helped, Sven,' she added hurriedly.

Byson squeezed his eyes shut and mumbled to himself. 'New Alexandria.'

'What?' Tornqvist's eyes widened.

'We're about to land on New Alexandria.' He opened his eyes and smiled. 'Will I meet my father?'

Tornqvist put his arm around him. 'Of course you will; and Tegan and I will tell him how brave you've been.'

Tegan simply laughed with relief. 'Crystal Bucephalus, here we come.'

The moment that the TARDIS had been dislodged, the Doctor had dispatched Turlough and Kamelion to the Legion tank and had then started pulling the console apart. He now stood in the centre of a ring of components, tied together by reels of golden bladamite tubing. It was hard to imagine that it had once all belonged to the polished wood and brass horseshoe.

'How long before the buffers overload?' he mumbled, three pieces of wire held in his mouth.

'Sixty seconds,' Monroe replied, looking up from the analogue clock set in one of the lecterns. She turned to Lassiter beside her. 'What's he doing?'

He shrugged. 'This is totally out of my league.' She could hear the envy in his voice. 'I'd swear that he's doing things with the Grid control systems that contravene the laws of physics.'

'He's a Time Lord – they make the laws,' she laughed nervously.

'I just wish he'd explain what he's doing. When the buffers go, the time spillage will rip this star system apart, and I don't fancy being in the middle of it.' He stopped as the Doctor beckoned him over.

'Hold these,' he ordered, handing Lassiter two thin red wires. 'And don't let them touch yet.'

'What are you trying to do?' asked Monroe.

'Something extremely clever and possibly blasphemous,' he replied. 'How long now?'

Monroe remembered her monitoring duties and ran back to the lectern. 'Twenty seconds.' For all her qualifications and intellect, she felt like a glorified lab assistant compared with the Doctor.

'I hope you've checked your wiring,' said Lassiter, nodding at the jumble of components on the parquet floor. 'Because I wouldn't have the first idea where to start. Will it work?'

'A wing and a prayer, Professor, a wing and a prayer.'

'Five seconds,' Monroe informed them.

Lassiter sighed. 'In the end it's all a matter of faith, isn't it?'

'Now, Alex,' urged the Doctor quietly.

He brought the wires together with a crackle.

'What's supposed to happen?' asked Monroe. At least they were still there, she realized gratefully.

Then she heard it. At first, the sound was almost unnoticeable, and she had to strain to convince herself that it was real. But it rapidly grew from a whisper to a trumpeting roar, and then to a pulsing, almost melodic whine which filled the Crystal Bucephalus.

The noise swept between the rings of Cubiculi and the avenues of pillars, past bauhaus and art deco, through the rose windows and across the elegant statuary, rustling the ferns and stirring the diamonds that hung from the chandeliers before it passed beyond human hearing. For a second, Monroe was reminded of *The Apocalypse*, the last book of the Codex, and she grabbed her Inf. She began to recite the Codex's final words. ' "May Lazarus's grace fill the heavens —" '

' "And His enlightenment fill our hearts," ' finished Lassiter, reaching out and clasping her hand.

And then everything began to fade away.

Throughout the Crystal Bucephalus, every piece of equipment associated with its function as a time machine vanished. From Legion tank to Grid Control, everything dematerialized: Cubiculi, Navigus, Legion pit, pillars, lecterns, time rotor, consoles – and the collapsar annihilator at the core of New Alexandria. Within seconds, the Crystal Bucephalus had become nothing more than a vast, empty auditorium.

'That's it,' the Doctor announced to the now bare room. 'The entire time travel mechanism for the Bucephalus is now firmly in the past.'

'What about the spillage?' queried Monroe. 'Whether it was unleashed now or in the past, the results would have been catastrophic.'

Lassiter's eyes suddenly widened in understanding. 'It didn't have any effect – it was projected back with too small a reality quotient!'

The Doctor broke into a broad grin. 'Exactly. A place for everything and everything in its place. Speaking of which, I didn't have time to reset the coordinates.'

Monroe began to say something, but Lassiter interrupted her. 'Sebby would have been heartbroken to see it all like this.' Despite his best attempts, he began to cry.

The Doctor stepped back and cast his eyes to the floor as Monroe hugged Lassiter and started stroking his back. 'It's finished, Alexhendri,' she said softly. 'It's over. All of it.'

She stopped as the room was yet again filled with a rhythmic trumpeting. Something was entering reality in the spot where, until moments ago, the Cubiculo had stood. Slowly, almost painfully, the outline of a large box filled out and went from transparent to translucent before finally solidifying about an inch from the floor. After hanging there for a gravity-defying moment, it fell with a heavy thump.

'The TARDIS!' shouted the Doctor, reaching into his jacket and retrieving a key. 'Battered but unbeaten.' He ran over to it.

Monroe suppressed her shock. The object in the corner bore only the slightest resemblance to the quaint shack she had first seen in the clearing. The regular lines had been replaced by a melted, blurred blue covering, as if it had been made of wax and then held over a flame. 'What's happened to it?'

The Doctor stroked the TARDIS with his palm. 'Fractal degradation of the outer plasmic shell, I should imagine. If that's the only symptom of what she's been through, then the old girl's come off lightly.' In the absence of anything that resembled a lock, he touched the key to the irregular blue surface. Nothing happened.

'Problems?' asked Turlough from the doorway of the Suite. Kamelion was standing next to him.

Frowning, the Doctor examined the key. 'The primary threshold systems don't seem to be responding.' He sighed. 'Oh well, time for a little laying on of hands.' He leant against the TARDIS, hands outstretched and eyes squeezed shut.

A feeling of almost sepulchral calm had fallen over the TARDIS. Tegan tentatively stepped closer to the edge of the platform and gazed out over the landscape. To her surprise and delight, some of the domes were already repairing themselves. The odd thing was, nothing seemed to happen while she deliberately watched a dome, but if she turned away and then looked back, the dome was whole again. 'If the Doctor can regenerate, why shouldn't his TARDIS?' she muttered.

'Sorry?' Byson was standing next to her.

'I was talking to myself, Garrett. The TARDIS seems to be recovering.'

He nodded, smiling. 'I hope so. It's nice.'

She turned to the Prelector with a reassuring smile. 'So Sven: how are you feeling?'

He gave a deep sigh. 'I'm not sorry about, about

earlier, you know. Despite the truth about Arrestis, and the Intent's plans for him, I do hold great store by my faith. And when everything seemed to be coming to an end, it was all I had left.'

'No problem. Actually, I did find myself praying at the end, you know.'

He gently slapped her on the shoulder. 'That's my girl; there's hope for you yet. As Saint Alexis said to Krystal —'

'So what do we do now?' interrupted Tegan, not really in the mood for another parable. 'I don't fancy spending the rest of my life stuck up here.' She broke off as a rectangle of shimmering mercury appeared about five feet away. 'What the hell is that?'

The quicksilver flowed apart as the Doctor walked through.

'Doctor!' she cried, running over and smothering him in a tight hug. 'Am I glad to see you!'

'Obviously.' He untangled himself from her grasp and tugged his jacket back into shape. 'Although I'd like to know what you've been doing with my TARDIS.'

'I'm sorry about the mess,' she said apologetically, doubting that it was enough to pacify him.

'Are you?' he growled. 'Anyway, I think it's time we all made our goodbyes, don't you?' A sudden thought seemed to hit him. 'Where's Professor Matisse?'

'My mother's not here, Doctor,' said Byson quietly. 'I'd rather you asked Tegan, if it's all the same.'

'Your mother?' He gave Tegan a panicked look. She nodded. 'Oh. I see.' He gestured towards the silver doorway.

'It'll be all right, won't it?' asked Byson. 'It likes me.'

'The TARDIS?' He gazed at the violated landscape. 'As right as rain, Garrett. Anyway, she was well overdue for a refit.' He smiled. 'Come on.'

'Doctor?' It was Tornqvist, his hand around his Inf. 'What happened to Arrestis?' he whispered.

'Lazarus is back where he belongs, if you understand me.'

Tornqvist deflated like a punctured balloon. Tegan

moved to support him. 'Back?' He started shaking.

Tegan looked over to the Doctor for help.

He coughed theatrically. 'Actually, Your Grace, I think I might be able to help. I am breaking every law in the Time Lord book, but what are a few rules between friends, eh?'

'What do you mean?' The Prelector was frowning.

'When I arrived here, the future was fairly well defined – please excuse my use of tenses, by the way: on Gallifrey we have two hundred and eight tenses, but they don't translate well. Anyway, in about a hundred years, the Union fell, to be replaced by the Junta, a military dictatorship that evolved from the Elective. And the Junta will crush the galaxy for over a millennium before the Confederation displaces it.' He lifted an eyebrow. 'That wasn't exactly a barrel of laughs, either.'

Tornqvist stopped shaking. He went white instead. 'That's the future?'

The Doctor gave him a reassuring pat on the shoulder. 'Not any more. It seems that you've made quite a difference, Your Grace. In twenty years, the dominant force in this galaxy will be the Concordance, with President Tornqvist – based on Clavidence, by the way – ushering in a new age of fellowship and harmony.'

'Me?'

The Doctor nodded sagely. 'You've saved the galaxy, Sven.'

'Doctor, I –' He stopped and broke into a wide, toothy grin. 'President?'

'Time to leave, I think.' He waved Tornqvist and Byson through the doorway.

'How did you know all that?' asked Tegan, watching them vanish through the silver surface.

He raised an eyebrow. 'I didn't. I guessed, interpolated.'

She felt her anger boiling up. 'You did what?' she yelled. 'You're trying to rewrite history!'

He looked a little abashed. 'My handwriting is better than most, Tegan.'

She shook her head in resignation. 'You know best, Doc.'

He sighed. 'If only . . .'

Monroe was relieved when Tornqvist and Byson emerged through the mirrored doorway of the TARDIS. She stepped forward. 'Where's Matisse?' she asked. She wasn't looking forward to that reunion.

'She paid the fine for overdue library books,' said Tornqvist quietly, but Monroe wasn't listening: she was staring at Lassiter.

'You must be my father.' Byson held out a massive hand.

He tentatively reached out and took it. 'You're Garrett?' he said incredulously. Byson nodded.

Monroe felt for him. The unusual nature of Matisse's son had been an open secret on the galactic grapevine, and it had only served to fuel her hatred of her. But Garrett was a nine-year-old boy who had never met his father, until now.

'Nice to meet you.' Lassiter looked terrified. 'Son.'

Tegan came over. 'It's good to see you again, Diva. Or should I call you Professor Monroe?'

Monroe clasped her hand. 'Soon to be Professor Lassiter-Monroe, or Monroe-Lassiter; I haven't decided which sounds better.'

'You mean?' Tegan broke into a smile.

'I hope so.' She frowned. 'Although I haven't actually asked him yet.' The two women started laughing.

The Doctor moved between them. 'I'm sorry to intrude, but we must be on our way. Tegan, Turlough, Kamelion?'

'What did happen with the Bucephalus?' interrupted Turlough. 'You did send an awful lot of time spillage back.'

'Indeed,' said the Doctor. 'But I'm sure everything sorted itself out.' He reached into his jacket and pulled out a book. 'I picked this up on Pella Satyrnis; it might explain a few things.' He handed it to Turlough, who looked at the small grey volume with surprise.

'*The Codex of Lazarus?*'

'Exactly. Take a look at the Gospel of Saint Clavis, Act Fifteen. The Sign of the Lights is quite interesting.'

With the destruction of the statue, the spillage found itself venting into the real universe, a situation that defied all the laws of physics. Time spillage wasn't supposed to exist in normal eleven-dimensional space: it was completely incompatible. With a final shrug of resignation at those laws, the spillage transformed itself into an explosion of radiation that rivalled the creation of the galaxy: a torrent of radiation which was instantly shoved into the Time Vortex by the Bucephalus, too fast for it to have a chance to interact with its surroundings.

The time bubble that contained the explosion exited the Vortex about five thousand years in the past, erupting into reality and dissolving. The radiation spanned the galaxy in about an hour.

In the skies of nearly every world, breathtaking aurorae burnt and flared as the radiation was forced to decelerate. But those of the faith noted that the display was centred around Sontara. It was the Sign of the Lights.

As the Doctor and his companions entered the blurred blue box, Lassiter reached out and grabbed the Doctor's hand. 'We'll always be grateful.'

He leaned forward. 'It was nothing.'

'Nothing?' protested Lassiter. 'Don't underestimate yourself –'

The Doctor put his arm round Lassiter's shoulders, pulling him closer. 'No, Alex – I mean, *nothing*. I wasn't here,' he whispered in his ear.

Lassiter laughed. 'I understand.' As the Doctor released him, he remembered something. 'You're not angry with me, then?' He looked rather sheepish.

The Doctor sounded puzzled. 'About what?'

'About building the Crystal Bucephalus here, on New Alexandria. My conceit, I suppose.'

The Doctor shrugged. And smiled. 'Where else? All I ask is that you declare this world off-limits.' He nodded at Tornqvist. 'Ask the Prelector to put it under a Lazarine Interdict. I'd rather this planet rested in peace; it deserves it.' With that, he followed the others into the TARDIS. Just as he reached the quicksilver threshold, he turned back. 'And by the way, I wouldn't count on my financial backing to rebuild this place — I'm just about to write to my bank manager.'

'Where the hell are we?' Tegan looked around. Instead of the familiar console room, they were standing in, well, nothing. And on nothing, come to that — it was as if they were in the middle of a vast white void. The only distinguishing feature was a thin metallic pillar in front of them, stretching upwards and downwards to infinity.

'Until I can repair the TARDIS, Tegan, this is the console room.' The Doctor seemed to materialize beside her, throwing open his arms. 'Emergency default.'

'Very impressive,' said Turlough with a trace of sarcasm. 'But where are we going?'

'Where we were originally going: the Eye of Orion. The ambient tranquillity is just what the old girl needs to make a speedy recovery.'

Tegan decided to ask the question that had been nagging at her. 'How did you end up in the Bucephalus after the Exemplar blew up?'

The Doctor tapped the pillar, paused, and tapped again. The familiar noise of the TARDIS, albeit slightly strained, filled the new console room. 'It seems that Hellenica activated a gate from the Bucephalus to Hexdane — and Tanthane happens to lie between the two. I was caught in the gate, and when the Exemplar was shut down, I was dragged to New Alexandria.'

Turlough looked sceptical. 'Very convenient.'

'Quite,' said the Doctor mysteriously. 'Perhaps I have friends in high places.'

'I will remain in my room when we reach the Eye of Orion,' stated Kamelion suddenly.

The Doctor spun round to face him. 'I beg your pardon?'

'I cannot be trusted,' he intoned. 'Both Arrestis and Lassiter were able to control me.'

The Doctor smiled understandingly. 'That's life, Kamelion.'

'No, Doctor.' He transformed into his mirror image. 'If I cannot be sure of my probity, I cannot guarantee my loyalty.' He tugged at his lapels. 'I shall stay in my quarters until I can be sure that I am not a threat to my fellow travellers.'

'Good riddance,' muttered Turlough.

'That's enough, Turlough,' the Doctor warned. 'Besides, Kamelion, your quarters are probably in the same state as everyone else's: in lots of little pieces. See how you feel when we reach the Eye of Orion – at least we'll get some rest there.' He examined the replacement console room. 'Actually, I've been intending to redesign the console for quite some time.' He sighed. 'A brand spanking new time rotor, ergonomic layout of controls, structural integrity field to prevent Cybermen from taking potshots . . .'

As the Doctor outlined an increasingly incomprehensible list of improvements, Tegan turned to Turlough. 'We never did finish our dinner, did we?'

He raised an eyebrow. 'Actually, Tegan, I didn't really care for the company.'

Coffee and Just Desserts

'**Y**ou have betrayed us, Arrestis!' The Sontaran that rose from the throne had no name save Imperator, but that was sufficient to maintain absolute control of his Empire. 'You promised us the codes for the Rutan Centroplex, and yet you return here empty-handed.' His eyes were venomous slits in his domed brown head.

Arrestis instinctively took a step back. All Sontarans looked nasty, but their Imperator, in his scarlet armour, looked even worse. At least he wasn't a reptile. He glared at him. 'I honestly thought I could get them,' he protested. 'It was my agent on Ruta 3 who let me down.' This was it. He wasn't going to get out of here, and his followers were about to learn that their saviour died on Sontara. He just hoped that the idea of the Lazarus Intent was going to work.

'Honest? Honest?' The Imperator marched up to him and grabbed his throat with a stubby three-fingered hand. 'I didn't think that was a word in your vocabulary, Arrestis.' He leaned forward so that his face was inches away. 'I should have realized that you would betray us. Unfortunately, I have already sent the stealth bombers to Tersurus – the Sontarans know the meaning of honour.'

'Listen to me!' Arrestis could feel himself sweating. 'I've given you the defence strategies for both the Federation and the Imperial fleets. Isn't that enough?'

'No, it is not,' hissed the Imperator, hurling him to the floor. 'The Rutan are the real enemy. The machinations of your crumbling Federation are nothing more than an enjoyable distraction.'

His voice began to waver. 'I'll get the codes –'

'Save your empty promises.' The Imperator unholstered his blaster. 'You have outlived your usefulness.' His fingers tightened around the gun. 'Saviour of the galaxy? I'd like to see you get out of this.'

Arrestis saw the red bolt leap from the barrel.

Suddenly he was somewhere else.

On Pluto, Lassiter's refusal to hand over his little secrets had led to Arrestis's flight to Hexdane, where assassination, bribery and blackmail gave him control of the Elective. His second attempt on Lassiter using Matisse had failed, driving Lassiter to the Crystal Bucephalus. On Tanthane, he saw his first successes in genetic engineering and the army of clones that resulted. From Hexdane, he began undermining the economies of the Union and the reptile empires that surrounded it, before making his third attempt on Lassiter. But Monroe's *double jeu* had put paid to that, leading to the fall of the Crystal Bucephalus. And then he had escaped through the time gate to Hexdane.

Arrestis reeled as he emerged from the gate. He was immediately aware of his surroundings: he wasn't on Hexdane. Although he hadn't seen it for over ten years, the room was instantly recognizable, with its rich tapestries over dark stone walls, an impressive metal throne, a squat figure in glinting red armour. 'No!' he screamed in the vain hope that Monroe was watching. 'Take me back!' All the safeguards he had designed to ensure his immortality were useless: the machinery to transfer his consciousness to another clone was five thousand years in the future. Blind terror began to overwhelm him as he faced up to his worst nightmare. He was going to die. All his planning, all his ingenuity, all of it: ending where it should have begun.

The Imperator ignored the outburst. 'You have outlived your usefulness.'

Panicked déjà vu gave Arrestis a slight edge, as he dived to his left to avoid the blaster fire. He hit the wall, feeling his arm break with the impact. Trying to ignore the pain, he started to get to his feet, but the Imperator kicked him back and fired.

Maximillian Arrestis finally experienced the truth of the Lazarus Intent.

The Imperator stepped over the charred body without a second glance. 'Saviour of the galaxy?' he muttered. 'I'd like to see him get out of that.'

Available in the Doctor Who – New Adventures *series:*

The next Missing Adventure is *State of Change* by Christopher Bulis, which will feature the sixth Doctor and Peri.